Silk for the Feed Dogs

JACKIE MALLON

BETIMES BOOKS

First published in the English language worldwide in 2013
by Betimes Books
www.betimesbooks.com

ISBN-13: 978-0-9926552-0-4

Cover image © Jackie Mallon
Cover design by JT Lindroos

For Chris

CONTENTS

Give fools their gold, and knaves their power; let fortune's bubbles rise and fall;
Who sews a field, or trains a flower, or plants a tree, is more than all.

—John Greenleaf Whittier

It's no good running a pig farm badly for thirty years while saying 'Really, I was meant to be a ballet dancer'. By then, pigs will be your style.

—Quentin Crisp

EARLY TRENDS IN FARMING

I heard the engine of the old red Massey Ferguson fart into life and I emerged running, scrambling to get my wellies on. We were on a rescue mission, Da and me. A cow was refusing to feed her calf. I'd seen it born that morning before I went to school, my bottom numb from being perched so long on top of the barred gate. But it was the animal's back end that bothered me, or what protruded from it: two spindly legs cut off at the knees, hooves pointed in the launch position. Uncomfortable as the cow had looked, she didn't seem inclined to finish what she'd started. I couldn't blame her - it looked exhausting. But she finally summoned the strength, gave two or three great heaves, and the contents of her belly slapped onto the ground. The calf lay sprawled and shivering. The noises he made, after a few moments of silent outrage, were more like those of a curious cat. As his eyes rolled slowly over this new, harsher environment, all the aloof heifers kept their distance, swishing their tails. I held my breath, willing them to be kind, but they seemed to want nothing to do with him. I couldn't leave him like that, crashlanded and splattered. It was only when I saw one or two cows join the reluctant mother in licking him clean that I jumped down and headed to school.

But throughout the day, he had stayed in my thoughts. As soon as I got home, I hurried to find Da. He said the calf had grown weak. The mother had disowned it. I had ten minutes to wolf down my tea, and we were off, soon turning onto our lane. It was pulpy from the rain and sported a shiny green mohawk that brushed the undercarriage. The hedges were higher than our heads, rampant with hawthorn, gooseberries, and whin. Sometimes Da let me drive on the lane and, as I let go of the clutch and we started to move, I felt the engine's gentle exhalation, its big and biddable strength. But today we talked little and he remained in his seat, his lips set in a tight line. The Massey didn't have a cab so the distant drone of silage spreaders, the flapping wind, the muted barking of a dog were our company.

From the dual carriageway people would see the Massey disappearing between the hedges and comment: "That'll be Dan Connelly and at his shoulder there'll be wee Kathleen, the great farmer. She'll run that place one day." That's what they'd been saying since I was old enough to understand. I always concealed my pride, never letting slip even a smile.

The Massey represented freedom, the open land. Every time Da raised his boot to the footplate, threw his leg over and lowered himself into the calloused seat with the threadbare cushion, I could see the silhouette of our Sunday afternoon hero, John Wayne. My position was beside him up on the mudguard of the back wheel. Unless for funerals, Da only ever wore a shirt opened at the neck, rolled up to the elbows, and chestnut coloured trousers with the shape of his knees wedged in the cloth. At six, I wore smaller versions of the same. I had his farmer's tan. My forearms, throat, and face were thick-skinned and freckled, my hair like tangled mélange yarn, often with a briar snarled in it.

We stopped in front of the cobbled-together cluster of byres with corrugated roofs, their numbers added to since granda's time. Da led me around the back to a clearing where the cows congregated before milking.

"Mind the nettles," he called.

I aimed to tread in his footsteps, but they were too far apart and my wellies sank, slivers of ground rippling at my heels like big wet tongues. I kept my toes clenched so the boots stayed on. While I'd been at school, Da had built a pen for the calf, using four iron gates tied together at the corners with twine, and scattered it with straw. That was where we found him, skinny limbs tucked underneath him, sleepy eyes trained on our approach.

"You stay outside, Kathleen. Right where you are is grand," said Da as he climbed in. "Now, lift that plastic bottle with the teat and hold onto it. You're going to feed him when I get him still."

With Da's help, the calf wobbled to his feet.

"Show him the bottle, Kathleen."

I stuck the bottle through the bars and, with his nobbly knees quivering and hind legs crooked like elbows, he pushed off towards me. "Booley-legged' was how Da described him, the same expression he used for neighbours he saw leaving The Farmer's Rest some afternoons. The animal sent his tongue to examine the offering, then stretched his neck and grasped the rubber nozzle in his mouth. For all the size of him, there was remarkable force behind the cute sucking sounds. Ears pinned back, eyes wide and unblinking, he headbutted my hand to alert me when I wasn't tilting the bottle enough. With my other hand I stroked the flat white forehead, imagined gliding a comb through those slinky albino eyelashes.

When he had finished, his tongue shot out again, but less suspiciously this time. Baby pink, as long as my forearm, the underside was a loofah exfoliating my damp knuckles. He went on to explore my shoulder and chew inquisitively on my collar. I squeezed my eyes shut as he discharged a gust of warm air in my face. The loofah worked its way over my nose and curled lazily across my forehead, finally inspecting what rested on my head: my 'rainbow tiara', constructed of three tiers of Caran d'Ache pencils adorned with clusters of M&Ms and trailing ribbons. Da laughed as the calf lapped contentedly at the candy, the ribbons tickling his nose, making him snort. When I opened my eyes, I noticed all the other cattle had gathered at the open gate and were looking on. The calf's mother had separated herself from the herd and was sauntering towards us.

"There you are, you see, Kathleen?" said Da. "Your creative side might not always be appreciated by your classmates, but here they're lapping it up. You just need to hang with the right crowd!"

Beloved though Da's tractor was, it was another industrial machine that forced its way in to dominate my childhood: mum's Singer sewing machine. Black and spiky, it towered over our kitchen like the arthritic nun that watched over school assembly. While the Massey pulled the plough that churned up the land, scattering new potatoes, Da proudly erect at its helm, mum sat hunched over the Singer, pressing the footpedal, easing the fabric to the needle, a crushed velvet waterfall tumbling over the side. She made curtains, or rather, *window treatments,* great bustled affairs with fancy names like 'swags and tails', 'tie-backs', and 'pelmets', garnished with rosettes, and little braided ropes, and tassels. People came from far and wide; she did a roaring trade making twitching net curtains for the parish to peer around.

I remember the day it arrived. I was doing geography homework in front of the fire when two neighbourmen carried it in and wordlessly set it on the tiles. And that's where it stayed. There was only room for one of us in the kitchen, and it soon became clear which one. I went to open the fridge door, and a bolt of fabric fell against me. At the doorstep, I kicked off my mucky wellies and trailed threads through the house instead. I swept the floor, but had to leave the sweepings so mum could pick the pins out. By the time she got round to it, it was all over the floor again. Da built an annex onto the kitchen, and we called it The Sewing Room. Mum stacked it to the ceiling with spools, thread, and cloth, crammed in a second-hand overlocking machine which drove her and the Singer back into the kitchen and me back out in the yard.

Cow dung was normal; thread balls were not. The loose gurgle of the tractor engine was music in comparison to the whirr of the Singer, which was neurotic, and monotonous, and drowned out the theme tune to "The Dukes of Hazzard". I hated to invite what few friends I had home because I knew our kitchen didn't look like theirs. They'd say mean things about mum and Da, and I couldn't have that; we'd be known as gypsies like Fiona Harkin's family who lived in a caravan. So on the afternoon my new friend, Siobhan Devlin, was due over, I asked if tea could be served in the hay shed; in fact it occurred to me that all my future entertaining could take place there.

An almighty row kicked off. Mum wouldn't hear of it. What were we, tinkers? She started to cry. Da came in and at the sight of her tears ordered me to my room until I learnt some respect. I didn't budge. He raised his voice, pointing to the door I was to disappear through. Just as he was about to go for me, he impaled the tender, paler underside of his arm on the Singer's spindle. We spent the rest of the day in the hospital getting Da checked for tetanus and his arm stitched up.

Still, mum thought I would go into business with her when I finished school.

"Sit down in front of it," she tried. "Don't be scared. I'll teach you the basics. There'll always be money to be made in curtains. People never get tired of their privacy."

But that beast had turned on Da. I thought of the old fable in which the King gives orders for every spinning wheel in the kingdom to be burnt because his daughter, cursed by an old maid, would prick her finger on one and die. Then to mum I responded, "I'll be staying well clear of it. In fact, if I never go near a sewing machine again, or thread, or needles, or fabric, I'll live happily ever after."

ST MARTIN'S

"**S**end that stupid Irish bitch in here!"

My pencil swerved across the graph paper, tearing a hole in it. A door slammed a little way down the corridor. The sound of scurrying footsteps. That could only mean me. I was the only Irish bitch she could be referring to. Jesus, I wasn't ready.

A second-year appeared at my elbow, slightly out of breath.

"Eloise wants to see you."

"Did she say why?"

"She said to tell you to bring whatever you have rustled up in the way of a final collection worthy of graduation, and it better be an improvement on what she saw last time."

"That's it?"

"Yeah, that's it. But you better hurry up. She's in no mood to be messed with this morning. A whole group of print students just left in tears."

I surveyed the puzzle of pattern pieces strewn across my table and looked up to see if anyone was watching, certain my panic was detectable, infrared and pulsating. So far, my only observer was the second-year. The sparkle in her eye suggested she'd taken easily to her role as harbinger of anxiety. I had five outfits near completion, three more in the early stages, and two unstarted. Other students were handstitching hems, working on hang tags, or sitting cross-legged in little camps on top of the tables like climbers who'd reached the summit of a mountain.

It was the week of Final Presentation. For the thirty-six of us on the BA, that meant unveiling our collections for the career-launching fashion show that would be attended by industry bigwigs with the power to pluck us from our East London flatshare-above-a-kebab-shop-obscurity and drop us in a glamorous atelier *dans le coeur de Paris*. There was no way around it; I would have to improvise what was missing. With four remaining days, I could pull it off. I might have to take my Mum up on her offer of flying over to help me sew.

I looked around jealously. They were all working with wool, obsessed with tailoring. I wanted everything to be light and airy. I was handling chiffon—layers of the stuff, and over-laid with lace. Afternoons passed as I coaxed the diaphanous wisps to approach the needle, only to watch the cranky old machines turn on them, snatching and biting. *This won't hurt a bit,* I'd promise and, moments later, have to rescue another gnarled ball of silk from the pit underneath the needle where the 'feed dogs' lived—two metal bars with diagonal teeth that lunged forward and reared back with every stitch. In another outfit I was attaching a sunray pleated skirt to a stretchy bod-ice, a fool's game with this equipment. My designs were fin-icky but worth the effort, they'd see. If I was guilty of any-thing, it might be overextension. My collection was different from the others, which made Eloise uneasy. And labour inten-sive, which was why she had forbidden the technical staff to waste any time with me.

"As you're here, you can make yourself useful," I told the second-year and yanked her arms straight out in front of her, zombie-style. Another year, and she'd have lost that smug expression, I thought, as I whipped a pleated dress from the mannequin, draped it over her arms, and scooped up everything else, piling it high so that her ogling eyes barely peered over the peak. Grabbing sketch books, folders, and toiles, I hurried her to the door. Edward put down his pinking shears and shot me a thumbs up as I blew past.

"Good luck!" he called. "Come find me after and we'll go for a fag break." Seeing the look on my face, he added, "You'll be *fine.*"

I caught up with the second-year just as she dumped everything on the floor outside Eloise's office and stage whispered "Good luck" before running off with a barely concealed giggle. At my knock, the irritated bray of the course director travelled through the door and hung in the corridor: "Just wait."

The bleakness of the corridor must have been designed to make students feel hopeless. No chairs, no art on the walls, chunks carved out of the paintwork, gaps in the floor tiles, the knocking of the pipes the only sound - although to what goal, I couldn't say as there was never any heat.

Yet this was the landmark I'd dreamed of reaching: London's Central St Martin's. A mythical place populated by misunderstood creative types, filled with malaise, who wound their way through the corridors, libraries, and stairwells to come out the other end in a puff of glittery smoke, destined for stellar acceptance. Ordinary unsuspecting folk passed by it on their way to buses or offices or pubs, oblivious of their proximity to greatness. Halfway between the National Gallery and Tottenham Court Road tube station, this mysterious genius factory lurked, in a building that was an unsightly hangover from the thirties, on a block once famous for sex cinemas and dirty book stores. The closest thing to glamour about it were the rainbow-coloured oil slicks that leaked from a parked fish and chip van pooling around the entrance during the rain, glimmering with the reflections of passing tail lights. But it was exactly where I needed to be. And I'd been accepted a year early, the youngest on the course, just turned eighteen.

Suddenly the pipes seemed to hiss: *That's all very well but if you don't want your future to be as bleak as these corridors, it's time to listen to what she fucking tells you.*

She was Eloise, the Fat Director. I gave her that title not just because of her outsized proportions but because it sounded like the Fat Controller. From Thomas the Tank Engine. It rendered her less threatening, I suppose.

"Come in now," she drawled from inside. Her voice had the long, nasal resonance of a foghorn. She never had to raise the volume, just force more air out the hole.

Oh holy Moses. I fumbled for the doorknob.

There were six tutors, with her at the centre, behind a long table. A model sat in a chair in the corner. They watched me stagger in with my arms full and kick the door shut. I dropped a pin box. A little silver river swooshed out onto the floor.

"Oh, get it later," said the Fat Director, rolling her eyes.

She was slumped over, legs crossed at the ankles, the narrowest and only part where crossing was possible, and she already looked bored.

"So, what have you got?" she asked.

"Well, I should begin by saying it's not all here. I've got a few outfits still to finish, but that won't be a problem. They'll be done. I can show you the sketches of what's missing. I plan to…"

She sighed heavily, so I stopped.

"Show me what you have got, will you. The clothes, Jesus. Is it too much to ask?" She slumped the other way. "That's what we're here to assess as our arses get numb on these chairs. Save what you're lacking for your fucking therapist." She made an impatient forward motion, and I grabbed the first half-sewn garment at hand and brought it to her. I asked the model to slip it on, and she walked back and forth in it. The Fat Director continued to mutely point, while I held things up or down until she had seen everything. The others said nothing.

"Anything else?"

"Oh, the illustrations! Here you can see what's left to finish."

I spread them on the table proudly. A mixture of drawing and collage, they captured the sense of movement and freedom I was going for since I dispensed with the templates I'd used for the past two years. Four of them cast a glance in their general direction. The sniffy Frenchman, whose speciality was tailoring and who had never been a fan of mine, half-heartedly pawed the corner of one, then slid it away again. He moved like a mime artist—little verbal communication, expressing himself with long fingers, restless limbs, and a melancholic but elastic face. The Fat Director exhaled through her nose while her eyes took another trip to the ceiling so that only the whites remained.

In 1975 when the Sex Pistols played their first gig at St Martin's, Eloise had attended as an impressionable freshman from an upper class family. According to interviews, she was instantly captivated by the idea of galvanizing a room of people by swearing, spitting, throwing beer bottles, even drawing blood. All these years later, she attacked blind hems, French seams, and notched armholes as savagely as Sid Vicious attacked his guitar strings; she berated her students as venomously as Johnny Rotten berated his fans. She boasted of last year's student who, pushed to the brink during an end-of-year presentation, made the evening news (great publicity for the school!) when he stole a classmate's collection and, with the passengers of the south-bound number 38 bus as witnesses, set fire to it in the City of Westminster rubbish bin outside the main entrance before urinating with gay abandon into the flames. Eloise's only regret was that the student didn't get to see the high marks she awarded him before the two officers led him away.

As I looked along the row of unresponsive faces and back to Eloise, I felt the frustration rear up in me. I was keen to give her the anarchy she craved. I imagined delivering a single finger salute, trashing the room, throwing a sewing machine from the window, and pogoing out of there. But I was the product of an education which didn't so much encourage you to respect figures of authority as to keep your disrespect to yourself if you knew what was good for you. So I waited quietly for one of them to speak.

"I just don't get it," said the Fat Director. Her weighty silver jewellery rattled on the desktop as she fixed me with torpid eyes. "You see, it's not that I think you're un-fucking-talented. I just don't think you did a very good job. You were stubborn and wouldn't fucking listen. You had your own ideas, went off in a different direction than what we advised, and this is the result. But I'm sorry. It's just not good enough. You've only got yourself to blame."

I considered the irony: the Sex Pistols' peddled noncon-formity and rejection of authority. My eyes sought an alternative verdict in one of the other faces. With the Frenchman I knew I didn't stand a chance, but even the visiting lecturer, with her lilac rinse and painterly smock, who had previously claimed to see "an unusual urban poetry" in my collection, deflected her gaze, showing no inclination to champion it further.

"We simply can't allow these garments to go on the catwalk," concluded the Fat Director.

It was like a shutter going down at close of trading. She wouldn't take those words back now they were out, and I knew the others wouldn't dare dispute her. They all had their elbows on the table, leaning forward, except the mime artist who was semi-reclining, arms crossed, his hands spookily white against his turtleneck.

I turned, in a hurry to leave and yet rooted to the spot. Summoning every morsel of energy I had I sprung forward, lunging at my collection and squashing it into a bundle in my arms. The floor-length chiffon gown inspired by a rare orchid—I could have grown one from the chiffon easier than sewn one—became the size of a tennis ball in my fists. The sunray pleating and the sweaters with rabbit fur stitched along their furrows were flung into a Boots carrier bag to lie tangled with the beaded headdresses I'd meant to show but forgot. When I was nearly done, I went back to gather my illustrations and threw them on top of the bag like documents for a faulty delivery of goods.

"Oh, and one last thing," said the Fat Director. She sounded amused. "You cannot draw. I'm sorry but some people just…Can't. Fucking. Draw. No matter how hard they try. And you, my dear, are one of them." She looked to her panel for confirmation. "Am I right? I mean, I'm only telling you for your own good. There's no use pretending you can if you can't."

Arms loaded up with all they could hold, the rest draped over my shoulders, I headed for the door.

"And while we're at it, what is that thing on your head? I mean, what message are you trying to convey? Is it a snood?

Is that what it is? You just look so *odd*. I don't get it. Do you want to explain it for those of us clearly unenlightened?"

The model snickered, then bounced up to get the door.

I could feel their eyes singeing the back of my collar and, as my heels crunched over the dropped pins, I was sure I made a lavishly downtrodden spectacle. No doubt they were wondering: "Will she wait till she feels the reassurance of the doorknob in her hand before she turns to unleash a tirade? Will this break her like last year's student who needed three months in a 'facility' to undo the psychological damage? Will she go back to whatever dot on the landscape she came from and bother no more with fashion? Will she cry?"

I didn't even have a free hand to slam the door.

EDWARD

E dward and I took up our regular position in Shut-
tleworth's, the bar underneath the Phoenix Theatre
across from college. We had been going there for three
years, but always before 8 p.m. to avoid the membership
fees. Seated on tatty crimson velvet surrounded by thespian
memorabilia, we'd put our corner of the world to rights and
squint at the vaguely famous people that passed through.

"Do you think I was too stubborn?" I asked him. "Should
I have listened to them more, done the collection they wanted
me to do?"

"Look, for what this school costs with its shitty bronze-age
facilities, I think the least you should get is to do the collection
you want. I mean, you're paying."

"Well, actually, the Irish government is. Ardnacross isn't
exactly what you'd call a fashion nerve centre. It's a hill. It's a
parish of turf-cutters and milkers. The centre of it is Toner's
Bog. People there aren't in the habit of swanning off to study
fashion in London, so they had a bit of a whip-round."

"All the more reason to stick to your ideas. You're a pioneer. You should be proud of yourself."

"I'll whistle 'I Did It My Way' all the way to the unemployment office."

"What's to stop you from still being Ballymawhatyamacallit's homegrown design star?"

I took a sip of beer. "You know, they wrote about me in the local paper. I'd hoped to give them an exciting follow-up, post-St Martin's, something new to talk about beyond the price of seed and the hurling scores." I rested my chin on my hand and my elbow slipped off the table, a combination of drink, defeat, and sleep deficiency. "Oh, Edward, my collection got ripped apart before it was even properly sewn together."

"Oh, rubbish! Who cares what they say? Get some photos taken, a beautiful portfolio, and off you go. You're only as good as the next person says you are." He swiped the air decisively as he was talking. His hands always ran riot when he was trying not to smoke. Down to five a day, sometimes he had to sit on them to keep them at bay. "Isn't that that bloke off the telly?"

"Which one? Nah."

"It is, it's the one from that show—you know, the political one."

"No, it's not. You know who it is? It's that famous chef, married to whatsherface."

"So it is."

"Well, do you think I spent too much time in here? I mean, do you think my social life got in the way of my studies?"

"Well, poppet, if it did, I was right there beside you all the way."

Edward's surname, Brandreth, fell just before mine alphabetically. This meant we shared a worktable on our third afternoon on the BA when we had to display our portfolios for our classmates. Not that I wasn't aware of him, even before that. He sparkled from wherever he was in the room. The sequined head of Debbie Harry—actual size—emblazoned the left boob and shoulder of his t-shirt, silver discs flashing like a smashed heart of glass.

His portfolio, however, was more unassuming in style, as was everyone else's, I was embarrassed to note: a corporate-looking, black, zippered, leather briefcase with a dainty handle. Mine was twice the size, green, sprouting sketchbooks like unruly offspring. I succeeded in closing it by jamming it under my armpit and clasping my strained fingers underneath while tugging at the zipper with my longer than average arms. I noticed how Edward rolled his eyes when I heaved it onto the table.

Before we set up our presentations, he lifted a measuring tape and began calculating the width of the table, found a halfway point, and laid the tape lengthwise.

"There, that's your side and this is mine." He seemed relieved to have settled it.

I looked around and saw no one else doing this.

"I feel cordoned off," I said.

"No, not at all. I just don't want our work to get mixed up, that's all." He flipped open his portfolio and muttered, "Although I'd say there's little chance of that." Slid into a side pocket was a book entitled *The Seven Rules of Highly Successful People* which he removed and dropped in his bag. I rolled my eyes.

Using all available space, I set about spreading out my work, stacking surplus sketchbooks under the table. To my left I saw Edward slide his portfolio to the centre of his side about the same distance from the table edge as the tape measure and equidistant lengthwise. He was spit polishing the surface with a handkerchief when he caught me watching him.

"What?"

"Is that all you have?"

"No." He retrieved something from his bag. A pile of business cards were placed on the left hand corner of the table. He neatened them with both hands.

"Well, they should last you a while," I said. It was freshman week. Who did he think would be requesting contact details? Did he have a secretary too? I returned to my display. Edward inched closer, until he was peering over my shoulder. He did smell nice.

"Why do all your women have bandaged heads?" he asked, pointing to several drawings.

"It's a commentary on the shallow and restrictive nature of the fashion industry."

"What are you talking about?"

"We're telling people how they should look. Doesn't that sound restrictive to you?"

"Quite the opposite. We're showing them the way when they don't know any better, bringing glamour and style to their semi-detached, my-dad's-a-builder, granny flat-above-the-garage, mum-has-her-herbaceous-border, mundane lives." He had the suave, clipped pronunciation of BBC wireless broadcasters in old war movies who addressed families sitting around their radios: temporarily reassuring yet prepared for disaster.

I would have liked to continue talking, but we were quieted by the sight of a huddle of people entering the room. As they worked their way through, complete silence fell. Although all the tutors had introduced themselves earlier, only two stood out for me: the first simply because she had pink hair and looked like the quintessential zany art teacher who made imaginative use of empty toilet rolls and pipe cleaners, and the second, Eloise Churchill, the course director, who was now speaking.

"So, first years, what you need to do now is leave your area and look at everyone else's work. It is of entry standard only. But it got you here over the three hundred other poor saps who vied for each space you now occupy for better or for worse. Now you will have to leave this standard far behind over the next three years. Some of you are already more accomplished than others, that's bloody well abundantly clear, even from where I'm standing. Later this afternoon we will announce whose work is of a higher level than the rest. They will be the ones to watch, the ones you will have to beat out for jobs, for interviews, for editorial, for fucking careers for God's sake. I'd start thinking about that now if I were you. So, go, look, despair. We'll be back at three."

It was like the room had been lifted and shaken, jiggling its occupants into the corners. Eyes on stalks, we began to shuffle inward, scanning each other's work, identifying our competitors, those potential thieves of our futures. I knew exactly where Edward was in the room by how he reflected the light.

My investigations revealed, as I suspected they would, plenty of talented designers. But fashion should be inspired by the world beyond it, and I saw none of that. My portfolio demonstrated variety: I had still-lifes, portraits, landscapes; charcoal studies and pastel drawings; church spires and animals in soft watercolour; of course, plenty of fashion illustrations too. But they were drawn large and unapologetically; my new classmates scratched itty-bitty stick figures, from which it was impossible to understand any detail or feel any spirit behind them.

When Eloise lumbered back in with her footmen, I was excited to hear what she had to say. I could just glimpse the side of her head through the tightly packed students staring forward alertly. She had divided her findings into categories: most fashion forward, best illustrator, best technical skills, best overall presentation. So far, all the awards seemed to be scattered between assorted Sophies, Sophias, and an Ann-Sofie. There was still no sign of my name when we got to the notable mentions. She named a Richard and a John and that was it, she was heading for the door.

"Oh, and Kat Connelly, where is she?"

I raised my hand. Eloise stopped. All heads turned to me.

Her eyes flashed like they were taking a snapshot. "You clearly need to focus. However, I recommend you never again present me with work spotted with the remains of last night's TV dinner. Or I will fail you. You and Edward next to you will partner up for the next few months. I think you can both gain a lot from each other." And she was gone.

Horrified, I grabbed a handful of pages in my portfolio and flicked, scrutinizing them for the villainous food specks, feeling somehow double-crossed. I glanced to my left and saw Edward staring at me with a bewildered expression.

"I don't know what she's talking about," I said, letting the pages fall and folding my arms.

Sighing, he popped his business cards into a silver holder and flipped the lid shut with a click. "Do you want to go for a fag?"

"I don't smoke. But I'll come with you. Partners, eh?"

"So what happens now?" I asked, slamming the empty glass down on the table. "Apart from we continue to drown my sorrows, I mean."

"Oh, thank God you asked!" said Edward. He'd been shifting agitatedly from one bum cheek to another.

"Have you ran out of fags?"

He burst clean off the seat. "I got a job in Milan!"

I'm sure I shook my head to unclog my ears like in the cartoons. "What? When?" Had I been even more impervious to what was happening than Eloise claimed? Did I need to repeat the year? How had I not seen this steam train pulling into my platform? "*How?*"

"I'm as shocked as you, believe me. The college called one day last week asking me to come in on Saturday morning. The team from Italo Rocco were in town, wanting to set up a few interviews..." His eyes landed at another corner of the bar. "Oh! Breakfast TV weatherman at three o'clock."

"Dodgy jacket. Anyway, you were saying."

"Quite dishy, though," he said, before tearing his eyes away. "So I thought the interview went terribly and put it out of my mind, but, hey—" He raised his hands to the peeling turquoise ceiling. "Turns out they liked me!"

A sigh rose up in me that I managed to curb. "Congratulations, Edward. That's brilliant."

The Fat Director was known for doing that: dangling her favourite students in front of industry types, usually about six to ten every year. But I had no idea Edward was among this year's chosen. I concluded I must have floated semi-conscious through these final months, closed off from the rest of the world by my curtains of chiffon.

"It's all going to be a bit of a mad dash, really. I've got less than two weeks. I go right after the show." He clasped the back of his neck, then went to tug on an earlobe, while his right hand crept over his hair, mussing then smoothing. "Will you help me get things in order?"

"Not only is school finished, and I won't see you every day. Now you're moving to Italy, I won't see you for months. Talk about kicking a girl when she's down."

"My first flat, I'll make sure it has a pullout bed for you even before I get a proper one of my own. It'll wreak havoc on my proposed steamy Italian sex life but, hey, see the sacrifices I'm prepared to make? *Mi casa, su casa.* Deal?"

"Is that Italian?"

"Haven't the foggiest. But '*la bella vita*', that's Italian. Deal?"

"*La bella vita.*" I stuck out my hand and smiled. "Deal."

LYNDA

I opted out of the graduation ceremony so they sent my diploma through the mail. It was the act of opening the envelope and extracting the formal document with its embossed crest and calligraphy that sent me into a delayed crisis. That piece of fancy paper was all I had to show for the past three years, and it was about as much use as a bounced check; without the capital of the St Martin's catwalk show to trade upon, it was worthless. I started to look for work in London. What would Italy want with me?

I met Lynda in Portobello Market on a Friday morning just like many others I'd spent there. It was about two months after graduation, early, definitely before eight-thirty, because all the good stuff was still being unpacked, and the stalls were not overrun by fashion students and tourists. The stall holders were shouting to each other, setting up, and toting rounds of steaming tea and breakfast sarnies from the corner greasy spoon. In spite of the bright sun they were wrapped up against an unseasonable September cold and wore hats with furry flaps, parkas, and fingerless gloves. Naked fingertips handled money better, whatever the weather.

I could feel a demure femininity in the air—it wasn't as strong as the smell of bacon butties, but it was there. So I was looking for lace collars and cuffs, even infants' ceremonial bibs would do, from the twenties or earlier. I was going to stitch them onto Gap basics. I imagined the cuffs fluttering delicately over fine china. It would be at least six months before it became a 'trend' everyone hopped on. By then, the novelty would be gone for me. A basket underneath a table that was almost capsizing with fifties bathing costumes, scarf-covered lamps, and Bakelite jewellery caught my eye. I stooped down casually.

"How much are these wee bits going for?" I asked the girl. I'd surely find what I needed in here. I picked up a piece of card to which was pinned a simple silk square with floppy pleats and a central panel of tulle layered with one-inch tiers of lace. I could make it myself but the lace was from a time gone by and couldn't be replicated, yellowed like the pages of favourite novels. I would stick a brooch dead centre and attach it to a grey marl T-shirt. I touched another little trim, the colour and transparency of rained-upon snow. It mixed three different laces and was softer than the first. It could have been from any number of things—the trim of a parasol, the edging of a bonnet, it didn't matter; it would look great sprouting from the cuff of a grey school sweater. But one was no good to me. Ah, there was a second!

"How much did you say again?" I asked.

"I didn't. "The girl pulled a face. "I'm not the owner, you see. She'll be back in a couple of minutes. Can you come back?"

"I can't," I said, shaking my head ruefully. "I'm rushing to college. But if you like, I'll give you a couple of quid for each…" I shrugged my shoulders.

She looked about. "I'm not sure."

"They'll be hard to get rid of, miscellaneous little remnants like these. Probably why she keeps them under here. I don't know why I like them, I just do."

"I suppose I would take a tenner for the three."

"Oh, I don't think I'd pay that. Let me see." I rummaged in my purse. "No. I can give you seven ten, twenty...fifty. Seven fifty, that'll have to do. I really have to go."

"Oh, go on then. Hand it over."

I smiled. No doubt the owner had stashed them under there for safekeeping, to pull out when a discerning customer made the right enquiries; she'd have their history and origin down pat. Meanwhile, her assistant was giving them away for a song.

Next stop, old Ruby, whose stall was festooned with a banner claiming: "London's Only Remaining Rag and Bone Trader—Selling other people's junk since 1986 and no bones about it!" She loved to recount her family's proud trading lineage. Her father, ringing his bell through the East End during the sixties on his horse and cart, met her mother when he dismounted on her doorstep to haul away her old dresser. Ruby had shoeboxes of postcards and photos she let me rifle through from as far back as 1840: couples, families, young girls, in rigorous outfits of heavy fabric and arresting hats, their faces the only visible patch of startled white skin—except for the flappers who, with their bare arms and long arched necks, seemed to be lassoing the photographer with their ropes of pearls. I liked to imagine the lives they were all dressed up for, the men they were setting out to impress, if they were going straight home to change after the photos were taken. The flappers weren't going home.

Ruby had acquired nothing new since my last visit so, hands rammed in my coat pocket, looking neither left nor right, I wove through to my favourite stall way at the back, my last stop. Jean, who ran it, had given me a tip-off about the arrival of a set of vintage stage costumes from the era of the Gaiety Theatre revues and she was keeping aside a burlesque bodice for me.

"I had to call," she said. "It just whispers your name from its dusty folds. There's no one else it should go to."

Jean was the fairy godmother of quality vintage, retrieving troves from musty, neglected attics and crumbling stately piles across the country, securing trousseaus from little old ladies as they were being lowered into the ground, and seducing exotic artifacts right out of the hands of salivating collectors across the globe. As if by magic, this ghostly procession of orphaned vestments materialized in her back lot, where she freshened them up, sprinkled them on satin-covered hangers, teased them from hatboxes, and dangled them over screens depicting French village life to the tune of 'La Vie en Rose' from her pre-war gramophone.

That day, I found her serene corner the site of some unrest.

"It's not for sale," said Jean, with the impatience that comes with repeating oneself. She was addressing a blond, middle-aged woman in a long coat and green gloves. It was an expensive coat that had led the life of an inexpensive one. "And *please* do not handle the merchandise. Now if you don't mind." Jean all but smacked the woman's knuckles to have her release a silk negligee. Always particular about her treasures, and often with the high-chinned snobbery of a connoisseur, I had never seen her be so flat-out rude.

"Hey Jean," I said. "How's business?"

She broke into a smile and held up one finger. "I have it right here, my darling. Don't move."

She slipped behind some hanging scarves. The woman beside me upended a pile of silk underthings, and several slithered to the tarmac. She paid no mind, continuing to pat everything in front of her as if taking inventory. I stooped to pick up the stray things before Jean returned holding a pleated bodice of faded brocade. It had rows of hand-rolled loops girding tiny satin buttons down the front, the narrowest of sleeves that would finish in a dramatic point on the wearer's hand, and a chiffon capelet to flutter about the shoulders. Daylight shone through every tired seam, and all the edges were frayed.

"Oh, it's gorgeous." I laid my hand on the small of its back and pulled it close.

"I'll give you two hundred pounds for it," said the silk-scattering one from before. She was so close, her chin practically rested on my shoulder. "Right now. Cash in hand. Take it or leave it."

An uncomfortable pause followed. A sale like that would make Jean's morning.

"Jean, I can't give you that," I said, caressing the sleeve. "I'm waiting to hear about a design job this week but, I mean, much as I love it—"

"I won't hear of it," said Jean. "I held it over for you. You get first refusal. We'll discuss suitable terms *privately*."

"Two hundred and fifty," said the bidder, "and I'll take it off your hands. This one looks like she's just going to ask it to dance."

I scowled at her, and she flitted from my right side to my left. I knew Jean would have taken a dislike to the woman's pushiness for she felt nothing less than obliged to deposit her treasures into hands as delicate and porcelain as those of the genteel ladies who had parted with them. This character was an anathema to her.

"Look, lady," said Jean. "This is not an auction house. Now if you would please step back so that me and my friend here can—"

"Three hundred." She waved the bills right at her and looked me over. "You'd have to be stupid not to snap my arm off."

By then it looked more likely Jean would have snapped her arm off just to beat her away with it. Deaf to the woman's appeals, she enfolded the bodice in wrinkly tissue paper, slipped it in a brown bag, and handed it to me. With a promise to see her later in the week, I headed back through the market. I was just turning onto Elgin Crescent when the overbearing bidder appeared again.

"Looks like the best woman won," she said, falling into step with me. "I wanted to know if you would join me for a tea or coffee—"

"Look, let it go." I shifted the bag to my other shoulder.

"No, no, I don't care about it. I just wanted to compliment you on your look. It's very unique. Where do you like to shop? You're in fashion, am I right? Looking for work, I heard you say. And the shoes, where did you find them? The thing is, I might have a proposal to make to you, if you have five minutes."

I was curious and had nowhere else to be, so I agreed.

After we'd taken our seats in a corner café, she peeled off her gloves and laid them on the side of the table, while plying me with compliments on everything from my appreciation of quality vintage, to the sound of my accent, to how my hat brought out the colour of my eyes. She'd seen me around the market before, said it was clear I knew my stuff. Her fingers crept nervously over her cup, agitating the milky tea so that it spilled into the saucer. Each time she raised it to her lips, drops landed on the lapel of her coat, the blot blossoming into a crude brooch.

"You mix things in an unexpected way," she said.

"I do have a love of the unlikely," I said, flattered.

"There's something about you I like," she announced, after she had emptied the pot of tea. "Why don't you come and work for me?"

THE ORPHANAGE

The following Monday I stood in front of an austere, grey building in Hampstead at the address Lynda had given me. Ivy seethed on one gable and appeared to be throttling a rosebush that had peeked over into its territory. Fronds climbed onto the roof like a comb-over and tickled the black-framed windows in the front. I imagined the sound on the glass at night, like tapping fingernails, and it conjured up thoughts of Cathy, locked out on the moors, haunted by Heathcliff, her cries carried off by the wind.

I crossed the road and went to the front door. Although I'd never heard of Lynda Wynter Designs I'd become convinced over the weekend that the circumstances of our meeting were most auspicious: just as it befit a model student like Edward to make contact with his future employer through the traditional channels of his *alma mater*, it seemed appropriate that my destiny would reveal itself in a more unconventional setting: among tea-stained satin petticoats in Portobello Market.

Filled with a welcome sense of purpose, I rang the doorbell. A pleasant if somewhat harried girl with a Scottish accent asked me to wait inside. I read the inscription on a wooden plaque that hung on the wall, missing some words: *Princess Christian, in honour of her mother, Queen Victoria, is proud to celebrate the opening of this new wing... refuge for the broken remains of misfortune and accident...from a position of destitution which by no act of their own, vice or folly, they had been placed...July 9th 1904.*

After the darkness of the front hall, it took a moment for my eyes to adjust when I was shown into a much larger room illuminated with sunlight and artfully arranged objects. Exotic urns as tall as people manned the inside door, and feathered headdresses on wooden hatstands lined the wall to the window; shadows rippled across the floorboards from the ivy outside; sequined and mirrored Indian cushions winked from comfy chairs; a tower of battered old suitcases stacked stylishly behind a shapely armchair draped in ballooning silks with scalloped edging reminded me of the old movies in which well-dressed women waved handkerchiefs at departing steam trains. Framed artworks stood two or three deep against the base boards underneath shelves upon shelves of books. *And was that a Chanel jacket hanging on the back of that chair?* If rooms made first impressions, this one said, "Happy, stylish, well-adjusted, worldly, GSOH, available for fun and games or long-term commitment". I was smitten.

Finally, I spotted Lynda at the far end of a cluttered banquet table, behind a series of ceramic elephants, a bronze Buddha, a Bonsai tree in a birdcage, and an art deco vase containing sunflowers whose heads drooped as if from prior chastisement. At her shoulder was a girl, probably about twenty-one, with long dark hair. She glanced up briefly and gave a weak smile. Her face was small and pretty, as pale as a bowl of fresh goat's milk.

"Hello, Kat, this is my other designer, Celeste," said Lynda, without looking up. "Celeste, this is Kat. Can you just give me a minute?"

"Surely. Take your time." As I hung back, I watched Celeste turn the pages of a leather-bound book while Lynda scanned its pages.

"Okay, Celeste, you know what to do," she said. "Photocopy the pages I marked. Remember, the student will be back to collect it at four, so make sure everything is just as he left it."

Celeste scooped it up and turned away.

"Oh, and Celeste? Obviously, let him know we don't have any positions at the moment, we thank him for leaving his book, will keep his resume on file, blah blah blah."

As Celeste disappeared down some stairs, Lynda rose. "Now, Kat," she said, giving me her full attention. "Welcome to Lynda Wynter Designs!"

The fit model wore the prototype of a satin buttondown dress Celeste had put into work some weeks before.

"I don't like it anymore," said Lynda, and promptly ripped a page from *Elle*, brandishing it till it crackled. "Let's make it a onesie like this one. They're the latest thing."

"No can do," said Vera, from our Chinese factory, with scant regard for *Elle*. "It's the end of the fabric. We'd have to get our supplier to print more and, to be honest, we can't carry you anymore regarding minimums."

"What are you talking about?" said Lynda. "Turn the skirt into shorts."

"They've no fabric to cut them from," said Celeste, enunciating slowly, obviously annoyed that her design would be bastardized.

"Are you deaf or just stupid, Celeste?" asked Lynda.

I watched two wrinkles dance at the outer tip of each eyebrow, then two more join them, shimmying, flaunting their refusal to go down without a fight. The Botox needle that had pushed all activity to that region made me think of an overzealous clergyman forcing ravers to hold their rowdy dance parties outside the town perimeters. Lynda, wanting to bust out a few moves in the main square and finding herself unable, let out a roar of frustration and bolted from her seat.

"What's all this, if not fabric?" She pawed between the model's legs, startling her. She bunched the skirt in her fist and, with a felt tip, drew a shaky line up from the hem, crossing just below the girl's crotch, and down the inside of her other leg. "Sew along that line!" she said, replacing the cap with a smack.

Vera and Celeste shot each other an uneasy glance. I managed to keep my giggling under control. Garment construction clearly wasn't Lynda's forte. We all sat, dumbfounded, until Celeste elected to speak.

"Lynda, they need to cut new patterns to make the shorts fit right. Shorts need a…a crotch."

"Crotch! *Crotch*! I don't want to hear about *crotch!*" She waved her felt tip like it was a wand. "Just make it happen!"

"I have an idea," I said.

Lynda swung her head my way.

"The other factory in Shanghai has been calling. They want us to take the crepe meterage off their hands from the styles you cancelled. We could have them send it to Vera. I know it's not the same but it's got the same print. I think it might even look better because crepe de chine is less transparent, would require no lining, so there'd be less bulk around the hips. Here, let me show you a swatch." I ran to Celeste's desk and pulled it from the fabric file. Vera put on her glasses and felt its weight between her fingertips. Lynda looked at her, then me, with a mixture of suspicion and expectation.

"Well?" she asked.

"Absolutely," announced Vera. "It's the perfect fabric for what you want to do."

"I knew it. That's the sort of assistant I've been looking for, Celeste, you see? Kat, if you keep thinking on your feet like that and saving me money to boot, we'll get on like a house on fire."

While Lynda took her seat and Vera busily scribbled the fabric details and the name of her contact person, I could feel Celeste glaring holes into the side of my head.

Celeste and I were kneeling on the floor, arranging images for a mood board. She stepped back to approve the layout, her face creased up, and the tears fell. I looked at the mood board, but could see nothing there to trigger such emotion. She trailed a soggy tissue from her sleeve to her nose and looked at me accusingly over it.

"You have no idea what it's like in here. But you'll learn soon enough."

I'll have my hands full with this one, I thought.

"How do you like your new office anyway?" She had rubbed her nose red. "It used to be an orphanage, you know?"

"I saw the plaque by the door."

"It was built in the 1850s and stopped functioning only in the early 1940s."

"And what happened after that?"

"It became an institution where, instead of orphans, designers are left to die." She flounced dramatically onto the couch, but Lynda chose that moment to walk through, and

Celeste sprang back up with an engaging smile. Lynda floated by like she was unaware of either of us. When we were alone again, Celeste clomped back to her desk, whilst flagellating herself with several long, woolly scarves. Resting one heavy boot behind her on the chair, she leaned forward conspiratorially.

"Seriously, we're wasting the best years of our lives. I'm just telling you."

"Actually, I could get quite used to it here: the space, the gorgeous books, the vintage clothes. If I imagined a design studio, I don't think it would look much different than this. It's a true bohemian lair."

Celeste responded by shoving her arms into a second cardigan and hugging herself. She shook her head and went back to work.

The word lair was somewhat misleading; the place was more of a chasm. The room I had admired that first day, the middle slice of a gaping split-level space, had been the reception area where waifs and strays had been welcomed, their heights recorded, their teeth examined, and their fates sealed. A waist-high railing fenced off its thirty-foot drop to a basement floor about four times its length which had been the dormitory where staffers in grey uniforms scurried with bedpans, linens, and thermometers, one hundred and fifty years before. Where there were floor-to-ceiling bookcases, there had been cabinets containing medicines and bedding. Where there was a fuchsia wraparound sofa with artfully mismatched chairs and stools, there had been uniform, grey-blanketed beds equidistance apart; and way at the end, in the former laundry room, our desks, computers, printers, and photocopiers had replaced the four deep sinks no doubt constantly in use. Despite the modern fittings and exotic curios, I heard the echoes of dozens of whimpering children, and the chink of spoons against bowls licked clean of gruel, my head filled with what those walls would describe if they could talk.

"So how exactly did Lynda come to set up a design studio here?" I asked.

"She lives here too, you know. On the third floor." Celeste spoke with the air of someone who has the keys to a vault of information but is determined to dole it out only in timely doses or when it would yield most return. She looked up, saw that I wanted to know more, and, this time, provided: "Her father set her up. It's all him. He bought the building in the eighties—he has *buckets* of dosh—and although it sat empty, he never wanted to give it to her. She harped on about starting her business, and finally he agreed as the only way to get her out from under his roof. She's forever in his debt, and he never lets her forget it—Shhh!" She snatched a pencil and pretended to draw.

Lynda was leaning over the balcony. "Kat, just in case you're not aware, when you are working late I don't allow overhead lighting as it would discolour my collection of old books and textiles."

I may have looked up too fast because she seemed to be swaying slightly.

"You can use the table lamps I have provided at your work stations."

But I had already worked late two evenings, and the sixty-watt bulbs positioned at shoulder height, piercing the darkness like a rescue party's torches, made the pen marks swim before my eyes.

"And while we're on the subject," she continued. "I don't like the central heating to be turned up any higher either. For the same reason."

That explained the layers that trailed off Celeste's limbs, encircling her waist, dripping off her chair.

"Oh, and can you come here a second, Kat?"

"There she blows," said Celeste under her breath.

At the top of the stairs, Lynda led me to a couple of low stools, swept several pairs of beaded moccasins to the floor, and we sat down. "Right. I think we need to get rid of Celeste. I need you to start collecting resumes for me to look at."

"You want to get rid of her?"

"That's what I said. I just don't think she has it anymore. That 'it' factor, that sixth sense, that mix of talent and drive that we have. She's tired, and it shows in her attitude. I've been considering it for a while." She breathed heavily. "Don't you agree?"

"I've only been working with her a few days. I don't feel I could fairly say."

"Well, I would expect you to know by now."

I had believed—based on what, I couldn't say—that Lynda secretly appreciated having Celeste around and vice versa. It fit in with my casting of her as Fagin, and Celeste as the Artful Dodger: together they formed a hauled-up-by-the-bootstraps, feisty design duo who, instead of picking a pocket or two, pilfered an idea or two. As the newcomer, I was the one who was supposed to consider herself at home, while proving herself worthy of staying.

When I returned downstairs, Celeste looked up from her computer. "Was that the talk about replacing me then?"

I opted for a light-hearted tone. "As of this morning, your neck is indeed on the chopping block. Know anyone good?"

"Don't worry. She wouldn't do me the favour of sacking me." She went back to work.

"And those are the themes for the next three deliveries," I concluded. "Has anyone got any questions?"

"Love it!" said Tamsin, the Head Buyer of Wovens, nodding approvingly. "The styles feel really right for spring, and the sketches are beautiful. Impressive presentation, girls."

I shot Celeste a quick smile. Her humour was as flitting as a deer dashing from clearing to thicket, but we'd bonded through our boards of Marianne Faithful, Marc Chagall, and Dries Van Noten. She sent over a hesitant smile in return.

Tamsin turned to Lynda. "You seem to have found your dream team, Lynda. Now, it's all systems go. We have high expectations for these next few deliveries, right, ladies?" Her assistants chimed in agreeably. "Kat, that skirt you're wearing, could we do our own version of it? Change the print, which might be a little too out there for us, but the shape is lovely."

"Oh, it's from the fifties. The pattern piece is actually a complete circle." I grabbed either side and held it out triumphantly so that the fabric fanned. "It'd take yards of material, but we have that inexpensive cotton/linen blend in delivery one with the nice crunchy hand. What do you think?"

Lynda did not participate in the spirited discussion that followed. She sat in her chair looking like she'd just collided with it, her fingers playing with the bells decorating the border of a throw cushion. Her eyes seemed bloodshot as they roamed over the group, landing back on Tamsin.

The buyer of Knits sat forward. "Kat, will you be extending these themes to the knit portion of the deliveries? I don't want you concentrating solely on Wovens now. Don't forget about the lucrative sweater business. Have you any ideas I could look at? I'd be interested to see."

"Oh course. Celeste will take the floor."

Celeste, naturally drawn to cold weather wear, had concentrated on the Knitwear while I sketched the Wovens.

"Let me see that," said Lynda, snatching the file from Celeste. "Have I approved these?"

"Well, you loved them this morning," said Celeste, drily. "But that might mean nothing."

Distractedly, Lynda shoved the file back at her. "Exactly what did you mean by that earlier remark, Tamsin? Are you suggesting I wasn't running a tight ship before?"

I heard Celeste suck air through her teeth.

"What comes out of this studio represents half of your business, are you forgetting that?"

"I didn't mean anything by it, Lynda. I was just complimenting you on your team."

"I've always gotten good people. Celeste has been with me over a year now, and she's the best. I know how to find talent—mostly it finds me. But some inevitably drop by the wayside, can't handle the pressure. It's one thing to make nice drawings, but drawings won't stock your shelves with merchandise, Tamsin. Customers don't buy drawings. We'll see how Kat is with measurements and production fittings, and delivery schedules. Let's not start counting our chickens." She shot me a warning look before pointedly concluding, "We've been down that route before, haven't we?"

The Head Buyer of Wovens, of Knits, their respective assistants, and Celeste sat in an uncomfortable silence.

A CABINET OF CURIOSITIES

"I don't think you should get rid of Celeste. We already have a rapport, she's a good designer—you said so yourself—and with her around I'll learn the ropes faster."

"When did I say that?" Lynda narrowed her eyes. "You think she's good?"

Without Celeste, my only other ally would be Sherry, the Scottish maid, who was amiable to have around but whose jurisdiction lay above: the kitchen, bathroom, reception, and laundry room; Lynda let her have it if she was found downstairs "fraternising."

"I do. I think we work well together."

Lynda had a way of looking at me sometimes, a glance that was so distrustful it was as if she could hear my secret thoughts, as if she had wiretapped my brain. All I knew was that the more time I spent there, the more I wanted to cling to whatever small familiarities each day brought; Celeste was a small familiarity.

"Have it your way," she said. "I hope you know what you're doing."

It soon became clear that I didn't, because a strange, new dynamic developed between us. While I had expected Celeste to be relieved, even grateful, that I'd come to her defence, she was pragmatic about it, riding the upswing of her fortunes with barely a glance my way. *Laissez les bons temps rouler!* But one morning, she pulled up a chair beside me as if overcome by a sense of duty.

"Listen, just a warning about what's coming up: the old classic disregarded sibling complex."

"The what?"

"She plays people off against each other. It's the pattern." She looked up to see if Lynda was likely to surface, then continued, her mouth curling into a sneer of contempt. "Lynda's the middle of three girls, you see, and, well, the least attractive. Her father only wanted boys and takes it out on her, leaving the other two alone. Because she's not a looker, he's angry not only that she's not a boy, but that she's not even a worthwhile girl. But she has to toe the line and take all his criticism if she stands any chance of getting a share of his fortune."

"Interesting. But what's that got to do with me?"

Unfortunately, I detected a presence from the corner of my eye and glanced up to see Lynda looming from the railings.

"Shut up," hissed Celeste.

She reverted to basking under the glow of Lynda's renewed favour, and I regretted not having gathered that hefty stack of resumes. Then, Celeste would be nothing more than a name scrawled along the stiff spines of some of the more expensive French magazines. Instead, her and Lynda joked, gossiped, and ate together like two sorority sisters, and I found myself disagreeing with them just to have my voice heard.

"It looks like some sort of rare skin disease," I remarked of a watercolour print they were both rhapsodizing over. When they discussed Lynda's next trip to Berlin, Celeste clearly angling to be invited along, I piped up, "*The Sunday Times* reported yesterday that Scandinavia's where it's at now." When they pored over take-out menus, debating over sushi or vegan for lunch, I called from the other side of the room, "There is increasing concern for women and the amounts of mercury they're consuming. They say the biggest culprit is sushi."

They usually responded with blank looks except for the time Lynda got up, lifted a file from Celeste's desk, and let it drop on my desk.

"Can you draw up these ideas? Celeste's busy with other things."

I opened the file; it was brim-full of pages torn from this month's magazines, items circled with a red Sharpie.

"You want me to copy them?"

"I'll expect them by the end of the day."

Lynda Wynter *Designs* read the name on the file's cover. I'd seen little evidence of it.

"Isn't Celeste pretty, Kat?" said Lynda over her shoulder.

"Girls, I have one of my headaches. Carry on with what you're doing, and I'll see it tomorrow. I can't make it into the office today."

The first time it happened it struck me as funny. Lynda teetering at the top of the stairs, the shoulder pads of her dressing gown squaring off her elbows, her face as puffed as her hair was limp.

"You're already *in* the office, you silly cow. You make it sound like you have to catch two trains from suburbia, a car service, and a lift to the twentieth floor to get to work."

I shot a surreptitious glance in Celeste's direction. I hadn't meant to speak out loud. She just giggled and broke into a *sotto voce* chorus of "It's a Long Way to Tipperary".

Over time, I noticed those days happened quite frequently, but they made more sense after my encounter with the hooded stranger. Fishing for my keys one morning, determined not to buzz Sherry, as she had already cut two sets for me and made me promise I would be more careful with the third, I was joined on the doorstep by a man.

"Lynda?" he said, from behind the hood of his sweatshirt. He held out a brown paper package about the size of half a dozen eggs.

"I'm not Lynda."

He nodded, regardless, pushed the package into my hands, and retreated quickly. I watched him bob away, fists sunk into his sweatshirt pockets, head down, until he disappeared onto the high street.

Inside, Sherry had removed everything from the grand table onto the rug and was polishing it vigorously as I shook off my coat. Coffee was steeping in the press. Its woody aroma combined with the lemon of the cleaning spray made for a pleasant welcome.

"Her Ladyship's not coming down today," said Sherry. "She has another one of her heads."

"I've just had a mysterious delivery for her." I gave it a shake. "What do you think it is?"

"I'll soon show you." With an air of sufferance, she laid down her duster and spray, tore open one side of the paper, and watched as six stout little bottles rattled like maracas tumbling onto the newly shined antique oak.

"Adderall, Dexedrine…" I read, "…Ritalin, Lithium… are all these for her?"

She scooped them up, carried them to a corner of the kitchen to a penicillin-green cabinet like the ones doctors had in their clinics during the fifties, an unassuming enamel press with brass feet, turned-out ankles, and panels of frosted glass reminiscent of a housewife's apron from which a lollypop might be produced if you were a good girl. Sherry unlocked and flung open its doors to reveal a veritable munitions hold, an arsenal of pharmaceuticals.

"Are we expecting an epidemic to befall Greater London?"

"We keep a full bar. Uppers, downers, and in-betweeners, whatever's her tipple."

"So there's nothing wrong with her?"

Sherry snorted. "There's nothing right with her." She slotted in the new bottles while reciting a grocery list of disorders and the medication employed for each. "This week, she claims she's bipolar, so we got extra of these. Her father called her up to tell her she's just loony and gets it from her mother's side, so she drank a half bottle of Jameson with a handful of these from last month when she complained of chronic back ache. Just last night, she downloaded a programme on ADD." Struggling to find space for a Ritalin and a Zoloft, she turned, agitating the jars as if gauging their weight. "And it ain't no doctor who shows up on her doorstep speaking no English, in tight jeans carrying an unmarked paper bag. You know any doctor like that? Some of this stuff isn't even available in this country." Rolling her sleeve up, she steadied two columns of similar-sized jars at the back, and lowered the last two on top. She closed the door and pocketed the key. "Of course, I didn't say a word, mind. Now I must get this coffee up to her."

Downstairs, I watched dust motes swirl against the windows. The distant alerts that I'd initially tried to ignore about Lynda were creeping closer, going off sharply now, a matter of daily routine. Meanwhile, Sherry busied herself above bringing the furniture to an enviable sparkle, and Lynda, above her, flapped about in dark corners like a bat in a belfry. An elaborate three-tiered charade.

I thumbed through the pile of sketches that the buyers were expecting me to put into work, but which Lynda had put on hold, then picked up a magazine. I flicked half-heartedly, but the sensation of my fingertips on the glossy pages had the soothing effect of a damp flannel on clammy skin. I spread my fingers, pressed down on the binding, and stared into a waifish face, translucent but shimmering; an apparition whose hair fit like a black lacquer helmet, and whose mouth, a swirl of crimson ribbon, wavered somewhere between seduction and derision. Grazing her square jaw, her earrings were an assembly of transparent plastic tubes locked inside each other, ready to disengage and propel themselves from the ramps of her shoulders like miniature prototype NASA capsules. She was half-human/half-alien, half-man/half-woman, half-high fashion/half-science fiction. I shifted my palm and read the willowy, white type across the bottom of the page: House of Adriani.

The successive page, a perfume ad, spotlighted the beautiful structure of her face, her eyes obfuscated like the lenses of sunglasses, revealing little. I hadn't yet peeled back the flap, but the fragrance had wafted out anyway, morphing into an unexpected medley of some of my favourite things… the whiff of long, rainy grass… watercolour paints…

"Earth to Kat, Earth to Kat. Hello?"

I hadn't heard Celeste arrive—unusual, considering the clatter she always made. The fragrance was intoxicating; it didn't so much grow on me as grow *around* me. I wondered if I was projecting my favourite smells on it or if it would have the same effect on Celeste.

I pushed the magazine towards her. "What do you think of this?"

She wrestled out of her coat and scarf and leaned over. "Oh, good, give it here. I didn't have time to put any on this morning." She tore off the square and, rolling up her multitude of sleeves, smeared her wrists across the scented teardrop.

"Do you know, I'd quite fancy working somewhere like that."

"Yeah, right. Good luck with that," she said and sent the magazine scooting back across the table. "Sorry to break it to you but I don't think either of us have set ourselves on paths that lead to the House of Adriani." She gave her wrist a dubious sniff. "This is as close as we get."

Which was as far removed from Edward's bella vita as I could have aimed for.

Edward's emails mentioned the word *"ragazzi"* on average about thirteen times; it meant boys. The *ragazzi* were gorgeous, the *ragazzi* were everywhere, *ragazzi* at work, *ragazzi* at play, here *ragazzi*, there *ragazzi*, everywhere *ragazzi*. To me it sounded like the name of a sportscar. Edward also repeatedly used the words *"moda"* and *"festa"*, but said his vocabulary was still limited. Boys, fashion, party. What more was there to say? I got the picture.

On the telephone, he substituted colourful new words for the good old-fashioned 'Hello': "*Vaffanculo, stronza! Va a cagare!* How are you, *Troia*? You have no idea how truly disgusting I am being. *Puttana!* You'd never get away with this stuff in everyday conversation at home. Italians are filthy!"

He was as chipper as a chaffinch.

I pulled up his last email while Lynda built to a quiet roar, reprimanding Celeste for reinstating a skirt style Lynda believed she'd cancelled, and it brought a smile to my face:

"*...Miu Miu bags and Marni shoes on the Metro! From schoolgirls to grannies, they know their labels. You wouldn't believe it. And everyone knows someone who can get you discount. They don't have those bizarre look-at-me styles you see trawling through London. I'm so over that. Here they just ooooooooze style. You see catwalk looks in the supermarket aisles. Go in for a jar of mascarpone and get an eyeful of Valentino as well.*

Be warned. It's not all glamour though. I had a harrowing experience at a place called the Questura yesterday. It's where you go to get your residence papers which you need to work here. Kat, I was thrown into the third world—smelly, chaotic, dangerous! Unclean! Unclean! Everyone crowded in the one big room, fresh off the boat: what looked like members of a drug cartel; sweaty, crying babies; Russian prostitutes, and me! All waiting for our numbers to be called. The sequence went like this: 1085, 313, 7, 430, 27... I didn't know if I'd be served in the next three minutes or the next three weeks! Tempers were beyond frayed. "I design for Italo Rocco!" I wanted to yell. Apparently, you can pay someone to line up and get all your papers for you. I clearly don't move in the right circles yet, but I'm working on it. Anyway, when I got home, I had two showers and a bath.

My landlady is an interesting old bird—she's always eyeing me like I'm up to something. But my flat is cute in a shabby chic kind of way. I can't believe I'm using that term! Italian shabby chic is different than English shabby chic, just so you're aware. Although if I'm using my electric shaver, I've been advised to disconnect the TV! Anyway, I'm sure the old dear will warm to me over time and consider me a responsible young gentleman. Most old dears love me on sight.

Have you decided what you're doing yet? Get your culo over here! Cazzo! You could work for me, going to the Questura, queuing for my papers, if nothing else! If you showed up pretending to be my girlfriend, I bet my landlady would be a little friendlier. In such a macho culture, doesn't she realize only a delicate flower like yours truly could live in her fragile little pied-à-terre?

Speaking of macho, have I mentioned the ragazzi? You'd fall over yourself for them. Not much action over there, is there, K? Admit it. Too much oestrogen in the orphanage? Not much in the way of outside diversions... I'm imagining you in a sort of Grey Gardens—like the poor handyman who went in with the intention of knocking in a few nails, putting up a shelf and doing a couple of odd jobs, but who got stuck between Little Edie and Big Edie with only the raccoons for sensible company... "

"Stop talking from your silly face, Celeste!"

Recently, they had been more fractious than usual. Maybe Celeste's cramps were coinciding with Lynda's flashes to discharge a fusillade of female hormones. If we had a cellar, I could hide there till the worst of it passed.

"I'm serious, Celeste! Just stop bleating excuses! And stop gawping like a moron! All I'm guaranteed with you is stupidity. That's all I can count on. I'm going back upstairs. I don't want to see you for the rest of the day. I mean it."

Celeste burst into noisy tears and ran to lock herself in the bathroom. Lynda set off on her laboured trudge upstairs. I checked about for raccoons.

One afternoon, Lynda braved a trip to the office after being out of action for three days with 'flu', arriving in time to meet with a print vendor, Sami, from a studio in South London. The four of us sat on low stools, Lynda swaying gently, with one leg by Kerry, the other by Cork. She looked like she'd thrown on her clothes with a pitchfork; her Dries Van Noten peasant dress was misbuttoned, and her hair hung in clumps which she pushed behind her ears to reveal three pulsating veins above her left eye. But in a nod to more elegant living, she wore a beautiful antique grid necklace embellished with pearls and matching drop earrings.

Just as we were about to review Sami's artwork, Lynda yanked herself upright and wandered off.

"Don't worry on my account," said Sami, with a gap-toothed smile in my direction. "I can wait."

Sami was part of a cottage industry of design graduates who made an excellent living flogging regurgitated ideas to past-their-peak industry types with more money than fashion sense. That was my take on it anyway. He bulk-bought cheap vintage clothes and, as I pictured it, sat in his Brixton bed-sit, a can of Heineken on one side, a spliff on the other, chopping the garments to pieces and reassembling their hacked, mismatching parts like a macabre back-street surgeon: an amputated knit sleeve from a child's dress tacked with garish thread to a floral bodice with too-large armholes, a row of motley buttons scooped from his collection and glued down the front, a lurid bow stapled at the neckline, and kerching! He would sell it for five hundred pounds to the likes of Lynda who would get it copied into a frock in China.

"And I'll take a herbal tea with that," Lynda called, returning to her stool.

When Sherry crept in and left a tray on a small African table containing the mug of tea and five coloured beads chasing each other around a saucer, Lynda absented herself again. She returned looking noticeably happier.

"We should have wine, not tea," she said. "Sami, wine?"

"Oh, no thanks, Lynda. I still have quite a few appointments. I don't want to be trolleyed in front of clients, at least not this early."

"Why? Who are you seeing next?" It drove her mad not knowing who else he sold to, but he remained evasive.

"Do you know, I can't remember. I forgot my planner. I'll just have to phone the studio after. Shall we continue?"

"Your suitcase might leave here empty, and there'll be nothing left for those other so-called clients of yours," said Lynda, her competitive streak rising.

Sami laughed his all-the-way-to-the-bank laugh.

"Laura Ingalls Wilder in Ibiza! How about that for the theme of our new delivery, Lynda?" I reached for two vintage Liberty print blouses from our work rack and plopped them down next to one of Sami's samples featuring orange plastic with neon stitching and another with a rubberized stripe. "A little house music on the prairie?"

"I love it," said Celeste, nodding like she could already see it in her head. "The nineties are coming back."

My guess was Lynda would need some convincing - it wasn't yet in the magazines.

"We could do pretty little apron dresses, with utilitarian detailing, floral blouses with plastic buttonstands and collars..."

"Humph," said Lynda, uncrossing and recrossing her legs the opposite way.

"You know, if that's your thinking," said Sami, swiftly unzipping a pocket of his case, "I was saving these for another client. They'd asked for something edgy and different, but as I like where you're going, take a gander!" He unfurled each sample with a magician's flourish, splaying his fingers and holding the corners between fingertip and thumb. Celeste and I pounced on each one.

"This is wicked, Sami," said Celeste.

"Thank you kindly. Occasionally, I like to challenge myself." He looked pleased but turned to Lynda, the source of his paycheck, to ensure her feelings were in concordance. "Can you see over there, Lynda? Should I come closer?"

"I can see fine," she said, sulkily, now swinging her crossed leg like she had better things to do, and we were all unworthy of her company anyway.

"Is this the kind of stuff you need, Lynda? I don't want to waste your valuable time."

She responded with one slow blink and a grunt. It was behaviour we saw every day, but it spooked Sami.

"I have other stuff in the car, archive stuff—girly, still feminine, and playful—but more traditional. Would you prefer to see that?"

It was the same crotchetiness she exhibited when her father made business decisions without her. Even though he funded her entire operation and had every right to capitalise on his investment, ultimately benefitting her interests, she was incapable of seeing past her out-of-joint nose. Similarly, Celeste and I had designed three well-received deliveries that had just begun to hit stores, registering higher than average sales, and still she didn't trust us.

"Lynda, don't you think this could be the basis for the update on our best-selling top from summer?" I asked, waving a sample.

Her nasal labial folds were parentheses embracing her obstinate pout.

"And this would be great for knits," said Celeste. "Just what the buyers have been waiting for. Right, Kat?"

Sami looked uncertainly from us to Lynda.

She lurched forward with a sigh. "You have good stuff, Sami. As always. It's not that. I just don't like what these two are pulling. It's not young, it's not modern, it's not relevant, it won't sell. It's not the direction we should be going."

"Alrighty, not a problem." Sami whipped the samples from our hands and zipped them back in his case. Positioning his stool next to Lynda and his back to us, he said, "Now, start from scratch with this pile here. Right up your street. If there's something that takes your fancy, pull it aside."

The meeting continued between Sami and Lynda, while Celeste and I sat glumly back, chins in hands, and watched the adults talk.

At the meeting's close, Lynda had lightened Sami's suitcase by three thousand pounds' worth. Celeste gathered the samples, Lynda fetched her checkbook, and Sami and I casually discussed his newly acquired holiday home on the Costa Brava. The front door had just closed behind him when the afternoon took its turn for the insane. Lynda came forward, her arms shaking like there were insects up her sleeves. I thought she was hamming it up to compensate for her previous moodiness. Transfixed by her bulging eyes, I had no idea what was in store as she picked up speed.

"I will not have you talking about me like I am not there. Do you understand?" She clutched me by the shoulders and began to shake me. "I've known him longer than you. You're just lucky I keep you around, remember that. You will never ever discuss me with my colleagues or peers. Do you hear me?"

I felt my head whip back and forth on my neck; it was as light as the head of a dandelion, its seeds being tossed asunder until nothing would remain but the naked stem.

"Stop it, Lynda!" cried Celeste. "You'll hurt her!"

I could see hands flailing between us and only realized they were mine when, in an attempt to push her off, I caught my fingers in the spidery strands of her necklace. I heard a pearl ping on the floor and watched as the gold grid split neatly in two and slithered almost in slow motion off her reddening throat. When it hit the ground, it unleashed a troupe of pearls spinning and reeling off the artworks and baseboards.

Sherry and Celeste got her off me by tugging on each arm. Her eyes, no longer protruding, had locked at the level of my breast bone like they had run out of energy to lift themselves higher. Beads of perspiration clung to the fine hairs of her eyebrows.

"It makes me angry, that's all," she said, weakly.

I dropped onto a stool. "I never said a word. No one even mentioned you... no one." My ears rang, the contents of my skull still settling. "You're cracked in the head, Lynda."

Sherry rotated Lynda and coaxed her back to bed. After a few steps, Lynda turned, her glassy eyes straining to settle on anything.

"You know, girls, maybe we don't need to see Sami any-more. See to that, will you?" As she was about to ascend the stairs, she mumbled something. Sherry tightened her arm about her shoulder, but she wriggled away and said, inclining her head so that her voice carried, "Isn't Celeste pretty, Kat?"

The room still resonated with the sound of rolling pearls. Celeste dropped down beside me and began to cry.

While Sherry nursed Lynda into a medicated sleep and Celeste anxiously patted her brow with cold water in the bathroom, I rose and went downstairs. The first thing to catch my eye in the dim afternoon light was the Chanel jacket. It was squashed on a rail, backed up against a bookcase, mixed in with her flea market finds. The most beautiful thing in this entire mausoleum, and it had no business being there—literally. Lynda had bought it on a trip to Paris but, in a world where fabrics cost three pounds a meter or were sent to China to be copied, where factories used the same pattern blocks for every style, and where buyers wouldn't know a Chanel shoulder from chopped sausage, it had languished untouched. I always made sure I could see it from wherever I was in the room. I ran my fingers over it like some people rub a lucky stone. Staring at its Lurex weave bouclé was like gazing at the great shiny constellation of fashion beyond the garret window. It was proof that when innovation, quality, and precision met, the result was too elusive, too enigmatic, and too formula-defying to be cobbled together in some corner of China.

I felt no sense of aftershock—apart from a slight whistling in my ears. I was mostly filled with awe at the vast tundra that must be Lynda's mind, where reason just detaches itself from any living thing, drops, and dies; where chunks of cohesive thought spiral by only to be dashed against the rocks or flung to the bitter winds. Lynda's assistants, like tundra plant life, needed to be tough, ground-hugging, and fond of darkness. Those seeking growth need not apply.

During the attack, I had been conscious of the impulse to reach for the nearest weapon; a birdcage or Buddha to the head would penetrate the fog more effectively than any pill. But a strange calm had descended right after, and I felt no inclination to retaliate. I had needed that shaking, deserved it. If I could have administered it myself, I might have come to my senses sooner. For old desires had been agitated and floated to the surface creating an odd exhilaration. And another thing, I was better for having spent those months with Lynda. My eye was more exacting, my taste level honed, my hunger piqued. Every time Da had to work with a neighbouring farmer, he would come home and say there was a lot to be learned from observing how not to do things. In working with Lynda I had completed a full-immersion programme of post-graduate fieldwork.

I gathered only a few favourite pens and pencils, the magazine containing the House of Adriani spread, and slung my bag over my shoulder. On my way back through, I touched the Chanel jacket one last time. Then in a moment of ultimate serenity, I slid it from the hanger and buried it in my bag. It would be my compass for where I would go next.

MILAN

My head vibrated against the window panel. From ten thousand feet, Milan looked no different than Dublin on a sunny day. I had expected some distinguishing features at that height, but the area it lay in was flat, the roads were long and straight, the buildings square, the roofs scuffed. Even the distant fields seemed to have been sucked of their juice. It didn't resemble a pulsating epicentre of anything and showed no immediate signs of the contained bella vita.

Soon the pilot urged those on the right side of the plane to look out their windows where the turrets and tall spire of the Duomo cathedral could be seen rising above the city. A passing cloud cast a shadow over it, and it reminded me of mum's Singer, the spire its bloodthirsty spindle. That's when I knew I needed to relax. This was where Edward was; everything would be fine. I told myself it wasn't such a bad thing to feel a healthy dose of uncertainty after having been so resolute about St Martin's and so convinced by Lynda. But I felt intimidated just by the sounds of Italian being spoken in the seat behind me.

As we descended through the last of the clouds, a winged creature came into view, as if guiding us in to land. I wondered if everyone else saw it too. It was a gigantic neon eagle with widespread wings emblazoned with the words "Emporio Armani", and it graced the entire front of an Arrivals building at Linate airport. Its presence reassured me, and when we disembarked, it was towards those welcoming wings I ran, and the entrance just beyond. My fellow travellers were resistant to any kind of queuing system. We were a big, disorderly bundle expanding wider than what the double doors could accommodate but pressing on regardless. Like protesters, people went to light up underneath signs showing a cigarette with an X through it. They had broken out like battery hens escaped from cages, preening flattened feathers, and squawking indignantly. "*Cazzo!*", "*Porca troia!*" and "*Stronzo!*" were among the first words I heard, recognized from Edward's phone calls. His email: "What to Do When You Arrive in Linate!" instructed me to avoid the men in suits around the Exit offering unlicensed taxis, and head for the registered white cars opposite. I even knew how to ask for a beer in the bar where we would meet: *oona beer-ah purr fah-vo-ray*.

Legal my driver may have been, but patient with my stuttered Italian he wasn't; he snatched Edward's e-mail from me and flicked his thumb towards the back seat. We moved off in a convoy of other taxis onto a nondescript stretch of motorway past billboards with legs as tall as trees. When the airport traffic was behind us, my driver became a rodeo rider. This was about him alone in the saddle, asserting his one-handed mastery over the car. With a jaw-clenching swerve, he changed lanes and wiped his brow, realigned himself in his seat and floored it, yelling through both open windows while dragging on his cigarette. Rubber screeched on tarmac, and we hurried to a stop in order to let a woman in a tight dress cross in front. He hollered approval, the engine revved, and we bucked forward. Approaching the first built-up area, he was still showing the vehicle who was boss. Slanted at a forty-five degree angle, I understood we had completed a roundabout. My luggage bumped against the sides of the trunk and, all the while, like a nagging wife in the passenger seat, a female voice repeated information from the cab radio while the crackling transmission did its best to stifle her. The Marlborough Red plume billowing from the window heralded our arrival into the town centre and, after zipping around sharp corners of handsome buildings, like a beast pulled up short by an invisible electric fence, we lurched to a halt in front of Café Victoria, and I toppled out, my bags following close on my heels.

The venue of Edward's and my rendezvous was an airy salon with green walls, painted mirrors, and framed faces of Cinecittà. I dropped to a seat under a wild-eyed Anna Magnani. The floor tiles were like black and white fifty-pence pieces, and the wooden wraparound bar was tended by gentlemen in bowties who didn't speak above a murmur. The whirr of the ceiling fan sounded vaguely exotic and lulled me into feeling like a character in a thick novel.

"Darling, you look wonderful!" Edward stood on the threshold like he was addressing the room, and indeed several patrons looked up hopefully. Then, sailing past the staring barmen, he said, "Martini, grazie", swinging a tan leather case born of the same family as his St Martin's portfolio.

"Still don't understand what bloody well took you so long." He dropped his case and pulled me into a long hug.

Into his shoulder, I replied, "Oh, you know, being ambushed in broad daylight, thrown in an orphanage, escaping, that sort of thing takes time." I stepped back to look at him. "But I'm here now. You look great."

"Do I? I have a hang-over'd strip the hair off your legs." He settled back in the seat. "And I'm trying to quit smoking."

"So you're my same conflicted Edward?" I giggled and wanted to hug him again. I already felt more myself than I had in weeks.

"You can count on me."

The public schoolboy with nary a blot on his copy book by day, who sneaked out of school grounds after dark for mischief-making and moon howling, he looked just as I remembered him. The front of his hair doubled back into a quiff, perhaps worn a fraction longer than usual, and he sported the usual classic, open-necked shirt with small logo on the breast. Just the branding had changed: instead of the polo player, it was the green, white and red Italo Rocco skull and crossbones.

The barman placed his martini in front of him.

"You'll have one too?" Edward asked over the rim of his glass before burying his nose in it. "Ooh, now that hits the spot. Lovely." It was unclear whether he meant the drink or the barman whose departing figure he was keenly observing. "Anyway," he said, putting his glass down and rubbing his hands together. "Welcome to Fashionlandia! Where Glamarama is the tallest Rollercoaster in the world!"

"Good God!" I laughed. "What if I throw up my lunch?"

"Then you'll fit right in. Eating disorders are rife round here."

Making short work of his first martini, he began the second full of anecdotes about his boss, Italo, and his ever-present boyfriend, Gio. A young buck arrived in the big smoke of Milan from a small Pugliese village twelve years ago, Italo had launched himself onto the grand stage in a fanfare of neon fun fur, stretch satin, and peroxide blonde models—and that was just the menswear—and had never looked back. Italo was immediately christened the "enfant terrible" of Italian fashion and the bad boy moniker still stuck even in advanced middle age because, in the closed community of Italian fashion, houses didn't sprout up like in London or New York, they were passed down from one generation to the next, their figureheads often working until old age or death. Italo had been the new kid on the block for over a decade simply because no one had arrived to challenge him.

"So their new Shiba Inu chewed off the logo from Italo's special edition Motorola," continued Edward, "made with two hundred rubies, two emeralds, and one diamond—the very stone the dog scoffed. You see where this is going, don't you? We had to take turns waiting for it to come out the other end. Well, what with the tax evasion scandal hanging over them and Men's Fashion Week coming up, we just do as we're told."

"It's a far cry from boring old St Martin's coursework," I said.

"Not as far off as you might think," he replied. "So, of course, out it popped on my shift, didn't it? I'm your man for finding the diamond in the dog turd. How's that for glamour?"

"The kind that clearly agrees with you."

A group of women strode into the bar, and although their voices were aggressive and masculine, they were top-of-the-range examples of well-designed femininity: glossy and curvilinear above the waist, slim-hipped and sleek below. As they claimed a table in the corner they commanded the attention of every male in the room: a pride of lionesses settling under a tree by a watering hole.

I leaned in. "Whereas I, on the other hand, have to admit I feel a tad scruffy in comparison to the women here, like something that's been dragged through a hedge backwards."

"Yes, well," he said, appraising me. "*You* will be noticed. They'll peg you immediately as a foreigner, raise their sunglasses indiscreetly, wince a little in passing, that sort of thing. It's just what they do." He eyed the cigarette he had been rolling absentmindedly between finger and thumb, while I looked down at myself. I hadn't imagined I was quite *that* remarkable.

"What works in London doesn't necessarily work here," he said, with a shrug. "Now, what say, one for the road?"

Several more for the road later, sozzled, I followed Edward onto the rickety orange tram that would take us back to his flat. He lived above a pizzeria "on the Naviglio", whatever that meant. The aroma of crusts baking in the brick oven sent me off to sleep that first night.

Before opening my eyes, I played a game of trying to isolate the sounds coming from outside, sounds of a foreign city, rhythms of Milan: I identified tram doors shutting, and their lumbering, squealing wheels; bicycle bells and buzzing scooters; a rattle of dishes, probably from the pizzeria, all punctuated by snatches of incomprehensible conversation. The soundtrack was complemented by the smells: the citrus and mossy steam from Edward's bathroom; coffee and bleach leaking in from outside; a heat-soaked, ancient dirt rising from the ground or discharged from the walls - I wasn't sure, and the smell of hay left too long in the sun which almost definitely came from the couch upon which I lay. I opened my eyes and the first thing I saw were Edwards's walls: bumpy, curved in the corners, and the most delirious shade of yellow ochre ever seen indoors. Together with the terracotta tiled floor, it was nearly enough to give me the impression I'd woken up inside the pages of National Geographic.

"Morning, Beautiful," Edward called. Or rather, trilled. First thing in the morning, head surely still throbbing from martinis, he saw fit to trill. "How'd you sleep?"

I yawned contentedly. Not ready to move but curious about the view, I craned my neck but a grimy sunshine hung outside the balcony like a discoloured net curtain. "Your place is beautiful."

"Isn't it? The Naviglo is an area of historic significance, you know? Naviglio means canal, which you can see just outside. The historic significance bit means, among other things, that the balcony doors don't really close, which is okay because the good weather's coming, that sometimes the ceiling flakes, and I can hear Signor Castelletti from below, singing "La Donna Mobile", through the pipes in the bathroom some mornings when I'm having a shave. But hey, it's home."

"I love it. It's dreamy."

"I must run, but there's tea and marmalade in the cupboard. Nothing to put it on, but there's a corner shop the other side of the canal." He drew my attention to a list of contacts on the table: names and numbers. "Get cracking! Dazzle, talk, or kill your way into a job. Leave no rhinestone, Blarney stone or headstone unturned!"

"Have a good day at the office, dear," I said.

"Can't wait to hear all, this evening," he called as the door closed behind him.

A nail holding a photo of Edward's grandparents popped out of the wall, and the old couple hit the floor. I could hear Edward's leather soles swishing down the stone steps.

I stepped out onto the balcony and watched a little sliver of Milanese morning unfold: the waiter washing down the flagstones in front of the pizzeria and the man at the newsstand paying for his paper, tucking it under his arm and entering the corner coffee bar where the grumpy owner in the apron fired up a row of espressos for him and the other customers hunched eagerly over the counter. I spotted Edward buying his cigarettes from the man on the corner, the one he had pointed out the previous night, who sold cheap, black market goods from a battered suitcase—fags, cigars, lighters, small leather goods, statues of Our Lady. Even though he wasn't watching I waved to Edward as he stepped down into the Metro station and watched the top of his head till it disappeared from sight.

The waiter had stopped washing the pavement. He was leaning on his mop looking up at me, and possibly up my shirt. "Ciao *Bellissima!*" he shouted.

I quickly stepped back inside.

FASHIONLANDIA

I flopped onto the Duomo steps, exhausted and sweaty, with sunburnt shoulders. Milan wasn't quite the hamlet Edward had me believe: "It's so small, everybody and his unmarried uncle knows your affairs." After getting through to no one by phone, I'd set out to deliver my resume to every design house on Edward's list and managed three. The metro didn't seem to go anywhere near where I needed to go, and I was reluctant to get on a bus or tram for fear I'd end up in the Alps.

Wedged between a pair of amorous natives on my right whose tongues were lapping at each other and their Japanese equivalent to my left lapping at a shared melting ice-cream cone, I stared straight ahead. On the main square it was rush hour, and a pageant of lustrous women had tumbled from behind their desks to catwalk among the pigeons. I thought I detected a trace of carousel music; it seemed to be coming from a row of stalls selling tourist souvenirs. I closed my eyes, and the sun put on a little fireworks display on my eyelids.

"Where are you from?"

There was some movement beside me, and I had a feeling the laboured pronunciation was intended for my ears.

"No, wait. I bet I can guess."

I sighed and opened my eyes. A dark-skinned, dark-eyed face hung there, so close to mine, it was blurry. I scooted farther back on the step.

"You are Irish." He smiled confidently.

"What makes you say that?" I said, covering my burnt shoulders with my hair.

"*Le lentiggine.*" He tapped his nose repeatedly with his finger. "I like the Irish.

They are very like us Italians. *Ma piu fortunati, non?* More lucky! I want to go to Ireland very much, but it is true it always rains?"

"Well, they have to keep it well watered. For the shamrock crop, you know." It was my third conversation so far that went along these lines.

"You are on holiday?"

"Not exactly."

"You are nanny?"

"Well...not yet anyway."

"Of course! You are *stilista*—how you say...fashion designer?"

"Jesus, I'd make a disappointing international woman of mystery."

He looked confused. "You speak very fast."

"How did you know that?"

He looked sheepish and pointed to my portfolio. "Anyhow, it's not so difficult. Everybody comes here to work in fashion."

"I think *everybody* might be a bit of an exaggeration," I said and put my sunglasses on.

"You have beautiful eyes."

"*Grazie mille.*"

I could almost hear him formulating the next phase of his maneuver. I shouldn't fault him. I understood that this was what they did: they made foreigners swoon with some reeled-off, hackneyed old pick-up lines delivered with a florid accent. Maybe they thought we expected it, part of their welcome wagon. But I bet he wouldn't do it with an Italian girl.

"Irish eyes are not smiling?"

"Not these ones." I looked out across the piazza. I hoped he was ready to be on his way.

"I have cousin," he announced instead. "She work for Versace for many years."

I kept my eyes fixed ahead.

"I could introduce you, if you are looking for work," he said, musingly.

I slid my sunglasses down my nose and looked his way.

"If you join me for drink." He raised an eyebrow as if to say: it's a fair price, take it or leave it.

I sprung up. "Well, I must be going now. Nice to meet you."

"Whoa! What is your name?" He jumped off the step. "I am Dario. I walk with you?"

When I shook my head, his hopeful look turned infantile, deflated.

"At least you tell me your name before you go," he called after me.

I reached the bottom of the steps.

"We can go get *gelato.*"

I crossed the piazza.

"*Un aperitivo?*"

At the tram stop, I couldn't help wondering, what if he did have a cousin in Versace, and I'd just walked away from an opportunity because I objected to his patter? It was a bane of mine to always be so sure of everything. The guidebook described the town square as the heart of Italian daily life, so it might be customary to make important career connections outside the Duomo during rush hour. More likely, the cathedral steps served as a kind of Casanova casting couch. I didn't want my *bella vita* to have any murky origins; the novel in which I felt like a character wasn't that kind of novel.

I felt a tap on the shoulder and turned to find him standing there.

"I give you my cousin's number," he said, holding out a card. "You can tell her I - how you say? - *ti ho raccommandato*. Then, next time we meet in Piazza Duomo, you can take me for *aperitivo. Vabbene?*"

I looked down at the glossy little rectangle with the Grecian border. When I looked up, he had already squeezed through the grumbling commuters and was gone. I felt like I'd been given a free pass to get on the rides.

Scoring a phone conversation with the Creative Director of an Italian design house ranked somewhere between glimpsing a unicorn grazing in a glen and spotting a comet. And they did not do email. My mornings went like this:

"Call back in twenty minutes."

"But you told me to call back in twenty minutes!"

"She'll be back on the fifteenth."

"Well, can I make an appointment to see her then?"

"I'm afraid she'll be out of the office then."

"But you said she would be back then?"

"Yes, but she will go away again."

"Did she get my resume?"

"What did you say your name was again?"

"It's Kat, K-A-T—"

"Oh, I'm sorry. Can you hold the line, please."

"Hello... Hello..?"

I thought of those colourful split-screen segments in old movies: first there were two, then four, then eight people in boxes talking on the phone, me at the centre, then the boxes disappeared one by one, and it was just me, full screen, left holding the phone.

At night, Edward and I sat on plastic chairs on his balcony comparing the velvetiness of a Nero d'Avola with the spiciness of a Barbera d'Alba, holding forth on how today's Barolo measured up to yesterday's Barbaresco. But one spring evening, when the Naviglio seemed to be prematurely overrun with mosquitoes, and we were their early bird special, he was unusually taciturn. I smeared myself with repellent as he viciously stubbed out a chain of cigarettes in the window box.

"I grew geraniums in these when I first arrived," he said morosely.

All sign of life had been paved over by a mosaic of fag butts.

"Anything the matter?"

"Oh, they're playing silly beggars at work with me and another designer called Colin. One day they take pot shots at him, and I'm their pet; the next day, they switch. Today was my turn to be invisible."

"Lynda used to do that. It drove me mad. What's the point of it?"

"Haven't the foggiest. Oh, it's probably nothing. I just need to toughen up."

That was all he would say on the matter. Edward rationed glimpses of his vulnerability the same way he rationed correspondence with his family, like the partial untightening of a pressure valve to release air flow.

At Versace, Dario's cousin explained that she had no available positions, assured me I was talented, and then launched me on a thrilling, high-speed loop de loop of Milan's design studios. First, she sent me to see her friend, Pietro, at Bottega Veneta, who could fit me in immediately—despite being unavailable all the times I had telephoned. Dressed in black, neat as a pin and just as thin, he introduced himself while slipping around the barely opened door, and shook hands with me as the door whispered closed. It was like he was drifting along on draughts of air.

"*Bene*," he said. "You already have your work out."

My book opened with photographs of my much-maligned graduation collection. The Fat Director's words still taunted me, but the work had been drawing compliments so far. Da's words came back to me truer than ever: I just needed to find 'the right crowd'. But when I looked at Pietro, I doubted I'd found it. He was taking the corner of each page between the extreme tips of his finger and thumb and laying it on top of the last like he was laying it to rest.

"I must say it's refreshing to see someone with a unique point of view," he concluded. "Your style is quite romantic. Our style is much cleaner. You have a nice sense of colour. But it's not right for here." It sounded like the beginning of a limerick.

Then he called a friend at Fendi who called a friend at Costume National who called a friend at Cavalli who suggested I come right over.

"Oh, it's not quite for us," said the interviewer at Cavalli, scratching her head with a pencil. Her hair was spun high like cotton candy. I was waiting for the pencil to get lost. "But you know who would love you? Rosalba," she declared definitively. She made a call to Rosalba Valle at Intermezzo, and arranged my appointment for the following Monday at noon. "You're just what she's looking for, I'm sure of it," she said, extracting the pencil triumphantly.

❧

Back on the balcony, like Statler and Waldorf, Edward and I discussed my day's performance.

"I have a Madame Zanetti here I really want to get," I said, studying my list of Creative Directors like targets in a shooting range.

"Tomorrow's news headlines," said Edward. "'Fledgling Fashionista Faces Stalking Charges: Offers a season's sketches in exchange for fashion asylum.'"

"You could print t-shirts with my face and the words "Free the Fashionable One" and hand them out during rush hour in Piazza Duomo."

His loud "Hah!" shot off through the silent streets. He looked happier than he had been recently. "Oh! Here we go." He poked me sharply in the ribs and nodded towards the street. "Look, Kat. It's your favourite waiter gazing up at you again." He waved and called out, "Hallo, there. Yoo-hoo! *Buonasera!* Why don't you just flash him a little smile?"

"Thank God you said smile."

"He finishes his shift soon. You could ask him to go for a little nightcap."

"You seem very familiar with the waiter's movements."

"When there's a cute boy underneath me, you can be sure I know what he's doing." He drained his glass dramatically.

"I have other *pesce* to fry, remember?" I said. "I didn't come here just to get laid."

He looked aghast. "To be taken for a native round these parts—and considered employable in the sex industry that is fashion—you must have the scent of an illicit rendezvous about you at all times. Either just had one or on your way to one. So get busy."

"Actually, the men intimidate me almost as much as the women," I confessed.

"Look, Jane Eyre, this is the stuff of classic romance right here: Juliet on her balcony coyly observing her Romeo waiting below for a mere moment of attention, even a glance." He stared at me through cigarette smoke. "A dropped handkerchief?"

"Oh, give over!"

"It's the weekend. I could push you off. You could land on him."

"Subtle, Edward."

THE FORTUNE TELLER

I had breakfast at a sidewalk café in Brera, Milan's picturesque historic centre. Edward had booted me out of the flat, cleaning implements of all strengths and purposes lined up behind him like troops.

"I do it every weekend," he said, slipping on a pair of rubber gloves. "Although this week the mess is somewhat more evident. I just need to contain it. My humble lodgings may be rustic, but I pride myself on having a place for everything..." He reached down the side of the couch and gingerly pulled out a lace bra by its strap. "And everything in its place."

I snatched it from him. "I'll help you tidy."

He rested his weight on one leg and tilted his head. "No. You'd be the sort of person who does their ironing sitting down."

"Suit yourself."

"I'll come meet you when I'm done," he called, closing the door. I heard the photo of his grandparents hit the floor again and him mutter, "Oh, bugger off!" then, "Sorry, Gran."

Cappuccino in hand, I gazed from under my hat at the tourists shuffling along the cobblestones, paying particular notice of a guided group of teenage boys that gawped shamelessly at every passing pair of boobs while listening to a description of the area's architecture. Scooters revved at the ankles of foreigners who broke into a little two-step to get out of the way. Elegant women carrying finely crafted leather handbags emerged from the outer doors of the *palazzi* which banged loosely like stable doors. I glimpsed courtyards full of greenery and flower pots and striped furniture, periwinkle window shutters, even a flock of roaming flamingoes, their pink pageantry squandered in their secret location. Edward said that the bourgeoisie, known as *i milanesi,* did all their entertaining behind these wobbly doors, a secluded well-heeled courtyard society sealed off from the chattering classes by a single bar bolt.

I considered the buildings' handsome pumpkin and mustard facades, dulled by pollution, violated by turquoise graffiti. I tried to visualize myself turning the key in one of their doors, cursing the uneven streets in fluent Italian for slicing up my posh heels. Could I call this dirty city with the shiny people home?

Edward burst through the crowd and stood over me. He was in good spirits, high on life and industrial cleaning fluids. "Let's go to Lake Como for the day!"

"What's Lake Como?" I asked.

"It's a vision of loveliness. You need a break from trying to pin down your elusive fashion career." He looked me over. "Is your top on inside out?"

"I dressed in haste for fear you'd Swiffer me off the balcony with the other dust bunnies."

That got a smile. "Just promise me you've not done that at interviews."

An hour later we were on a train ploughing through the Lombardian flatlands. Edward sunk into the seat with *The*

Economist, frowning at the small type. "I need to find a boyfriend in banking."

I turned my attention to the tattersall landscape flashing by and the occasional solemn farmhouse wedged flush to the corner of a field. Clusters of cypresses rose black against the midday sun. There were no animals, no sign of sogginess, and it was much less unruly than most expanses of Irish countryside. Fields with low-growing crops were crinkly like raffia, those mowed smooth were like cashmere, and one farm of land was so raked and tailored right to its sharp corners defined by trim hedgerows that it reminded me of a Max Mara wool crombie with fur collar I'd admired recently in a magazine. Then for miles swathes of seemingly uninhabited landscape stretched either side without a bump like a freshly unrolled bolt of woven cloth. The warp and weft left by the tractor wheels were visible as we sliced cleanly through it.

I was unprepared for the spectacle of Lake Como. It looked like the gods had been doing their laundry. The lake, a vast blue sheet strung between the two posts of Como and Lecco, rippled in the breeze. Bobbing along its edge like coloured pegs were all the pretty boats. Fresh green hills tilted towards Alpine peaks and a perfect sky, a sky that seemed to have sprinkled powdery flakes that collected at intervals to form villages all the way down to the edge of the water.

"George Clooney's got a place over there," said Edward, pointing to a group of pastel lake-side villas. "Maybe we'll see him scoot by on his Vespa."

We slowly wound our way into the walled town but looked back often to check the lake was still there, that it hadn't been folded and stowed away in the gods' hotpress. The walls finally obscured it, and the road ahead became darker the farther along we went. The clear sky of only minutes before had turned moody, but it was with delight we happened upon a street market twinkling with fairy lights. As I browsed the stalls of local produce, I felt an insistent tap from behind.

I turned and looked down at an old lady about the height of my shoulder in a long, black dress with silver hair slicked tight to her head. Her hooked finger, post-tap, was still raised, and she stood behind a weird, two-wheeled contraption with two shafts for handles so that it could be pushed along like a barrow. Its central structure, painted with folksy flowers, resembled a miniature church organ, but where the keys should be was a red lacquered drawer divided into compartments that held coloured cards. From various appendages ornaments tinkled, and riding on top as if on lookout duty was a bow-tied canary. Worried the exotic wagon might knock the old dear off her feet when it began to roll backwards, I reached out to steady her. But she brushed me away; what small amount of space she occupied, she did so tenaciously.

She looked up at me through heavy lidded eyes and spoke earnestly.

"Quick, Edward!" I tugged at his sleeve. "What does she want?"

"Well, I don't bloody know, do I!" he said, staring at her fast-moving mouth "Oh! Hang about, she wants to read your fortune, that's it… Forty euro."

I inclined my head, both playful and curious.

"Can't hurt," agreed Edward, eyes roaming over her psychedelic vehicle. "Leave no stoned old biddy unturned."

"She's not stoned." At my nod, she quieted down and beckoned the canary. It perched on her forefinger, and she drew it close to the cards. With a tweet, the bird flew in a circle before hovering over the drawer, selecting a card in its beak and returning to drop it into the tray below. It approached a second compartment, paused, and then with the same swift motion, chose another card. After selecting a third from the last compartment, it returned to its perch to clean its feathers. The lady intently laid the cards face upwards. She spoke in the same cracked monotone as before; this time her expression shifted from grave to serene to joyful and back to grave again. She shook her head and extended her arthritic pinky finger and thumb in some sort of symbol. All this animation, provoked by my future no less, and I was privy to none of it.

In desperation Edward had been stopping passersby eventually arriving upon a young woman who agreed to translate. As she listened to the fortune-teller, her face grew concerned.

"*Il malocchio!* You—you have been hexed, by a dark presence. Quite recently, it seems. The evil eye follows you. You have brought it with you."

"So much for your playful Irish wit and charm," said Edward.

"Well, what can I do about it?" I asked.

"There's nothing you can do," said the translator, "except hope it lifts—and watch out for accidents, misunderstandings, and betrayal. That card spells chaos." She paused again to listen. "With your head in the clouds you will suffer many falls. She says you will reach a... a maze, is right? Where each path looks the same? And inside it you will get lost. It might also signify a... a *sfida*, how you say? A psychological challenge." She tapped her temple with her finger and listened again.

"Never mind cards, we all need our head read for listening to this," said Edward out the side of his mouth.

"It's hardly enlightening." I wondered if the translation was lacking.

But the young woman looked to be gaining confidence. "You are entering the field of politics."

"Oh, for pity's sake," said Edward.

The old fortune-teller clicked her tongue reprovingly at Edward while the translator explained: "She says your success and money cards are intertwined and signify power struggles and, uh, *spionaggio,* how you say… to spy?"

"Espionage?" I asked.

"*Esatto,*" said the translator, nodding.

"Oh, she's been at the sherry," said Edward.

"She says you should be loyal to the colour red."

"I wear a lot of red."

"Well, forty euro well spent there, then," said Edward.

"She says you will be at the side of an international figure. He's not too tall, but he casts a long shadow. It's a mysterious and complicated relationship. He will throw aside another for you."

"Oh, oh! Don't tell me. A tawdry affair with an Italian politician?"

"Such lofty aspirations you have for me, Edward."

"There's money to be made if you choose to go that route. This is Italy. You'll have to get a boob job, though."

"The canary says no," said the translator. "Romance is not in her immediate destiny. *Il malocchio* is too strong. It destroys all affairs of the heart."

"Bollocks! We are going to get you laid this week," whispered Edward. "I will not stand by and watch this happen." A thought came to him, and he rolled his eyes before asking, "What about *bambini?*"

"*Niente bambini,*" said the fortune-teller.

Edward looked devastated. "Never?"

A crack of thunder sent the old woman into a frenzy of hand gestures and talking in triple time. "She wants her money," said the translator before dashing off. The old lady gave me one more warning look before snatching her money and steering her prophecy wagon off through the slanting rain, her silvery head like a diminishing lamplight. *She wheels her wheelbarrow, through streets dark and narrow...*

"Should we make a run for it?" asked Edward.

"We're already soaked," I replied. "Why be out of breath as well?" I loved the feeling of giddiness that getting caught in the rain left. *Alive-alive-oh!*

The fortune-teller's words hadn't made much sense even with a translator, but it didn't matter. London and Lynda already seemed a lifetime ago. Italy had seduced me in less than a week with colours as spicy as its smells, four euro bottles of wine, flamingoes, laundry-day lakes, and shadowy streets erupting in fairy lights and evil eyes. It made me even more determined to get a job despite the fortune-teller's ominous lack of specifics in that regard.

"Should I have the house risotto or be good and stick with the salad?" asked Edward, as we dried out in a little trattoria afterwards.

"What would the canary have advised?" I said with a smile.

INTERMEZZO

Sitting on a plush red throne, hands curved around gold armrests, surrounded by blue sky with picture book clouds, I thought this must be how St Peter feels every day he shows up for work as bouncer at the gates of heaven. I was sitting in Intermezzo's Surrealism-inspired foyer, awaiting my interview with Rosalba Valle. I had worn the Chanel jacket, effectively announcing our return—mine *and* the jacket's—from fashion exile, as I now regarded our shared time in the orphanage. Its metallic thread caught the light jubilantly and the curls of the bouclé looked puffed with a sense of occasion. The buttons, signature gold camellias nestling in clear plastic shells, gleamed like medals from the cuffs and pockets.

A girl stepped from behind a pair of velvet curtains tied with rope behind which a red staircase led deeper into the clouds—she arrived so silently it crossed my mind she may have floated down on one. She smiled as if that smile was all she had to concentrate on, and she wanted to get it right.

"I am Simonetta," she said. "Come with me."

She led me to what appeared to be a painting of a door floating among the cumuli but when she pressed a button it sprang open. We squeezed inside a tiny lift. Its interior was painted with stars.

"Curiouser and curiouser," I ventured.

"Com'é?" said Simonetta.

At such intimate quarters, the only part of her I could observe, without being rude, was her shoes which, to give them their due, held my attention well. They were in the form of ladybugs: red patent leather with black spots, their eyes positioned to forever gaze dolefully up the wearer's skirt, two leather tentacles wrapped around the ankles. The ladybugs stepped briskly out of the lift and I hastened after them. We came to a stop on a black-and-white checkerboard floor.

"Just take a seat," said Simonetta, indicating a white chaise longue. "Signora Valle will be along shortly." She marched the ladybugs from the room.

The room in which I found myself seemed furnished for a seduction rather than an interview. A dressing table, black and shiny, took pride of place in one corner and vintage perfume bottles sparkled from its surface: rose-tinted cut glass, amber with brass detailing, fitted with atomizers, and one with a stopper in the form of a female nude. A glorious tribute to narcissism, it boasted three mirrors, spotlights, and a plump stool with shapely legs and a bold striped seat. Bette Davis or Mae West would have preened and powdered at such a podium. *When I'm good, I'm very good. When I'm bad, I'm better.* I pouted into the glass, and three identical doubt-filled faces pouted back.

"*Buongiorno.* I am Rosalba Valle."

"Oh!" I whirled around, sticking out my hand as I went. "It's a pleasure to meet you," I told the stylish woman in her late fifties.

"Likewise." Her hand grazed mine in passing as she led me back towards the chaise longue. "Were you admiring yourself?" A wrist flicked in the direction of the dressing table, her cigarette leaving a meandering trail.

"Oh, no, I was admiring the table."

With another flick—of her ankles, this time—her slingbacks fell to the floor. She tucked her feet underneath her and surged forward, acquiring a dowager's hump, the summit of which was visible above her head.

"Diana Vreeland said, 'I loathe narcissism, but I approve of vanity. Well, that was my sentiment. She heard that from me at a party." She blew smoke, her smile stretching thin and wide after its release. "So, I already know a lot about you... except why you think you should be a designer at Intermezzo." She drew back in her seat, her movements like ripples or like she was operating on a series of well-oiled pivots and hinges.

"Well, Intermezzo has been a company that has inspired me since I first became interested in fashion." I'd gone over this answer with Edward on the balcony the previous night. "It represents all that's modern and cool, but irreverent and tongue in cheek, and it never loses its femininity. I can see how my design approach would fit in here."

"Hmm." She stubbed out her cigarette and turned away, "That's disappointing."

And she truly looked disappointed. Her veiny hands tugged at the already-standing collar of her shirt like she wanted to cover her ears in case I decided to say more.

"And what if I told you we dress footballers' wives and insignificant, lesser-known royals, sugar daddies and their trophy whores?" She still didn't look at me but smoothed her hair, chestnut accentuated with grey.

"Well, um..." Edward and I hadn't covered this line of questioning.

Her eyes flitted to my face. "Why don't you try again," she said, wearily. "Why should I hire you? Leave out the prepared statement. Gut instinct—you've been in the building for twenty minutes."

I worried I was leaving sweat patches on her chaise longue. It hit me that Rosalba Valle didn't have to hire me, no matter that her friend at Cavalli thought I was "just what she's looking for." Unlike Lynda, there was nothing desperate or grasping about Rosalba; the brains behind a house with a long history and unique aesthetic, her catwalk alone provided Lynda with the majority of material her assistants would knock off every season. If I didn't make the right impression, there would be another graduate along any minute who would. And yet somewhere in my deepest, most audacious thinking, I had believed I was guaranteed this. Suddenly, I was the one desperate and grasping—for a response that would please her.

Rosalba Valle rearranged herself; she returned both bare feet delicately to the floor, one in a black square, the other in a white. Outside the door, thick red carpet stretched in all directions.

"This weekend, a fortune-teller told me to follow red," I blurted, "and I notice you have a lot of it here."

She laughed a throaty laugh. "Now, that's an answer to the question. It's *an* answer." Her eyes were drawn to the portrait on the far wall of the company's founder, Franco Manzoni. "Franco did have a thing for the colour red, it's true. The passion, the sex, the suffering, the death..."

The portrait caught Franco posing cross-eyed with a red stiletto covering his mouth; he looked like a clown whose make-up had smeared.

She blew him a kiss and lit a new cigarette. "You see, inside is always different from how it seems from the outside..."

I remembered the fortune-teller's warning to keep my head out of the clouds, flashed on the foyer's walls, and wondered briefly about the coincidence.

"If you think you'd fit in, we don't want you," continued Rosalba. "We want the ones who don't know where they fit in. They're the special ones. What are you waiting for? Get out your work."

I reached for my portfolio, and she grabbed my arm. "Where did you get that Chanel jacket?"

"It was a gift," I said confidently.

"Franco considered Chanel couture a lighthouse illuminating the choppy waters of prêt-à-porter for the rest of us. So much so they sued him three times in five years. He considered it an honour. One would beg, borrow or steal for Chanel, wouldn't one? J'adore, j'adore, j'adore Chanel."

"Oh, moi aussi," I replied.

Come on, mum, pick up.

The volume would be way up on the TV. Since her hearing started to go, you had to break through a wall of noise just to get to her. Her small, cluttered kitchen was a pulsating, angry pod to outsiders, but to her it was as serene as a confessional. I checked my watch. Not yet time for *Deal Or No Deal*. *Come on, mum.*

Tentatively breaking through—beaming in from her pod—I heard her cautious "Hell-oo-oh?"

"Mum! Guess what?"

"Oh, it's you. I nearly let it ring. I was out the back pulling rhubarb for jam—"

"Mum, I got a job!"

"A dog?"

I rolled my eyes.

"Put your hearing aid in!' There was some fidgeting and the faraway squeal of it coming to life in her ear.

"I got a job, in Milan."

"Oh, holy Moses!"

A large spaniel stopped in front of the bench I was sitting on and delivered his own message of congratulations for me. His sexy owner flicked her hair, tugged his leash and trotted on, leaving it to steam gently.

"Is that the real top shelf stuff?" asked mum. She misguidedly referred to goods so expensive they were out of normal folk's grubby reach as "top shelf stuff". I was not about to contradict her with reference to Juggs or Hustler.

"Intermezzo, it's one of the big Italian design houses. They make gorgeous things. It's in all the magazines."

"Oh, wait till I get a pen to take it down. Or I'll not mind it as soon as I hang up."

I heard her burrowing through the stack of papers next to the phone: the Christmas cards devoid of glitter, flyers for whist drives, windowed brown envelopes, and unused pages from old diaries. The urgency of her to-do list was always somewhat undermined by the fact that it might be written on a page bearing the date of Shrove Tuesday eight years ago. My mother had been a pioneer in early recycling initiatives, although neither of us had been aware and confused it for hoarding.

I spelt it out for her, and she mispronounced it back to me. I tried again then figured whoever she would be telling wouldn't know any better. Intermezzo wasn't a name much bandied about in Ardnacross.

"She just said 'I love your work. When can you start?' That was it."

"Well, sure, isn't it well-deserved? Did you bring those lovely drawings you did when you were last home?"

"Of Hughie's Lake? They only want to see drawings of clothes, mum. They live, eat, breathe fashion here."

"Well, tell me, who was this you spoke to? Was she the Big Woman?"

Before getting married, years before the Singer-in-the-kitchen era, mum cycled three miles a day to her work in Daintyfit, a factory that made bras and knickers. Respected by the other "girls" and promoted often, she knew the importance of staying on the right side of the Big Woman. When I had announced I wanted to go to London to meet inspirational people and study fashion design, I might just as well have announced I was running off to join the circus to meet lion tamers and study fire eating. As mum plumbed her past for parallels, Daintyfit, a self-contained, mostly female microcosm of personalities and hierarchies, located a grateful distance from her parent's pig farm, was deemed a close enough fit to gain her approval.

"Her name's Rosalba Valle, and she looks like Dentist O'Brien's wife, mum," I explained. "Very well-dressed, lots of jewellery, not a hair out of place, but tanned." And *bendier*. Mrs O'Brien had bad knees and would never have been able to wind her way into a chair the way Rosalba Valle had.

"Dentist O'Brien and his wife are lovely people. Everyone says it. You'll not go wrong there whereas that gipsy, Wynter, that old string of misery, sure it was the scrapings of a job, that. Good riddance. She was a toe-rag of the darkest dye; this'll show her, the ill-bred ruffian…"

"She's history, mum. I'm sure I'll never lay eyes on her again. We won't exactly be moving in the same circles."

"Now does this mean your name'll go on the inside of those lovely clothes then?"

"That's not how it works, mum. Intermezzo goes on the label."

"Well, will you get money every time somebody buys something—if it turns out you designed it, I mean?"

"No, but it's more than I earned in London. It's the opportunity that's the biggest thing."

"Well, I know, and that's all very good, but it's maybe something you should have looked into before you signed up. Negotiations, as they call it."

"Those things aren't up for negotiation, mum. It's not *Deal Or No Deal*. It's not Daintyfit."

"Oh, Daintyfit wasn't like that either. But times are different now, aren't they? And it's this fashion design path you want..."

She went quiet. I think she had begun to intuit that a career in fashion might not prove to be as stable as a position in Daintyfit. Mum believed hard-work, good timekeeping, respect for your co-workers and your uniform should be enough to guarantee you security for life. So far, my career didn't seem to be following those guidelines. There were two artists who lived in Ardnacross, both depressive sorts, frugal bachelors who liked a drop too much to drink, drew the dole, and sold a painting once in a while, usually coming up to Christmas. She seemed to understand their career easier than she could mine because at least they had stayed at home to indulge their creativity. I felt guilty for thinking *Da would get it. He'd know just what to say.*

Then when she spoke, I couldn't hear her. She was softly spoken at the best of times, but the hearing aid which amplified the sound of other people's voices and distorted her own, making it boom and echo in her head, often had her dropping her voice further. I strained and caught the words: "He would have been so proud."

I swallowed the lump. "Yeah, I know."

"He always said you had it in you. 'Particular' was the word he used."

"Not 'peculiar'?"

"I just said you had peculiar ideas. I'm sure that's why they hired you at this new place. They don't want someone who thinks the same as everyone else." Little hiccups of laughter erupted from her suddenly. "What was that thing you used to say when you were no age? Dander on me own. That was it. Dander on me own. And off you'd go on fat wee legs, wouldn't take my hand, just away like billy-oh on pork sausage legs, never looking back. Oh, you were a funny wee thing..."

"Well, it's nearly time for your programme now, mum. I should let you go."

"Oh, is it that time already? Nobody's managed to beat the banker in ages."

"I'll ring you soon, okay?"

"Alright, now, Kathleen. And that's great news," she said, before retreating back into her pod. "Great news."

Brandishing a bottle of champagne tied with a red bow, Edward burst through the door which smacked against the wall, causing plaster to fall on his head. With a high-pitched squeal, he popped the cork which dislodged more wall fragments after ricocheting off the kitchen cabinet.

"We have much to celebrate. First and foremost, to being not just gainfully but glamorously employed! Intermezzo! Congratulations!"

"*Salute!*"

"And I got an unexpected raise at work. So, dinner's on me."

"Things are looking up. *Slainte!*"

"Can you picture it? Just a couple of swells we'll be, mincing along the Naviglio, attending flash soirees and—oh, come here a minute, will you?" he said, frowning. "A jauntier angle is called for." He adjusted my hat so that I could see nothing beyond my own two feet and the toe of his brogues. "That's better."

"To being in the right place at the right time," I said. "And to Dario, my little Duomo angel, bless him."

"To Dario! Now someone who was in the wrong place at the wrong time..." said Edward as we retired to the balcony. "Colin. He got fired. *Salute!*" We knocked glasses again.

"Your rival in the popularity contest?"

"Yup. It seems he was showing up at all the same parties as Italo and Gio, hanging around like a desperado. Colin always claimed they asked him along. They got tired of it and sent him packing."

"So he was as invited as potato bread at a wedding?"

"I have no idea what that means." He looked down at a group of lads strolling by, then gave them a dismissive sniff. "Anyhow, Italo and Gio travel in a pack of gorgeous, Adonis types, sailing, tanning, partying—they'll welcome a celebrity on board for an evening, but otherwise it's closed ranks. Colin broke rank. Brought it on himself."

"Hmm, I doubt that's the whole story. It just doesn't add up."

"Whatever. I felt sorry for him for all of twenty seconds and then nabbed his desk by the window."

"You are ruthless, Edward."

"That's how it goes. Don't say you haven't been warned." He held up his glass. "While you, *Principessa,* are being cordially invited up the grand staircase of Fashionham Palace, stepping on scattered rose petals to the sound of harps playing, someone else is being escorted out the servant's entrance with his personal effects flung after them in an old laundry bag. *Salute!*"

We had planned to go somewhere fancier for dinner, but our champagne wave washed us up only as far as *Le Tre Marie* below the flat. The tall, wooden doors opened onto a typical family restaurant packed to capacity at its busiest hour, and we wove around the tables, over sprawled dogs, around men's foppishly tasselled and loafered feet, past fast-moving waiters who delivered pizzas on silver rostrums with a flourish like they were presenting awards.

"Back in a jiff. Bubbles go right through me." Edward disappeared.

I studied the specials board.

"Ciao," rumbled a male voice at my shoulder.

I turned to see the smiling face of our favourite staring waiter. For a change, I was the one looking up at him.

"Ciao," I responded. "*C'ome stai?*"

What I had gleaned from a phrase book propped against the cereal box could form little in the way of meaningful dialogue, but the champagne convinced me a full conversation was not out of the question. I regretted it soon enough. He took me careering through a series of rolling r's and looping l's, at a pace that whipped from my head any words I might have recognized and battered me with an onslaught of unfamiliar ones.

"Whoa! My Italian's only a week old!"

He laughed. "I was just saying you are the girl from the balcony that…"

"Oh, hallo there. I'm Edward." Edward remained standing and offered his hand. "This is Kat. And you are…"

"Davide. *Piacere.*" He was still smiling at me. It was infectious. "Where are you from?"

"*Irlanda,*" I said.

"Ireland," he said, looking delighted by the news, and I prepared myself for the usual patter of shamrocks and rainbows.

"Anyway, we're celebrating tonight," interrupted Edward. "Therefore, we will be needing some wine; house white, if you please."

"Because I got a job!"

"*Ah, si? Qui, a Milano?*" asked Davide. "You come to live? Then we go out sometime for a drink, just the two of us." He hurried off purposefully, his voice sailing across the tops of people's heads. "*Allora, una carafa di vino bianco!*"

"And what am I, Scotch mist?" asked Edward. "I could have been your fiancé of five years, for all he knew."

"I think he might have seen you prancing off to work in your sequined Debbie Harry t-shirt of a morning and drawn his own conclusions."

"Whatever happened to '*I didn't come here to get laid*'?"

"I should probably sample some local delicacies now that I'm going to be living here."

"Jezebel!"

"Jealous!"

Edward's eyes found another comely waiter. "We'll be driven to distraction, the pair of us."

I ate my Margherita self-consciously, imagining Davide watching from hidden corners, and then felt disappointed when he wasn't the one who brought us our bill. I dragged my feet when we had to free the table. But as we pressed through a new swell of people arriving to eat, I felt a tug at my elbow and turned as Davide gestured for me to follow him. He leaned against a dresser. Bottles of olive oil and balsamic vinegar tinkled.

His hand cupped my elbow. "So, we go for *aperitivo* one evening, *non*?"

"Why not? You know where to find me."

"Okay. I watch for you. We go on my day off." He lifted my hand to his lips and, maintaining eye contact, raised his head so that my fingers dragged his lower lip down and my knuckles knocked against his teeth. Then he bit me. I snatched my hand back, squirmed out of reach, and threw myself at the door.

"Phew!" I said, sitting down on the kerb next to Edward who was smoking. "Every day is like the Seduction Olympics here. They're highly trained competitors, eyes on the prize, eager to set a new record. The Irish never win at the Olympics. Unless in boxing."

"It's not the winning," said Edward, exhaling. "It's the taking part."

KATWALK!

For the next few months I felt like I was inside one of those montage sequences in the movies set to upbeat music where the protagonist's blossoming is represented through a series of shopping trips, hat changes, and bicycling through a new city with fresh flowers in a basket while the seasons change around her. I moved from Edward's couch into a shared flat a few blocks over, still on the Naviglio. I came across an ad for it in *Secondamano,* the free newspaper, lodged between an announcement for the upcoming San Ambrogio flower show and a plea to give a home to a litter of Golden Labrador puppies. When I went to view the flat, my potential flatmate was waiting in the doorway. She was one of *those* women: the ones that intimidated me just passing them in the street, a *lioness.* Prowling the stairwell, she sized me up. I hovered between the penultimate stair and the landing and was considering making a run for it when she grabbed me by the wrist.

I was plunged through a floral-perfumed curtain—which turned out to be her hair—to emerge blinking in a sitting room where soft lighting, mismatched rugs, and reading lamps on short-legged tables were not what I was expecting at all. It was low-key and homely—everything she wasn't. A well-stocked kitchen was cluttered with exotic foodstuffs, cooking instruments that resembled gardening tools, and pans hanging overhead like misshapen tin fruit—everything that Edward's wasn't.

"What are all those jars?" I pointed without thinking. "With the coloured lids."

"Come! I show you. *La mamma*, she sends me from *Napoli*. She thinks I will starve up here in dirty, *orribile Milano*. I am Ginevra. This is pickled mushroom."

"Pleased to meet you. Kat."

"Try this, Kat. Wait, I get a spoon—you can eat just like that. This one is eggplant. And this one?" She opened it to check. "Pepper relish. Are you hungry? I can make some *bucatini*."

It was all I could do to stop her firing up a pan. Her hands and wrists were unusually dainty; her fingers, though busy, barely seemed to brush the surface of things. When we went over to the couch, I noticed a framed jigsaw puzzle of Monet's Water Lilies on the wall. I thought it a little odd, tacky even, and a sign of someone who should get out more. But by the time I was ready to go, I had changed my mind: it was quaint and intriguing, suggestive of the parlor pursuits and indoor diversions of literary heroines like Jo Marsh or the Bennet sisters.

"I like to do puzzles," she said noticing how my attention returned to it. She pronounced it *"pootzlay"* which made me snort with laughter. "What? That is how we say it," she protested. *"Pootzlay.* But it is written the same."

I saw us whiling away the winter months seated at her low furniture doing calligraphy, pressing flowers, maybe even trying our hand at lace-making.

"I would like to go to Ireland one day," she said. I waited for "If it wasn't for the weather," but she continued, "It must be beautiful there. I lived in Brussels for four years. I should have stayed. I had a lot of friends."

"Why didn't you?"

"I couldn't take the weather."

"You don't have friends in Milan?" I asked.

"Milanese people, you will find, are not very friendly. I do not like them so much. People from the south, they are different. You will see. The landlord, he is from *Torino*. He has been promising for months to come and fix the boiler. But, look! I cannot wash the dishes while you have a shower or you would be soup. I will call him again today." She smiled and her eyes sparkled "You like the apartment?"

"I do." And that was how that part of the *pootzlay* fit into place.

Then there were my dates with Davide, the waiter. He was good-looking, no doubt; that was obvious at first glance. But right from our first date he laid it on thick with ostentatious pledges of devotion. I was too self-conscious, too unaccustomed, too *Irish* for that palaver. You can't make a silk purse out of a sow's ear, and while I wouldn't usually compare myself to a female pig, the romantic sounds both our ears were used to hearing were not worlds apart. If all Italian men talked this way, how would I ever communicate for laughing? In time, if I applied myself like I did with Irish in school, I would train my memory to recall the right words, learn by rote the phrases, grow familiar with colloquialisms to eventually use in sentences. But how would I train my thinking? I imagined placing my brain in a colander, straining it of all subtlety, marinating it at high temperature in the juice of bodice-ripping novels, and squashing it back in my skull, engorged and sticky.

But I was put out of my misery in an unexpected way. One evening, while looking for the bathroom in his flat, I came upon Davide's bedroom by mistake. When I hadn't returned after many minutes, he came looking for me. He found me kneeling on his bed intently studying the map of the EU above his pillow. Initially, I'd been curious about the Italian flag emblazoned across the belly of Ireland: it had my name written in it. Then I'd noticed that *Il Tricolore* fluttered over other countries too: it was marked "Dorota" in Poland, "Dagmar" in Germany, "Jane" *and* "Christina" in England…

With poorly concealed pride, he described his aim of sleeping with a girl from every country, his base of operations, the pizzeria. *Le Tre Marie* had been mentioned in a popular guide book, so the project was well under way and not entirely unachievable. I suppose he couldn't believe his luck when the Irish candidate sprouted overhead ripe for the picking.

"The trouble with foreign girls," said Ginevra, afterwards, "is that they always think Italian men mean what they say. Just because they say it with passion."

"Oh, believe me, not a word of what he said meant anything to *this* foreign girl," I corrected. "No. The trouble lay in what he didn't say: that his penis had overtaken the euro as the common currency of sixteen countries."

So I told Davide what he could do with his flag and threw myself into my new job. So much for sampling the local delicacies.

Intermezzo was as different from the orphanage as day was from night: we designed in collections, not deliveries. How the buyers would merchandise the clothes in stores was their responsibility; ours was simply to create an original and powerful message. I didn't copy from magazines and the factory didn't use the same old dressmaking blocks, instead I draped fabric on the mannequin, pinning and pleating my way to new forms which the factory studied in order to create their patterns. I carried tomes to and from their extensive library. Books weren't flashily displayed and temperature-controlled; they were housed in a custom-built space behind a cloud-scaped door, managed by a librarian. On any given moment, my head would be filled with anything from a wistful sea-green and cyclamen tutu Karinska created for the Ballets Russes, to a couple of Schiaparelli dresses Man Ray gave to the bohemian Kiki de Montparnasse who cut them in two and sewed the opposite halves together. I photographed people on my way to and from work with a Polaroid camera and watched inspiration develop within seconds in my hands. Life was truly heavenly: every day I ascended through the clouds to my office on the second floor.

The peal of the church bell wrenched me from my pillow the morning of Intermezzo's catwalk show—and every morning, for that matter. Like a parent saying "You live under my roof, you'll do as I say," living under the six-hundred-year-old bell of the Chiesa della Santa Maria del Rosario meant I started my day when it did: 7:15 a.m.

A blanket of fresh coffee wrapped the flat in its folds; Ginevra was already up. Toweling my face, I opened the door and peeped around to say hi.

"Ciao, *cara, un caffè? Che fantasma!* You need some sun."

"Cheers," I said. "I'll have tea."

"So, come, tell me all," she said, crossing her legs and patting a chair. Bunny rabbits hopped all over her pyjamas. "How's everything looking? Is Rosalba pleased?"

"She seems to be. She just keeps warning us to *separate the fashion from the fiction,* whatever that means."

"You should make *le corna.*" Ginevra touched the table top, then her nose, and finally stuck her index and pinkie finger out: a trifecta of inoculations against a last-minute bout of bad luck.

"Let me read you what she said yesterday. I wrote it down." I dragged my bag across the floor, pulled a sketchbook from it, and found the page. "Here we are: 'The collection must be a surprising realisation for the audience. More than a curiosity, it must whisper forbidden promises like a hot breath at your collar. It must stop you in your tracks, reveal to you the life you want to live, the person you want to be, the people you want to know...'" I looked up helplessly. "I mean, what?"

Ginevra shrugged as if it sounded perfectly reasonable. "Well, does it do that?"

"*Whisper forbidden promises?* How am I supposed to know?"

She made a worried face. "My friend in PR at Prada said Miuccia's changing everything. She woke up yesterday *hating* the forties. She collected all her designers and seamstresses in a room, each with a tailor's dummy, and made them drape for one entire day. New silhouettes, new forms; she wanted volume. Then it was passed right over to the *modellisti* to cut. Total chaos, no prototypes, barely any fittings, twenty-four hours to go. *Un bordello!* Then, specially made buttons didn't arrive in time, so she is holding everything together with thin belts. Of course, it'll be a roaring success." She shook her head in admiration. "*E troppo brava, Miuccia.*"

Ginevra relished such bulletins: working in the show-rooms during sales campaigns, she never felt close enough to the front-line action of Fashion Week.

"I'm not going to worry until I need to," I said. "As my Da used to say, you never plough a field by turning it over in your mind."

She looked confused. "You are speaking from, uh—what Edward calls the—how was it, the *Penguin Book of Lucky Leprechaunisms?*"

"Oh, Edward thinks everyone should talk with bowler hats and brollies in their gob."

"To that, of course, he would say if you didn't have the likes of him to take you under his wing, teach you how to talk in polite society, you'd leave mass confusion everywhere you went."

"That's Englishmen and their inflated sense of self-importance for you."

The ribbing that went on between us was a leftover from when the three of us were first sussing each other out. It grounded us, as language barriers and cultural differences left us scrambling for footing. When Edward and I launched an attack on Italy, its customs, politics, driving, Ginevra stepped in and fearlessly held her own—although even she had to concede a few of our observations were valid. A diet of mild abuse and political incorrectness kept our friendship growing big and strong.

"What about you? How's the new guy—Gianluca, isn't it?"

"*Che miseria,*" she responded. "He's young."

Of all the catwalks, the one Ginevra cared about most was the one she dreamt of walking herself some day: the one festooned with flowers, an altar at the end of it. At thirty-two, she bemoaned her passing years and solitary status relentlessly: "I'm just an old spinster without love, without children," she'd lament, sounding like the gypsies begging for money on the metro who mourned, "I'm just a poor widow without work, without family." I guffawed when I first heard her. But I soon learned she was as serious about husband hunting as the gypsies were about hustling money.

"So is being young bad?"

"I just don't think we want the same things."

"How can you tell after only a couple of dates?"

"He wears his trousers so low, they're practically falling off. All I ask for is a man who can hold up his own trousers."

"You could always buy him a belt," I called, heading back towards the shower. "I hear it's this season's must-have at Prada."

"*Fa le corna!*" she called back.

As the tram rasped along the tracks, a sliver of Jumbotron screen from a half-hidden piazza flashed catwalk images from earlier in the week. I got off at Piazza Cinque Giornate to walk. Traffic was stock-still; drivers sprouted angrily from windows and delivered passionate steering wheel soliloquies while swinging their arms to a chorus of horns. *Carabinieri* officers blew whistles. Sealed off in the back seat of each cab, exacting-looking women in their early thirties, their hands in laps, eyes downcast, were caressing key pads like the beads of a rosary, utterly remote from the chaos outside. It was the infamous Fashion Week stand-off between locals and out-of-towners.

My stomach had begun to turn. I sympathized with the locals—hadn't they every right to go about their daily business without this upheaval? And the out-of-towners—although it seemed like they just swanned in and created disruption, weren't they just doing their jobs too? Everyone around me, whether sounding off or feigning obliviousness, blaring his horn or cursing under his breath, was authentic. I was the lone imposter streaking through the centre of it, going unnoticed. I was the pretender; the hick who had rolled into town in stolen Chanel and deceived everyone.

But by the end of the day, all would be revealed. I would know and so would everyone else. My three month *periodo di prova* would be over. It was a common practice to put new designers on trial to see if they understood the aesthetic of the house, the dynamics of the company, the nature of *la moda Italiana.* Ginevra's comments this morning had touched a nerve. If the show didn't go well, if Rosalba changed her mind, if the reviews were bad, these and any number of other upsets could be blamed on me, for I was the only new element in the equation.

I reached a side street clogged with trucks and equipment. A caravan of rolling racks trundled by carrying four outfits to a carriage, the merest teaser of their exotic colours and textures offered by a transparent plastic window next to the zipper. They were like guests of honour arriving early to a gala, being drawn through grounds that were still being made ready. In the courtyard, I stepped aside to allow a company of men to pass carrying heavy sound equipment. I avoided wriggling ropes and cables underfoot like cracks in the pavement. Farther inside, the DJ was yelling at a sound technician and a photographer from the *Corriere Della Sera* was taking pictures for the evening edition while people milled, someone handed me an Access All Areas pass, and the music became louder as the DJ ran through the sequence one last time.

The whole city was a stage. Fashion Week was one big show comprised of many smaller ones. I felt a respect for every single player in this ensemble cast, no matter how small his role, no matter how reluctant, from tram drivers whose routes were disrupted to newsstand owners who ordered extra copies of the dailies. I envied the regularity of the gig, their familiarity with it and, most of all, their pure, blinding proximity to the lights, camera, action. After tossing my coat and bag in a backstage locker, I walked into the fray, rolled up my sleeves and, wearing a smile from ear to ear, joined in the preparations for curtain up.

"Everyone into their first outfits now! Not a moment to lose! And *where* is Svetlana?"

The girls had gone into Hair and Make-up looking like a bunch of high schoolers and emerged as exotic as a herd of giraffe. At the announcement, they responded leisurely at first, loaded eyelids blinking, long necks crooking, gangly limbs knocking. Still without rush, they began to peel off army sweaters, unwind scarves and kick off scuffed boots, their vertebrae bobbing just under the skin like multiple Adam's apples. As the outfits were pieced onto their bodies, they became less like wildlife and more like tribal figures, subjects of a sort of dressing ceremony in which elders draped skins, beads, scarves, feathers and jewels on the clan's youngest, most beautiful members. Adrenaline pulsated in my ears like a drumbeat as I watched them transform into the goddesses from the glossies.

"Find Svetlana," I heard Rosalba growl. "Her agent says she's here." I watched her retreating figure with her overhead choo-choo cloud of smoke and realized the growl had been directed at me. I set off running, in circles at first. *How should I know where she is? What information on her whereabouts could I possibly have that Rosalba, the model booker, and the model's own agent didn't?* I considered the possibility that Rosalba had gone off me; she was a capricious sort. On a hunch, I pulled open the heavy metal doors to the real world outside. Svetlana was gliding up the pavement in rollerblades with fluorescent wheels and smoking a cigarette, while flirting with three boys who were trying to impress her with their skateboarding tricks.

"There you are," I said, spinning her around on the spot, a giraffe on wheels. "You need to go immediately to Hair and Make-up. You're really late." I clamped the heavy door closed and steered her to the make-up artist who looked at her unmade-up face in horror.

On my way through, I stuck my head out and saw the venue had filled up as journalists and editors took their seats somberly. Many still wore sunglasses. The shoes in the front row reminded me of a coastline of beautiful villas, each one more extravagantly built, more architecturally challenging than the next.

"Agnese! Ana D! Lara! Fucking get in line! Then I need Raquel, Natasha—Svetlana better fucking be here. Listen for your name and *get in line*! Agnese, Ana D…"

"I'm here, I'm here!" Svetlana whined indignantly from the make-up chair.

The man who inserted one curse word for every three names was red-faced but wore an impeccable grey three-piece suit and carried a clipboard. He had half-dressed models crashing into each other in their panic to react to their names.

"Who *is* that guy?" I asked Grace, my creative director.

"Oh, that's Martinelli, an old friend of Franco's. Most of the time, he's okay. He does the hiring and firing, contracts, money, all that stuff. He's scary when he has to fire someone, but he's worse backstage at the fashion show. He's been doing it for fifteen years, and every time it's like he's going to have a stroke."

The air was heavy with hairspray. The lights dimmed outside. Rosalba put her finger to her lips and everyone was silent. The file of thirty-five girls—including Svetlana, urging her fingers into a pair of leather gloves—wound around the backstage area. Martinelli stared menacingly. The music began, and we saw on the video screen the heads of everyone in the audience pivot towards the narrow slit that separated our collection from their judgment. Their studied boredom had transformed into something else, a throwing down of the gauntlet: "Go on then, surprise us!" A current streamed between us and them, travelling underneath the wall and across the floor, an anticipation uniting performer and critic alike before the show would separate us again into opposing camps.

Rosalba gave the first girl, Lara, an encouraging push. She squared her shoulders, threw her upper body backwards like she was suspended on strings, and strode out. I saw her kick and stomp until about halfway down when she was diced alive by flashbulbs. When the third girl exited, Lara had returned and her body popped back to normal. She broke into a run, peeling her dress down off her shoulders, hopping out of her shoes, breasts jiggling while her dresser ran to meet her with arms outstretched. Martinelli thundered from behind his clipboard and the file of girls kept advancing.

After the second outfit change, I sneaked out, re-entered at the photographers' benches, and leaned against the wall to watch the remaining minutes. I took a shaky breath and was grateful for the darkness: it hid the salty tears that were tumbling down my face. I thanked the ninety-odd blinking shutters for drowning out my sobbing. I'd overlooked an important fact: this was the first time I had seen clothes I designed on a catwalk. Those were my ideas parading by under the glare of flashes.

Stray words gained strength and crowded in to crush any feelings of triumph: *"Here at Central St Martins, if we feel a student's collection is below standard, we have the right to refuse him, or her, the opportunity to participate in the graduate fashion show. I am sorry to tell you, Kat, that we will not be allowing you to show your designs."*

But before me my designs were promenading by in the finale, as if on a carousel, alongside creations by the other team members and even a few reworked vintage pieces from Rosalba's seventies wardrobe. The audience rose to their feet. It had been a wonderful collaboration, I thought, almost mournfully, then smeared my sleeve across my damp face and returned backstage. It wouldn't help my prova to be discovered missing before the show had barely ended.

Models had already begun discarding the garments over racks or on the floor, ducking back into their boyfriends' jeans, thinking of their next booking. The mood was festive as an anchorman from TV *Rai Uno* shoved a microphone under Rosalba's smoke-emitting nose and yelled, "Brava, Signora Rosalba!"

She was flitting between one interview and the next when she pulled me to her.

"Kat, before I forget, Martinelli will be waiting for you first thing tomorrow morning." She paused in her husky whisper to blow smoke at me. "It's about time we made you officially one of us, don't you think?"

She sailed off into the embrace of another round of flashbulbs.

GUCCI PARTY

"I think I might be entering withdrawal," I wailed. "I don't want to come down!"

The models had disappeared, the last interview had wrapped up; I was ready to celebrate, but I was alone backstage. Everything was quiet but for the heavy footsteps of anticlimax coming for me down the hall. So I called Edward.

"I had a feeling this might happen. Post-partum blues," he said. "So I convinced a guy at work to get both our names on the list for the Gucci party tonight—just in case."

"Oh, that's what I call forward thinking, Edward. Because we need a party...I passed my *prova!*"

"As if there was ever any doubt. Now, you may refer to me as Baron Ruffles Von Dazzlington this evening."

"By a funny coincidence, I just happened to bring my nineteen-thirties tea gown with the power shoulders and the boned waist—just in case. It's fire engine red; you'll see me coming."

"Well, I better see you coming in thirty minutes. Porta Venezia. Hurry!"

The floor was littered with water bottles, stray napkins, and paper cups spinning weary semi-circles under the dying fans. The champagne on the catering table was all drunk, and the bottles' festive foil top hats and bowties discarded on the floor. But the cork would just be popping on fashion week events all over town, and the Gucci party was the most anticipated of them all.

I got into my dress and new Prada shoes, smeared Ravish-Me-Red on my lips, and arranged the netting of my hat over one eye. I grabbed my coat and couldn't get out of that draughty warehouse fast enough. Instead of traffic, the streets were now filled with attractive girls and boys striding purposefully in every direction like they were part of a city-wide ad campaign. Confidently, I clipped along as if one of them. I turned the corner off Viale Piave, and the crowd changed. I passed the newsstand that was twice the size of all the others to accommodate its extensive range of porn magazines and DVD's, vintage and current. I was slightly curious to know why it drew such solid business but not enough to raise my head. I hurried by the ogling men and across the intersecting tram tracks.

Edward waited by an entrance policed by dark-suited bouncers wearing earpieces. Despite the dark, the gleam from his patent shoes reflected the animation of the city as he paced back and forth, and Debbie Harry twinkled from underneath his tuxedo jacket. I snuck up behind him as he self-consciously arranged a ruffled evening scarf over his shoulders like some grand dame waiting to be escorted on board her transatlantic passage.

"God, I thought you'd never get here!" he said. "I'm bloody freezing."

"Von Dazzlington, I presume?"

"C'mon, let's just get in and get a drink down us. I could be wearing five of these patches, I'd still kill for a smoke."

A girl consulted a list, the bouncers parted, and we tip-toed through. There was another triad of bouncers and two more imposingly draped entrances through which the sounds of a DJ flown in from London beckoned from somewhere just beyond. Edward, unable to contain himself, stopped and broke into a shimmy causing me to crash into him.

"Steady. Keep it together," he cautioned, importantly toss-ing his scarf and swatting me in the nose with it. "Let's not get chucked out before we're even in."

We stepped through the final curtain and gawped.

"Bloody Nora!" I spluttered.

Edward concealed his first impressions more successfully. "How entertaining," he remarked.

Like a pair of boulevardiers, we strolled along a bar that stretched the length of one wall. Its lacquered surface was laid with rows of cocktails, an invisible line dividing the gin tonics from the vodka tonics, the rum and cokes from the whisky sours. All the straws faced east like the whole regiment was engaged in a formal salute of welcome. As drinks were snatched up, the infantry of topless barmen swooped in and lowered fresh ones into the gaps.

I selected a gin tonic but Edward hovered indecisively.

"Gin makes me sin."

I could almost see the film reel of possibilities unspool-ing in his mind. But after a quick scan of the room, he said, "What the hell, it looks like I'll be in good company."

We withdrew to an observation post, twirling and stab-bing our straws in our glasses. What had been a state-of-the-art raised catwalk that afternoon had become a pulsating dance floor for a jumble of twiggy, writhing bodies. They were silhouetted against a grid of lights and the effect was almost pagan, like watching a bonfire's flames dancing between the tinder. There were low-hanging chandeliers and gold-trimmed cushions of Brobdingnagian dimensions for communal lounging: a tricky proposition as women in skimpy printed dresses tugged at hemlines but continued to reveal too much, and men with slicked back hair and baroquely patterned shirts aimed for a macho, spread-legged nonchalance but resembled toads on lily pads.

Out of the half-light a figure came bounding; I had just assembled in the correct order the mop of blond hair, oversized glasses, ankle-baring patchwork trousers, and red shoes before being crushed in a lanky hug.

"Winnie!"

"Shammone!" said Winston, releasing one arm to slap Edward's shoulder benevolently. "My peeps! Trick or treat?" He released us both, and with a spirited capriole landed in front of us. "Bona drag, Gorgeous," he said to me. Then he surveyed Edward, pinched his chin between thumb and forefinger and deadpanned, "Trick."

Edward returned his gaze dourly. "Right back at you."

In a city full of interesting characters, Winston was one of its highlights. He was Scottish but spoke in a baffling hybrid of cockney rhyming slang, eighties rap lyrics, Polari, and other odds and ends, for no good reason anyone had yet determined. He didn't speak Italian, so maybe he thought if he created his own language, it might go undetected. He also worked at Intermezzo on the menswear team, but I saw more of him on the party circuit than I ever did in the studio. Often a little the worse for wear at work, he had been known to fall asleep during fittings, but they hadn't yet acted on their threats to fire him because Rosalba found him delightfully droll.

Edward and Winston treated each other with ambivalence on the best of days. Edward disapproved of addressing everyone as Shammone, speaking in riddles, and dancing around like a boxer. Winston thought Edward "looks like he got a root canal done from the wrong end".

"So, VIP-wise, here's the cackle," said Winston. "Mariah's quite the hoofer but only to her own tunes. Usher's representing in bespoke. Some TV dolly-birds and a field-full of footballers, but I've been saving the best for last: Kylie is upping a surprise whistle laters, peeps. Spinning around. All truth. Hang out and bear witness."

That was the other thing Edward didn't like about Winston: his unfortunate habit of spitting when he spoke. He had large teeth and a hell of a time finding enough space for his restless tongue to scamper around.

Casting a pointed look in Edward's direction, Winston turned to me. "Well, that's all *I* got. You are up to date and fully acquainted. Check with you laters. Join me for a slide if you're hanging loose on the piste. And remember, one love." He disappeared into the darkness from whence he came. Edward grabbed a napkin and made a great show of mopping his face.

"Pillock!" he said, delving inside his shirt to pull his nicotine patch from his arm and slap it on his chest.

"Are you trying to stop before the ban kicks in?" I asked.

"Don't talk nonsense. A smoking ban in Italy? It's ridiculous!"

"That's what they said in Ireland. But it happened last year."

"Not here. No chance. It would never take. There'd be rioting in the streets. I'm just cutting down for myself. But these things don't half give you weird dreams, and bring you out in a rash—I have to keep moving them around. No one's going to tell me not to smoke. I've been doing it since I was fourteen. This is not the neurotic states of fucking America, this is Italy. Long live the great European traditions!"

"Actually, Ireland was the first country to ban smoking in the workplace, you know—I mean, in the world?"

"Well, I'm glad you finally came first at something. No smoking in the workplace, well done. So more time to shag sheep, then?"

Before I could think of a smart retort, a troupe of men glistening like statues dropped upon us. Five bronzed and buff Bacchus figures pushed me aside with a cursory "Nice dress" but scooped Edward into their centre. Pale and boyish but seemingly at ease, he struck poses as they fenced him off. I noticed how their black tailored trousers strained against their athletic thighs. With the lights bouncing off his t-shirt Edward resembled a sparkling festive Maypole. I glanced about to see if anyone else was witnessing the odd scene and when I looked back they were gone; Edward had been abducted by the gods.

I spotted Winston near the dance floor. "Let's dance!" I called.

"For inspiration," he responded, and led me towards a group of semi-familiar faces: flotsam and jetsam that floated by on Milan's nocturnal currents. Winston crouched on the floor and spun slowly on his hunkers, eyeballing us as he turned, creating momentum for the moment when, like a champagne cork, he spiraled into the air. When he landed, he really got going, flipping his limbs about, making faces and striking ungainly poses, freezing mid-position, trembling with the effort, falling over. I laughed till I could hardly breathe from the boning in my dress. This was the kind of celebration I was due. I was a fully-fledged designer, tomorrow a recognized member of the Intermezzo team. When Winston heard, he picked me up and spun me in a blur of lights and colours. How refreshing to be this close to a male without any complicated sexual tension! In Italy, it seemed that every time a man and woman interacted, however briefly, there was an undertone, a move being made, a story waiting to be played out into a three-act opera. The nation lived in a state of constant sexual alert: in the supermarket, at the bus stop, in the bank. It was so palpable it could bring on a migraine.

Winston stopped flailing. "Oh, aye. Looks like you've claimed the eye of my bro, Fausto. Looks like he's been jiggery-poked, good and proper."

I turned to find a gangly fellow dancing behind me. Winston winked and made a magnanimous gesture with his hands, as if to say "Go forth, multiply. Shammone."

I had no choice but to dance with his friend, but I drew the line when he wanted to sway cheek to cheek. The lure of physical contact for Italian men was similar to my compulsion to scratch mosquito bites; they were unaware they were doing it until the swelling became chronically inflamed. I heard little above the music - only that he was a photographer and lived in Milan. What was most striking about him was his hair: it was the most unlikely colour of red, almost that of my dress but more copper, and probably natural because his eyebrows matched. He stood out on the dance floor like a Jersey in a field of Friesians.

"What's all this? Do my ogles deceive me?" interrupted Winston, pointing. "How'd that transpire?"

I followed his finger to the roped-off area where Edward, sandwiched between Usher and Cristiano Ronaldo, was sliding a bottle of vodka from an ice bucket. He jumped up abruptly and gyrated while Italo and his partner Gio looked on. They raised their glasses. Edward stopped dancing, grabbed his drink, came to the toast a little late. He was flushed and sweating, running his hand through his cowlick to keep it from falling forward.

"Your guess is as good as mine," I said, unable to decide if I was more impressed or baffled. I waved to get his attention but became distracted by the sight of a familiar face in the crowd. "Mother of God, is nowhere sacred?" I said, lowering my hand.

"What? Who? Where?" said Winston, looking left and right.

Davide the waiter sauntered right past. I gabbled nonsense in Winston's ear and pretended not to see him. He'd once mentioned something once about having a cousin who worked in the Gucci press office. I'd forgotten that everyone in this town knew somebody on the inside. However, the sighting reminded me to proceed with caution in matters I knew little about. Later, when Fausto asked me if I wanted to go somewhere quieter to talk, I said no but gave him my phone number. Maybe I'd get to see what his hair looked like in daylight.

Sometime around one, Edward reappeared looking dishevelled. "I thought you'd gone," he said. His words were slurred and his tone accusing.

"No, sweetie. I've been here the whole time. It was you who ran off with He-Man and the Masters of the Universe."

"Well, by the power of Grayskull, I declare this party dead."

"What about Kylie? Don't you want to stay for that?"

"She's not coming. Italo told me. She decided at the last minute not to do any fashion week parties, just the shows. Gone back to her hotel. If it's not good enough for Kylie…" He hiccupped.

I caught sight of Davide again as we were leaving: he was in a corner chatting to Svetlana, the model from our show. If I remembered correctly, she was from Slovenia.

Fausto called and we arranged to go for an aperitivo. Edward insisted on coming over to help me pick an outfit, but really he just drank my vodka and made me late. I was at the mirror when I heard a series of quacking sounds from the street. I ran through to Ginevra's balcony and saw that it wasn't as it sounded, a flock of valiant ducks steering a course along the canal, but Fausto aboard what looked like a skateboard fitted with an engine, saddle, and handlebars. He hit the horn again for another loud "*MWAK!*" and some birds fled a nearby tree.

"Oh, holy Moses," I said, as Edward joined me and clapped with glee.

"How very....*enjoyable!*" he said. "Oh, and a redhead, too. You know they're becoming extinct? There's nothing like knowing you're working with rare materials."

I ran around the room throwing things in a bag.

"So I shouldn't wait up?" Edward called as I flew out the door.

I secured myself on the back of what apparently qualified as a scooter. I figured Da's old Massey would have reached higher speeds. The most bothersome thing about this arts and crafts project would probably be the noise. Edward stood on the balcony, his glass held aloft like a proud patriarch from a Jane Austen novel watching his last daughter be swept away in the style to which she should become accustomed.

"Ready?" Fausto revved the engine.

"Tally-ho," I replied, feeling intrepid. I waved to Edward and flicked my hair, anticipating the sensation of a little wind threading through it. The engine gave a pop, we jerked forward, and went hurtling along the canal at such breakneck speed that my breath caught in my throat, and I was sure we'd left some of my internal organs behind.

"Next time, I'll just meet you there," I said, after twenty minutes of see-sawing around badly lit corners with my knees almost scraping the ground. At the last traffic light, when we shrieked down the middle of five tightly packed aisles of scooters, the rider next to me had asked for my phone number. Lack of personal space was a characteristic of everyday life here. Brushes with total strangers I came to expect, but brushes with death I struggled to accept as routine. Outside the small locale nestled in the shade of the *Sforza* castle, Fausto had to pry each of my fingers from his belt buckle.

"You need to relax more," he said. "Trust me. *Dai.*" It was a term of encouragement like '*come on*'.

Die. I evaded his hand pressing the small of my back. *I'll go the rest of the way under my own steam, thank you.*

Inside the coffee bar there was a lot of calling and back-slapping between Fausto, the barman, and a couple of regulars; this was clearly one of his haunts. I felt like the punch line to an earlier joke. The machismo was so stifling I suggested we sit outside in the rush hour pollution instead.

"I'm a fraud," said Fausto. "I lead a double life. I pretend to be an AC Milan supporter with those guys, but my father would disown me if he thought I supported one of the northern teams. My heart belongs to Napoli."

As I sipped my cocktail, I noticed his hair was the colour of the Himalayan goji berries Ginevra had started eating for breakfast to keep her skin from ageing.

"So how long have you been a photographer?" I asked.

"Oh, I'm not a photographer. I'm a photographer's assistant. I help out my cousin. It's his business and I've been there three years. It's not bad. You meet lots of interesting people."

"Great for meeting women, I imagine." I could have throttled myself.

He laughed. "Yes. Some women. Now and then. But there is opportunity for that everywhere if you look for it. It's all around, no?" He looked up through long eyelashes of that same unlikely red, and a perverted curiosity about the exact hue of the rest of his body hair barged into my brain. I had to keep a clear head. That *it* was all around was indisputable. Milan was a sexual amusement arcade, and we were all just an assortment of jingling, jangling, flashing knobs and buttons to be pressed and slots to be filled. With little chance of hitting jackpot, the cheap thrill of seeing one's number come up turned the brain to tinsel. I was just the sort of new-to-gambling hillbilly that would rip through the kid's college fund in a weekend.

"Let's speak in Italian for a bit, see how I do," I ventured. That should act as a cold shower. But he shook with laughter at some of the things I said which sent me scurrying back to English in which he was fluent. I silently vowed to start lessons immediately: no motivation as effective as ridicule.

"I got accepted to study English literature at Oxford," he admitted shyly.

"I don't know if that makes me feel better about not speaking to you in Italian or worse. So you lived in England?"

"No, I couldn't go," he said. "That summer, my mother died. Cancer. My father, he went to pieces, and I am the oldest. He needed me. I still go home as often as I can."

'I'm sorry to hear that."

"It was eight years ago." He shrugged and took a sip of his mojito. "She was Scottish. That is where the hair comes from. So, watch out, I tell you. It turns out we both have fiery Celtic blood in our veins. What do you think of that?"

What did I think? That Celtic blood can only be held responsible for so much. No Scotsman I had ever met boasted that golden skin, those lofty cheekbones, and that big aquiline nose casting a noble shadow over the proceedings.

"And then my father is a cantankerous little Umbrian, so you have been warned."

I laughed while continuing to study him. He had the sort of face that demanded to be painted, in a rustic palette of oils. In fact, with the castle looming behind him, if he turned in profile, he would make a convincing Renaissance-style portrait.

He asked me where I was from in Ireland and what it was like, and told me he was originally from Alba, and that his father was a truffle farmer.

"I'll bring you some truffles next time I go home. Or maybe you can come with me, and we can go foraging."

"I thought they used pigs for that," I said.

"Yes, pigs, dogs. But people too, for the pheromones that are in the truffles. They give a very powerful, natural high. Being a country girl, I bet you'd like it."

"Well, it sounds more interesting than gathering spuds. But why are truffles so expensive?"

"Because they're considered an aphrodisiac. Didn't you know? Sex and nature—can you think of a more desirable partnership?"

By the time night had fallen and the moon had risen behind the castle, Fausto's hands were lying comfortably on top of mine on the table. After another Caipiroska I was conscious of his knee nudging my thigh. But standing in the street afterwards, when he urged me to come back to his place while nuzzling my neck, one of Ginevra's earlier insights came to mind: "Italian men are complicated. First of all, always make them wait even for a kiss. It's *importantissimo* if you want to see them again. Yes, we are old-fashioned but what makes us modern is that we know it, no?"

But Ginevra's rules seemed to contradict the sexual glow that pulsated from every living being. While he was occupied nibbling at my ear, I had but a moment to decide. I chose the only reasonable course of action: I fled the scene and tried to project my desire to see him again through the rear window of my departing taxi. As he stood there in the shadow of the castle next to his scooter, with his hands hanging by his sides and a woebegone look on his face, I was sure I'd blown it.

And yet he did call again, and sooner than expected. Despite my initial attempts at caution, I quickly realized that dabbling with the libido of an Italian man was no trifling matter and, by our third date, we were tearing each other's clothes off in the cramped kitchen of his shared flat while his roommates watched the AC Milan qualifier in the next room.

COME ON, BABY, LIGHT MY FIRE

"I've started acupuncture," said Edward. "Had my first session this morning. It was really good. She stuck needles in my ears, my wrist, my feet, everywhere really. It hurt but it was worth it. I haven't enjoyed the taste of a single cigarette all day."

"How many have you smoked?"

"About twelve. And I'm not craving them either."

We were sitting in Atomic, my favourite dive. It was a bunker: black walls, no windows, red strip-joint lighting lending everyone a bohemian glow. For me it acted as a time capsule: one night it was 1985 and I was in London, at Taboo, surrounded by body art and boys with pretty faces in pirate clothes while I wore a quilted mini-crini I'd made myself; the next I was transported to the Kit Kat Klub of 1930s Berlin, dabbing my lipstick with a yellowed silk handkerchief as the master of ceremonies introduced me onstage.

I studied tonight's crowd. The DJ switched seamlessly from Visage's *Fade to Grey* to electrotrash, and lit a cigarette which he handed to a girl to hold until he needed to inhale.

"We have the usual skinny boys in skinny jeans with skinny hair—"

"—and skinny wallets," grumbled Edward.

There were the accompanying girls in garçon stripes and polka dots, raccoon eyes, and Miu Miu shoes. They were hard and sugary like lollipops. A group of out-of-place Milanesi stood at the bar in business suits, their tan belts, briefcases, and well-shined shoes looking like they'd been cut from the very same hide. I was surprised Edward hadn't perked up when they walked in.

"I could never date a man who wears a suit," I said.

"That's just foolishness talking," said Edward.

I felt a pair of eyes drill into my temple. The barman had been doing this since I arrived. He didn't break his gaze, just gave me a wink and a grin. I looked back at Edward tearing up his beer mat.

"Okay. What's up?" I asked.

His frown remained even while he announced: "Italo and Gio invited me to come and spend a weekend on their boat in Portofino."

"Really? Wow! You're in tight there, Edward."

"It is. I am. This is the same boat that J Lo parties on, and Madonna. It's such an honour. No one ever refuses these invites. It'd be unheard of. And, of course, if I go, my career is solid gold. They're very loyal to their boys. It's...yeah, it is."

"So, what's the problem? Go. Drink a cocktail. Soak up the sun. Come back with an autograph or two."

"Hmm...right."

"I'm envious."

His head hung but he looked up from under his eyebrows. We used to have a dog that did the very same after being caught chasing the neighbours' sheep. He dived under the stove to hide from Da's wrath only peeping out hours later when the coast was clear. The sheepish-looking dog.

"Well, you see... rumour is that's when they intend to make their move," said Edward. He raised his eyebrows as if to say *do I have to spell it out for you?*

The vodka I'd gulped too fast went white water rafting down the wrong channel, sending bubbles shooting through my nose, turning my throat inside out. "You *are* joking." I hoped my streaming eyes and coughing conveyed my sheer horror. "Wait a minute. Is that why they gave you that unexpected raise recently?"

"Ask no questions and I'll tell you no lies," he said with a smirk.

"That's disgusting! You can't even consider it. You don't know what you're saying."

"Don't be so naïve, Kat. That's how everyone gets ahead in this business. I'm like a nineteen-fifties typist in a typing pool. I could be there for years unless I take advantage of such opportunities."

"Don't be stupid! You're too good a designer for that."

"Stop being so judgmental! People get flats in the centre of town, promotion, travel—"

"Oh, *shut up.*"

We sat in silence, him staring defiantly the other way, me staring incredulously at him.

I tried appealing to his ageism: "I don't know about the other one but Italo is *old,* Edward." His sizeism: "And fat. You really couldn't."

"Oh, don't look at me like that," he said after a while.

"I'm not looking at you any way."

"Okay, I'll admit I was kind of tempted but I didn't say I would go. You just jumped to conclusions."

"Well, thank God, sanity prevails! You had me for a minute. No designer of your quality needs to be lost to the harem of that pair of old queens." I held his chin so our eyes met. "Promise me you won't consider it again."

"I won't consider it again. Now quit getting your knickers in a knot. I'm sorry I even mentioned it."

"You have no intention of going?"

"Absolutely none."

"Good," I said. "Now have you noticed the way that barman keeps looking over here..?"

"Kat, can I ask you a question?" said Ginevra like she'd been waiting a long time to ask. "Do you *mean* to wear your clothes inside out?"

I laughed and nodded.

"Oh. Well, good then. I was worried there wasn't enough light in your room."

"Sometimes the inside's more interesting than the outside," I said. "Take this top. You can see all the stops and starts the embroiderer made, all the threads that dangle, the labour that went into it. Why hide that? And see how the colour inside is a few shades lighter but the turn-up of the hem makes a dark border. See how perfectly sewn the seams are? I think that's beautiful. Sometimes the joy is in the work more than the result."

Ginevra looked skeptical. She had tried grooming me as one would any little runt that turns up on the doorstep. When she quit pushing the idea of a boob job on me, she found me slightly more responsive, but we both knew I would never be her magnum opus.

"Thankfully, it's not what I think that matters," said Ginevra. "What's important is that Fausto appreciates these individual flourishes of yours."

"So far, no complaints. He thinks I am *interessantissima.*"

She gave me an indulgent smile.

"Which reminds me. It's our one-month anniversary this weekend. I wanted to cook—try to cook—something special. Make it a romantic night. Any ideas?"

"Which night?" She looked up sharply.

"Saturday."

She made a pained face. "But I've invited Stefano to dinner. I'm making four courses: veal, pasta, at least four cheeses, Aleatico wine—"

"Okay, okay. Don't panic. I'll work something out." I had no intention of getting in the way of her romantic plans: it was the equivalent of big game hunting at close range, while what I had planned was more like an amateur-level clay pigeon shoot. "Maybe I can cook at his place."

"Oh, thank you, Kat. I will make plenty so there will be leftovers. It's an important night. At the end of it I will know if Stefano is right for me."

"That'll be some powerful wine you're serving."

As it turned out, Fausto's place was unavailable too: his flat mates had invited friends over to watch Lazio play Real Madrid. Just when I was getting disheartened, Edward called wondering if I could water his plants that weekend as he had been roped into helping out at the opening of a new Italo Rocco store in Rome.

He agreed to loan me his flat with the words: "Just don't forget to show my Begonias some love too."

I'd glazed a salmon in garlic and lemon just as the recipe instructed, and filled Edward's place with flowers and candles, just as I'd seen Ginevra doing in our flat a few blocks east. Tea lights flickered on the balcony, and church candles cast shadows from the bookshelves and around the bathtub.

"This is a revelation," said Fausto, mopping his plate with bread.

"It is," I said, getting up. "And there's more."

"You look oddly cute in the kitchen, you know."

"Of course you'd say that," I said, placing sliced banana in the pan and adding sugar. "You're Italian, but just remember, domestication is for pets."

"I mean in an untraditional, post-modern, ironic kind of way. You don't remind me of my mother or anything," he added cheekily.

"Domestic *Science* or Home *Economics,* that's what they called it at school. What a con. There's nothing scientific about it. And what do flour and eggs have to do with economics?" I added a big splash of rum. "I chose woodwork and made Da a very handsome hen house." I struck a match and everything was engulfed in a column of blue flames. I staggered backwards and fell against Fausto who had leapt out of his chair. "No, no, sit! It's supposed to do that. It's flambé. It just took me by surprise, that's all." I shook the pan from side to side and the flames petered out.

"You saw I was ready to be a hero though?" he said.

"Relax, big boy. I'm not going to burn Edward's place down. I'm not *that* undomesticated."

After dinner, we went onto the balcony to look out over the canal. I slid one of his Marlboro Lights between my lips and leaned in so that his lit tip touched mine till it flared.

"I didn't think you smoked," he said.

"Only now and then. Everyone in fashion does, and it pains me to be like everyone else. But I do love the sensuality of smoking. And the feeling that even if you're alone, you're really not if you've got a cigarette - you're just mysterious. Cigarettes go so well with hats too. Edward once told me I didn't look right smoking."

"It's true, your grip is kind of odd. Like a child with a candy cigarette." He demonstrated a more stylish pose.

"Do you think people will smoke less when the ban comes in?" I asked.

"No way. Italians don't respond to any form of social engineering. Look how they tried to limit driving cars into the city on alternate days to lower pollution. Pollution's increased. They want to pay couples to have more kids, and the birth rate goes down."

I shivered slightly, bare-armed in the night air.

"Come with me, little girl," said Fausto, leading me back inside. "I'll light your candy cigarette for you."

The easiness of us surprised me. I had thought a relationship with an Italian man would be fuelled by arguments and accusations, judging by the amount of couples I came upon in the street doing their impression of a Punch and Judy show. I hadn't wanted to acknowledge the old stereotypes until I realized Italians wholly embraced them: women liked to be whistled at because it signified an appreciation of their femininity and the efforts they made with their appearance; men wore the lothario label proudly as a tribute to their manhood; both sexes considered outlandish exhibitions of jealousy a sign of devotion, and any reference to their highly strung personality was amended with the word 'passionate' and accepted with a shrug.

However, in Fausto, I had stumbled upon the anti-type: reflective and trusting, he was an example of the

less-chronicled new model of Italian male. He would come
in from a football match and rustle me up a risotto. Next
to his slickly presented countrymen, his hair never conceded to his wishes, its colour alone preventing him from
ever appearing coordinated. Among the sprawling herds of
Vespas, Aprilias and Piaggios, his scooter, which he named
Quasimodo, was the proverbial black sheep, a triumph of
individuality. He didn't own a cell phone carrying instead
a battered volume of Italian poetry in the back pocket
of his jeans. I enjoyed his cooking—especially the truffle
dishes—preferred his dishevelled manliness to the plucked
and tweezed variety, and even developed a grudging respect
for Quasimodo which he had assembled with his brother
over the course of a summer mostly from scrap parts. The
poetry he recited was from the thirteenth-century and had
nothing to do with modern Italian established in the seven-
teenth century, so while I loved how it sounded—scholarly,
lyrical, romantic—I didn't understand a word. All in all,
Fausto and I had the kind of relationship I couldn't even
have dreamt up for myself.

At around midnight we got dressed. I kissed him good-
night as he had an early start the next morning and I stayed to
eliminate any sign of our tryst. Steam from our bubble bath
still coated the balcony windows and curled about the exposed
wood beams of the ceiling where a landmass of plaster was
now missing. I smiled as I locked the door behind me, listened
to make sure Edward's grandparents didn't hit the floor, and
felt confident that Edward wouldn't be able to detect even a
whiff of heterosexual activity, something which always gave
him the heebie-jeebies.

I whistled all the way along the canal.

With my career on track, love life in high gear, I felt ready to build on an area of my life in much earlier stages of development: the mechanics of interacting with other human beings native to this foreign land, ie. talking Italian. Fausto's English now sported a subtle Irish twang while my Italian was too basic to exhibit any personality. It was like a square, white-washed room with wooden floorboards and a mattress on the floor. There wasn't even a hook on the wall to hang something. I needed to begin furnishing it if I was ever to live in it.

I had started reading *The Little Prince* in Italian with a dictionary by my side. I spent so much time between the pages of the dictionary I dropped *The Little Prince* and just read the dictionary. Every Sunday and Wednesday evening I made the journey to a depressing 1960's high school on the outskirts of Milan where Italian lessons were offered free to foreigners courtesy of the *Commune Di Milano*. I was returning from class the following night on the number forty-three tram, lurching through thick fog, with the textbook, *Ciao Italia!*, unopened on my knee, when its cover photos of the leaning tower of Pisa, La Scala and the Vatican prompted me to think Fausto and I should plan a little trip in the spring.

I wriggled my gloved fingers against the cold and looked at my feet. I now regretted being seduced by the dangling signs shouting '60% Off All Marc Jacobs!' in the window of the new discount emporium where I had bought my high-heeled, peep-toed booties; I'd gone out expressly for sturdy-soled, insulated winter boots. This town was full of those places. Each season, accessory designers from New York, Paris and London descended on a cluster of hillside towns outside Florence and deposited their sketches in the hands of the local artisans. Shoes and bags were already christened—Lola, Margot, Beatrice, Gilda—before they were even born. Out they popped six to eight weeks later. Surplus stock, discarded prototypes and samples were swiftly transferred to the shelves of Milan's discount stores where I came along, snapping up my draughty Marc Jacobs for half the price American girls paid.

The first day I wore them to work, Rosalba had sidled up behind me and ordered, "Take those shoes off immediately!" Seeing my startled expression, she explained, "I want to try them on." Those passing lingered until a group of about twenty had gathered on the stairs and draped themselves over the banisters.

"*Sono un amore,*" she said. "*Davvero, sono da Dio.*" *They are love. Truly a gift from God.*

The congregation murmured respectfully—those seated on the red-carpeted steps were like genuflecting figures of a fresco, their heads tilted towards the same vision. There was no denying it, Italians worshipped fashion.

On the subject of fashion worship, as if on cue, there they were. Just as the tram arrived at the bridge, the transvestite prostitutes emerged from the fog like a pack of she-wolves hoisted up on hind legs and strapped into six inch Gucci heels. They had the same groomed aggression as the lionesses: every undone button, every glimpse of lace, every flash of stocking weighed for its killer seduction value. They were a colourful interlude to an otherwise dreary stretch of Via Ripamonti. Stalled in traffic, I looked around for my two favourites whom I'd named Coco and Chanel.

As I watched the pair of them bantering, strutting, and circling each other in that familiar way, I did a double take: Chanel was wearing the Marc Jacobs booties as well! I lowered the brim of my hat. If she caught me gawping, she'd storm the tram and beat me with her classic Speedy until the LV logo swam before my eyes. Despite her feminine adornments, she looked like one scrappy broad. Coco, Chanel and their crew were reportedly among the biggest spenders in the boutiques of Via Montenapoleone. They could afford full price Louis Vuitton thanks to the droves of husbands who, seeking a break from marital bliss, spent countless hours in their company. With their women's wares on display for all to see, it seemed many Italian men were drawn to a femininity that still held a few hidden surprises.

The tram pulled off and my thoughts turned to Signora Quadrona, my Italian teacher. She was as far removed as you could get from a world where she-wolves and lionesses fought over handbags. Her look was a feat of dowdy sobriety. Unfortunate plaid trousers: check. Belted high on the waist to create pear-shaped posterior: check. Chalky fingertips and neat short hair requiring no maintenance from chalky fingertips: check. Novelty plastic earrings of a dangling design, perhaps parrots, suggesting sense of girlish fun: check. Sensible lace-up shoes to show that learning the language was, in fact, not girly or fun but a serious one requiring both feet firmly placed on the ground, arches well-supported: check.

"Okay, who wants to describe their week so far—in Italian, of course?" she purred at the start of every lesson. No matter how many other hands flagged the air, she would invariably ignore the more enthusiastic student and ask, "Kat, how about you?"

The tram doors opened and an old tramp dressed in every stitch he owned clambered up. I was ashamed to find myself admiring the way he had layered three cardigans on top of each other, misbuttoning the inner layers with the outer one for a most charming result. He stamped on my frozen Marc Jacobs toes and flung himself down next to me, lacing the air with swirls of whisky and urine. I drew the textbook close to hide my watering eyes. From Vuitton-toting trannies to dapper-cardiganned tramps, this tram journey was a trip. I slid over a bit, the tramp grunted and slid after me. Past Participles of Irregular Verbs was the title of the page we were to work through. The verbs he was slurring into my ear I had yet to come across; they sounded *highly* irregular.

The sound of my phone ringing lifted me from my thoughts: it was Edward.

"Oh thank goodness, I am saved," I said. "I'm on the tram of the damned, miles from civilization, hurtling through the frozen inner circle of hell. Keep me company, Edward. Tell me stories so I don't fall asleep and end up God knows where."

"Okay. How's this for a story? I lent my flat to a friend for an evening, and she burnt the fucking place down."

LOVE IN A WARM CLIMATE

S everal hours later, covered in soot, I squeezed through the narrow doors of our flat. Ginevra who had been stirring the contents of a large, scuffed pot, stopped the motion of the spoon and stared.

"*Mamma mia*, Kat! From the inside-out clothing to *this?*"

I sloped across the floor and dropped onto the couch, but not before she scurried ahead and shoved a dishcloth underneath me.

"I set fire to Edward's flat."

"*Ma che dici?*"

"It was an accident. I've been helping him clean." I slumped back against the couch, but she had another towel ready and I leaned forward while she arranged it over the cushions. I let my head fall in my hands.

"Tell me," pleaded Ginevra.

"Last night, after Fausto left, I thought I'd blown out every candle. But it seems I forgot one, up on the cistern of the loo, the epicentre of the devastation. It burned out and melted most of the plastic toilet; the bathtub's completely black; his precious Kiehl's products are congealed on the radiator; the shower curtain stuck to the tiles—even his rubber duckie's a goner."

The only noise from Ginevra was the drip of the sauce from the spoon she held as it hit the floor tiles. When I closed my eyes, the image of Edward's belongings covered in a thick black ash was all I saw. The smell of the melted materials still stung my windpipe.

"But neither of you should be in there," said Ginevra. "You need to let the fire department deal with it."

"The damage was done when he got there. He doesn't want trouble, and he's worried what his landlady might do. She already doesn't like him. It *was* our fault, remember—my fault."

"Yes, but you can't just keep it to yourselves and what, pretend it never happened?"

A funny visual appeared through the memory of the debris; it bubbled up, and I couldn't resist sharing it: "Edward said after just two minutes he came out looking... looking like Al Jolson."

Ginevra's eyes glittered. A smile leaked out but she wiped it away. "You two." She shook her head hopelessly. "So what does he intend to do?"

I groaned. "His landlady's coming up from Mantova tomorrow night. I have to be there to convince her that the loo just melted like an igloo in a heatwave. He says his Italian isn't good enough, and it's the least I can do." I dropped my head back in my lap. "I should go look up some words."

"Can't Fausto be there? I would, gladly, but I have late meetings with buyers all week."

"Unfortunately, he's out of town till tomorrow night on a magazine shoot. We'll just have to play the helpless foreigners and hope for the best."

"*Porca miseria*, Kat" she said, turning to tend to three gurgling pans. "*Che cosa hai combinato?*" It was a common phrase meaning 'What *have* you done?'—*what have you combined?*—but to me it conjured up a witch stirring a wicked brew, cooking up her recipe for chaos, and cackling; all I'd meant to cook up was a piece of salmon, a flambé for afters.

I got up and followed her into the kitchen. The countertop was strewn with coloured lids and saucers heaped with the harvest from the jars: moist little mounds, pickled, peppered, and oiled. The grill glowed against her knees. It was certainly a comforting spectacle, but I wondered: "*Che cosa hai combinato tu, Ginevra?*" For she tended to cook with every ingredient in the kitchen when she was most upset. A good rule of thumb was: the more herbs in use, the spicier the problem.

"Are you getting a head start on food parcels for Edward when he's homeless?" I lifted the lid of a pan and inhaled. "This whole thing could work to his advantage."

"But where is Edward? He must come and stay here tonight."

"Nope. To cheer himself up, he's gone to stay in a *pensione* filled to the rafters with male models."

"Really! Is that all that boy thinks about?"

"Getting his end away? Yeah."

She began chopping parsley with what I could only describe as a vicious sense of purpose. "You haven't eaten, have you?" she asked. Bless her over-cooking heart.

"They haven't got the canteen up and running yet at Cell Block H where I take Italian. And the only thing Edward ever keeps in is vodka and a jar of mascarpone—both of which survived, incidentally."

"Will you take your chimney-sweep face out of my sauce!"

As I scrubbed myself clean in the shower, I thought of Edward crawling about his floor with a pair of tweezers and a magnifying glass, looking for evidence his landlady could use against him. Ginevra was banging pots like it was New Year's Eve when I returned. She sighed and began thrusting cutlery in the general vicinity of the table.

"Okay. Before you start launching the hot soup, tell me. I've walked in on an epicurean exorcism, haven't I? Stefano?"

"*Che palle,*" she said, ladling soup. "*Un bambino.*" She slammed the pot back on the stove. "And before him there was that *testa di cazzo*, Luigi, who made me pay for my own lunch. Is it too much to ask that a banker might make a good impression and treat his date to lunch?" She flung open the oven door. "There was Marco, the week before, who turned out to have three other girlfriends, one of whom wears his great grandmother's engagement ring—a family heirloom, no less—and the big day's planned for spring. Is it too much to ask that a man, when he gives a ring, might take himself off the market? I mean, at least until the wedding!" She dumped the contents of the oven grill on the cutting board. "Have a *friselle.*"

I was at a loss. I'd already introduced Ginevra to three of Fausto's friends to no avail. I had no idea what she was looking for and seriously wondered if she even knew herself.

"I know what'll take our mind off things," I said, jumping up from the table. "Let's turn on the TV and laugh at the *Veline*, then we'll watch the news."

The female newscasters were as titillating as the dancing girls. Like porn stars tossing their hair and pouting at the camera sideways, they delivered updates on Middle Eastern conflict; Lara Leanover (And Look Down My Blouse) and Lucia Legover the weathergirl. But to Ginevra these women had reached the zenith of their feminine potential. They would marry footballers by the end of the year, open a series of trendy nightspots in Milan and Rome, and be media royalty;

photographs of their nuptials would sell for unearthly figures, appearing in the magazines to which Ginevra routinely subscribed, in turn, making her yearn for her own big day and ultimately feel even more dejected.

So I put the TV on mute and returned to the chick pea ravioli. Then we attacked a cheese plate after which she went to the shelf above the cooker and proudly produced a Tupperware container.

"You baked too?" I asked.

"Uh-huh." She sliced two generous portions of her speciality apricot tart.

"You are thorough, Ginevra."

"Thoroughly alone," she said with her mouth full. "And soon thoroughly fat."

The decadent flavours had sedated me temporarily. But when we finally stopped eating, the feelings stormed forward stronger than before, a flotilla of anxiety. I flashed again on Edward's flat. Like the vandals who spray-paint graffiti on the Brera museums that house the nation's treasures, I had defaced something precious. During my first days, those sunny, humpy walls and terracotta floor had soothed me after hours spent dodging lionesses and chasing creative directors. Only after moving out did it occur to me that the rudimentary design of Edward's small studio, its primitiveness, and the earthy colour scheme had made me feel so at home probably because it resembled a barn—even Edward's couch smelt of a hay shed. Only its canal location, the sights and sounds from the balcony, gave it its exotic lustre. It had been the best of both worlds, a refuge. Then I had galloped through trailing turmoil in my wake. I was an oaf and a barn was the best place for me.

Fit to burst, Ginevra and I dropped onto the loose-springed couch and watched in silence as two politicians snarled at each other on a talk show while a miniature screen showed one of them pitching a pen like a dart, hitting his adversary squarely between the eyes. Then the miniature screen expanded to full size as the struck politician removed his jacket, loosened his tie, and advanced towards his opponent while other members of parliament hopped and tumbled over chairs and each other, their fists in the air, like a scene from the Keystone Kops. I couldn't sleep for guilt that night and desperation to make things right; my only hope was that Edward's landlady wasn't as hotheaded as the men that ran the country.

"Just as long as you know that everything will be said in the present tense," I told Edward. "That's as far as I've got: page nineteen, *Ciao Italia!*"

Despite having lived in the country twice as long, Edward resolutely refused to converse in anything other than the Queen's English. He went to buzz in Signora Palmira, his landlady. I could sense his apprehension by the way he was chewing his inside lip.

Signora Palmira cut quite a swath both entering and contoured against Edward's once-cheery walls. A bugle call preceding her would not have seemed out of place. Dressed in velvet and plaid, in a palette of forest hues, she might have shopped for some of her wardrobe in the same place as Signora Quadrona. But her most singularly striking item, a military green cap with a machete-shaped feather slicing the air, together with her Mogdigliani-esque features, lent her a sangfroid my homely Italian teacher could never claim. Sternly she greeted Edward, ignored my extended hand, and went barreling towards the bathroom leaving Edward and I to scuttle after her. With as much conviction as I could muster,

I launched into what a shock it had been for poor Edward to come home to this.

"How could a fire have started in the toilet?" she demanded, feather twitching.

"Clearly there must have been something faulty with it." Edward nodded to me, and I duly translated this pearl of wisdom.

"Toilets are not prone to catching fire *in this country*," she responded.

"He always keeps the place immaculate," I said, "As you can imagine, these conditions are intolerable for him."

"Tell her maybe it was the pipes of the radiator, we can't be sure," said Edward. "We're as confused as she is. Tell her I get electric shocks for no reason and bits of the ceiling land right in my dinner sometimes. This flat is not without its...issues."

Her response was a look of disgust before she pulled the towel from the rail and knelt on it to examine the remains up close. Plaid rear in the air, feathered bonce stabbing at the floor, she looked like some sort of pecking highland cockatoo.

"Luckily, I live close by so Edward can have his morning shower at mine," I said. "But it's hardly convenient."

She glowered up at me. Getting up and dusting off her hands, she said, "It's my guess you left something burning, like a candle."

"*Assolutamente non!*" said Edward, leaping over the language barrier at this offence. "I'm not that careless, Signora." Then he glowered at me.

Signora Palmira said she would return the next day with a plumber friend who would tell her *precisely* what had happened. With a look that said, "I'm on to you. You've gotten away with nothing. Don't leave town," she bowed to fit through the doorframe and was gone.

"Did you notice she made no mention of notifying the authorities?" I said, sitting opposite Edward in Atomic afterwards. "She wants no legal situation either is my guess."

"We're not out of the woods yet. And I haven't forgiven you. Just to be clear."

"That's completely fair," I said as the waitress brought our drinks. "I feel terrible. Anything I can do, just say the word." I waited but he just sat there, quiet and grim, nursing his drink, and exhaling cigarette smoke like he was trying to expel the worries of the world.

Then he turned to me squarely. "A colossal lorry-load of shit is about to hit the fan."

"Let's wait and see what her plumber has to say…"

"No, no, not that." He stubbed out his cigarette impatiently. "I mean I haven't been entirely honest with you. There was no store opening. I was in Portofino. On Italo and Gio's yacht."

He left the news to settle on the tabletop like a spinning coin. I became overwhelmed by a buzzing in my ears and a blurring of my thoughts that rendered me incapable of speech, the selected words sitting in a row on my tongue and I unable to spit them out. I had been struck mute. Slowly, I turned my head. The barman, the same one as before with the stare, seemed to be the cause of my condition; it was as if his gaze hadn't broken since last time. My right ear was lit up like a neon sign on the side of a motel, while my brain had become the dusty grey mattress in the adjacent room, bathed in its gaudy flashes. I turned back to Edward's anxious face.

"Let me get you another drink," I said and slid off the chair.

"Oh. Okay," he said, looking down at his glass, still three-quarters full.

The barman's eyes were locked with mine as I approached the counter. They seemed to dance with a fire just behind the pupil. His black hair spiked every which way and his wide smile looked almost sinister outlined by a thick goatee like the ones people draw on posters at bus stops. When I ordered the drinks he blinked his acknowledgement, then, feigning reluctance, slid up the bar still watching me as he dropped ice cubes, one by one, into two glasses. He had the head of a devil and the air of a shipwreck. Languidly he lifted the Tanqueray bottle and poured, then the Smirnoff, then the tonic water which, with a squeeze of the trigger, sent electric blue bubbles frothing over the ice. With be-ringed fingers he hooked a juicy wedge of lime over the lip of each glass and a single lime tear slid down the length of one. He pushed the drinks towards me, pressing them into the counter as if testing their strength.

Unable to withstand such high-octane interaction I turned abruptly, carried the drinks back, and insisted we move to a table farther away from the bar.

"So are you going to say something?" asked Edward when we were relocated. "Or are you going to sit in quiet judgment of me for the entire night?"

"What?—oh sorry! I don't know what came over me." The eyes of that atomic Beelzebub of the high seas, that's what. I was conscious of my heart pounding. "Tell me everything."

Edward began with a deep breath. "There were about fifteen of us in all—the usual circle plus a couple extra. It started off fine, well, obviously a little weird, but fine. We were up on deck of this really *huge* boat. It was fabulous, with a glass atrium, smoked glass walls, black lacquer everywhere, and zebra print—it was like some sort of floating theatre. The sun was going down. I was chatting, looking at the water, everything was lovely. I hardly felt nervous at all. And with a few more drinks, I definitely started to relax. Some more cocktails were served and then we had dinner down below. After, everyone started doing coke. I was, like, give me some of that. We were dancing, drinking, and I had totally forgotten about it...then shit, before I knew it, the others disappeared and I was alone with them in a room—" He gulped a mouthful of vodka and lit another cigarette. Italo comes towards me—"

"Oh God, Edward, I don't think I can hear this."

"I couldn't help thinking, uh-oh, haven't thought this through, and, well, I felt I was going to have a panic attack. I *was* feeling funny. He comes over, plants one on me; I start to giggle which makes him upset, then he starts to unbutton his shirt and puts my hand on his chest. Now, I don't know if it was the sight of his saggy boobs, or the last daiquiri alla fragola but..." Edward moved his glass out of the way, laid his forearms solidly on the tabletop, and lowered his head into the space between, hands dangling over the side. He held this position for a few seconds before he began to repeatedly bang his forehead off the table.

"Edward, stop it!" I had to grab him to hold his head still.

"I threw up on him. Risotto alla Milanese, tuna carpaccio, panna cotta. All over Italo Rocco." He looked at me helplessly. I was holding him by the ears like his head was a winner's cup.

"Where was the other one?" Some perverse curiosity in me needed to completely capture the scene.

"Oh, what does it matter?" he cried. "He was around; I think he burst out laughing. But Italo wasn't at all amused. In certain circles it's not considered appropriate dinner etiquette to vomit on either of the hosts, last I heard. It *can* raise eyebrows."

"Jesus, what did you do?"

"What could I do? I jumped."

"Jumped where?"

"I ran up on deck and jumped overboard. I just had to get out of there and I knew we were close to shore. Although, it was pitch black and pure luck I even swam in the right direction." His eyes were darting about the bar as he relived it, squinting as if trying to discern if what lay between the tables was land or just the shadow of a big cloud. "Did I overreact? I'm not sure. Could I have explained my way out of that situation? We'll never know. So there you have it."

He looked so distressed I didn't know what to say.

"It's the mixing of the coke with the fruit of the cocktails, that's where I went wrong," he said, decisively. "Anyway, you can't imagine how glad I was to find the station and get the next train back. That is, of course, until upon my return I find you had casually set fire to my home."

"Oh, Edward, what a palaver. What are we like?"

He nosedived onto the table again with a thud.

I looked around; no one was paying any attention—well, no one except the barman who was watching through a porthole in the wall next to the bar. Once again, it took some effort to pull away; I felt at the mercy of some kind of Atomic magnetism.

I laid a hand on Edward's shoulder. "Did you see Italo today?"

"I rang in sick, didn't I." He sat up and ran his fingers through his quiff. "What if he wants me out? What if they relegate me to packing boxes in the warehouse? What if I never design in this town again?"

I walked to Edward's from work the next day tortured with thoughts of how I had added to his problems and filled with a new dread of what we were walking into. We were quite out of our league: there surely weren't two other words that, when placed side by side, could strike more fear into the hearts of foreigners than '*Italian*' and '*plumber*'. Of course, I would fork out if there were damages to pay, although I'd have to call mum for the money, and revealing the truth of my steamy night with an Italian man would make for a cringe-worthy mother/daughter chin-wag. For once, it would be a blessing if she forgot to put her hearing aid in. It could turn out to be one costly piece of salmon Fausto had chowed on. Provided mum didn't send a fleet of Catholic priests to whisk me back to chastity, Fausto and I would have to live on sex and spaghetti for the next six months—on the bright side, that was probably the secret to looking like a lioness.

Deep in such thoughts and rounding the corner of the Naviglio, I almost toppled someone coming in the opposite direction.

"Whoa! *Merda!* Kat? Ciao!" It was Davide, the geographically horny waiter.

"Oh, hallo."

"You're in a hurry. Where's the fire?" He was beaming but put away the smile and composed his face into the picture of thoughtfulness. "How've you been? I've been looking out for you but I haven't seen you in ages."

"Been working."

"Of course! How's it working out?"

"Fine."

"You still living...?" He pointed in an upward direction; he might have been indicating the sky, a tree, the bell tower of Santa Maria del Rosario church.

"I moved."

"And how are you finding life in Milan?"

He was behaving as if international relations between us had never been breached. There were no flags hanging at half-mast above his bed; each one flew without embarrassment or regret. He smiled and winked and dazzled to his own backing track of olive oil bottles tinkling on a dresser. He had more front than Donegal Bay. And my sullen responses bounced off him like raindrops off Bundoran surfers.

I said I had to go but he joined me walking. When he asked why the haste, I dropped my guard and found myself inexplicably disclosing every detail of my imminent appointment.

"I'll call Astrid," he said. "She's close by."

"Who's Astrid?"

"A friend."

"I see."

"I bet she'll be able to help."

"No. It would only make it worse. Bringing a posse might look…aggressive. I've already done enough damage."

"She'd deal with this sort of thing over breakfast. She's amazing. Trust me."

We arrived at Edward's at the same time as Signor Palmira—her head boasting two feathers on this occasion, like crossed swords—and her plumber, an even greasier-looking chap than I had imagined. I overheard him informing her, "It's completely out of the question. I installed those fixtures. I should know. The damage is that English boy's responsibility, and this'll be a simple matter of showing you the proof. He's only making this more difficult for himself."

"Okay, call Astrid," I told Davide.

Edward opened the door to his landlady, her plumber, my waiter, and me, greeting us all with composure, and only a faint quizzical look towards Davide. In the end it was La Signora's feathers that were most ruffled. Giacomo, the greasy plumber, while agreeing it was unlikely a toilet could set itself on fire, much to his surprise, could find no evidence whatsoever to the contrary. It was less of a surprise to Edward who'd taken his formidable cleaning skills to a forensic level; he had extracted any anomalous matter from the rubble with a surgeon's precision. Edward Tweezerhands.

Signora Palmira, furious but undeterred, was threatening to set her lawyers on Edward as if they were dogs, when Astrid strode through the open door. Miss Netherlands in a designer suit, her tiara a pair of blinged-out Dolce & Gabbana shades restraining thick blond waves, said "Pardon me," and began surveying the place, jotting down notes on a legal pad without a word or glance to anyone except Davide with whom she maintained a coquettish dialogue with her eyes. Signora Palmira looked her up and down, unsure what to make of the prepossessing stranger tapping at the walls and peering at the ceiling.

"Who is this?" she asked.

Astrid stopped in the centre of the floor and addressed the room. "Astrid Vermeer, junior partner of law firm Giardini, Giamatti, and Vermeer. Excuse my breezing in but I only have a few minutes so I will be plain. This apartment is in disrepair, clearly has been for quite some time. La Signora—" She consulted her notes. "—Palmira, as owner of this property, is in violation of a list of codes as long as her arm, and, just looking at the ceiling alone, my firm, Giardini, Giamatti, and Vermeer, could make a case for this dwelling being ruled uninhabitable until large scale renovations are undertaken. I avert La Signora that, if she chooses to pursue this further, she could be out of pocket a substantial sum in enforced improvements before being able to continue renting the property, a procedure which might, of course, take years." She turned to Edward's landlady. "Do you understand, Signora?"

Flushed of face, Signor Palmira stammered an affirmative. With a chastened air, she picked up her coat and bag, headed for the door, and, while avoiding all eye contact, announced she would send men to install new bathroom fittings the following weekend before disappearing. Astrid turned to Davide and kissed him passionately before slipping from the scene as swiftly as she had arrived. While the plumber packed up his equipment, Edward and I didn't dare look at each other for fear of betraying our disbelief. The last to go, Davide, seemed almost reluctant to do so.

"See you soon, Kat?" he asked, the stain of Astrid's lipstick still on his mouth.

"I can't thank you enough, Davide," gushed Edward. "You have contacts in all the right places."

"Yeah, thanks," I muttered.

"Oh, no worries. I knew she could pull it off. She's an opera singer, only here for three months, but she has a great sense of theatre, a real presence about her, speaks five languages. She can really work a room, don't you think?"

"Bye now." I pushed him out and closed the door on his chuffed face. Edward and I adjourned to the balcony and watched them make their various exits from the Naviglio.

"Well, I'll have an interesting tale to tell Signora Quadrona in class when she asks about my week," I said. "Here's to life getting back to normal, Edward."

"Oh, yes, please!" he said, rolling his eyes.

STREET SCENE

"Who was that guy you were with?"

"What guy? Aren't you going to give me a proper hello? Boy, do I need to fill you in on the last twenty-four hours. You'll hardly believe it."

He folded his arms and pulled back.

"Fausto, what's wrong?"

"Go on then, fill me in. Who is he?"

"Who's who? Will you come inside? Did the shoot not go well?"

"Don't play games, Kat. I do everything bar lose my job to get back in time to help you out with the landlady and when I get here, what do I see? You strolling along in broad daylight with some other guy." His colour had risen so that his face started to clash with his hair.

"What other guy..? Oh, I see! You mean Davide. Well, wait a minute, will you, and all will be made clear."

"Brava!" He paced a few steps and I thought he was trying to compose himself, when he whipped around to face me. "Who the fuck is Davide? Eh, Kat?" With a karate chop, he struck the helmet, the one I had bought for him in a fit of concern for his well-being, from the saddle of Quasimodo and spat a string of curses after it. "Whoever he was, he went into Edward's with you anyway, that much I know. Your phone was turned off. And I know that because I called for two hours straight last night. What the hell were you doing?"

"Have you gone raving mad?"

"Two hours, Kat. Answer me!"

"Afterwards, Edward and I went to Atomic," I responded, bewildered. "You know there's no signal there."

"Oh, right. And I'm sure you both had your little heads together preparing that story. Of course, he'll back you up. You spend more time with him than you do with me. Well, fuck the little *froccio!* While we're at it, fuck you too, Kat! Fuck both of you!"

"Now I can see what a loss it must have been for Oxford when you turned down their Languages programme."

He stared at me through narrowed eyes then transferred his frustrations to Quasimodo's front tyre, kicking it till a cloud of dust rose. I pulled my eyes from him and caught the glances of passersby just before they delicately averted their eyes. I saw the smile playing on their lips and the flicker of dewy nostalgia cross their faces; in fact, I could almost hear them thinking: Ah, love's young dream. We were the stereotypical young *innamorati* screaming abuse at each other in the street; this was the inevitable rite of passage I'd thought we would avoid.

A motorbike came to a stop beside us and then we were three.

"Hey, Kat, is everything okay? Need some help?"

It was Davide astride a shiny, purring, red Ducati. The only help I needed was for someone to explain what in God's name had come over everyone.

Fausto stopped kicking. "Well, speak of the devil and he'll fucking appear!"

"Whoa, *Bello*," said Davide. "It looks like you need to calm down."

"Thanks for stopping by, Davide, but I'm fine," I said. "You'll be needed at the pizzeria. I wouldn't want to keep you."

"A *pizzaiolo*, Kat?" said Fausto, bouncing with disbelief. "A *pizzaiolo*?" I wouldn't have dreamed he was capable of such venom.

"*Allora*," said Davide, dismounting slowly like he was getting off a stallion, inexplicably looking to me as if for a signal. But I wasn't taken in by this sudden show of chivalry. We'd happily ignored each other for months, and our one recent fortuitous encounter did not make me so grateful I now wanted him a daily feature of my life. When he wasn't seducing tour buses and had a few minutes to kill before his shift started, this would do nicely as another way to flex his manhood.

"Davide, get back on your bike. This is between us two. You're intruding."

But Fausto wouldn't hear of it. "Put your helmet down, *Pizzaiolo*. Come over here and we'll discuss it."

Davide readily obliged and they began circling each other. I heard the lock rattle against the palazzo doors and looked to the sky, fearing we would now be joined by troublesome old Signora Costanza, the *portinaia*, but hoping for an intervention of a more celestial nature. I tore my eyes from the skies: it was Ginevra who stepped out.

"You ran out so fast and left the door lying open," she said. "I became worried."

"Fausto refused to come up, demanded I urgently come outside." Now I knew Italians actually *chose* the street for their showdowns; they didn't just occur there in the heat of the moment as I had previously thought.

"What's going on?" she asked, stepping gingerly across the cobblestones past the two grappling men. I updated her briefly.

She nodded, adopted a wide-legged stance, then appeared to think twice and slipped out of her heels. She rolled her shoulders back, then forward, before stretching her arms above her head and flexing the fingers of each hand. Her expression was inscrutable so when she reached over, seized a handful of Fausto's warrior hair, and yanked him staggering backwards, both he and I yelped. With her tumbling tresses and prominently displayed bosom, she called to mind a saloon madam stepping between two cowboys who were brawling over one of her 'girls'.

With a solid grip on Fausto's now entirely enflamed head, she went nose to nose with Davide on her other side, and ordered him to back off. There was a moment of silence as she, a pillar of pursed-lipped womanliness, stared down the two men who were wriggling and frothing with anger. Then she let forth a rapid fire onslaught of regional dialect, an incomprehensible torrent that spilled into the otherwise silent street while the whole neighbourhood including myself stood entranced. With both men fully restrained, she returned to an Italian I could understand.

"Davide, go." She pointed up the street.

He threw his hands up, his mouth fell open, and he jerked his head around as if to share his indignation with everyone watching.

"I have no idea what you're doing here anyway," I added.

Fausto snorted derisively.

I turned to him. "And you can go too."

"Don't worry," he muttered, marching over and snatching up his helmet from the middle of the road. "I'm long gone."

In unison they lifted their legs and slid into their saddles. The corridor-like street was filled with the combined output of Davide's 900cc engine roaring off in one direction and Fausto's 50cc spluttering defiantly the other way.

"Don't you people have dinner to prepare and families to take care of?" yelled Ginevra before picking up her shoes, identifying a patch of smoothed cobbles and skipping inside.

We had offered Edward a place to stay while the workmen were in his but he declined, shacking up instead with a French model named Pascal he'd met in the *pensione*. "Keep your saggy, loose-springed couch; I have a firm-chested Frenchman to lay my head on!" He was impossible to get hold of for the next few weeks. In the meantime I avoided daily voicemail messages from Fausto in which he begged forgiveness, claimed his behaviour had been entirely out of character, and swore that it was something only I brought out in him that would never happen again.

Ginevra, to my surprise, came out in his defence. "We are a passionate people," she said, like the leader of a tribe defending its customs. "You have to understand that," like it was some deficiency in my pale-faced character, a result of my frigid northern upbringing, that would ultimately prevent my integration and acceptance. "Jealousy is the fuel that keeps passion alive," she announced with such confidence she could have been reciting from a treaty—*Amore: The Terms and Agreements Act*. It should be rolled into a scroll, tied with a green, white, and red ribbon, and pressed into the hands of everyone entering the country who qualified for a *permesso di soggiorno*.

Passion. The word had grown to trouble me. It smoothed out as many unsightly bumps as a little black dress. Everyone looked good in it; it was forgiving. Designers depended on it for their creativity more than fabric or nicotine; *Rai* news reporters changed to a more sympathetic tone when citing it as an explanation for murder; fruit sellers in Via Benedetto Marcello forbade the handling of produce, so passionate they were about the plumpness of their *pomodori*; the sea was passionate; the mountains were passionate; passion seemed to swirl like pollen in the air leaving the entire nation powerless.

But when I thought of Fausto, I didn't think of passion, at least not anymore. With his popping eyes and red face, his entire being dancing and wobbling with fury, I thought of Elmo: a funny-looking Muppet with a falsetto voice. When Ginevra insisted I give him another chance, I fired back with something she said often: "*Meglio essere solo che mal'accompagnato.*"

Better to be alone than badly accompanied.

BOYFRIEND BLAZER

We had entered my favourite phase of designing a collection: the research phase, during which I buried my nose in books and among the dusty rails of vintage stores and collectors' fairs to sniff out that first line of the romantic narrative that would set me aflight. A decaying crocheted scarf from the 1920's, exhumed from the depths of a neglected bin and fragile as old newspaper, sent me into paroxysms. When I suggested to Rosalba we chop it up, patchwork it back together with some leopard print, and have it reproduced as a fabric, I foolishly expected a similar level of excitement. Instead, she gave an imperious nod and wrapped herself tighter in her nicotine shawl—a garment which fit her body so well, it was almost part of her flesh, preserving her, kippering her. Yet, deep beneath her seasoned shell, I suspected a kindred spirit lived: a Miss Havisham that had escaped the mansion, tore her wedding dress above the knee, and ran off on tour with a garage band.

Now that Edward was frolicking through the menswear racks of Via della Spiga with his new *amant* on weekends, I began meeting up with other young designers for afternoon tea at the Four Seasons hotel, a treat we granted ourselves because the pots were large, and we could share their multi-tiered sandwich and pastry tray. Hearing of their experiences in the other houses, I counted my blessings. One girl, grown worryingly thin, had erupted in severe stress-related adult acne. Another less frequent member of our circle worked weekends, late nights, and public holidays, for a creative director who demanded she design ten collections for every one needed, so that she could dispose of the rest in a perverse shredding ceremony with the epitaph: "Below standard; must never see the light of day." Another formerly chatty, carefree soul had become a gibbering wreck from being hit regularly by hurled bolts of fabric and from being summoned by a referee's whistle she now heard in her sleep.

At Intermezzo I seemed to have sprouted through pure luck in a fertile little nook that allowed me a cautionary view of the egos and power games but left me safe to bloom, untouched. I remembered an article I once read about organisms that existed in polluted environments using the chemical activity to light up their tails for attracting a mate or finding food or to help them maintain a mutation rate sufficient for evolution. I felt I was in a period of similar development. Every morning I stepped under a Marlboro mushroom cloud, called "Buongiorno!" to the occupant of each office who invariably held a pencil in one hand and in the other, a cigarette slim and proud: a row of little chimneys pumping out the leftovers of what was needed to fuel our factory of ideas.

I shared my office with a fussy French man named Serge who trawled the internet and chirruped on the phone most of the day. When he did put pen to paper, he assaulted his drawings with cries of *"C'est dégoutant! Répugnant!"* and balled his sketches between long fingers, throwing them in the rubbish bin already so full it spat them back onto the carpet. It was like tennis practice: he launched balls, and they were lobbed back. Serge worked on menswear, but he was just as dismissive of our work, scowling as I pinned images, buttons, swatches to my inspiration wall, and muttering "*Bricolage. Je déteste le bricolage.*" The only thing that cheered him was gossip; he worked his phone constantly *à la recherche de scandale*: fellow designers' drunken outbursts, embarrassing hookups, tragic break ups, and career catastrophes; he was a tabloid hack in designer's clothing.

My Italian was improving, although it still provided moments of unintended hilarity. At a recent Production fitting, a debate arose around a desired sleeve length. A senior male patternmaker was adamant it should be elbow-length, but as it was my design, I configured my verb, cleared my throat, and forced my voice to resonate over the babble.

"It should have a capped sleeve. That's what I had in mind when I came up with it."

The room fell about laughing.

What I had actually said was: "He should have a blow job. That's what I had in mind when I came up with it." The difference between '*pompierino*' and '*pompino*' was big yet infuriatingly small.

If I had one lament about my job, it was that I was forever skint. My meager monthly paycheck granted me at most four days of operating outside of overdraft, and my bank manager had taken to requesting bi-weekly meetings.

"I am due a raise any day now," I said on my most recent visit.

"Ah yes? When exactly will it take effect?" His pen was poised.

"Probably soon."

He put down the pen.

"Look, Signorina Connelly, you cannot keep going into overdraft like this. It is not our policy."

But having deferred my student loan, scooped out three-months rent for the landlord, and paid my taxes, I had no room for his policy. The Italian tax system was an imbroglio of clauses and loopholes benefitting the employer and the government. Like all the other foreigners within the company, I had been given the details of an Intermezzo accountant whom I visited every few months but who did little to unravel the mystery surrounding the amount of taxes I paid.

The accountant's name was Signor Maltempo, which, appropriately enough, translated as "Mr Badweather", because he certainly made off with any rainy day savings I may have had. Grey-haired with whiskers, he sat behind a wooden desk in the centre of a green room. All around him, cardboard files were stacked precariously on the floor like shanty town buildings on the outskirts of the landlord's estate. There were computers in the other offices but none in his. I carried piles of paperwork to his office when summoned and left mentally and financially depleted but with an armful of new paperwork.

Rumours circulated that Intermezzo was mafia-run. When I finally broached the subject of a raise, I was offered a 'loan'. Apparently this was common practice, and the man to speak to was Martinelli, the six-foot-three, bear-like individual with the porn star moustache and three-piece suit who screamed the models' names at the catwalk show. Amid all the backstage commotion, I had failed to notice he also sported an artificial leg; no one knew exactly what misfortune had befallen him, but the mystery just added to the trepidation in the belly of anyone having to cross the street, enter the other building, and make their way to his office.

'Loan' requests were met with few words; he would open a drawer behind him, pull out a roll of banknotes, and drop it on the table, scribbling a note on a pad. On my visit I was so anxious to get out of there, I scraped up the money and lunged for the door without ever enquiring when it needed to be repaid. I figured there would be plenty of time to settle the tab.

On the afternoon of the unfortunate incident, I was tucked away upstairs studying the lace patterns of Victorian bloomers. What occurred three floors down was described to me by Enzo, our receptionist. With detail provided by Serge.

It was just after lunch, around two. Rosalba was returning from a hair appointment in time for a meeting with Martinelli. As soon as she stepped out of the town car she would have seen the young redheaded gentleman pacing the foyer through the window. He was just so *noticeable*. Even Enzo, a simple suburban heterosexual, couldn't fail to admire how the hue of the boy's hair coordinated with the décor, matching exactly the foyer furnishings which Rosalba had cleverly juxtaposed against the cloudscape walls. It was as if she had added him herself, her piece de resistance, a titian-tressed cherub.

Martinelli had just exited the building across the street; he was dropping his inanimate leg off the kerb with the usual practiced movement when Enzo rose to go open the door for Rosalba. Serge was the only other person on the scene, sitting in the foyer throne, leg thrown over a gilt arm, phone pressed to ear.

Before he left his post, Enzo had reassured the visitor, "I will call Kat and let her know you are waiting. Please take a seat."

"I don't want you to call her," said Fausto, and Enzo detected the growing impatience in his tone. "I want you to take me to her office."

Enzo explained that would not be possible. Fausto stared at him with such an air of suspicion that Enzo admitted he began to *feel* guilty, although he had no idea why.

"I've been calling her all week. Where's it got me?" Fausto slammed his palms on the reception desk. "Don't waste any more of my time, I'm warning you."

As they eyeballed each other, Enzo silently cursed Fausto's timing; from the tail of his eye he saw Rosalba reach the door.

"I'll have to call you back. Shit's about to go down," whispered Serge and flipped his phone closed.

With gentlemanly courtesies thus interrupted, Rosalba sighed and opened the door for herself.

"What's going on, Enzo?" she asked.

"Rosalba Valle," uttered Fausto, momentarily starstruck. Like everyone in Italy, no matter how far removed from the fashion world, he knew all the major players; it was like coming face to face with a TV star or a footballer.

"Buongiorno," she replied, smiling graciously. "*Lei com'e sta?*" She went to pass, but he laid his hand on her arm. She froze and looked down at it.

"Signora Valle, I'm here to see Kat," said, Fausto, recovering his sense of purpose. "She's one of your designers. Can you tell me where I can find her?" He threw a scornful look Enzo's way.

Serge had left the throne and was leaning against the wall intently watching Rosalba eye the hand. As Fausto's agitation increased, his grip tightened. Wrinkles had begun to form down the sleeve of Rosalba's jacket.

("The dusty pink twill Marni one," specified Serge.)

Enzo threatened to call the authorities. Fausto dared him to do just that. Was it against the law to call by your girl-friend's workplace for a few words? He didn't think so. Neither man noticed that Rosalba had started to jerk her arm.

"Release me now," she hissed through clenched teeth.

The men, intent on proving which of them was cock of this walk, seemed oblivious to Rosalba's distress until, with a burst of unexpected force, she heaved her arm upwards and smacked Fausto squarely in the chin, knocking him sideways. He moaned and brought his hand to his mouth to grab his tongue which he had chomped down on. With his other hand he reached for the desk to steady himself but accidentally brushed the vase of tulips, the only ornament Rosalba allowed on the reception desk. The next thing Enzo knew, the con-tents were overturned into the handbag Rosalba toted in the crook of her arm.

("The hand-woven, straw-coloured shiny calf Cabat by Bottega Veneta," said Serge.)

The water that didn't collect in her bag pooled at her feet.

("Satin square-toed Manolo Blahnik mules.")

By then Martinelli had made his ungainly way across the road and down the drive. As he entered, everyone stood in shocked silence, but one look at an open-mouthed Rosalba standing on a bed of tulips was enough to tell him all was not as it should be. True to his motto of act first, ask questions later, he grabbed the stranger by the collar and propelled him through the door. At a discreet distance, he hoisted Fausto about an inch off the ground and began to whack him relent-lessly with his free hand.

("Fausto's head was swinging back and forward like one of those little air-filled punching balls boxers use," noted Serge.)

From the doorway, Serge and Enzo watched as Martinelli delivered his closing argument. He chucked Fausto to the ground like a heap of firewood and, with his prosthetic leg, ground down on the hand that had previously attached itself to Rosalba's person so ferociously. The grating of skin against gravel made both of them wince and look away.

When Martinelli returned inside, Rosalba had hurried off to try and save her outfit. He rolled his eyes and growled to Enzo, "Women! They can never seem to keep their bedroom affairs from catching up with them in the office." He'd obviously mistaken Fausto for one of Rosalba's scorned lovers. Serge, positively ablaze with *scandale*, put that rumour immediately into circulation, just in case there proved to be something in it.

Enzo reckoned it took Fausto about fifteen minutes to get to his feet and walk away, sporting a gait much like his aggressor's. His flopping hand, he cradled in a sling fashioned out of his blood-spattered sweater.

ALL'S FAIR IN LOVE
AND LUXURY FABRICS

B y mid-afternoon, the incident had swollen into legend; Ginevra got wind of it from a buyer in the Versace showroom. However, the tale she relayed back to me was unrecognizable: it depicted Rosalba as a sort of Lucrezia Borgia enthroned at the heart of a love triangle between a young ill-tempered Vulcan figure and a dapper Long John Silver—that would leave Serge as Captain Flint, the parrot, nibbling on seeds. Surprisingly, it was Martinelli who emerged from the melodrama most sympathetically, considered ingeniously cast as the poor unrequited lover driven mad with jealousy, forced to wreak vengeance with his prosthesis.

"Never mind, it'll blow over," said Winston, patting my shoulder. "It's my boy Fausto with the long-term damage to his princely stride. Rosalba'll take herself off to Manolo for a new pair of how-do-you-dos, and all will be forgotten. My best china plate's in pieces." Winston's 'china plate' being his mate.

"Rosalba will be cool," agreed Grace. "She's all for sexual intrigue and foolhardy acts of passion. Don't forget, she went to Studio 54 in the seventies. She'll get a kick out of the idea that she can still set people's tongues wagging."

I had to go and make sure.

Through the open door I could see Rosalba sitting poker-straight at her desk, hurtling through a magazine, pinching the corner of each page and slapping the back of any that dithered. At my knock she looked up, and the page crackled to attention. She smacked the magazine closed and coiled back into her chair, tilting her head for me to come in. I wasn't asked to sit down. Her bag had been emptied and turned upside down on the window ledge, the newborn leather bearing a large port-wine birthmark.

"I wanted to apologize for what happened, Rosalba. I'm mortified. I had no idea he would show up like that. We're not even together any more. I would never have allowed him to come here. I'm—I'm terribly sorry."

For an uncomfortably long time, Rosalba's gaze focused on a point somewhere near my hairline.

"And I feel terrible that, no matter how unknowingly, I put you in such a spot."

Ash had turned her cigarette into a drooping ghostly finger. She turned to watch the tip break off and hit the floor. Then she twisted the stub into an ashtray, rose, and walked around her desk. Her breath rattled when she inhaled as if with something suppressed. She was standing by the door before she spoke.

"You never ever bring that sort of thing to work. It has no place in my studio. Is that clear?" She seemed to be ushering me out. "Is it?"

"Absolutely," I said, backing over the threshold. "I mean, technically, I didn't bring it to the office this time, but I can assure you it won't happen again."

"Good. It won't. On that we're clear." She shut the door in my face.

"Off to the fair you go," said Grace. "It'll take your mind off things. You're automatically registered. If you have any problems, just call me, but I'm sure you'll be fine." She waved the brochure of exhibitors at me. "It seems everyone's there this time, so you should definitely dig up something unexpected."

The fair in question was, to use Grace's words, "a select group of international speciality print, textile, and embellishment merchants in town for three days to sell their wares." I conjured up a mental picture of men on camels arrived from the east unfurling bolts of perfumed silks, bejewelled scarves, hand-loomed damasks and brocades, in a bustling mercantile perhaps next to an oasis. But the car dropped me off at the Fiera: a vast multi-pavilioned stadium of steel, glass, and concrete, with suspended walkways and galvanized steel pergolas custom-built to house Italy's top industry shows. The line of brightly attired people winding around its front was like an unruly flower bed.

I hurried past the queues and flashed my pass to enter the cavernous foyer. In case I got lost, I identified the banner indicating the entrance to "Fancy Fabrics " as a sort of North Star and studied my map. There were four huge pavilions just like this one, packed tightly with rows of cubicles like a honeycomb around which I could already recognize queen bees from the world's top design houses, their buzzing only dissipated by the high ceiling. Taking a deep breath, I set off but my name echoing from somewhere nearby stopped me in my tracks. I turned just in time to avoid being knocked sideways by a fast-moving fur ball. The delighted face of my new friend Chintzy peeped over an outrageous mink chubby.

Chintzy Toile, not her real name, of course, but a variation of her Polish birth name, Lechsinska Tola Trzebiatowski, which, she learned years earlier as a student in London, carried too many consonants for your average English person's liking. Residing at the time in a bedsit above a Shepherd's Bush showroom specializing in French reproduction furniture and soft furnishings, she adopted this more pronounceable handle which also expressed her avid interest in Marie-Antoinette and all things Versailles; the *Toile de Jouy* 'chintz' with its pastoral scenes of couples strolling under parasols, nowadays mostly used to cover couches or for curtains, was a favourite of the young queen's. Chintzy made it a feature of her graduate collection and subsequently her wardrobe, until it became her signature. Today's incarnation: a jauntily tied neck scarf. How appropriate I should find Chintzy Toile in the 'Fancy Fabrics', I thought.

"Good to see you," I said, attempting a hug, searching for the form beneath the fur. "Aren't you a little overdressed for this time of the morning?"

"Oh? I cannot evoke Rita Hayworth *and* drink espresso?" asked Chintzy without irony. She pouted her vibrant red lips, and her skin looked sallow under the lights. "Actually, I have been burning the candle at the two ends and I am thinking this disguises it a little."

Chintzy was a freelance designer about town, older than me, but by how much she wouldn't disclose. She had cultivated an impressive air of mystery around herself, and her walk-in wardrobe probably possessed more skeletons than the *Cimitero Monumentale*—like the husband she had acquired in Britain in order to get her papers and then promptly abandoned. She had accompanied a mutual friend to one of our

Four Seasons teas, and I immediately liked her spontaneity and persuasive way with heavy jewellery. But she never came to another. "It's like a brood of old ladies whining about their aches and pains and blowing on their Earl Grey." We went shopping or dancing together instead.

"Anyway, I can hide in this," she said, nestling down into the fur so that only her eyes were visible like a creature in a hedgerow. "You're sure to run into someone you can't bear or who can't bear you or who you've fired or who has fired you. It's best to move by in a bit of a blur."

"Let's go around together," I suggested. "Can you manage in those shoes?"

"It's not worth bothering with anything less than six inches." She went ahead leaving me to ponder the statement's ambiguity.

Chintzy had once boasted of owning two hundred and eleven pairs of designer shoes and was probably the most materialistic person I'd ever met. I put it down to living behind the Iron Curtain until the age of fifteen and having to queue for hours for Coca Cola and bananas.

We spent the morning combing the aisles of the first pavilion and found a few inspiring items, but after lunch we made a beeline for Aisle H to hone in on the world's most beautiful laces and embroideries.

"H4...just up here on the right," I said, checking the map before coming to an abrupt halt. It couldn't be. I listened again. It had to be. There wasn't its equal anywhere. *That* voice: arch, offended... slurring.

"What do you mean I can't come in?"

Every hair on my body shot straight up in outrage on its own little goose pimple platform. Chintzy had rushed ahead to the booth, only looking around when she got no response from me to something she'd said.

"I'm sorry, Signora but we cannot let you in to see the collection at this time," said the representative to the woman ahead of Chintzy.

"Why ever not *at this time?* This is a fair, isn't it? Where you show your collection to clients?"

Her head quivered with umbrage. I was almost upon her as I checked off the ratty highlighted hair, the mistreated coat with this season's shoes, all accessorized with her unique air of vagrancy. But this time she had set her sights a good deal higher than Jean's stall in Portobello Market. What strings could she have pulled to get in? The criteria for entrance required you be a member of the luxury goods sector whose company had established relationships with exhibiting vendors. Last time I checked, the Lynda Wynter Design Studio was not uttered in the same breath as Louis Vuitton Moët Hennessy.

"Mind the floorshow," whispered Chintzy as I tucked myself in behind her.

The representative had taken Lynda's business card and gone inside. She has the protocol of a cockroach, I thought. Her coat displayed more embarrassment than she did; it looked downright ashamed of its circumstances. The man returned shaking his head, saying "I'm sorry" more firmly. A red crescent formed on each of Lynda's cheeks. It looked like a six-pill situation, all different colours. With a herbal tea.

"You have no right to treat me this shabbily. I will be in contact with your father."

"Signora, it was my father who gave the orders not to allow you to view the collection. It has come to his attention you were taking our ideas and having them copied in China. Exclusivity is something we pride ourselves in. It is important to our family and business. We ask that you respect our right

to maintain the reputation we have built over three generations. Now kindly step aside."

Chintzy showed her business card.

"Welcome, ladies. Good to see you again, Signorina Toile."

I held my business card in front of my face, pulled my hat
low, and buried my nose in my armpit. I was nearly in when I
heard an intake of breath.

"Kat, is that...?"

I saw her Adam's apple rise and fall, and the predictable
mechanics of her brain kicking in. She gulped down her pride
and, with eyes trained on me, her expression a hybrid of a plea
and a dare, she said, "You've made a mistake. I'm actually with
these ladies. Now if you don't mind..."

"Oh, how embarrassing," said Chintzy, burrowing deeper.

The rep regarded us all with suspicion. For the merest
second, it seemed like Lynda would trample over me in
her determination to get inside. It struck me as divinely
twisted running into her after all this time at another 'marketplace': at this booth, home of my favourite fabrics, after
having first met her at Jean's stall, home of my favourite
vintage.

I stretched my arm across and blocked her way. "She's not
with us."

Lynda flinched like she'd just been slapped. She seemed to
go cross-eyed with indignation. Her jaw flexed as her tongue
busied itself to produce saliva.

The rep lost his patience. "Signora, I will call security and
have you physically escorted out..."

"Who was *that?*" asked Chintzy, emerging hesitantly
from her fur as the rep's brothers greeted us bearing
espressos and wine from their family vineyard, and their
colleagues displayed swatches of Chantilly, Valenciennes,
and filet crochet that shimmered with silver and gold but

were so light they looked like they might disintegrate at their touch.

"That, Chintzy, was the Ghost of Fashion Past."

I made arrangements to see Chintzy at the weekend and got out of the taxi at Piazza San Babila. I wanted to walk the tram route home. Feeling reflective and in need of the half hour alone, I considered the fading lukewarm sun the ideal companion. Lynda and Fausto's surprise appearances had unnerved me, coming so soon after each other—it was a two-for-one wake-up call reminding me how far I'd come but also how fragile everything was. If I'd emerged unscathed from the Fausto debacle, it was only because Rosalba, who'd seen it all and was difficult to shock, was in possession of an impenetrable glamour and confidence. Although she didn't tend towards nurturance of her designers, nor was she a bestower of shallow reassurances or praise, she was a far cry from Lynda: there was no yelling or manipulating. No throttling of staff at Intermezzo. Rosalba cast the same indifferent, smoke-glazed eye over everyone, remaining consistently cryptic and reliably abrasive. Admittedly, some of her personal comments could leave a piquant aftertaste, but only on the most sensitive. It's true she was partial to the male designers over the female— Winston's behaviour went unchecked, Serge's productivity remained low, only females were ever spotted running in the corridors—but that had to do with her hiring men who reminded her of her dear Franco. Every day we pulled the red velvet curtains closed on the world outside because inside there were always blue skies. Rosalba was the gatekeeper of a dreamland that she let us run around in, a playhouse for overgrown children, but she was also the enigmatic helmswoman of an elite creative think-tank of which I felt I had become an integral part. That was good enough for me.

Some days at Intermezzo I even experienced an actual flutter of belonging. The sensation was reminiscent of the freedom I used to enjoy on the tractor with Da, sealed off from the rest of humanity, although, ironically, the situation had more in common with mum sitting at her Singer. Pins glinted from my clothes, lint clung to my skirt, swatches fell out of my pockets—I was turning into her! Eyes crossed from tracing layouts on the lightbox, fingers ink-stained, knuckles pencil-bruised, wrists scissors-stiff—these stamps of my profession I sported proudly even after work and all through cocktails and dinner, often waking up with them the next morning.

I walked on skirting Piazza Duomo and its crowds, finding satisfaction in the familiarity of the old, broken-up side streets. I knew most of their names by now, and when the cobbles weren't attacking the delicate heels of my shoes, they made for agreeable walks. I passed through the heart of the business sector where the *palazzi* containing central banks and government operations seemed vacant, through to the smaller squares teeming with trams and shoppers and emerged in one of the wide, tree-lined *viali* where the rich people lived. I crossed to the other side, cut down a narrow street and entered a neighbourhood that always cheered me. These streets had a honed demographic: old ladies who always seemed to have a smile for me. They lived in two-storey houses with exuberantly-painted facades that quivered in the heat and made me think of individual flavours simmering on a stove: a smidgen of *aromatica*, a dash of *piccante*; a glaze of mustard, a coating of honey, paprika, olive, sun-dried tomato...

"Oh!" I cried.

Sun-dried turd. It must have been lying in wait a while because its outer crust had faded to about the same colour as

Edward's walls post-fire. I held onto to a lamppost and scraped my sole on the kerb. Milan was a mecca for dog-worshippers, every day a festival of pooch devotion. But no one had been put on cleanup, and the party raged on. Dogs as large as milking cows dropped turds like empty beer cans. They were kicked about the streets until they finally just disintegrated or until the rain came. Meringues of dung lying in wait on the farm, quivering with mischief and bluebottles as big as raisins, never bothered me to the same extent. I wore wellies on the farm. Le Milanesi springing by as light-footed as their four-legged, Gucci-leashed BFF's, in white jeans and strappy, bejewelled sandals, had me baffled. How did they magically avoid treading in it? This cologne that rose from the poshest streets, this spice distilled in the air, this *eau de toilette* seemed to bypass their highly-held nostrils to settle only under mine.

I noticed two scuffed Converse boots had pulled up alongside my one stationary espadrille as if waiting to be introduced. My eyes travelled up two skinny poles for legs, clocked the guitar case, skimmed over the lean torso and sharply angled face to lock again with familiar eyes. I had to quickly replot the coordinates of his face. Like when you see someone from TV in real life, and they look different, he looked different in the street than he did behind the bar.

Atomic Boy.

His eyes crinkled at the corners. "Ciao."

Big teeth.

"Ciao," I responded.

"*Finalmente!*"

"Si." I continued to shuffle my feet, worried about the smell.

He looked down through the corridor of our bodies. "*Nervosa?*"

"*Non. Merda.*" I showed him the sole of my shoe. I nodded towards the guitar case. "*Suoni?*"

"Si. *Basso.*"

I touched his arm, and we both stepped back to let a slim woman pass with three cantering red setters. He asked if I lived around here, and I explained that I liked to walk this way when I needed to think. It wasn't clear if his face wore amusement as its default expression or if he found me amusing. After about four heart-pounding minutes, I gave him my phone number. He hadn't asked for it—Ginevra would throw her hands up in despair—but the corners of his eyes sprouted a few more creases when I did.

With a nod, he tucked his phone back into the pocket of his army shirt.

"*Come ti chiami?*" he asked.

"Kat."

"Kat," he said and we shook hands. "*Piacere,* Kat. Massimiliano."

His palm was warm and smooth. He released my hand slowly, I thought, unwillingly. Then he seemed to catch himself, emitting a slight snort like a horse. He glanced sideways before turning back with his hand outstretched again, this time dispensing a business card. I took it and felt implicated in something. He reaffirmed his grip on the guitar case and moved off, still amused.

"Ciao… Kat," he called over his shoulder and loped down the street swinging his guitar; a fire-eyed, swashbuckling troubadour. I looked his card over. It was silver but covered in little cracks and dents, rivet marks from riding in the back pocket of his tight jeans. The word '*atomic*' in blue print with a little red rocket zooming around it was on one side, on the other his name containing a lot of vowels, his telephone number containing a lot of sixes.

Massimiliano. Under the sun the letters danced against the silver, playfully changing places. *Massimo Milano.* The maximum Milan had to offer. They jumped and swapped again and by the time I'd walked to the next corner he'd gone from Atomic Boy to MaxiMan.

TAILOR'S DUMMY

"*Incroyable!*"

Serge had been swiveling decadently on his chair, kicking the floor with his right foot, his left tucked underneath him, when he came to an abrupt halt and planted his elbows on the table. He had been working the office phone since he sat down, peddling the daily cycle of buzz, hearsay, testimonies, tittle-tattle, and prize-worthy fiction.

"*Mais non!*"

I glanced up. His mouth formed a perfect O to match his eyes.

"*Je ne peux pas le croire!*" He sang the words like a series of breathy notes on an ascending scale. "*Oui, oui. A plus tard.*" Disconnecting himself from the cord, he replaced the receiver gently and chewed on a pencil. For some reason, I looked up again. Maybe because he usually slammed the phone down, the act had a gravitas. Also he spoke in French to maintain secrecy when he was on the trail of something juicy. I heard the scrunch of paper, the noise of it hitting the bin, the plop of it back onto the carpet.

"*Ooh mamma!*" He jumped up, sliding his phone into his pocket. When I caught him looking sideways at me, he swung around, studied the pictures on the wall as if seeing them for the first time, wheeled towards the window to check the weather, frowned at his watch, picked up his jacket, put it down again, and called "*J'arrive!*" to no one in particular before finally fluttering out, his vintage Nike Air Rifts making no sound. All the better to sneak up on people, I thought, and went back to work.

Finally I got the call I'd been waiting for to go see Martinelli. With the renewal of my contract, I was confident they would give me my long overdue raise. For once, crossing the street, entering the other building, and pressing the button for the third floor, I wasn't apprehensive at all.

"Buongiorno, Signora," I sang to the stooped charlady scrubbing the steps. She raised her head, but I had already disappeared into the lift so she dunked her brush in the mop bucket and carried on.

"*Che bella giornata oggi!*" I called down, my voice drifting out through the wrought iron gates and echoing on the stairs as I soared upwards. The cleaning lady muttered irritably to Our Lady of Sorrows.

And a fine day it was, a day to grab hold of and hang upside down by the ankles till all the good stuff fell in a pile at your feet. Martinelli was just a big teddy bear with a gammy leg. Don't go attempting to hang *him* upside down by the ankles though, I joked to myself, and emerged into the cool dark corridor. Slants of sunlight curled like fingertips around the half-closed shutters as I went over possible negotiation tactics in my head. I announced myself to the po-faced secretary, and she nodded towards a chair. I would ask for a salary *adjustment,* and he would locate a dust-covered bundle fastened with a rubber band that had lost its elasticity, still marked with my name, although the letters were barely discernible from the passing of so much time.

I took a deep breath as I stepped into his office but most of the intake was his cigar smoke, and I stifled a cough. He greeted me with a rumble that began in his belly, gained power and, when it hit air, turned into the words:

"Buongiorno, Kat. How are you this fine day?"

I sat down with my brightest smile. Teddy bear.

Exactly eleven minutes later, as bore witness by the clock on the secretary's wall, I left his office and walked unsteadily to the lift. Inside, I let my head flop against the cool plywood and stared through the bars as the floor of the third storey became the ceiling of the second, felt the blast of air from the tiled corridor, then another floor became a ceiling, until it trundled to a stop, and I pushed the gate across. The charlady straightened when she saw me, exhaling with the effort, and rubbing her back. She said it was indeed a beautiful day and eked out half a smile for me. But this time I passed her in silence. The sound of water slapping onto the floor as she flung her scrub brush into the bucket indicated she was sorry she had bothered. I heard her summon again Our Lady of Sorrows as I stood on the other side of the wall reviewing what had just happened.

They were not renewing my contract. Changes were being made internally. My position was no longer available.

"We really appreciate everything you have done for the company," Martinelli said. "You will receive an extra two month's salary in your paycheck this month as a token of our gratitude. That will tide you over till you find something else."

I asked him if it had anything to do with what had happened and explained that I'd already squared things up with Rosalba.

"I'm acting on orders directly from Rosalba," Martinelli replied. "She feels you are no longer the right fit for the company."

I took refuge in the rather facetiously named *Happy Bar* around the corner because I knew no one from work went there. Sipping lukewarm tea, I pulled at the threads of the torn seat and studied the fabric; early computer-age graphics of red and black triangles tumbling across a grey and white grid—it was like a teenager's duvet cover from nineteen eighty-three. I looked around at the signora in the corner with the blue rinse sharing a croissant with her beribboned Shih Tzu, then at the three stool pigeons by the counter drinking grappa, back at the septuagenarian owner with the circus-worthy handlebar moustache. He had chosen these covers in a bid to attract a younger, hipper clientele, I surmised; they were the result of a decision to "brighten the place up". Either that or to hide stains.

I ordered a grappa and when one of the old timers raised his glass and winked, I ignored him, then felt worse. My phone rang, and when I saw Edward's name, tears came to my eyes. I tried to speak, swallowed repeatedly, but couldn't make my mouth work.

"What's wrong?" he asked.

Three fat tears dropped one after the other on the table. I held the phone away; my throat made noises like cracking twigs.

"Kat, what's wrong?"

"Everything."

He asked me where I was and said he'd be right there. In the time it took for him to arrive, the barman had left the bottle of grappa on the table, and I had agreed to go dancing with the old-timer I'd previously blanked. Even without looking I recognized the sound of Edward's heels clicking across the floor. He'd had his head shaved; his cow's lick was gone and his ears stuck out. When he held out his arms, I catapulted off the seat.

"It feels like ages since I've seen you," I said, breathing in his smell: Hermès. "What's with the new edgy look? You're all loved up, aren't you?"

"I am. What do you think? Pascal loves it." He ran his hand uncertainly over the crown. "Anyway, never mind all that. Let me just loosen my stays and I'm all yours." He took off his coat and lit up.

"You're smoking Gauloises? You always said they were poncey fags for poncey fags."

"Yeah, well, Pascal got me onto them. Anyway, as of tomorrow smoking is banned in this once fair land, don't forget. It's like the last days of the Roman Empire all over again. Vive la France! You can still smoke there. And 'cigarette' *is* a French word, so Gauloises it is. Till the bitter end. Bastards, all of them! Now what's got you so upset?"

The barman brought another glass while I untangled the events of the week, and he sat not saying a word. When I went quiet, he sighed.

"Bloody hell, Kat. I just turned my back for five minutes."

"Oh, don't be ridiculous. This wasn't my fault."

"I am now beginning to think *ragazzi* might be the ruination of you." He pointed an unlit cigarette at me in mock reproval, which was similar to how Signora Quadrona waved her chalk at me in class. "Sex, although available from all good outlets nationwide, is not a toy. I steer clear of the natives now, myself."

I could certainly see his logic after recent events. "What about you? Are you back in the flat yet?"

"I told Signora Palmira to shove it, the old bat. She didn't seem too bothered to see the back of me. Pascal and I got a short term lease near Garibaldi. Just signed yesterday." He beamed. "Our first home."

"And everything worked out okay at work? You were worrying for nothing?"

"I guess you were right. Crazier things happen at sea. I'm not such an original after all." He lifted my face up by the chin somewhat tenderly but then brought the other hand up, mashed my cheeks together and laughed. "You look like a pet goldfish I once forgot to feed. Is that a new hat?"

"When I'm down in the dumps, I always get a new hat."

He looked at me mischievously. "I always wondered where you got them."

I arranged one side of my mouth into a brief smile.

"But, listen, Kat, seriously, you know what you need to do. I'm going to France with Pascal—just for a week. A little holiday. While I'm gone, get stuck into your portfolio—all those lovely designs, catwalk shots. With this new experience under your belt you'll be able to work anywhere you want."

"And fuck Rosalba?" I muttered.

"Fuck the old crone, she'll be begging you to come back. But one thing: give the men a rest. They are at the centre of your most momentous downfalls. You don't seem to have built up a tolerance. I mean, don't get me wrong, you've surpassed all my expectations. They really seem to go for your jumble-sale, inside-out, lily-white, freckly brand of charm. But lay off a bit. You've proved your point, okay?" He gave me a look. "At least till I get back?"

"Okay, but will I get to meet this man of yours?"

"You will indeed. He's dying to meet you too. All this emotion! And now my lighter won't work!"

"*Prego,*" said the signora with the Shih Tzu, leaning in with a Harley Davison zippo.

"Signora, are you ready for tomorrow?" he asked. "Have you heard how much they'll fine us if we're caught? What do you make of it all?"

"Bunch of Nazis!" she erupted, setting her dog to bark shrilly. She and Edward fell into a discussion of the myriad ways they intended to overthrow the new regime. Edward's Italian seemed to have improved considerably since taking up with a Frenchman. Maybe it was the desperation to connect with his fellow condemned that brought it out in him.

"…I really don't think they'll enforce it," he was saying, not a verb out of place albeit with an atrocious English accent. "How could they? That would mean changing the national policy of bone idleness. Let us praise the Lord for it!"

The signora looked momentarily put out by this brusque assessment of her nation's work ethic, but then she shrugged and raised her grappa; he was her brother in arms on the eve of deployment.

"I'm giving up giving up," declared Edward. "It's a relief to say it."

"So are you kids waiting for bingo to start in the community centre next door?" asked the signora.

"Not us," said Edward, motioning to me. "Actually she's just been dropped like this season's Prada hems. I'm here to get her drunk." He held up the empty grappa bottle.

"Ooh, I see," she said, her eyes twinkling from inside their blue-veined settings.

A man strode in, went directly to the bar. He was not tall or particularly striking but for his mop of dark curls. I waited for him to turn around with a vague sensation that I knew him. It wasn't anyone from work. He ducked under the counter straight to the coffee machine where he knocked back an espresso then chatted with the owner who was counting cash at the register. I still couldn't see his face.

"Hello?" I called, then again loudly and waved.

"Another bottle?" asked the owner.

I shook my head and pointed to his friend just as he turned around. He looked momentarily confused and then broke into a smile of recognition. He ducked back under the counter and came over.

"I thought it was you but wasn't sure," I said. "If I recall, I still owe you a drink."

I saw Edward glance up and shake his head. "After all we've just been saying," he muttered loud enough for me to hear.

"Edward, this is Dario—remember, from Duomo? Dario, my friend, Edward." They shook hands, then Dario greeted the signora whom he referred to as Duchessa. "Ciao, Milka," he said, affectionately rubbing the Shih Tzu's ears.

"I'd often wondered what happened to the Irish girl with the nice drawings. I asked my cousin if she had bumped into you since but she hadn't. But, I see, you're still here."

"By the skin of my teeth."

"Your Italian has improved anyway."

I'd seen Dario a couple of times in the past six months but always at a distance. I'd been whizzing by on a bus, or he'd been passing on a motorino. I'd yelled hello in the street once, but he hadn't heard.

"I'm really glad I finally get to settle the score and buy you that drink," I said.

"Not tonight, you don't. In this bar we drink for free already." He raised his hand and beckoned to the owner. "Papa, I want to introduce you to some friends. And bring more grappa! I've been telling him for years he needs to modernize this place and finally he's agreed." Dario and his father co-owned Happy Bar. Dario was convinced he could make it one of the top aperitivo spots in the city. "It's going to be cool," he concluded in chewy English, and threw his arm around his father's shoulder.

"Know what'd be cool?" Edward piped up. "If you install the right ventilation for smokers. Now that would be cool. Are you thinking of doing that? Do you know how people would flock here? That would be cool."

While Edward grilled Dario on the extent of his commitment to cool, a tall boy with unruly blond hair, wearing a ripped vest and bleach-spotted jeans approached them, scowling. His hands were rammed into the pockets of jeans so tight, they looked like they were trapped there. Happy Bar was suddenly happening, I thought.

"Pascal, you made it!" said Edward jumping up and kissing him. He made us all squash together so that Pascal could perch by him. When Pascal extracted his hands from his pockets to introduce himself, his fingers looked bloodless.

We managed to persuade La Duchessa to skip bingo and, together with the three gentlemen at the bar, we formed teams to play gin rummy, which I'd never played before. Edward blazed a determined trail through his Gauloises until he looked at the filled ashtray, and turned to me aghast. "Would you cut me off, Kat? For fuck's sake, cut me off!"

I put the packet in my bag. Fifteen minutes later he demanded I return it and stop being such a Nazi.

"What do you think?" he asked when Pascal had slipped off to the bathroom.

"Not what I was expecting. A departure for you. But as departures go, a bloody cute one."

"I couldn't have put it better myself."

But the biggest 'departure' of the evening was yet to come. Ginevra arrived and squeezed onto our eighties duvet where we were all now talking over each other, our limbs knocking like guests at some multigenerational slumber party. She took one look at Dario, and something happened: she forgot about every six-foot, athletic banker with a yacht that might be stalking the streets of Milan on the lookout for the love of a good southern woman. Instead, she hung on every word that came out of this short, curly-haired, scrawny boy with espresso-dark eyes that drank her in as if she'd disappear were he to blink. For the rest of the evening she and Dario might as well have been sitting by themselves while around them the gin rummy got steadily more raucous. The three old gentlemen turned out to be hardened gamblers, cursing up a blue streak and prompting La Duchessa to caution that there was at least one lady present; Edward and Pascal snogged like teenagers upsetting the Shih Tzu who howled for some attention of its own. I smoked several watershed cigarettes which, along with the grappa, wiped the day from my memory and wrote off the next day too for recovery purposes. And still the grappa kept flowing. Only Ginevra barely touched it. Hers was inebriation of a different sort.

PLASTIC FANTASTIC

The heat of too many bodies crammed into a small space was making me itch. I straightened my hat that had slithered forward during the skirmish to get in—a felt 1940's style with a velvet bird nestled in the crown, its long feathery tail grazing my jaw. Confident headwear could do wonders for a flagging spirit. Blowing the feathers from my lip gloss, I plunged through a strobe light sequence vaguely on course for the bar. Dynamic cocktails were the willing accomplices of confident headwear.

The DJ set off a wailing siren over a series of beeps and blips. The crowd's movements were controlled and robotic, and I crossed the dance floor with ease. But they were ready to spring. When the siren faded, the DJ dropped a base of electronic belches, followed by some surprised pops, and then a grinding synthesizer, and the crowd soared. It was as if the speed of their dancing was directly connected to the DJ jerking his hands, as if he had them all on strings which, when he pulled sharply enough, yanked them clean off their feet.

When I reached the bar someone linked their arm with mine. It was Chintzy, her dimpled face flashing under the strobes. Tonight the fabric for which she was rechristened had been whipped and boned into a corset that hoisted her bosoms so high her chin rested on them.

"We're in our usual spot," she said, pointing.

All the familiar characters were in place: Winston in a bowler hat and tails offering Luciano the DJ a sip of his cocktail; Johnny, who, after ten years, had lived in Milan the longest, dressed in his usual washed-out blacks. Up on one of the cubes that were scattered about for dancing, head down, swaying and hugging himself, a curious hybrid of shoegazer and go-go dancer, he emerged from the rippling neon gradually like the images that appeared from the trays of chemicals in his dark room. Then the tall figure of German Jolanda loped over (there was no other Jolanda to require the specification of *German* Jolanda, but I liked the vaguely vaudevillian sound of it). Moving her shoulders like pistons, she threatened to put Winston's eye out. German Jolanda's frosty gaze and ski-slope cheekbones belonged in a different altitude; travelling down along the steep vertical descent of her, clothes were hastily erected held in place by pole-like limbs. She was as much in demand as muse as she was designer. Nonchalant about her beauty, lazy about her design career, her role as muse she played with total dedication, permanent props being a cigarette, a glass of something stiff, and an experimental glint in her eye.

Since Chintzy first brought me to Plastic, I had returned faithfully every weekend. We were like an international troupe of gipsy exhibitionists, toiling during the day in the fields of fashion and photography but settling on this dance floor once a week. Our camp fire was the DJ's box which warmed us with the energy to get through the next seven days.

DJ Luciano's voice came over the music: "Okay, Plastic People! Everyone's in the house. Let's see the *Carabinieri* try and shut us down again!"

The entire crowd cheered but *we* were the Plastic People. Luciano had given us this nickname to honour our commitment to his weekly parties. Chintzy and Johnny, the Plastic pioneers, had stuck their flags next to his booth and behaved like they owned that plot of land ever since, bringing in other nomads as the weeks progressed. In Milan, designers hobnobbed with designers, photographers frequented other photographers—except Johnny who thought the girls in fashion were better looking, furniture designers hung out with other furniture designers. I'd never come across any artists or sculptors. This was a city of applied arts as opposed to fine ones. It used to be a haven for writers, poets, and painters; a bastion for like-minded great thinkers to feed their souls and cultivate their intellect. Now it was a stage for fey boys and gawky girls to frolic and mingle and flaunt their individuality in front of the natives. Oddness, deviancies, quirks, and foibles were our stock in trade. The Plastic People were the unlikely consultants of cool, arbiters called upon to define glamour for an international arena, making the rules by which others would be judged.

Sprinkled about I could see the combined design talent of the houses of Prada, Gucci, Dolce & Gabbana, Armani, and Versace in various stages of being drunk and falling down, the head designer of Marni fast asleep on the comfy couches at the back. I had been one of them, even just last week I was one of them. Now I wondered if I could legitimately count myself a member of their tribe or if I'd be asked to detach my wagon from the caravan and fall behind.

Chintzy arrived at my side. "What's that look for?"

"Oh, I was just thinking."

"Are you okay?"

At that moment Davide, the ever-present waiter, passed right in front of me trailing a young Nordic-looking companion. In the amphitheatre of Italian dating, he was what I now referred to as my admission fee. After the spectacle he put on with Fausto, we had reverted to ignoring each other. But his darkening of my path once again seemed nothing but ominous.

"You know, Chintz, my teachers at school were determined I should take myself off to the Gaeltacht. It's in the farthest north west of Ireland, where the country crumbles off into the Atlantic and becomes floating bits of turf populated by fishermen and old spinsterwomen in shawls. And on one such piece of turf, I would speak Irish until I was fluent. If I stuck it out, I'd be presented with this little pin to wear, a *fainne,* and get to be an Irish teacher. Can you imagine?"

"Sounds alright," said Chintzy. "If I'd stayed in Poland, I'd be an alcoholic steelworker's wife, cooking beef tongue and chicken liver, still dividing my mascara into six tubes by diluting it with water."

"Okay. But my point is…" This time I was thrown by the sight of Fausto entering the club with his arm in a sling. "Good God, sometimes Milan seems as small as the bloody Gaeltacht."

Confused, Chintzy followed my gaze.

"I forgot you never had the pleasure. Fausto. Arm in sling."

"Ah," she said, scrutinizing him at a distance.

I switched places with her, so that my back was to the room. "It feels like we're cows slapping about in our own messes, flicking our tails against the flies. I'm giving men a rest for a while. I need to concentrate on my career."

That got her attention. "What has come over you?"

"Italian men are bad news," I said. "*Brutte notizie.* They're like red meat: difficult to digest, can cause heart disease; what I need are some leafy greens and white meat. It's my new diet." I put down my drink. "I feel a migraine coming on." It had been working on me for ten or fifteen minutes maybe, a premature hangover: Plastic's cocktails were strong. But I had been of a questionable state of mind all day. My thinking had a waywardness to it that I thought a night's dancing would cure. Now that I was here, dancing wasn't what I wanted.

"Let's go dance," said Chintzy.

The buzzing in my ears continued as I trailed aimlessly after her and worked on shaking it off. Winston was trying to inspire me with some moves when I happened to glance up and saw an unexpected sight. He hadn't been here on previous nights. His movements were slow yet the frenetic; crowd parted for him as if relenting to a force. His eyes were closing the gap between us, making straight for me like two just-launched missiles: MaxiMan. He slid in next to me while the crowd pulsated around us and breathed some words in my ear, which I didn't catch but which seared the root of every hair follicle. With a raised eyebrow, he slipped away again.

"Come on, girl," said Chintzy, popping up beside me. "We miss your usual sparkle." It had happened so fast, she hadn't seen it.

"Temporary blackout," I said. "Trained professionals are working to restore normal service without further ado."

"Listen to me. Job, career, all that will work itself out. Always does. You're here to have a good time. Forget everything else."

Later, as I was making my way to the bathroom, I stepped right into his arms and did just that, forgot everything else. He had appeared from nowhere, as if he'd been waiting for me, and when he suggested a dance, I didn't refuse. We stopped at the edge of the dance floor and began moving gently, hip bone to hip bone, even though the music was fast. A few minutes later, we were kissing like there was no one else around. His sweat smelled metallic. I felt the pounding of the music in my bones, in my teeth, through every strand of hair, and felt it travelling from me to him and back. But around us everything was muffled like a bell jar had been lowered upon us. When we pulled apart, the onslaught of lights and noise was over-whelming. He suggested going somewhere quieter and while he grabbed his coat, Chintzy caught up with me.

"What are you doing? Who is this guy?"

"I've no idea what I am doing," I answered. Then he took my hand and led me towards the exit.

"But what about your diet… the red meat?" called Chintzy.

"It starts first thing tomorrow," I called back.

I sat up in bed the next morning and looked at the sleep-ing figure beside me. With his eyes closed to the world, long lashes splayed out on brown skin, there seemed to be nothing threatening about his face, even though his hair jarred against the white of my pillow, and his beard still carved his chin into a point. His chest rose and fell, and one long arm mapped with veins and tightly packed little mounds of muscle hung over the side. His body had no excess flesh on it whatsoever; a feat of aerodynamics, he pulsated with energy but carried no weight. I felt corpulent next to those hips. The closest I had seen to legs like his—not counting models who were usually in their early teens—were those of my Aunt Josie who had died of lung cancer in her early forties but who had always been as determinedly thin as the Marlboro Reds that were her downfall.

I had no explanation for last night other than those eyes made me do strange things; they messed with my wiring. I looked over out of the corner of my eye but, thankfully, the dangerous orbs were still under cover.

I scrambled to answer my telephone. It was Chintzy, unable to get ready for work until she knew what the hell was going on.

"I take it all back," I whispered, stepping into the bathroom and pulling the door closed. "Women need red meat; when it's lean, it's a good source of protein and iron."

EDWARD'S DEPARTURE

When Massimiliano—I stopped thinking of him as Max-iMan, né Atomic Boy, for fear of blurting it out in his presence—was working and unavailable to satisfy my omnivorous cravings, I wore one of his old biker jackets whose smell of damp ashtray and mandarin oranges I couldn't seem to get enough of. I was wearing it over a cotton peasant dress when I answered the door to Edward the evening he returned from France.

"You look like the dysfunctional spawn of Heidi and Elvis," he said, flouncing onto the sofa. "Was that desired?" But then he waved his hand dismissively. "No—no. Don't bother, I wouldn't understand anyway."

"They say a friend's eye is a good mirror," I replied. "Sure, it's a pity mine's cracked."

"Are you speaking Lilliputian again?"

"Pog mo thoin!"

He swung his crossed leg. "But if you've been fermenting potatoes, I'll have a glass, to be sociable."

I went to check the cupboards. "There should be a bottle of Amaretto Ginevra uses for cooking around here somewhere. Here we go. So, tell me, how was your holiday?"

"I had tonnes of fun." He stared at me as I poured. "What's that look in your eye? You've been up to something."

"Ah, well, you know the barman in Atomic..?"

"Oh Lord." He swirled the liquid in his glass. "First things first, have you been on any interviews?"

"I'm still working on my portfolio. But it's nearly done. So, um, the holiday—" I paused and took a sip. "—do you realize how lucky you were that they gave you time off on such short notice? To go on holiday, I mean."

When he finically rearranged a few things on the coffee table and set his drink down, I thought he was preparing to give me a talking to, a chastisement on priorities, procrastination and portfolios. But that's not what I was on the receiving end of at all.

"Oh, did I forget to tell you?" he said. "They fired me."

"What are you talking about?"

"After Portofino. But no matter. They did the same thing with Colin, remember?" He flung his hand loftily. "You move on, don't you?"

"Wait a minute. Not so fast. *Move on.* Why didn't you say something?"

He took a sip and made a face. "What was the point? You warned me not to go. I didn't listen. They've already replaced me. Some young twink from St Martin's." He pulled a set of complicated facial contortions after another hearty gulp.

"I wish you'd talked to me."

"You were going through your own... episode, shall we say. Anyway, I've enjoyed these few weeks of larking about. But larks must come to an end, mustn't they?"

"You're so calm, Edward, at the strangest times." I shook my head in wonder. "It's like that time in second year when that idiot copied your work and then accused you of copying his. And Eloise made you do a new project. You didn't bat an eyelid."

"Then it comes out he'd been expelled from Middlesex for the same thing. There's no point in losing one's dignity. If I did that project I could do another. There are other jobs to be had too."

"I admire your sense of self. I'm still waiting on some of it to rub off on me."

"Oh, bollocks! You're doing fine. It's just what I've always said, one day you're the *piatto del giorno*, the next you're *fuori menu*."

"On that you don't need to convince me! God, what are we like, the pair of us? Oh, well. Things might be desperate but they're never serious." I knocked my glass against his.

"You're right there!" He executed a neat seated jump as if to announce a new topic. "Now, I don't want you to get upset that I didn't say anything, right?"

I sat down on the arm of the chair. I had a feeling of déjà vu.

"I didn't want to jinx it." He paused for effect.

"You've found a new job."

"I've found a new job."

"Congratulations! Flies don't get a chance to settle on you."

"It was actually thanks to Pascal, bless him. He knew some people."

"I didn't even think he'd been in town all that long."

"I'd already had two phone interviews before the meeting."

"Oh, is that how it's done, now? I'll keep that in mind."

"So they flew me over, and when—"

"Flew you over? So it's outside Milan? But you'll still live here, right?"

"Sweetie, I'm not quite at the level yet where I can commute daily to Paris. That's for when I get my private jet.

Although Paris is literally just over there." He pointed in the vicinity of the cooker. "You can come for weekends. I'll get an inflammable home this time. A stainless steel bathroom. I'll allow myself a celebratory ciggie. It's bonkers. What perfect timing though, because I've been feeling kind of over Milan. The spark's gone, everyone says so. It's gotten dreary. I've always wanted to live in Paris, you know."

"You never said anything to me before."

"Oh, absolutely," he said. "Ever since I saw Shirley MacLaine in *Irma la Douce* at an impressionable age."

They might just as well have announced they were taking the Duomo from the centre of Milan; Edward was the axis upon which my orbit pivoted. All other friendships, routines, and pleasures I'd put in place for myself suddenly seemed hollow. This new life—this bella vita—was a bit of a con, really, if Edward could jack it in so easily. He was following Pascal to Paris—of course, there were great opportunities for designers there, too—but he hadn't explored his possibilities in Milan; they didn't even know what he was really capable of; they hadn't uncorked his potential. In Paris you could still smoke. It didn't escape me for one second that this would play a significant part in his altogether deficient reasoning. *Milan's lost its spark.* My eye!

Ginevra tried to convince me that I was especially upset because it followed on the heels of the Fausto disappointment and losing my job and everything being insecure. But her excitement at having a place to stay in Paris, her favourite city, and her talk of long weekends there, tacking on an overnight stay in Brussels to see old friends, just depressed me more. Massimiliano's advice on how to cope with my impending loss was no better: "Play Led Zeppelin on the guitar. Those chords really got me through some tough times with a Californian chick I knew. She was the reason my first band broke up." He grew wistful. "It was a tragic loss. I still think about those guys and the times we had. Just let it out, babe." His beautiful eyes welled up as he handed me the pick, closed the door and left me and his guitar to bond.

When the day of Edward's departure arrived, I took custody of three potted plants of unimpressive stature, while Edward whittered on about a hodge-podge of matters weighing on his mind: his unfortunate allergy to most French cheeses; the land of lost socks; if he ran out on his overdraft in Banca Popolare di Milano, would they be able to track him down. I focused on keeping my emotions in check.

"Of course, interfering do-gooders would say my smoking stunted their growth," fired Edward.

"Huh?"

"The plants. They ought to fare better with you."

"Oh, don't say that," I said, choking up. "You were as good to them as you could possibly be."

He gave me a warning look. "It's a cheese plant and a couple of begonias. No call for water works."

We were sitting on the floor of his and Pascal's flat. Pascal had left a few days earlier to arrive in Paris in time for casting calls for men's fashion week. As we inched the zippers closed on a pair of slick black hold-alls that he'd stolen from Italo Rocco, I was struck by how quickly all of Edward's worldly goods had been packed away.

"Did you leave some stuff behind in the old place?"

"No. I travel light, sweetie." He finished wrapping the last of his collection of snow globes in tissue paper and added them to a box. "I'm a magpie. I swoop in, attracted by shiny things, and then fly off." He sealed the box and sat back on his heels. "That's it."

I felt like a once-shiny thing that had lost its appeal. Only I was less portable than a box of snow globes.

Edward's personal effects amounted to four misshapen nylon bags and one medium-sized cardboard box that I was to mail him in a few days. More material possessions might have better represented the loss for me. This felt like a poor turn-out.

We had planned to have a last lunch along the Naviglio. But he glanced at his watch and said, "Sweetie, it looks like it's going to be a bit of a mad dash. How about we grab a slice of pizza at the airport?"

After sitting side by side in the quietest car journey we'd ever made together, we sat opposite each other at a tall table in the Malpensa *Autogrill*, separated by the half-gnawed crusts on paper plates of previous diners. I pushed away my unfinished slice. Edward ran the napkin over his mouth and pushed his away too.

"I'm giving you my Debbie Harry T-shirt."

"I can't take that. You love that T-shirt."

He fished it out of the side pocket of a bag. "Don't argue. I know you'll take it out to flirt with glamour once in a while. That's my only condition: it must be spotted on a dance floor at four in the morning at least once every few weeks. It's built quite a fan base here, become well-known around town." He ran his hand over the discs, smoothing out some rogue ones till they all lay flat like fish skin.

"I sewed every sequin on by hand, you know. It pissed my old man off something rotten. When he came home from work to see his only son on the couch reading fashion magazines or handling a needle and thread, he'd go ballistic. He wanted me to follow him on the building sites—a hard man like him, in a hard hat. Instead he got a sissy who sewed. He threw it in the rubbish numerous times, you know, one time in a skip at the end of our road when they were renovating our neighbour's semi-detached. But I got it back every time. That's why this sleeve is a slightly different colour, if you've ever noticed. He set fire to the original one with his cigarette."

He hurriedly folded and lobbed it across the table at me. "Now you must carry on the pursuit of sparkle to which I have dedicated my very existence and disowned my very father. No pressure."

I stroked the soft cotton, rearranged it in my lap. Then I put it to my nose and backed away again quickly. "You might have dry cleaned it first! I can smell every debauched Saturday night you've ever spent trawling about in it."

"If you could bottle that scent, you'd have your fortune made, sister, let me tell you. Have you any idea how much it costs to dry-clean sequins?" He looked at his watch, then clapped his hands twice. "Now, you strapping cow-herd, give me a hand with these bags."

"Charming. I won't miss listening to that," I said, trailing the smaller hold-all and following him. "Why didn't you check this too?"

"Just in case my bags get lost or don't arrive, I have everything I'll need for my first week. Can you imagine showing up at your new life and not having a stitch to put on?"

A little later, we stopped in front of Departures and dropped the bags again.

"So, you're okay?" he asked.

"I'll have to be, won't I? Got no choice."

"You know that pair of sour old queens bad-mouthed me all over town—Gio was actually the worst. I went for a couple of interviews. I knew as soon as I walked in that they already knew me. Or knew of me. Gio wanted to fuck things up. Milan's too small for that. This way, it's a clean slate. I'm excited. Just don't have me leaving all worried about you. Portfolio, job, Atomic Boy, in that order, okay? I'll be checking. Now, give me a hug and let's get this over with."

"You smell lovely," I said into his shoulder. "Don't go all French on me. It would suit you even less than going all Italian."

"Which I never did."

"No, you never did. Anyway, I'll be over to drag you back soon enough. As soon as I get back on my feet, actually. So enjoy it while it lasts."

"Bye, poppet!" He broke into an exaggerated mince because he knew I was watching but it ended in a lurch as the heaviest bag whacked against his hip. Before disappearing behind the wall, he turned.

"We'll always be best friends," he said, almost too softly for me to hear, and gave me a wink.

I waved and nodded through tears.

"I'm not going far." He blew me a kiss and was gone.

I stood alone amidst the muffled airport sounds. I was about to turn when, clearer and crisper than anything that was coming over the loud speakers, his voice sailed back around the corner. "Don't just stand there, Farmgirl! I can't wait to find out what you're going to do next. You're not done here. Now watch out for those *ragazzi*! Call you at the weekend!"

MAMMONE

In festive spirit, Massimiliano had been passing out free drinks since I arrived. It was his thirty-third birthday, and if he had to work, he was determined to make a party of it. Then again, he always had to work as I was quickly learning, and after closing he hung around with friends, sometimes hit a club, getting home just before sunrise to sleep all day and then do it all over again. God knows where he'd been going that day I ran into him in the street, but such occasions were an anomaly; Massimiliano only showed himself under cover of darkness.

As a result, I had been going drinking more than usual. From Ginevra I began to hear comments such as "Irish booty on tap, next to the Guinness." It wasn't her disapproval that bothered me, it was that her English vocabulary included the word '*booty*'; I had been living in the country coming up on a year, and my Italian was nowhere near as comprehensive.

Chipping at the ice cubes in my glass with a straw, I looked up to see where he was. To watch Massimiliano at work was to observe a man thrilled with his life, truly tickled pink; his cup runneth over or at least was always half-full—usually with

Jack Daniels. He felt that to be a good barman you had to be on the same wavelength as your customers, which basically meant having the same blood alcohol level. Behind the bar of Atomic he was the ringmaster, joker, ground control, and lead guitar; he poured second-rate gin into half-washed glasses, and girls treated him like a rock star.

But I was glad of the party atmosphere as I was still missing Edward, and a sense of aimlessness had settled over my days like a fog.

Massimiliano leaned in and gave me a peck on the cheek as he deposited some empty glasses on the bar. The DJ was playing only The Rolling Stones that night at Massimiliano's request.

"Did I tell you the last concert the Stones did in San Siro, I went backstage and hung out with Keith? We got on like brothers. That was one wild night! He's coming back in a few months and going to look me up. I'll introduce you. Get her another!" he yelled to his colleague. Then he lit up that demonic smile. "You're coming back to my place tonight. I'll show you Monza, where I live."

I don't know if I believed I would meet Keith Richards, but I knew he believed it when he said it. I was more interested in Monza: I knew it was famous for the Grand Prix at the *Autodromo* and for its beautiful walled park, one of the largest in Europe, neither of which would be open at night. So the beaten path would have to wait until another time. But it was the opportunity to glimpse Massimiliano in, I couldn't say his natural habitat as that would be the bar, but in another context intimately associated with him, that I found so irresistible.

"I get what you see in him," said Chintzy from the barstool beside me. She was watching him move around also.

"You do?"

"Oh yeah. Those eyes. They blaze with something."

Later as we sped along the *autostrada* in his rusted Fiat, I asked, "You know that time we met in the street? And I gave you my number? How come you never called?"

He snorted with laughter and threw his head back. "Why didn't you call me?" His eyes flashed in the dark.

"Oh, come on. It's always easier for the guy. Ginevra says Italian men are very traditional that way."

Another exhalation of mirth and I had to wonder if I didn't have a hidden gift for comedy. His face settled on an expression that read 'Whatever *will* she say next?'

"It's a serious question."

"I don't like to force these things," he said. "I'd seen you around enough. I knew we'd cross paths when we were meant to. Don't you think so?"

"I suppose so. Milan's small. Sometimes it's harder to avoid people than anything else."

"Well, there's your answer."

"It hardly leaves me feeling special though."

He let out a long laugh before squeezing my leg. "Did you feel special before? In the bar when I said I'd take you back to Monza? I don't take just anyone, you know."

I shrugged.

"So don't ask silly questions and you'll still feel special."

This last comment sounded a bit slurred, and his eyes were dancing like devils in his head.

"Exactly how much have you had to drink?" I should have made the calculation before I got in the car: Italian driver + Jack Daniels - Airbag = Brain-dead.

He screwed up his face dismissively. "I always drive after drinking. I'm fine. Don't I seem fine to you? I'm that rare creature—alcohol makes me do everything better."

I decided not to distract him with any more talking and, without incident, we pulled up to an ornate white gate, he pressed a gadget attached to his keys, and we drove through. I couldn't see what was ahead but the push of another button took us down a spiral tunnel into an underground car park. He slid the Fiat between a Volvo family car and a small Nissan with two baby seats in the back. He didn't lock it but hurried me into a lift which, moments later, silently deposited us outside a split-level villa. As conspicuous in these surroundings as the Child Catcher at the gates of the local junior school, he approached the front door without glancing right or left, and I became suspicious of his reasons for inviting me. Could it be he was here to burgle rich people and I was his accomplice? If I had known the Italian for 'casing the joint', I might have dared ask. I watched him whip a bunch of keys from his pocket and deftly separate one from the rest using one hand.

"So what, you live here?"

He rattled the keys in the door which gave way with a chink.

"*Casa, dolce casa,*" he said, ushering me in.

As he pressed the door closed, he motioned for me to keep my voice down. He turned on a lamp; we were in a small hallway perfumed with lavender. I looked around at the peach walls, gilt mirror, ornaments on doilies, painting of The Last Supper, and statue of Padre Pio. While I hadn't expected his pad to include these items, what threw me was the utter absence of what I had expected: the framed Hendrix posters, the scattered electric guitars, eardrum-splitting amps, the pyramid of empty beer cans.

Massimiliano stopped creeping and froze on his tip-toes. I, naturally, did the same. We remained like that, holding hands and perfectly still, eyes trained on the spiral staircase up ahead, and the sound of slow, descending footsteps. A pair of floral bedroom slippers popped into view from which sprouted two brown twig-like legs. There followed an expanse of quilted housecoat which was topped off with the head of a little old lady, her hair in rollers. Calmly, she completed her descent then stood before us with her head tilted inquiringly. I eyed Massimiliano, then her. He didn't say a word but if looks could kill, she would have been flat on the floor with X's on her eyes. The suspicion returned that we were 'on a job'.

Then the old dear spoke: "Massi, would you or your guest like a *panino?*"

Massimiliano bellowed at her to go back to bed—so loudly I was sure I saw her rollers slacken their hold. But she shuffled off into the kitchen, her bedroom slippers swooshing across the tiled floor.

"How was work, dear?" she called.

"Ma!" He chased after her; I remained in the hallway and peeped around the door. They were having an angry, whispered exchange, or at least, Massimiliano was. His mother, considerably shorter than him, was just attentively gazing into his face. Then he followed her across the worktop, returning items to the cupboards from which she had just taken them, snatching pots and forks from her busy little hands.

"Ma. We're not hungry. No tortellini. Ma. *Ma!* Just go to bed." He threw his hands in the air and, crossing the kitchen in three strides, took my hand, and pulled me towards the stairs.

"Nice to meet you, Signora," I called.

We took two flights, to what seemed to be a converted attic space, ample enough to house a large bedroom, bathroom and separate dressing area.

"*Questa e la mia vera casa!*" he announced and went directly to an intimidating system of music equipment stacked next to three pillars of vinyl; an entire wall of sound. He selected something obscure, the intro of which was a swelling guitar solo. I suggested lowering the volume, but he responded by hanging over the staircase and letting another holler out of him.

"Fuck!" He strode back across the room to lift his cigarettes.

I stood stiffly in the middle of the floor. Now I was surrounded by everything I'd been expecting: the T-shirts and flyers for clubs; overflowing ashtrays and empty beer cans; collector's copies of *NME*, *Melody Maker*, and three different guitars. On a ledge, I spotted the Acqua Di Parma cologne that always smelled so masculine on him. But after passing rooms furnished with overstuffed couches, needlework mottos, and a full French style kitchen, and even up here, in what he referred to as his *vera casa*, his real home, among the expensive cherry wood, travelling lavender, and polished parquet, Massimiliano's belongings looked less like rock and roll paraphernalia and more like wishful thinking. These were like souvenirs of a place he had yet to visit. They were no different than Lynda's grouped *objets*, her birdcages and Buddhas, on display to convince people she was an interesting person.

I recalled photos of seventies rockers prowling elegant hotel lobbies or sprawled about a five-star suite, in the background, the unmade bed in which they'd just entertained a beautiful groupie. They usually wore a look of disdain for such trappings, as revealing as their skintight trousers. Massimiliano, despite his contempt for his mother's fussing, suddenly seemed to move about with a pampered impertinence.

I lay near the edge of the bed pretending to be asleep. For there would be no hanky-panky with his mother downstairs cutting the crusts off sandwiches. Oh, how Edward would enjoy this, when I told him! I could almost hear him screech.

The next morning, while Massimiliano lay open-mouthed, and still emitting snorts, this time of deep slumber, I dressed quickly and crept to the stairs. After completing two floors with no surprises, except the sudden celestial chiming of a clock in another part of the house, I turned the last bend and placed one foot on ground level. I had just lowered the other and was poised for a quick getaway, the front door a mere three feet ahead, when I found myself once again confronted with the mildly inquisitive face of Massimiliano's mother.

Shiny and alert, she was minus her rollers, her hair like a plate of rigatoni. A gruff and wheezing gentleman in cardigan and pyjamas joined her carrying an espresso and the *Gazzetto dello Sport*. He had the same dancing eyes as Massimiliano; he would surely have been one to watch in his day. But if those eyes hadn't been pinned suspiciously on me, I wouldn't have noticed their vibrancy, hidden behind the folds of sagging skin and tired lids.

I introduced myself, declined the mother's offer of breakfast, and complimented her on her home. After enquiring if it was fresh lavender or pot pourri that lingered so pleasingly through every room, I swung the door almost off its hinges and did the hundred-yard dash. At the gate, I could see no means of exit. I looked back but there was not another living soul to be seen, not a twitch of net curtain, not a hunky pool boy, not a barking dog nor fearful postman. Just me and my shadow stranded in a compound of identical houses lined up on equal-sized plots of landscaped garden. The sun was already hot, and I could see no other option but to scale the gate, about ten feet high, so I slid my evening bag through the bars and hoisted myself off the ground. What was left of the previous evening's makeup slithered off my chin the farther up I went. Swinging my leg over the top, I ran into difficulty only as I began my descent. The ironwork was more intricate higher up, and the footholds narrower. As one foot stabbed desperately for a ledge, the heel of my shoe tore a panel out of my dress, revealing a decent slice of thigh and, at that height, generous portion of right buttock. My toe slid into a suitable crevice just as something dropped from my pocket. I eased myself down but, impatient to feel the ground underneath me, jumped the last bit, landing squarely on my arse in the dirt. A passing car horn squawked gleefully starting up its own dawn chorus. Squinting into the sun, I could see the fabric flapping in the breeze like a memorial flag honouring the fallen.

On the ground beside me, my lipstick had become separated from its lid: Ravish Me Red. Dirt clung to the shaft like frosting. I picked it up and placed it on one of the ledges below the spike that held aloft my skirt, a sort of altar to celebrate walks of shame being embarked upon everywhere, and set off kicking up dust. I had no idea where I was going. About half a mile along, I came upon an old man sitting on a deckchair manning two petrol pumps.

"Excuse me, sir, could you tell me how I get back to Milan please?"

To compensate for my questionable appearance, I spoke in my finest Italian, but he barely glanced my way. Maybe there was a steady stream of bemused-looking females that tottered to a stop in front of his unleaded pump, lost after having set out for walk on the wild side. He wordlessly pointed off in the distance.

"I get a bus to Milan up ahead?"

He nodded.

"Thank you for your time, sir. I appreciate it. Good day."

Continuing under the blistering heat, I reflected on the difference a day makes. Disillusionment was a swift and immediate attacker; I recognized it as a strain of the greater disorder I'd been suffering from over the past few weeks. Disillusionment contaminated everything. Last night, I had imagined I was going home with a bad boy, yet I woke up with a mamma's boy. Without a guide and on the trail of something completely different, I had happened upon and observed in its natural habitat one of Italy's most talked about indigenous species: the *mammone*. A much scrutinized creature, he stalks the wilds of the great metropolis, oozing testosterone and mating freely. He's the epitome of independence but, come nightfall and in his thirties, he will still seek refuge in a nest feathered by his mother who provides constant nourishment and an ever-watchful gaze that protects against foreign predators.

It is recommended to bring binoculars, photographic equipment, even a picnic, and enjoy these colourful creatures from afar. But under no circumstances should one try to entice them away. Their allure is known to quickly fade if they are plucked from their secure environments. It is best to leave them to flourish undisturbed and move quietly on.

EVA

A few days later, I received a call from Signor Maltempo, the accountant at Intermezzo, notifying me that there was a small matter of outstanding taxes to be paid from my time with the company. I had been expecting his call, and they do say that the only things you can rely on are death and taxes. I was on my way to his office when a freak summer *tempesta* burst over Milan. Rain was rare during high season, but when it came in those short, violent bursts, it was like a shootout had erupted in the heat-clogged streets. Barkeepers leapt, cursing and blinding, to fasten down awnings; waiters sprung from inertia to snatch menus from dazed tourists and tumble them from plastic chairs; taxi drivers refused fares, and Vespas were abandoned in clumps. By the first clap of thunder, the streets were deserted, with huddles of people peering apprehensively from the doorways of banks.

I splashed through a deserted Piazza San Babila under an umbrella. It wasn't common practice in July to carry one, but coming from the north west of Ireland, I considered it more of a challenge not to. There were actually three things you could rely on: death, taxes, and rain. Not that I was ever heard bemoaning the rain. Not me. I liked to gaze out the windows during storms and watch the Italians run. When they waxed lyrical about how everyone looked better with a tan and how people were happier in sunnier climes, I shared my theories that everyone looked better wet, that marital infidelity was probably stoked by excessive heat. People shag in the sun; real romance happens in the rain. No trips to the seaside for me on summer weekends; I preferred beaches in winter. The wet weekends that trapped me indoors as a child, igniting my passion for reading, had introduced me to the eclectic cast of literary heroines who'd turned up in my designs ever since. So it could even be said that rain was one of my earliest inspirations.

But there was something more fundamental about rain that I liked: it cut to the chase of the matter, hence the phrase "right as rain". At home, we referred to the need to get our head *showered* when things became too confusing. A rainstorm was a burst of realism, clearing the air for a fresh start. So the sound of it outside the window that morning comforted me as I took a seat in that green office to focus on what Signor Maltempo had to say. By the end of it, this is what I could make out:

Tot up this and that, subtract such and such, minus the cost of thingummy combined with the rate of inflation, times two for good luck and carry your one... Ta-da! Before you know it, you're worse off than you thought you were and buona giornata!

Martinelli's generous parting gift of two months' salary was swiftly manhandled back into the company's coffers, and I was back out in the rain.

At home and dried off, I felt ready to dig out my portfolio. I took a sheaf of blank paper to the middle of the floor and sat cross-legged on the rug drawing quickly: thumbnails, silhouettes, details. Sun rays of sketches were emanating from me like the tax files encircling Signor Maltempo when a draught from the doors swinging open scattered drawings everywhere.

"Ginevra!" I snatched to safety a penned evening dress poised to jump from the balcony. "You're back. I forgot it was today."

"*Ciao, Bellissima!*" she sang and then looked perplexed. "What's all this? What are you doing home?"

I helped her get her suitcases through the doors. She and Dario had been on a two-week package holiday to Egypt. Her face looked like an exotic sun-ripened fruit.

"You first. Tell me all about Sharm el-Sheikh."

"*Oh mio Dio!*" Her eyes sparkled madly. "You will never guess what happened."

A lot can happen in two weeks. But she was right; I wouldn't have guessed what was to follow.

"We're engaged!" She nodded with an endearing disbelief, and I hugged her and joined in her breathless gabbling until her tone turned serious.

"As I said, Dario and I have decided we would like to move in together. Why haven't you responded to my messages? You'll need to look for a new place unless you intend to take on the rent by yourself. The landlord's e-mail that I forwarded you says he wants to raise it from next month and only have one tenant. I got no reply from you. Did you read it? Have you worked something out? You'll be alright, won't you?"

My financial situation was hanging by a thread. I had no choice but to make the call I had been dreading.

"*Hell-oo-oh?*"

"Hello mum, how's it going?"

"Oh, it's yourself," she said. "Not so bad. I'm just in from a set and blow dry. Any word of a new job?"

"These things don't happen overnight, but you'll be the first to know."

"You know, you've given this fashion thing a fair go. Would you not try something a bit more realistic?"

"Like what?"

"Well, Maureen Murphy is looking for a trainee to start in the salon. At first, it would just be washing and sweeping—no perming or anything like that—but once she sees you're good, you'd move on to that. It could appeal to your artistic nature."

"Mum, Maureen Murphy runs her salon out of her kitchen."

"And sure what she doesn't pay in rent for some fancy premises, wouldn't she be putting in your wages?"

"Every time you go in, you come out smelling of fried liver and potato bread."

"As she likes to say, 'It's a happy man what smells liver on the pan'. Her Malachy would eat it morning, noon, and night. It's not like you'd be asked to eat it. It's her tea I object to; it's nothing but coloured water. She stews the same three leaves over and over again on the stove. I wouldn't wash the outside step with it. And, of course, she hasn't a titter of wit in her, but apart from that, not a bad soul."

I took a deep breath and launched myself: "Mum, there's something I need to ask you. Could you transfer a bit of my Ballyloughin money?"

When Da died, he left me a fourteen-acre plot of land in the adjoining parish of Ballyloughin. It was the farm his father had left him, and it amounted to four good grazing fields and a patch of bumpy, unseeded ground only fit for goats. I had sold the lot for a fair price to Uncle Eugene, mum's brother,

when he expanded his head of cattle. By then, my interest
in the farm was merely as the subject of my romantic watercolour period during which I painted soaring pastoral landscapes; tending the aminals amounted to anatomical studies
in pencil or oils of gormless, chewing, staring heads or swollen
pink udders capped with bullet-like nipples. Towards the end,
Da was sensitive to my shifting interests and encouraged me
to follow my own path. The farm was the largest animal of all:
a living, breathing, helpless, demanding organism, but it was
the only thing left of Da. I had struggled to turn my back on
it, consoled myself somewhat when we were able to keep it
in the family, and vowed I would use the money to make Da
proud. I had not foreseen pulling my precious legacy asunder,
because I was unemployed in a foreign land, unable to pay
my rent but unwilling to accept a life peddling blue rinses to
senior citizens in Maureen Murphy's front room.

"But that money's for when you get married to build yourself a house," said mum.

"*Is* it, now?"

"Isn't it?"

"Well, if it is, I'll have it replaced by then. Anyway I don't
need it all. It's my rainy day fund." Pointedly, I added, "And
it's raining here, mum."

"Is it? God, we had a couple of wee showers early in the
day, but it was dry all afternoon. I got the sheets out on the
line and walked up to eight o' clock mass and down again.
Only as I was turning in our road did it start to spit."

"No, I mean raining in the sense of needing something to
tide me through some unexpected circumstances. Here, I'll
give you my account numbers."

I heard her scrambling to unearth a pen, then the receiver
knocking against the wall as she left to scour other corners of

the kitchen. Five minutes must have passed when I started yelling for her down the phone. "Mum! MUM! I'm still here!"

Then, some exasperated mumbles until her voice came through clearly.

"What? I know! I was looking for the pen and came across a card from Dymphna, my cousin. I clean forgot. She's coming over from England on Saturday. It's a good job you called or I mightn't have come across that."

"Glad to have helped. Now have you the pen?"

After she took note of my bank details, she said, "I'll go into the town first thing and do that. By God, I'll walk if this weather keeps up."

"Thanks, mum. I'll call at the weekend and speak to Dymphna."

"Alright, Kathleen. And you know what you're doing now?"

"I'll have it back before the builders arrive."

"Are you sure you don't want me talk to Maureen?"

The coffee bar I sat in, barely larger than your average bus stop and of the kind routinely being replaced by chic and spare Wi-Fi cafes, was a great spot for sketching people: from the steady stream of fashionable espresso fiends, teetering momentarily at the counter, to the old gentlemen behind their newspapers whose skinny legs were wrapped around their stools like trees roots resisting urbanization. My sketchbook acted like a one-way mirror; I saw them in great detail but they didn't notice me behind it. As the sun slunk behind the bank across the street, I shaded furiously with my nib at a slant; it had become imperative I capture the light bouncing off one man's bulbous crown. These small challenges of seizing fleeting moments, expressions, and movements with my 4B pencil brought some gratification to my day. I'd finished my portfolio, and two weeks of solid interviewing hadn't gotten me anywhere so far. Houses proved keen to meet with me but my portfolio seemed to entertain and simultaneously alienate them. They all expressed the same concern: "Intermezzo's style is so playful, ironic; what we do here would probably be too serious for you." I volunteered to do some sketches for them, but they were weirdly reluctant. I was left with the impression that Intermezzo was a curiosity to the other houses, like a fantasy island doubling as a tax haven—something fun and exotic but not entirely legitimate.

Having polished the man's noggin to a gleam, I considered two young women at the next table and found a clean page. I'd guessed as soon as they came in that they worked in fashion, but by their general air more than how they were dressed: a jacket and trouser combo in listless greys rejecting any notion of the female form underneath.

"Do you think Silvia has finally lost it, then?" asked the first, with bulging eyes.

Her companion looked stupefied. "She locked people in the *Sala Bianca* overnight. I can't get over it. And then the string of hateful phone calls. That's after she threw her tool belt at one of the girls in the factory who had to get five stitches. Heaven help us, she's firing on all cylinders!"

"Oh, Martina, how will it end? I mean, some of us don't even feel safe on the third floor." She sent a fearful look towards the door as if the rampaging Silvia had expanded her reign of terror beyond the third floor to prowl the streets below.

"Well, the rumour is one of her girls announced she was pregnant, and that's what set her off. You know she takes that as a personal insult."

"Just because she hasn't dusted hers off in decades, she thinks no one else should get any action either." The girl laughed distractedly and picked at her food.

Martina made a disgusted face before putting a napkin to her mouth. "Anyway, she got rid of all three of them. Has another batch of assistants starting tomorrow. I didn't even get a chance to learn these ones' names."

"I just wish I could work with you instead," said the other. "I have to choose yarns with her in..." She looked at her phone. "Shit! Look at the time! I need to go."

They gathered their bags in a flurry and ran out leaving the bar in silence except for the sound of the till opening and a woman paying. I rolled my eyes. Some designers should be on the stage of La Scala, their propensity for melodrama was so great. They had put me in bad humour. I gathered my pencils and reached for the bag at my feet.

"You have a very nice hand and interesting eye. Beautiful lines," said a voice. I returned upright to see a woman in her mid-thirties standing over me.

"Oh, thank you. I've found some good subjects in this bar."

"Are you an artist?" she asked, rolling down the top of her takeaway bag. "Do you mind?" Her hand was already holding the corner of my sketchbook.

"No, work away. I wouldn't call myself an artist. I'm a—I'm in between jobs, interviewing, you know?"

"Lovely as these are, there's not much of a career in this kind of...oh, but these are beautiful." She was looking intently at a page of studies of fashionably dressed lionesses that had passed through earlier.

"My career's in fashion. I don't know what I'll use these for yet."

"Oh? Where have you worked?" Her eyes were pink-lidded and attentive. "For who?"

"Intermezzo until a couple weeks ago."

She pulled out a chair and lowered herself onto its edge. She was dressed in muted colours but carried a poppy-red Birkin bag which she placed on the table next to her elbow. "Have you any of your fashion drawings with you?"

"You're in luck. I had an interview earlier..."

She practically seized my portfolio from me. What a strange little thing! She flicked through the opening pages, making twittering sounds.

"You know, we might be able to help each other out." Her hand crept inside the Birkin. She slid a business card across the table without lifting her eyes from the book.

Before I even lifted it from the table, I read:

Eva Vermicelli. Co-coordinator.

House of Adriani.

I had never before felt such a powerful sensation of wanting to rewind and start again. I wished I had dressed differently, that my tone had been more professional, at least, that I hadn't said I was unemployed. I couldn't have made a worse impression if I had turned my hat upside down on the floor for her to toss me some spare change.

Although I had heard that the House of Adriani was located somewhere in this area, on one of these pretty streets, I preferred to think of it as a mysterious mansion on a hill secluded behind tall gates. I saw it lit up by bolts of lightning, a place that the villagers gossiped and speculated about, but had never been inside nor met anyone who had. Chintzy had told me that anyone who got in never left. If by some extremely rare occurrence they did, they never talked about their experience inside. She made it sound like Bluebeard's locked room.

I thought of the House of Adriani ad that I'd pulled from the magazine in the orphanage, carried to Milan, and pinned to my bedroom wall, the same one that I'd Xeroxed fifty percent smaller and pasted in the inspiration book I carted around in my bag. When I first arrived, I'd asked Edward if he had any contacts at Adriani, but he shook his head with a sigh. "No one. Absolutely not a one." Like he'd failed both himself and me. But that was before I understood how it went. Adriani was the king of Italian fashion. You didn't telephone there for an interview. Designers stepped down from those positions as from thrones, and successors were waiting in the wings already groomed.

Yet for all this elusiveness, Adriani's presence was felt all over the city; he had reigned for more than thirty years, seeing pretenders with various-sized followings come and go, but no one who had been able to topple him. I felt intimidated by this alert little woman and her powerful title as I asked meekly, "What do you coordinate?"

She gave me her full attention. "You could say I liaise between Signor Adriani and those who craft his message." Then she returned to the pages of my portfolio. That was all I was getting.

In my confusion, I found myself describing all the ways my portfolio did *not* reflect the clean, androgynous, minimalist style of the House of Adriani; how Intermezzo probably represented something too different for them. I was inexplicably regurgitating the contents of two weeks of unsuccessful interviews when she held a finger aloft.

"Ah, but, you see, we happen to be looking for someone whose work is not typical of the Adriani style. We need conflict, different styles, that *collision,* to bring about something unexpected. Do you see what I mean?"

She looked around before continuing. I felt a shiver of privilege, like I was receiving highly classified information.

"You see, that is how we move forward. Otherwise the House of Adriani would remain stagnant, passé, a relic from another time. We need someone with a young, raw eye who is forthright in their opinions. Someone with the kind of character you show in your life drawings." She blinked excessively as she made her petition. "But with the modernity of your designs. Strong, yet sensitive. Do you see now?"

I felt my head bob along to the rhythm of her blinking eyes. It was like her heart was beating just behind her eyelids.

"It requires a certain quality of designer."

When can I start?

"But, it must also be someone who is diplomatic and understands how to work with an extremely successful man, a man who has a very strong vision but a planet-sized ego; a primadonna who doesn't like to be disagreed with or contradicted, whose style is revered the world over but criticized by fashion insiders."

It was an interesting sell.

"Your portfolio is very original. You could be just what we need…"

Her face was almost feral but she appeared to have exhausted herself. "I would like to put you in front of him and see how he reacts."

Put me in front of him? I felt like a court jester who would be tried out for the first time in the king's court.

When we said goodbye, I went straight home to dust off my cap'n'bells.

AN AUDIENCE WITH THE KING

I was sitting in a box room somewhere in the west wing of the House of Adriani, in the centre of the city's historic quarter, at the heart of the country's history of fashion. After waiting thirty minutes, my excitement at meeting the great man had somewhat waned. I stared at the unadorned walls until they started to loom. If I stretched my arms out without leaving my seat, I could touch all the walls with my fingertips; that was how I established that they were painted the exact shade of calcium-deficient fingernails. Ten more minutes passed. Just when I was sure I had been forgotten about, Eva arrived. It seemed it would be just the two of us again when, before the door closed, a small man hopped out from behind her. It struck me as comical but the small man's expression betrayed no humour.

I recognized him immediately; his face represented his country like that of the pope or prime minister. My eyes, so attuned to every nook and crevice of it from seeing all the close-up portraits in magazines accompanying articles that attempted to get to the heart of the man, dashed ahead, drawn to the other parts, briefly alighting on his hair. Although slick and stylish in photos, live it looked like a helmet of baked clay. Then my eyes dropped to the diminutive feet encased in gleaming white sneakers, and back up over the body outfitted in navy to the hands and face, the colour of rotisserie chicken. He was compact, polished, and stiffly pressed, like he would be slid back into his display packaging when we were done. "Made by Mattel" might be stamped on his arse.

Eva nudged me. My hand was sweaty touching his outstretched one, but the two brisk shakes he gave it were over so fast he may not have noticed.

"Buongiorno, "he said under his breath, almost reluctantly and with no eye contact. Instead he scanned my upper body, then swivelled towards Eva.

"Chanel?" he barked. "*Ma che cazzo?*"

She shrugged.

I was wearing the Chanel jacket over Edward's Debbie Harry t-shirt. I wanted to give the impression that I belonged among luxury things to the extent that I treated them with nonchalance, even irreverence. I'd read somewhere that, along with his mother, Coco Chanel was one of Adriani's earliest inspirations, and it was indisputable fashion lore that a Chanel jacket chicly navigated one through any situation. And the sentimental total value of both items worn together couldn't fail to bring me luck.

"E poi, la giacca, la porte come un taglialegno."

With a look of distaste, he flung the chair back, sat on it, and pulled my book towards him. He started flicking through it at speed, like he was looking for something in particular, something he may have lost or misplaced. His small, age-spotted hands, set like the claws of an animal, still looked like they could inflict pain—and the willful set of his mouth suggested there was plenty of desire to. A heavy gold ring worn on the third finger of his right hand knocked against the table top providing the only noise.

Eva, in contrast to our previous meeting, was tight-lipped and careful, blinking less. She sat forward, occasionally drawing his attention to something by pointing, but the few times I chimed in, I was conscious of my words bouncing redundantly off the walls. The air conditioning turned itself off and, without its hum, a new layer of silence insulated us. My swallowing sounded cacophonous. The rise and fall of his well-maintained pectorals through his fitted t-shirt held my attention for an unnaturally long time. His clothed parts could have belonged to a man much younger.

Just as the silence seemed to drain all oxygen from the room, Signor Adriani spoke.

"*Vabbe', arriverderci.*" He nodded to Eva, and was gone.

The door hurried after him attentively but in the last few seconds sighed to a close. I was struck immediately by my own wastefulness. I had let the meeting be carried on without me. If I ran after him and tapped him on the shoulder, I doubt he would have even remembered me; for him the Chanel jacket was probably the only thing of note about the entire encounter.

I looked at Eva.

She smiled calmly back.

"Didn't he like my work?"

"He seemed to." She got up. "I will know more when I speak to him later. Thank you for coming in. Goodbye."

The door closed a second time. When I packed up and stepped out into the empty corridor, the assistant who had accompanied me on arrival was nowhere to be seen. I took a right and turned a corner into another corridor at the end of which I assessed a similar landscape and took a left. Another passage stretched ahead that became a series of right angles like ever decreasing squares. It was a beige maze. Maybe this was what Chintzy meant when she said if you got in you didn't leave. Breadcrumbs would have been lost in the neutral carpet even if I'd thought to drop them. I emerged in a corridor lined on one side with windows; the sight of the trees and sky loosened my breathing. There was a lift at the end of it.

The joke was on me, after all. I didn't belong in a place like this with its labyrinth of unmarked passageways, unspoken interviews, and stiff little kings with earthenware hair. I stepped out into the street and felt the air hit me.

But if I didn't get a job soon, it would be no jesting matter.

"I'm looking at a picture of him right now in *Paris Match*," said Edward. "Is he really that orange?"

"He is."

"I can't believe you met him. A Kat may look at a king, hah!"

"That was the extent of it, Edward. A look was all I got. Pleasantries were limited to 'Buongiorno' and 'Chanel, what the fuck?'"

"He had a point, Kat. Who wears Chanel to the House of Adriani? That would be a major faux pas. I bet it put him in a foul mood."

"Oh, I thought he'd appreciate it, didn't I." As the hours passed, I'd developed a muddled resentment of the esteemed ruler of fashion and our meeting which had been a royal disappointment.

"Did he say anything about your work?" Edward asked.

"He only said one other thing, still on the jacket—I had to come home and look up the word to be sure—He said... he said I wore Chanel like a lumberjack."

Edward whooped with laughter. "You are cheering me up no end and boy, did I need it!"

"I'm glad you find it amusing."

"Oh, never mind, Pumpkin. When did they say they'd get back to you?"

"They didn't. The interview ended in a great hurry, and I was left to find my own way out. I could have run out of water and not been found for days in there."

"Oh, well. I couldn't picture you in that world anyway. You wouldn't have lasted the week, let's face it."

"Why not?" I couldn't hide the edge to my voice.

"Totally not your style. Sparks would fly."

"For your information, that's what they're looking for. A 'collision' was how this Eva woman put it. 'Conflict' was the word she used."

"Yeah, but he's probably looking for someone who looks a certain way, draws a certain way, who is already a disciple," continued Edward, undeterred. He must have noticed my silence because he did a sudden about turn: "Of course, it goes without saying, he should be seeing your portfolio in his dreams."

"Impossible. He only dreams in beige."

He paused to take a drag from his cigarette and exhaled into the phone. It made an eerie whistling.

"In my experience, what they project is never what they really are. I mean, take this nut I work for. She took the world by storm with her girly boho blah-de-blah chic; she's the epitome of glamour and good taste, attending all the beautiful events in her chiffon and chignon on the arm of her handsome art-dealer husband. The world waits breathlessly for her first menswear line that yours truly is slaving over. And guess what, Pumpkin?"

"What's that, Parsnip?"

"She's a gnarly old crackhead. The posh English rose is a dirty junkie, a sack of bones, but put her in vintage Halston, prop her against a wall at the Serpentine, and she looks like a fashion illustration. Her dealer sits in on our fittings!"

Edward's boss, a willowy, blond St Martin's alum not much older than us, courted by cultural and popular media alike, was one of the handful who really made waves in the fashion world; a visionary. Even though I could understand his frustrations, I couldn't bring myself to voice comparisons between her and Lynda, no matter how familiar his revelations sounded; it was more than I could bear in my current frame of mind, so I just let him rant.

"Sometimes her eyes roll in her head so much, she can't even tell the difference between a highland plaid and a windowpane check." He announced it as if that alone captured the height of the dysfunction. "*Where* is the glamour? I've searched high and low. It doesn't exist. It's all just smoke and mirrors. We're illusionists."

"Disillusioned illusionists," I echoed.

"At least Adriani stands for something more," he said. "There's a history there, an aesthetic, a discipline. It doesn't matter if he's not the coolest kid on the block any more. He owns the block, baby, the town, the *county*."

"Oh, shut up about Adriani, will you. I've heard enough."

"Gotta go!" he whispered. "She's back."

I was left with the dial tone.

As it happened, that was nowhere near the last I'd hear of Adriani. During breakfast the next morning, I got a call from a Signora Alessandra Arpaia. She was the head of Human Resources at the House of Adriani and wanted to know when would be convenient for me to come back in. There was a contract waiting on her desk with my name on it.

THE HOUSE OF ADRIANI

"I should have worn my glass slippers."

My voice descended spookily behind me on the grand stone staircase, like the rustling train of a gown or the subdued murmurs of ladies-in-waiting that might have been gliding obediently along at a respectful distance. High above, cherubs manned each arched support, blank-faced and oblivious to the majesty that was leaving such an impression on me.

"We like to take new people along the scenic route," said Eva's assistant without cracking a smile. "On the first day."

I watched my hand slipping along the satiny balustrade like it was someone else's. The stone was the colour of skin. This was a staircase that demanded respect; it warned all who went there of the importance of three things: history, power and money. I couldn't help thinking of Intermezzo's red-carpeted stairway to the clouds; how camp it seemed now. We passed through a series of arches, crossed the road, and entered the statue-lined grounds of another *palazzo* cloaked in the same monastic quiet but for the gentle trickling of a series of fountains. After a lift ride, we stepped out into a corridor like the one I had struggled to find my way out of: beige and noiseless, but with a row of windows on the right and a succession of glass offices on the left. I looked in, and the tenant of each looked out. They reminded me of cattle lined up in tie-chain stalls, chewing their cud, and gazing disinterestedly as the world passed by. Right at the end, I was shown into another glass box, about three times the size of the others, which housed Eva behind a desk.

"Ah, there you are," she said, standing up. "So you're all sworn in, then? Congratulations. I wanted to welcome you in person."

"Thank you. I'm very happy to be here."

"So. A few things, uh, Kathy. Would you mind wearing your top how it's supposed to be worn? It's inside-out, right?"

"Well, I prefer it this way," I said, looking down. "And the name's Kat."

"And then go to the third room in the archive corridor and get yourself a jacket."

"I'm warm enough, thanks."

"No."

"No?"

"Signor Adriani is only comfortable working with people in jackets. If he sees you like this," she made what looked like a benedictory sign of the cross, "it would be starting off on a very bad foot."

Not Chanel jackets. "I have a leather jacket here—"

"*Una giacca di tailleur*, Kathy—Kat. From Adriani. Come, I'll show you." She set off at a smart pace, out the door, past the glass stalls, and I trotted after her. "Think about tying your hair back too."

I automatically put my hand to my hair.

"Here we are." She opened the third in a row of nondescript doors which led into an equally nondescript room of decent size with plenty of light. It was like a vacated crate; unless the air in it was somehow precious, I couldn't see that it contained anything else. But you didn't enter to see what was inside, I soon realized; you went in to see what was outside. The room's sole feature was the commanding view of a courtyard below. I crept forward to take in the fountains and statues, hedges and bushes, all engineered in a surreal landscape in which nature had been neutered. Water seemed almost frightened to stray beyond the fountains, trees were clipped into submission, squares of exuberant green were corralled by black gravel paths, even the lemon trees bore their fruit symmetrically. Each element of this eerie landscape was as plotted as the placement of pieces on a chessboard, and the addition of a human being would have thrown the entire design into disarray. It made me shiver.

I was to be groomed like the foliage.

"Your size should be in here," said Eva and pressed a button.

A panel in the wall slid open to reveal a deep closet with jackets lined by colour like documents in a filing cabinet. The blacks faded into charcoal, then navy into grey, continuing into light neutrals behind an adjoining panel.

I slipped on the charcoal wool she handed me and felt immediately hoisted straighter. This jacket would make me behave; it would keep me in line, I thought. Maybe they were colour coded like in some parts of the military, charcoal denoting that I was in training, had not yet gained black jacket status.

"How does it feel?" asked Eva.

"A strait jacket couldn't feel any snugger."

"Good enough," she said, running an appraising eye over me while the wall closed up. She turned and left.

"Does Signor Adriani check how I've made my bed and shined by boots too?" I asked the empty room.

"Only when he gets to know you better," Eva called back.

❧

If only they would wear name tags. Francesca, Federica, Alessandra, Alessia; Franscesco, Federico, Alessandro...Adriani's slim-hipped, sleek-haired subjects marched by in uniform succession, exhibiting little to tell them apart. Male or female? My best bet was listening for the vowel at the end of their names. At regular intervals, like members of a strange ministry, they crept up on me to deliver new teachings from an encyclopedia of eccentric doctrines. This is a reading from the Book of Adriani...

"Never wear yellow. Signor Adriani hates it. It's to be worn by daffodils, not people." "Conspicuous Prada makes him hopping mad, especially the pantomime dame's bags and shoes." "Combat trousers are for Desert Storm." Furthermore, I was to "beware hysterical jackets" and "avoid gum disease" - a shade of pink, not a dental condition. Every time I made a gaffe, they sniggered or exchanged pointed looks. To them, I was an alien. To me, they were Adroids.

Weirdly, I retained every one of their dictates but couldn't recall the directions to the photocopier, how to work my clock-in card, which series of corridors led to my office, or how to use the highly evolved telephone system, and I still hadn't taken care of my most pressing need of all: to find a new place to live.

On the third day, I was instructed to go to the custom-built theatre known as the *Pedana,* located directly under the design studios.

"The *Pedana* is hallowed ground," said Eva. "It's where Signor Adriani has presented every collection since he started over thirty-five years ago. Its front row has seated royalty, from Princess Diana to Queen Rainier, from Jackie Kennedy to Hollywood stars, La Paltrow, La Jolie, everybody!" She stood up and gave a twitch of her head. "It'll be impossible for you to find as you don't know where you're going. You'd better just come along with me."

The system of linking corridors seemed to occupy an entire street in the centre of Brera. I had strolled along it often like every other tourist and wondered what went on behind the terracotta walls, baroque columns, and portals holding aloft such glorious roof gardens. Now I knew: the daily operations of the House of Adriani; at number nineteen, the Administration offices; next door, the sprawling PR department; across from that, the Design studio; Adriani's private apartments with gym, movie theatre, and pool; and then today's discovery, the *Pedana*, located *below* street level. The only indications of its existence from the street were the tall black gates with the name Adriani discreetly woven into the ironwork.

Safely deposited in *Pedana* and awaiting the arrival of a tardy Signor Adriani, I had plenty of time to take in my surroundings where I would be spending the coming weeks helping prepare for the Spring/Summer show. Everything was black save a lit up strip in the centre of the floor: the catwalk. Lining either side like the fruit trees along the courtyard paths of number nineteen were shoulder-high racks displaying colourful hats, scarves, and belts. Sunglasses, necklaces, bangles, bags, and purses lay in trays on the ground like flower beds; leathers and jewels, metals and silks, twinkling and coiling under the hothouse glare, ripe for the picking.

"All ready for your first *Pedana* session, then?" asked a fine-featured woman with a pixie cut, in floppy trousers and a waistcoat. Andrea? Alessandra?

"I think so. I'll just keep my mouth shut and observe for the moment."

"Just as long as you know that quiet people make him nervous."

"I'll speak if I have something to say, of course."

"Just choose your words carefully." She slipped away.

Eva appeared. "I just got off the phone with Marco." Everyone stopped buzzing about to listen. Marco was Signor Adriani's much-mentioned personal assistant. "Adriani had an interview with *The Wall Street Journal* this morning that's running late. He'll let us know when he has more information. Looks like we still have quite a wait."

A chorus of groans greeted the announcement. Three women opposite me dropped to the floor in yoga poses.

"Oh well, that does it," said a voice to my right. "More journalists asking when he's going to sell the company, if the buyer will be LVMH or the Saudi Arabians, who is going to take over when he retires, and he'll arrive in a foul temper that'll last all day. Lucky us."

I glanced around to see two women armed to the teeth, measuring tapes, safety pins, scissors, pin cushions strapped on like punk jewellery. One, a watchful elderly lady, conspicuous in her largeness, carried further munitions in a plumber's tool belt around her ample waist.

"Don't talk like that, Martina," she said, folding her arms, her chest spilling over. "Signor Adriani's going to live forever. He'll outlive us all. We should feel honoured just to have the opportunity to work alongside him."

"Yes, Silvia," said Martina, looking at me and rolling her eyes. I recognized her as one of the two I had been eavesdropping on in the coffee bar the day I met Eva. The other harmless old matron was the fearsome Silvia?

I headed for the fruit trolley where two blond women lingered. From Sales, maybe. Or was it Production?

"Not the grapes!" said one, and rapped her colleague's hand. "Don't you know they expand inside your stomach and cause bloating? Your waistline could be one and a half centimetres thicker by the weekend."

Her friend gasped. "Good God! Well, I can't have a banana—it'll throw off my saline level. Oranges I can only eat at breakfast because of the acid reflux." She looked distraught; her hand hovered like she hoped the right choice would arrive by levitation. "I'll just have water," she said and limply lifted a bottle.

"I have a herbal digestive aid if you want to try it," said Martina, looking happy to have escaped the fat lady's company. "Just add a spoonful to your water and sip on it throughout the day."

The younger woman, from Production—or was it Sales?—accepted it gratefully and watched as it turned a ditchwater brown. The world is a grim place if even the humble grape has a dark side, I thought, and popped three in my mouth at the same time. All three women frowned.

It never ceased to amaze me how in tune with their digestive systems Italian women were; it was like they had a direct line to their metabolism and were constantly negotiating with it for the best deal. Certain foods encouraged at midday became unthinkable in the evening; eating this meant cleansing with that; ads on TV for pasta were followed by ones for fat-blocking agents. By mid-morning, half the women in the Pedana were carrying water bottles filled with bile-coloured liquid.

Although I was apprehensive about working with Signor Adriani, whom I hadn't seen since the interview, I could feel the tension from everyone else too, and because we were underground, it had nowhere to go but hang in the air in globules. I was returning from the bathroom when I overheard a conversation between the Creative Director, the grand-sounding Arturo de Carlo, and Eva, that didn't do anything to ease my nerves:

"Should she really be here? I mean, who is she?" Arturo asked. Getting no response, his whispers grew more insistent. "Eva, we don't know what temperament he's going to be in. She's just arrived from I-certainly-don't-know-where. I know nothing about her. Who knows what she'll say or do or how he'll take to her. You know he hates new people, Eva. I just don't think it's a good idea, not today. It's asking for trouble."

"Arturo, don't start," said Eva. "Of course she should be here. He hired her, so she's part of the team. You've had a week to get used to it—"

They were interrupted by the sound of an approaching hullabaloo and everyone sitting up straight or rising to their feet, like a congregation hearing the first bars of the opening hymn. Eva and Arturo joined the others in looking forward. Signor Adriani appeared at the top of the stairs, fulminant. His arms jerked stiffly by his sides as he yelled, it seemed, at no one in particular. Three suited men materialized and tumbled after him, as he blazed an angry trail down the stairs taking particular issue with one holding architectural plans.

"I don't care that the store has already been built, do you understand? I requested quartzite veined sandstone, not quartzite veined sandstone *effect!* All the walls must be rebuilt. That rare stone was dug from underneath a fucking mountain range for my new China flagship. So you just go back to your hot shot team, tell them this is not what I asked for, and have it put right. And if you can't follow simple instruction, I'll find some other idiot who can." He punctuated this statement by slamming his fist through the plans, so that the halves hung limply from the bearer's white-knuckled grasp as he stammered further complications to Signor Adriani's retreating back. With veins bulging in his neck that I could see from where I stood, Adriani reached the bottom of the stairs and halted.

"Dickheads!" Beads of saliva exploded from his mouth.

He took off again. "Nothing but dickheads and imbeciles! If the Chinese government doesn't allow the import of that particular stone, for the purpose of urban building, as you so eloquently put it, then find a way to persuade them. That's what I pay you for! My Shanghai store will be built how *I* want it, not how the damned Chinese want it, thank you very much!"

With a swipe of his arm, the three men vanished. Signor Adriani came hurtling towards us. Eva urgently shepherded from backstage three gangly young models dressed in flesh-coloured body suits, as shiny and sterile as department store dummies. Signor Adriani touched down on the landing strip of the runway, his sneakered feet a blur as he showed no inclination of coming to a stop. Then, just a short distance from us, he veered right and, pouncing on a pair of shoes atop a tower of shoeboxes, stopped dead.

"Eva! What's this piece of shit? Is this the sort of rubbish your so-called designers come up with?"

Eva had opened her mouth to address the origin of the shoes but not before he flung them to the far reaches of the theatre, knocking the tower over with a kick.

"Shut up! They're ugly, make me want to be sick!"

Arturo sidled up to him, standing closer than anyone would surely have advised; unusual behaviour for someone who, since the day I arrived, had lurked around the sidelines. He had regarded me the way you would a new desk or standard lamp, evaluating it with a glance, registering its position in the room to avoid bumping into it, but, other than that, having little to do with it. Yet the soft placement of his feet, the gently spoken words, the prayerful hand gestures were having a calming effect on the riled king of Italian fashion. The great man nodded compliantly. The tension left his face. He gave Arturo's shoulder a sprightly tap and Arturo stepped back. Signor Adriani turned his attention to the job at hand, sliding a tailored jacket off a rack and onto one of the models. The rest of the *Pedana* broke into motion, people sprinkling themselves at various spots, looking alert.

"*Dammi un pantaloni!*" Signor Adriani commanded.

Six people sprinted down the four steps to backstage and, in a matter of seconds, tumbled back out, elbowing each other up the steps, and charging towards Signor Adriani with trouser options. With a nod, he approved of a grey wool pair, and they were passed to the model. Plucking a handbag from a table, he rolled it like a newspaper and forced the model's hand closed around it.

"No. I want it like that," he said, although no one had challenged him.

When he stepped back, about twelve people stepped back also. Squinting, hand on chin, he studied the outfitted model as she posed, and the twelve behind him adopted a similar stance. He—and they—turned towards the trays of jewellery, and that was when his gaze landed on me.

"Who is this? Eh? Who is this here?"

Holy Moses.

Eva stepped forward.

"That's the new designer, Signor Adriani, the recent hire. Kat. You interviewed her yourself."

Unsure whether to move forward, shake his hand, doff my cap, or execute a curtsy, the decision was made for me. He turned sharply and resumed piling necklaces onto the model who was threatening to buckle under the weight. I stepped off to the side, and twelve people closed in on him like the postern gate of the castle that kept the commoners out.

Signor Adriani began each session by layering clothes and accessories onto the model, packing her up like a dray horse, seeing how much she could hold, and as the day wore on, lifting most of it off again. I had chosen a perch in the second row where I could watch and learn without being conspicuous. The whispered caution, "Signor Adriani does not like new people", still reached my ears.

I quickly grasped the dynamics and hierarchies at work. The Adroids clucked approval at Signor Adriani's every decision: if he said "white", it was met with enthusiastic nods; if he abruptly changed to "black", they chorused anew in the affirmative. When he talked down to them, they agreed wholeheartedly, and when he told them they should shut up, they were in even heartier concordance. Their docile laughter when he made them the butt of his jokes turned uproarious when he shoved one so violently she skidded along the catwalk and crashed into a stand of hats.

I made a new friend called James who was the knitwear designer, part of what seemed to be Adriani's inner court, although he said he had only been there a matter of months; I suspected his cute baby face and blond curls had helped him gain his privileged status. But I feared for him when Signor Adriani, after having installed on the model a strange series of frills and furbelows in shades of cornflower and lavender, turned to James and asked his opinion:

"It's beautiful, no? Very modern, don't you agree?"

James hesitated before replying, "Uh… seems more mother-of-the-bride than modern."

A silence crept through the theatre as Adriani demanded a translation. Some averted their eyes, others clasped their hands to their chests, Silvia the fat lady murmured, "That young man would do well to remember he is in the presence of a legend". Signor Adriani's mouth dropped open a fraction as he raised his left hand. He seemed to be contemplating striking James when, instead, he leaned in and gave his cherubic cheeks an extended pinch.

"You cheeky young monkey, eh! Now, let's keep the bride's mother out of it!"

The room collapsed in merriment.

Alongside James and Arturo, the inner court contained a mysterious, bloodless creature called Paola, apparently a one-time muse now past her prime, and, of course, Eva, who fell in step with me as I climbed the stairs at the end of the day.

"So how do you feel, Kat, after your first day? What do you think?"

"All good, thanks. I'm sure I'll get to know who's who and what they all do in time."

"No, I mean, what do you think of the looks Signor Adriani is putting together? Do you like them?"

"Well, um, some of it's a bit demure for my tastes, maybe for someone a bit older, but that's his vision and I—"

"No, hold on, Kat." She stopped. "You must make *your* views heard. You're the only young female on the design team. You must find a way to make him listen to you. That's why you're here. It's very important." She tucked her Marni bag onto her shoulder and set off up the street, tutting and muttering "*Importantissimo*" as she went.

I had a dream that night. The King was shouting, working himself into a terrifying rage while Eva raced around him, her pin thin legs encased in graphic black and white stripy tights as she fanned the Royal Highness with sheaves of architect's plans. "Now look what you've done!" she panted. "You know he doesn't like new people." The kafuffle had arisen because I had dared to suggest adding a necklace made of red grapes instead of green to an otherwise pastel ensemble. The grapes were increasing in size, big as oranges, then footballs before exploding all over everyone, while the King, crimson with fury—and grape juice—was yelling:

"Off with her head! Off with her head!"

THE BANISHMENT

Signor Adriani did not like heads; he liked faces but not heads. He squashed skulls into caps as snug as condoms; it was known as a signature of his. He balked at any existence of breast and considered the backs of women's knees repugnant. He liked wide shoulders, a concave torso, and the rest of the body to conclude in a wispy point like a question mark. He had yet to find a woman's body that naturally fit that description, so he continued to whittle it. Yet for years he had been glorified for his innate understanding of the female form and for offering clothes that allowed women to celebrate their femininity.

I took my place at court the next day and gave James a conspiratorial wink as Signor Adriani wrestled some unruly curls into a nylon cap, trapping his thumb in the process. He wrenched his digit free, stuck it in his mouth, and sucked on it. I thought the model resembled a robber wearing a pair of hose to hide her identity. Signor Adriani turned suddenly and asked my opinion.

"Bello," I duly commented.

"Bello. Si!" he confirmed, happily bobbing on his pristine-sneakered feet.

Then he motioned for Eva and muttered: "I don't want that model tomorrow. Too hairy."

When he waved a silk blouse and demanded some bottoms, I grabbed what I considered a perfect pair of Annie Hall checked wide-legs, and Eva gave me a barely perceptible smile.

"I know why Eva chose you," said James. "She's been looking for someone for ages, someone different, you know, someone outside the system."

"Well, it's certainly different for me too," I said, grateful for an ally. "How have you found it here?"

"So far, so good. I've been lucky. Adriani has a soft spot for blond English boys, so a little of what I say gets through. But the rest of them have been rattling about in here for years only telling him what he wants to hear. This house could be so relevant. Eva thinks putting the likes of you and me against Arturo and Paola is a step in the right direction."

"But he seems to trust them."

"Oh, he doesn't trust anyone—but they're as good as it gets. They've worked together for years; they know how to massage his ego. He's like a child responding to a tone of voice but paying no attention to the words. You see, he's so removed from the real world, he has no idea what's going on. But what filters through, he learns from them."

I watched Arturo and Paola leaning in to talk quietly to each other, pale faces almost touching like two theatre masks.

"When he gets trashed by the press, he comes down hard on everyone else, never them. So we're here as a sort of damage control."

As far back as I could remember, I had looked at photos of the Adriani shows and admired their magnificence, the beauty of the pieces, especially the eveningwear in his famous finales. But what James said rang true: the styling always seemed musty, like if I got too close, I might catch a whiff of the camphor from the mothballs.

"So Arturo and Paola always work as a duo?" I asked.

"Oh, they read each other's minds."

"And is it my imagination or do they also possess a freakish ability to float a few inches above the ground?"

James laughed. "Now you have some idea of what we're up against."

I struggled to isolate the exact moment it all went wrong or even who was to blame... Dolce & Gabbana? They had shown their parade of pulchritudinous predators in second-skin satin and boob-baring bodaciousness that morning, and the reviews were in: "*Sexy! Modern! Powerful!*" We could practically hear the wolf whistles echoing below ground. As far as Signor Adriani was concerned, they might just as well have filed through *Pedana*, arched their backs and pressed their breasts against him, writhed on a pole, and finished with the splits - he was so affronted.

"*La donna oggi vuole essere troia! Puttana! Vanno in giro nude, con le tette fuori. E loro—loro vestono delle zoccole!*"

This rant that women today wanted only to look like sluts was met with loud support from Paola, Arturo, and half the assembled Adroids; the declaration that certain designers' sole purpose in life was to furnish whores' wardrobes had every head in the court bobbing. Only James and I hung back; we had shared our appreciation of the Dolce & Gabbana show within earshot of Paola and Arturo about forty minutes earlier.

Wrapping a scarf around the model's head so tightly he might actually squeeze her brains out seemed to be Adriani's method of banishing the reviews from his own mind. No one went near him; he was still sparking.

Eva, however, was frowning from the sidelines, glaring and headbutting the air in an attempt to communicate with someone. I turned to see who and, at that moment, Arturo appeared at my side.

"Listen, Kat, this is where you must step in. It's late in the day. He's tired and frustrated and won't listen to any of us at this point. But a fresh voice has a possibility of getting through. Suggest something, offer *anything*. I know what he's like. He's struggling but won't ask for help. And if he's feeling insecure, to know that the new designer wants to contribute and has a vision, well, it could make all the difference."

His creamy voice was tinged with helplessness, his body language in marked contrast to what he'd displayed with Signor Adriani previously. But Arturo had barely broken breath to me since I'd started, and I giggled at the unlikeliness of the situation: Signor Adriani, the king of Italian fashion, floundering, and only *I* could help? I stopped giggling and eyed Arturo suspiciously.

"If I have to, I'll remind you, this *is* your job. It's why we hired you."

I felt his palm press against the small of my back and shove me forward. I landed there on the first illuminated tile of the runway while everyone else stood safely in the shadows. I had no choice but to keep moving.

Adriani stood alone clutching a tray of jewellery, his thumb grazing a mother of pearl necklace as he looked thoughtfully at the model. I stooped to pick up a pair of turquoise ankle boots and tried not to startle him when I cleared my throat. But he whisked around anyway, eyes searching my torso.

"What if we replaced the slippers with these, Signor Adriani?" I held up the boots.

He looked at the slippers—the model's toes visibly curled with embarrassment through the thin fabric—then he looked back at me.

It was another first: following on the heels of Arturo's first proper conversation with me, I experienced my first moment of eye contact with Signor Adriani. That stare, those flashing white-blue eyes, about as friendly as a Taser, made me long for the carefree moments of watching from afar and flitting about the fuzzy margins of his field of vision.

"What is it you don't like about the shoes I picked?"

No one spoke.

"It's not that I don't like them, it's…it's…" I waited for someone—Arturo, James, maybe Eva—to come to my aid.

His eyes travelled down my body, glinting dangerously. "Signor Adriani doesn't like that top you're wearing either, but what's he to do about it?"

I knew things had taken an irrevocable turn for the worse. The top was vintage Helmut Lang. From his last ever collection. A collector's item.

"Well, now, what do we make of all this?" he asked, turning to his Adroid court.

With their chins pulled into their necks, arms folded, they wore a collective expression that said, "We've already washed our hands of her. We knew she was trouble right from the start."

Signor Adriani's eyes did not settle on me again, nor did anyone else's. The Adroids closed rank relegating me into the shadows. After a while, I went and sat in the second row to rest my feet, and no one noticed. I was experiencing the repercussions of another broken law: Signor Adriani does not like turquoise on Tuesdays after two.

Later James slid in next to me.

"What the hell was all that about? After everything I told you. When he's like that, everyone knows to back off. What came over you?"

"Okay. Calm down. Let's not blow it out of all proportion. Arturo asked me to do something; he thought I might be able to help, and that's why I was hired."

"Eva knows why you were hired, not Arturo. He just has to like it or lump it. He doesn't like it and saw a way to jeopardize you. And you made it so easy for him."

I'd never known anyone for such a short time and have them look at me with such reproach.

"It was only an opinion," I argued. "There has to be some creative dialogue, even in a place like this. Otherwise what's the point?"

He gazed at me incredulously.

"So I'll know better next time."

He walked off shaking his head.

The next morning Eva called me into her office. With a resigned expression, she explained that Signor Adriani had cornered her earlier and expressed concern that she had brought someone inside the House of Adriani who was so far outside its style.

"He doesn't feel comfortable having you around," she said. "I recommend you stay away from *Pedana* until further notice."

"Well, will I get back in?"

"I honestly can't say. You could try to turn the situation around, but it will be a difficult uphill climb. No one's ever managed to before."

Afterwards, slumped in my glass office at the end of the long, deserted corridor, I felt like I had been dropped down a rubbish chute. While everyone else was frantically preparing for the show next week, I was chewing on a 2B pencil and staring out through the skylight. I knew the House of Adriani wasn't right for me. Yet, having been in and then unceremoniously shut out, all I wanted more than anything was to be let back in.

❧

The fashion show passed. I hadn't been given a ticket: even standing room was full, they said. But it had been far from a roaring success, and I garnered some satisfaction from reading the snide comments of editors about its irrelevancy and lack of direction. I began designing for the next season without being involved in the meetings with Signor Adriani during which he discussed his vision for the season ahead. I received all my information hastily, even dismissively, from Eva or in casual conversation with James. My bruised ego caught me sharply at the most unexpected times, like a toothache.

"So what are you going to do?" asked Ginevra as we stepped inside Geronimo Wedding Dress Emporium the following weekend.

Just like that. There it was: the twinge.

"I'm not sure yet. But I'll have to think of something. Today though, let's focus on you."

"How are you getting on with this Arturo guy?" Ginevra was not easily brushed off.

"There's no getting on. The only contact I have with him is when I bristle every time he breezes importantly by in his floppy trousers and tight shirts." My hand grazed an opalescent puffed skirt and gave me an electric shock. "It's a similar reaction to what's happening now at the sight of all this taffeta."

"You better think fast. Why would they keep you around if you're just a dead weight or an embarrassment to him?"

I turned to her, my mouth hanging open. But I knew she wasn't trying to be mean. She was doing as she always did, getting to the point. Her bluntness wasn't down to expressing herself in a foreign tongue; she was the same in Italian. What she said was true but hearing it was hard.

"Why don't you look for a new job?" she asked. "To be honest, I could never really see you there."

I couldn't begin to explain what it was.

"Things are not just going to turn in your favour. They're not suddenly going to feel sorry for you."

"That's the last thing I want."

"So, you need a strategy to get back in *Pedana*, no? I say *Pedana* because that's where Arturo took you down in full view of everyone. You need to find a way to reclaim your rightful place and their respect. Most importantly, it has to be in front of Signor Adriani. Arturo wasn't doing things by halves, and neither should you. I wouldn't turn my back on him for a second."

It sounded like she had in mind some gladiator spectacle of ancient Rome. Fight well or die well.

"*Buongiorno Signorine,*" said the shop assistant gliding in from behind a lilac curtain. I was grateful for the interruption. "*Vi posso essere utile?*" She spoke in a curious lilting whinny, and I glanced at Ginevra, hoping we could introduce a more jocular mood to the proceedings. But Ginevra was here on business.

"You start on one side and I'll start on the other," she commanded. This might easily have meant: you take the east coast, I'll take the west, because with the proposal under her belt, she now intended to scour the length of Italy for the dress of her girlhood dreams.

The shop assistant frowned as we prized apart dresses designed to look as light as air.

"Ginevra, I refuse to let you look like a cream puff that's gone stale in the window of Patisseria Garibaldi."

"Better that than one that's still sitting on the shelf, Kat."

We switched languages easily now, on this occasion, shifting back to English to avoid offending the shop assistant. I pulled out a confection of whipped ivory that made noise like a plastic bag caught in the wind. "Call the hotline. This is a clear case of abuse of innocent fabric."

The sales assistant cleared her throat and plucked it from me.

"*Mi scusi*," I said.

I freed a satin juggernaut with pointed breasts and sparkly rhinestones, waved it at Ginevra. She evaluated it for slightly longer than I would have liked.

"Let's move on to the next shop on our list," I said. "My expectations weren't that high to begin with but..."

"You're right, it's not here. Moving out."

The miniature church bells tinkled as we closed the door. Glancing back through the rosette-trimmed curtains, I saw the sales lady produce a pink feather duster and begin removing every trace of us from her aggressively feminine merchandise.

I felt another pang come out of nowhere.

THE COMEBACK KID

I hoisted another cardboard box into my arms and descended the stairs to the sound of Chintzy and Johnny laughing in the street.

"You better not be playing Frisbee with my hat collection again!" I called.

It had taken the sight of Ginevra packing up the room in which I sat, removing the very cushions that were propping me up on the couch, to finally push me into looking for a new home. I sneaked out each day while everyone else was holed up with Signor Adriani in meetings I was forbidden to attend. Although my circumstances at work were not ideal for committing to a new lease, I had to live somewhere.

"Only a few more boxes," I said. "Twenty minutes should take us there."

Chintzy and Johnny had given up their Saturday to help me. German Jolanda couldn't make it; she was posing nude for a Danish magazine. Her elongated arms and legs could have cut an hour off our loading and unloading time. Ginevra and Dario had also shown up, although I wasn't sure how much help they would turn out to be. Ginevra only allowed

Dario to see her without heels when she was lying down, and she wore make-up just to talk to him on the phone so, for her, this was a date like any other: she wore five inch spikes and stretch Lycra, and they continually pulled each other into corners to canoodle when they weren't following each other from afar with their eyes.

When he heard it had taken four trips in Dario's Punto to relocate Ginevra to the far side of Parco Sempione, Johnny replied, "Time's money, people," and persuaded Luciano to lend us his transit van. Originally white, pockmarked with rust, and fitted with a replacement red door, it was aesthetically challenged but would do the job in one trip.

"My flat has a red door," I said. "The only red door on a pastel street. That's why I chose it."

"Remind me never to have you invest in property for me," said Johnny. "Goodbye, Naviglio!" we chorused as the van jiggled through the Saturday strollers who were in no hurry to be anywhere in particular.

I was moving to the neighbourhood filled with old ladies - the one I liked to stroll through. It was the only area I looked in. My new street was just as pretty as the last time I'd seen it, all frosted sherbet houses with half-closed shutters lined up drowsily in the sun. Unlike the Naviglio which attracted travellers, partygoers, and foreigners, this was a residential quarter where people had lived for generations. My new landlord confirmed I would be the street's youngest resident.

Johnny pulled up outside the red door halfway down. I made everyone stand in a row while I put the key in the lock.

"Ready?" I stepped aside to let them file in. "*Ecco la mia nuova casa.*"

"Whoa! You weren't joking when you said it was small," said Johnny, the first to enter. "You'll need to drink your shrinking potion on the tram home."

"Oh, move in a bit," said Chintzy, pushing. "I can't see."

I entered last and, with the five of us, there wasn't space for a stick of furniture other than the IKEA basics already there.

"Lucky I'm not one for throwing dinner parties, isn't it?" I said as their eyes travelled the short distance around the room and back to me. "But there's an upstairs!" We trooped up the narrow, winding staircase to a slightly larger room above. Chintzy made for the main feature: an entire wall fitted with closets.

"Well, here's your shoe storage right here," she announced.

"And the alcove with the three shelves over there?" said Ginevra. "Perfect for displaying all your knick-knacks and ornaments, maybe put a little lamp in one of the corners."

Johnny broke into a mince and flung open a cupboard that had rows of hooks in the door, a deep interior and a slim drawer below. "Oh, and look! A place for your sex toys, harnesses, and, what luck, enough space to store a chained man while you're at work. *Casa, dolce casa.*"

"Do you mind? Those hooks are for my hats."

I noticed with amusement how Luca's head hung gormlessly to the right. He was six foot something and the ceilings were not. "So what do you all think?"

"If you line the two rooms together, it's actually bigger than the bar," said Dario. "You could do a lot with a space like this." Dario measured the potential of all spaces against the interior of Happy Bar which he was in the process of thoroughly renovating.

"It's a rabbit hutch," said Johnny.

"It's petite," I corrected.

"It's cozy," conceded Chintzy.

"What more could you need?" asked Ginevra.

"A litter tray," said Johnny.

"Shut up. I have a good feeling about it."

After we unloaded the van, I took them for a pint to the English pub around the corner. Its close proximity helped alter Johnny's perception of my new digs somewhat, a perception that was further elevated by the availability of Newcastle Brown Ale and the sexy Roman barmaid that told him he resembled Jim Morrison while leaning provocatively across the bar.

"Not a bad little neighbourhood, all things considered," he said.

I had found a book in a box of stuff Ginevra was throwing out. It was an introduction to Callanetics: a fitness programme promising a taut, lean body while building strength, flexibility, and endurance through "tiny but powerful movements". Most probably, it was left over from one of Ginevra's numerous attempts to tease a supermodel's frame from five foot two inches of burning potential, although the coffee mug stain on page six suggested the mission was aborted in its early stages. There was something about the woman on the cover— she wasn't an Adroid, she wasn't a lioness—that intrigued me. She looked dynamic, feminine and in control, in a magenta leotard and pastel blue legwarmers.

The only requirement for Callanetics was access to a dancer's bar, and while I didn't have much in my new place, I had one of those, of sorts. The handrail of the spiral staircase continued above, all the way over to the far wall, and three or four nights a week I positioned myself in front of it and worked through the routines. I relished the sensation of muscles strengthening and streamlining, and, in the process, thoughts simplifying.

Unfortunately, the bar crossed right in front of the window overlooking the street. Revellers, cutting through on their way home from the pub, would gather to watch, as if I was enacting some titillating ritual for their benefit, like a girl in the window of Amsterdam's red-light district. I'd gather myself off the floor, march to the window, and slam the shutters in their faces, spluttering "*Pervertiti!*"

Johnny, who had never worked out a day in his life, preferring to emulate the reed-like silhouette of a junkie, took an amused interest:

"Are you back up on your stage, moving your pinky finger to Gregorian chanting?" he'd say. "Got your ballet pumps on? Frightening the elderly neighbours again? Call me if you have an accident and break something, like a sweat."

But other people were noticing subtle changes. Making no sudden movements, I put down the serving spoon and stepped away from the pasta. Like most Irish, I had been saddled with a propensity to stock up on carbohydrates, which I can only attribute to be an enduring legacy of the potato famine of 1845: the fear of ever finding ourselves in a similar predicament, having to sell our meager silverware, up sticks and set sail for a new crop made us a chunky-thighed lot. In contrast, the Italian girls fuelled up on a diet of sun, sex and jealousy, sweetened with a dollop of Nutella for breakfast, and nourished with twenty species of lettuce for lunch. They rarely touched their country's prized carb.

The results became more evident: my shoulders looked elegant, my boobs dissolved into buds and my lower body became aerodynamic. I felt pocket-sized and nimble, ready to jump through hoops. I chopped off all my hair, adding an asymmetric fringe to the short back and sides, and went from freckly brown to a decisive black. Glimpsing the Adroids' stunned expressions and double takes, I felt redesigned, made to measure.

During the solitary work hours and afterwards at home, sitting on the fourth step of the stairs, I filled a sketchbook. The Adroids no longer bothered delivering counsel; I was a has-been, a troublemaker, a spy in the House of Beige. But I didn't need them anyway; I had already gleaned enough for what I needed to do. On a Sunday evening around eight, I closed the sketchbook, unsure what to do now that it was ready. I placed it on the table and walked around it for the rest of the night.

"*Molto bello,*" said Eva, running her fingers over a drawing of a vampy 1940's bias cut gown under a boating blazer. She studied it silently, then turned the page to a mannish wide-legged trouser suit accessorized with a veiled hat. "*Very* beautiful, Kat." She looked up wistfully, stopped at a pen and ink drawing of a girl in a cocktail dress and Oxford brogues dancing the Charleston. In silence, she turned the remaining pages, then pressed the book closed between her palms.

"Well, I can't say I blame you," she said. "Most people in your situation would do the same. You should have no problem getting a new job with work like this." She handed me back the book. "I know I said it would be difficult but I really am sorry it turned out this way."

Sensing peripheral movement, I turned as Arturo and Paola floated silently by like two characters from a Japanese horror movie, pale faces gazing alertly through the glass. Both wore black, their bottom halves billowing. I went and closed the door.

"No, Eva, I'm not leaving," I said. "This is for Signor Adriani. If you prefer, I can make an appointment to see him myself…"

I trailed off as a barely there smile crept over her face, but she corrected it immediately. Shooting to her feet, she reached for her agenda.

"Leave it to me," she said, flicking. "We have a fabric meeting late this afternoon in the Sala Bianca. I will personally make sure he sees it." She snapped the agenda shut, and the abrupt click of the two magnets reconnecting seemed my cue to leave.

"Brava, Kat," she said. "*In bocca al lupo.*"

It was a common good luck greeting that translated as 'into the mouth of the wolf'.

"By Jove, I think she did it!" announced James down the phone.

I sat back on the fourth step, my plate of roasted vegetables forgotten.

"What happened?" I said. "I really wanted to stay but I felt stupid just sitting around waiting, like I didn't have anything better to do."

The Sala Bianca was at the other end of the corridor from my office. Each time its doors swung open, I'd pricked up my ears, not even sure what I was expecting: first the hurried footsteps along the corridor—were they approaching or becoming more distant? I held my breath—then the disappointing sound of them making the journey back before the doors settled closed. Did I think I would be sent for, escorted back in? I'd strained to make out the hushed voices synonymous with the Sala Bianca, but caught only the thud of a fumbled clothes hanger hitting the ground, or someone striding purposefully across the wooden floor. I hadn't heard *him*. But then you rarely did, unless he was angry—then you would hear him in every avenue of the House of Adriani, out through the manicured gardens and still courtyards, across the road now spotted with romantic tourists, his anger echoing up and down the grand staircase, creating ripples in his heated pool. When Signor Adriani provided the rage, the building's acoustics provided the transport.

"So we were wrapping up for the day," said James, "and I noticed Eva turning the desk of fabrics upside down. Earlier I'd seen Arturo take something from the table and put it in the corner under a pile of Etro prints that Signor Adriani had discarded. I'd thought nothing of it at the time. I went over to see what it was. It was your book of drawings. He'd hidden it!"

There was no room for misinterpretation. Arturo wanted to send me back to the supplier like a pile of rejected organdy.

"So I brought it over to Eva who was, by now, ransacking the room. Like a mini tornado, she was. When she saw what I was holding, she shot Arturo a look that would have—well, put it this way, we were on the verge of a major fringe comeback because it would have shredded every fabric in the room."

"Then what?"

"Well, by this stage, we'd wasted a lot of time—you know how Signor Adriani is, you have to get in fast or he's gone to his next appointment. He was on his way out but Eva chased after him."

I was ready to reach down the line and wring James's neck. He was enjoying the story so much he was forgetting I was in agony. "Come on, what did he say? Stop being dramatic, will you?"

"She handed him the book. He looked through it. From start to finish, I mean, probably not every page - it was still all over in a flash, but he gave it due attention, for him. Then he came back inside and said"—another pause—"he said, 'You all need to see this.'"

"Really? He made everyone look at it?"

"You want to hear the really funny bit? He turned to Arturo and said: *'E bellissimo, non, Arturo? Molto moderno.'* You should have seen him; he couldn't have looked any more pained if he'd been asked to swallow the bloody book whole. I couldn't keep a straight face. It was classic."

"I would have killed to have seen that."

"Then Signor Adriani took Eva aside, away from Arturo and Paola—and, unfortunately, away from my flapping ears as well—and had a word. You'll find out soon enough what it was all about, I expect."

"What do you think it means?"

"I would say our plan to take over the world from *Pedana* headquarters is back on track, wouldn't you?"

As I rummaged for my clock-in card, the machine blinked, ready to register my arrival time down to the last millisecond. It was as if we could sense each other's hostility. This blockheaded bouncer had apparently never had a day off, never called in sick, and never wavered by a second in its calculations since its arrival twenty or so years ago. If all technology failed, darkness reigned, and Adroids were short-circuiting and conking out kingdom-wide, this thing would still be down here recording arrivals and departures like a compulsive train spotter.

It blinked 9:01, even though I had been standing there since 8:52 opening and closing the pockets of my bag. I was ready to kick its belligerent head in when my fingers landed on the bothersome piece of plastic, and I slid it between its thin lips. It gulped and spat back 9:04.

I threw it a look of contempt but I had another thought as I turned towards the lift. Maybe the *'machina per timbrare'*— the 'stamping machine'—was on my side. It marked me as belonging the minute I entered, like farmers marked their livestock before shutting them safely in the field. I'd found out the hard way that that conformity was survival in here. My finger danced on the UP button. Adroids were pack animals—and I wanted to be one of them.

Back in Eva's office, on the other side of last night's events, I waited for her to get off the phone to deliver my fate. She looked at me expectantly and seemed to have forgotten our current business.

"The sketchbook," I prompted.

"Yes. Of course," she said, blinking rapidly. "There's no question that your work was beautiful, Kat. But terrible though it sounds, the fact that you are now thinner helps our case considerably."

Yes, the man likes girls to look like boys. I get it. If he had his way, we would be required to arrive twenty minutes earlier than men in order to bind and strap down all wobbly bits in a facility located next to his obnoxious clock-in machine.

"You see, you can't ever be yourself in here because he judges everything," she continued. "That's just the way it is, and knowing that puts you at an advantage. Sometimes you have to learn the hard way." Her eyes drifted off somewhere distant, and it seemed like she was reminding herself as much as me. With him since the age of eighteen, half her life, she would have seen as much coming and going as the clock-in machine.

"Anyway, the truth is, he's still skittish. He liked your work but, once slighted, he holds onto the resentment. Look how he banned the *New York Times* from his shows for daring to question a belt choice. You have a second chance, but be warned."

I nodded.

"We have our next fabric meeting today at 5:30. See you then."

It was gone six and we were gathered around the long fabric-strewn table. Seated as far away from me as its length would allow, Arturo behaved like my presence was an inconvenience he was under no obligation to acknowledge. The phone rang. Signor Adriani had been called to an emergency sunglasses meeting. Someone had reported hearing him thunder: "People who wear twenty four carat gold lenses don't need UV protection! The sun doesn't harm their eyes, dammit!" Then the sound of a tray of sunglasses hitting the wall. I looked around in alarm, but everyone else accepted this report without reaction: a couple from the fabric department were arranging newly arrived collections of fabric down at one end, another Adroid was texting, Arturo was flicking through *Vogue Italia*, discussing noncommittally with Paola the naturalness of Angelina Jolie's lips, and James had nipped to the coffee machine, primarily concerned with keeping his hangover in check.

I sat biting my nails and reminding myself that there was life on the outside. This strongly-defended sovereign state, I decided, was like Monaco. It meant nothing to the vast majority of people on the planet. Adriani was a difficult old fart; that much I'd gathered in a short space of time. I looked around, fearing the Adroids might somehow be privy to my sacrilegious thoughts. No one looked my way. Granted, he was also a living legend. My mum had even heard of him; she could lean over the fence and discuss my illustrious career with the farmer who leased the back grazing field, and even he knew who Adriani was—as a brand, he rated below such greats as John Deere and Massey Ferguson, but nevertheless, he had made inroads even in the hard-to-penetrate Donegal farming circle.

The old fart—living legend arrived. Without greeting, he approached the table to murmurs of "Buonasera, Signor Adriani", sounds of chairs scraping the floor, a magazine falling, a telephone receiver being replaced, and the clip of Eva's heels and squeak of James' sneakers as they entered from two different doors. He attacked the first pile of fabrics in a pattern that went like this: he clawed at a swatch, and with a flick of the wrist let it whizz over his right shoulder; meanwhile his left hand took up another, and sent it sailing over his left shoulder. Repeat. Repeat at increased speed, until the table emptied and catapulted fabric lay all over the Sala Bianca.

"Che schiffo! Bruttissimo! Fa cagare!" he growled, the fabrics travelling so fast I couldn't see the difference between one and the next, a shimmering aqua-beige rainbow. The blunt crack of his fingernails against the tabletop was Arturo's sign to place a new batch in front of him, which he did with a solemn but administrative air.

Marco, Adriani's personal assistant, arrived at the door, dressed head to toe the same as his master. He received a wallop of paisley micro fibre to the face.

"Signor Adriani, c'e Sophia Loren al telefono da Roma," he announced, striving for dignity amid the onslaught.

Signor Adriani strode out to the hallway to take the call. I felt everyone let out a collective sigh of relief. Long before Hollywood had embraced him, Sophia Loren had championed his gowns on the red carpet; she would expect, if not chumminess, at least a civil tone. When he returned, indeed more serene, he began to seek our inevitable murmurs of agreement as he placed his selection in rows, forming proud little rosettes of the more colourful swatches that punctuated his beloved neutrals. *See? I am capable of whimsy, of flights of fancy, of brights,* they seemed to say.

He sought Arturo's opinion of a Gerani jacquard, and both he and Paola launched into a rousing endorsement. But Adriani's eyes closed dismissively, then travelled along the table till he caught sight of me peeping out from behind James's hangover.

"*La piccola gatta, vieni qua!*"

The little cat?

He motioned for me to come forward.

In one swift motion, his eyes logged my hair, body, shoes. He was prompted to exclaim how cute I was. Eyes flashing with amusement, he repeated, "*La piccola gatta!*"

Then shoving me sideways, he addressed Arturo regarding a polka dot chiffon. He ignored Arturo's fawning opening and turned the question on me. I wasn't sure if it was a trick. I'd been here before, and it wasn't that the rules were any clearer this time. Polka dots didn't seem to be something that would appeal to his minimalist tastes, I reasoned.

But, oh, wait a minute...

His eyes were downcast, all other movement arrested, except for the fingertips of his right hand naggingly fondling the frothy lilac. He turned the piece of cloth over, pressing it in miniature accordion pleats.

"*Bellissimo,*" I hazarded. He released the fabric, and it hit me in the face.

"*Disgraziata!*" he spat. His eyes landed on me for a millisecond before darting off. He gave a tight little smile.

Oh, happy day. '*Disgraziata*' was a term I knew from observing him in *Pedana*: it meant 'unfortunate wretch'. He used it when he wanted to express affection. I pinched James's bum.

I was back in!

THE NEWSPAPER STORY

A dutiful Adroid-in-training during work hours, I whipped off my uniform almost as soon as I escaped the beady eye of the clock-in machine. My new lithe body inspired me to aim for ever more adventurous feats of sartorial daring—like balancing on a cube in Plastic in a pair of blood-stoppingly snug, stone-washed jeans, crawling with gold embroidery, and smattered with rhinestones that would have made Dolly Parton's tour wardrobe seem understated. Signor Adriani would have had an ictus.

But thankfully, Signor Adriani was far away, perhaps swimming nighttime laps in his pool, or eating a controlled portion of pasta with a small rosette of salsa al pomodoro. Perhaps he was at rest under a beige eiderdown, his clay helmet making a deep indentation in the crisp pillow, his fulminating eyes dimmed for the night, his fists slack by his sides. I was equally at peace where I was, pumping the air, stamping my foot, whooping, and hooting while the floor seethed with gyrating bodies. Wiping sweat from my eyes, I looked out across Plastic through the flaring lights. There were designers from all the other fashion houses bouncing, shaking, drinking, laughing, and dressed to stand out. I was exactly where I belonged.

"Can you get down, please?" squeaked the voice I had been attempting to shut out for several moments. This time it came accompanied by a tugging on my arm. I looked down and saw Fifi Bambinella, the new girlfriend of the club's angry lesbian bouncer, Pinky, who sat on a stool outside in all weathers, hand-picking who would get in. Fifi wanted my place. If I pissed off Fifi, Pinky would slide off her perch, crack her knuckles, and with a mafia boss head flick, she'd say "You, outside". The following week, that's where I'd be: outside. I clambered down, begrudgingly—and without much grace, unable to bend my Dolly Parton legs.

"I wish it would hurry up and be summer again," I said to German Jolanda as we stood at the bar. The same seasonal ennui descended on me last year around this time. Winter didn't offer the bursts of rain or snow I had expected, just a relentless fog that shrouded the city and a chilling damp that swirled down from the mountains and pooled in the Po Basin inside which Milan sat.

"Oh yeah," agreed Jolanda and pouted. "Those hot sweaty nights, doors opened onto the street not lowering the temperature one bit, the traffic mixing with Luciano's tunes. The place just seemed to hop. Didn't it seem to hop? Everybody all fired up on each other..." She sipped her drink lustily. "Perspiration is so sexy."

Summer and winter in Milan were as precisely defined as countries with different customs. In the summer, everyone came into the streets to look and be looked at, exhibitionistic in bright colours, black banished by all but the diehard fashion intelligentsia. Everyone moved hazily, the chaos of the city muffled as if by a big, overstuffed pillow. At aperitivo hour, *ragazzi* sipping foliage-sprouting cocktails spilled from the glitziest locales. Love at first sight struck left and right. The festivities slid into late-night round-tabled al fresco banquets with everyone talking at once. The Milanesi stormed the beaches at the weekend to tan the bodies they would flaunt the following week, and suffered the dreaded Sunday evening's *rientro,* jammed for hours in motorway traffic. For those who preferred to sweat it out in the city, the steamiest boîtes created grungy beach pastiches and theme nights. The party culminated in the big August blowout, when the city shuttered its windows, located its passport, loaded up the car, and went on holiday for a month, leaving the tourists to fend for themselves.

In winter, the summer personalities all but disappeared, staying indoors concealed behind sleek clothing, looking out on frigid courtyards. When they had to go out, they wore ankle-length, dark, quilted coats that looked like they had zipped themselves into their beds. On Friday evenings, they took to the mountains, where they skied and consumed heavy food they'd scorn during summer, vowing five days of detox as retribution. The deep cold carried every sound, in particular the soggy church bells, through abandoned squares hung with wan Christmas decorations and cheerless lights. Ginevra got a head start on the *pulizie della primavera,* the spring cleaning, because she wouldn't want to do it when spring came and the weather improved. Television replaced socializing and prime-time ratings were high as casting for the new *veline* took place in towns all over the country to secure dancing girls for the coming season.

Pale and freckly though I was, with a scent that attracted mosquitoes all the way from Africa, I still preferred summer. Yet that night in late February, it was a creature of a more local variety that I attracted, engorged with hot blood, with a prominent proboscis all the same, who wasn't so much buzzing as breathing in my ear.

"*Hai sempre buon profumo,*" he said. *You always smell nice.*

Never mind my *profumo,* I thought, as his arms circled my waist, and the familiar combo of Acqua Di Parma and Marlboro Red washed over me.

"Massimiliano."

Jolanda raised an eyebrow. "Be careful what you wish for. We have now rolled six months back in time." She turned to click her fingers imperiously at the barman in leather trousers.

After months of avoiding Atomic, I was once again face to face with its biggest attraction. As I remembered him lodged cosily in his mum's upper floors, I thought of the treasured Iron Crown of Lombardy in Queen Theodelinda's oraculum in the Basilica of St John. But I understood now that I was responsible for Massimiliano's fall from grace, not him. It was my imagination that had raised him up so high, that erected a stadium for him to play air guitar in. And it was the lavender pot pourri, like a dose of smelling salts, that had finally brought me out of my swoon.

Although time apart hadn't dimmed the intensity of his eyes, I noticed.

"You look beautiful," he said, ostentatiously viewing me from head to toe.

"How have you been?" I turned to signal to the barman and, when I looked back, I caught Massimiliano staring at my arse.

"Why did you disappear from my life like that?"

His teasing tone left me lost for what to say next. He must have interpreted my silence as a sign to dispense with words entirely because, before I knew it, he was nuzzling my neck. I wriggled away and lifted my glass to chest-level as a barrier.

"So what have you been up to?" I asked.

"You don't come into the bar anymore. I miss that. And not even a phone call."

"I thought it would have been too awkward."

"It's really good to see you. You're different. You're thin, and your hair like that—what happened?"

"Just fancied a change," I said, swinging an arm casually on the bar for support.

"Me too. I started a new band. Me and some guys that come by the bar. They're talented, and I've lined up a few gigs. I sing and play bass. You should come along to rehearsals one night, see for yourself."

"Maybe."

"I still don't understand why you disappeared that morning. Weren't we good together?"

How could this mollycoddled mamma's boy in his thirties still hold such mystery? I couldn't fathom it. I was struggling again for words when Chintzy arrived. Words never seemed to fail her.

"Hey, guys! I'm not interrupting, am I? Oh, what the hell, I probably am. You look like you are in the middle of a deep and meaningful, but it's hardly the place so, listen, you'll enjoy this."

Massimiliano spoke no English except for the lyrics of his favourite songs which he had memorized by heart but which served him poorly in everyday conversation. He stood grinning at Chintzy shouting like a sports commentator.

"Oh, *scusa!*" she said, laying a hand on his arm and switching to Italian when she realized her rudeness. "Ding-a-ling-a-ling, let the catfight begin! You know Fifi, now with Pinky? Well, she was up on the cube, bumping and grinding with the sexy model from the Prada campaign... the *male* one. Pinky came barreling in and hauled both of them out the back door where it appears she is whipping his ass in front of the taxi rank as we speak. Who wants to go see? He doesn't stand a chance, it'll be over in a second, but we might catch her pounding the squeak out of her chew toy, Fifi, afterwards. That'd be worth the entrance fee alone."

Chintzy had recently been replaced by Fifi in one of her regular freelance gigs; whether shoes, dance floor real estate or jobs, Chintzy didn't take kindly to people touching her stuff.

"Suit yourselves," she said, and scooted off with an odd coquettish little wave.

"A friend," I said and smiled at Massimiliano's grinning face. "Crazy." I spun my finger next to my temple. "Polish."

"Ah," he said and nodded in comprehension.

After Chintzy's interruption, there seemed to be an understanding in place that we would stay a while in each other's company.

"I like your jeans," he said. "They're very sexy. You're very sexy."

Maybe if I didn't visit Monza any time soon, the fire stirring in my lower belly would blaze on, thought the pyromaniac in me.

Twice a year, the carnival came to town, its formal title the *Salone Internazionale del Mobile*. Milan's famous furniture fair boasted parties nearly as flash as those of fashion week and played host to an influx of sleek blond foreigners in dark glasses, and truckloads of trendy lamps and chairs. I sipped free booze under light fittings made from seaweed, beside kitchen cabinets blasted with industrial smog, in front of inflatable tables that doubled as life rafts to be stored away snugly in nylon backpacks when not in use, and felt reassured to know that if land should disappear during dinner I could sail to safety in time for dessert.

These parties were focal points of our calendar, invitations to down pencils and mingle with creative types from other walks of life. Chintzy was the point where all events converged; she was the party bus we all hitched our wagons to, gathering speed and overheating as the week progressed. At Moooi she introduced us to Rob, her friend from London, a freelance journalist covering the fair for *the International Herald Tribune*.

"It's really quite amazing how many English-speaking designers there are here," he commented, looking out over his vodka cranberry as we all chattered over one another. "All hidden away at your spinning wheels inside the major Italian design houses... There's just something so cute about that—" He clapped his hand over his mouth. "Of course! What a fantastic idea! I'll do a piece on the ex-pat designer community here in Milan! Are you listening? What really keeps the 'Made In Italy' moving, the anonymous individuals behind the international names, toiling away unseen. What's their story? Guys, guys, are you with me?"

The group's attention was suddenly directed at Rob.

"Let me see, I'll start with the usual thing," he continued. "Where you like to eat, drink, hang out, *make* out. It'll be a modern, youthful take on *Gli Scorpioni!*"

"*Gli Scorpioni?*"

"The group of English ladies in *Tea with Mussolini?*" I asked.

"The very ones," said Rob.

"You mean ladies in the royal sense, I take it," said a cute boy who worked at Gucci.

"Whoever's talking, I'm listening." And faster than you could say 'Rita Skeeter', he had pulled a spiral notebook from his trench coat, pushed his fedora back and, licked the nib of his pencil. Actually, he wasn't wearing a trench, and he just

pressed start on a Dictaphone, but it would have been more
of an event the other way.

In the cab on the way home I saw three messages from
Massimiliano: *"Where are you? Who are you with? Thinking of
you."*

"He's keen this time round, isn't he?" said Chintzy who
was sitting beside me.

"There's a voicemail too," I said, listening. "He's just fin-
ishing up at the bar, wants to come over."

"Have you changed your perfume or what?"

I didn't go into it, but the truth was I had been listening to
Ginevra. She held aloft her relationship with Dario like some
sort of diploma and insisted I benefit from her schooling in
the ways of the Mediterranean male, despite my rolled eyes
and comments about feminism turning away in defeat from
Italian shores, trounced not by the male's machismo but by
the female's defence of it.

"*Feminismo? Un disastro!*" she squawked. "You'll catch
more flies with a drop of honey than a barrel of vinegar, *cara
mia.*"

But outdated though her curriculum was, it had Massimiliano eating out of my hand like never before. It helped
that I was learning to relate to him on a more realistic level,
without the need for the fantasy I'd whipped up around him.
I bade Chintzy good night, hopped out, and hurried inside to
retouch my make-up and wait for what my next-door neighbour, Signora Fozzi, had named my "colourful gentleman
caller".

The ladies of a certain age of Via Gerolamo watched the
comings and goings of the street from their balconies and

front gardens, and regularly saw Massimiliano leave my place, just not before noon. Signora Rosa across in number fifteen, who'd got several good looks at him through her theatre binoculars, commented that he was just the sort of fellow her mother told her to avoid when she was a girl in the sixties. The sight of Massimiliano seemed to awaken in Signora Rosa some buried fantasies of her own.

Late again!
The clock-in machine flashed accusingly: 9:20. Across the courtyard I saw Signor Adriani being ferried in at the centre of his entourage through the formal entrance, and I scurried behind a fountain. His sneakers screeched to an abrupt stop, and his yelling punctuated the early morning calm. I tucked my head in tighter and prayed. But it wasn't me on the end of his wrath. I peeked out just enough to see him wagging his finger in the nose of a PR executive a good two feet taller than him. Tossing a final "Fuck you all" over his shoulder, he sped off again, his people falling into formation like a cavalcade, and disappeared through the doors to be enveloped in the layers of his day's schedule.

I brushed myself off and headed for the stairs. I would have to sneak in unobserved and give the impression I'd been in my office since nine. I bundled my coat into my bag, left it in a second floor cleaning closet, and climbed the last flight. I inched open the door and slithered through taking the corner like a spy; the coast was clear. Just three metres from the stairs to my office. No one would ever know I hadn't been oiling the wheels of industry for almost an hour already. I collapsed into my seat. Suddenly Paola was in the corridor, just hanging there like a black kite with her tails flapping. Sitting poker straight, I picked up the phone and murmured to the dial tone. She soared forward as if scooped up by a low wind and passed my office without looking in.

Flopping back, head lolling, I stared up at the skylight. *I can't keep doing this.*

"Kat?"

I straightened again. Eva in the doorway.

"We need to talk about your timekeeping. It has been brought to my attention that you just arrived several moments ago and, apparently, it's not the first time. It's something of a regular occurrence. You know that after 9:30 is unacceptable, so I have no alternative but to issue you with an official warning."

My phone started ringing. Eva turned and left.

"Hello. Edward? It's not the best time to talk right now."

"So I'm sitting in this cute little creperie where I go for breakfast," he announced. "It's just off the Rue Saint-Honoré, I'm minding my own business when, *quelle surprise*, your smiling mug pops out at me from the pages of the bloody *International Herald Tribune*. Can you provide an adequate explanation, *tout de suite*?"

"It's out already?"

"*Après moi, le déluge, ma chérie!* What's been going on in my absence?"

"It wasn't just about me, that story."

"No, it was an ensemble piece, that's true. But you feature predominantly. And a photo, too: you and that other riff-raff you pal about with when I am not around to steer you right. I'm feeling quite put out."

"Don't worry, it was just a *Salone* party with Chintzy, you know?"

"I most certainly don't."

"Well, what does it say? Is it good?"

"Hasn't anyone else mentioned it yet?" he asked. "Well, they will. I tell you, I almost lost the suzette from my crepe. Kudos to the House of Adriani. It gives the impression he's associated with the cool kids. A PR office couldn't set this kind of thing up. Good going, Kat. It lets them know they struck gold in hiring you."

I got a copy at lunchtime, peeling the pages apart in the park. The photograph caught my eye first; it must have been one of Chintzy's. There she was, far right, smiling widely, her hand on her *Toile de Jouy* clutch. No show without Punch. Next to her, German Jolanda leaning her unmanageable torso across the table, scattering glasses, and the remains of dinner. Johnny was steeped in shadows at the back, next to Winston whose spectacled face loomed over the heads of three other designers. Then there was me, dead centre, smiling from under the brim of a floppy felt hat, my arm around Jolanda's shoulder. It was taken a few months earlier in one of our favourite *trattorie*. We had badgered the overworked waiter to take our photo, not once but three times, till everyone was satisfied their eyes were open, chins were hidden, and bellies were sucked in. We'd given him a decent tip, but if I had known then it was destined for international distribution, I might have worn a more fetching blouse.

"Italian Fashion: A Special Report" read the bold type. *"How a Tribe of Aspiring Expats Are Rewriting the Guidebook to City's Urban Cool"*. It was part of an eight-page section on design innovations in Milan, with updates from the furniture fair interspersed with fashion and the arts. In general, Rob had presented us well: a team of fledgling explorers carrying out an underground cultural colonization of dusty old Milan. But I thought "steadily climbing through the established echelons

of the grand old Italian houses" made us sound like termites. Ambitious termites.

I was quoted describing the differences between living in London and Milan, my favourite shops and where to go for fun—I was delighted to see my shout outs to Plastic and Atomic, which "has the sexiest barmen in the city". Massimiliano could thank me later. I felt sorry for an English guy named Steve who was quoted at length describing his quest to track down Marmite, gravy granules, and HP Sauce. Who goes looking for Marmite?

When I got back, Eva called me into her office where she had her own copy spread out in front of her. I smiled, a little embarrassed.

"This," she said, without preamble, bouncing the back of her hand off the page. "Kat, it is not acceptable that you are credited as connected with the House of Adriani." She had underlined the words, *Kat Connelly, Designer at House of Adriani*, and was still circling them with her pen, an inch above the page.

"But I wasn't," I said. "I didn't speak about the House of Adriani. That's not what it's about."

She sighed. "That's beside the point, Kat."

I looked into her stern little face and felt annoyed that she hadn't even bothered to read it.

"Wait a minute. I didn't discuss what I do here or anything that goes on, nor did I mention Signor Adriani, nothing. I mean… unless Signor Adriani's favourite watering hole is Atomic, which I doubt, as I've never ran into him there, then you don't need to worry."

"Here it reads "Kat Connelly, Designer, House of Adriani", does it not?"

"That's my job title."

"Listen to me. You must understand that Signor Adriani is a very important man and does not like his designers being interviewed as any kind of representative of the house itself. It can become a legal and PR nightmare." She blinked in triple time for emphasis. "That's just the way it is here."

It was becoming her standard conclusion to all our conversations.

"Does Signor Adriani actually think no one knows he employs other designers?"

She reverted to her usual economy of words. "What anyone knows or doesn't know is not my concern."

"Mine neither."

She looked up at me with a squint, like she was trying to work me out. "You seem to be having some trouble understanding. But if you work here, there is certain protocol to follow. Do you know that there is a team in the PR department employed solely to record every single time his name is used in print, in publication, online, anywhere, and verify the context of every single mention? Now they are kept busy, believe me. Do you think they want to start combing through what members of his staff are blabbing over cocktails?"

I could feel the heat rising in my face. "And how could I possibly have known this? It's like working for the FBI."

She threw her hands up. "Now, you begin to understand. So you will apologize to Signor Adriani. Hopefully, he'll be able to let it pass due to your inexperience in these matters. As you said, you didn't know."

I left feeling sulky and went to find James.

"God, there you are," he said, rising to his feet as I sloped in. "I was looking for you earlier, but they said you were late. I wanted to warn you of a spot of strife perhaps heading your way."

"It's already hit. Is it to do with that article?"

"Oh. They collared you already? I was afraid of that. He was on a mission."

"Who was?"

"Arturo. He nearly knocked me down on his way to Eva's office with a face like thunder and the *International Herald Tribune* under his arm. You could hear him all over the third floor: 'Who does she think she is? Is she here for her own agenda? Where does she think she has landed? This is the House of Adriani for Chrissake!' James looked around to make sure no one was about. "He went on about it not being his responsibility, but if Eva wasn't prepared to do something about it, then he would. Then he stormed out. I didn't even hear your name mentioned, but I just knew. It was only afterwards that I found out what was in the article."

"So Arturo showed it to Signor Adriani?"

"Oh, for sure."

"Funny how when I'm right in front of him, he pretends I'm not there, but when I'm not around, I'm all he seems to think about."

"You do seem to get his back up," said James.

A company of cats used to come onto the farm when I was little. I was only ever allowed to keep one as we couldn't afford to feed them and I chose a fat, fluffy grey tabby that I called Katie. She had strong ideas about my wanting to keep other cats too—in that respect, her and Da were in agreement. She sprayed urine all over the yard, on the front doorstep, in her favourite sunny corners, near her dish. Arturo had been spraying urine since I'd arrived.

That night, I slipped the letter of apology I'd written into my bag and called Massimiliano. Not that he had much patience for these matters. He didn't ascribe importance to what he called "petty office politics that most people bore themselves to their deathbed with", and the extent of his knowledge of the fashion industry was that it was filled with pretty girls, and that no matter what trends they claimed were happening in menswear, his Jimmy Hendrix-on-a-shoestring was always the pinnacle of dapper. But sometimes his black and white approach was what was needed: he could be an unlikely agent of sense in an often nonsensical world.

The bar must have been hopping because it went straight to voicemail. Then Jean, my old friend from Portobello Market, called. She'd found the eight page section of the paper lying open on a table in one of the market cafes, probably left behind by a fashion student.

"You are my very own style guru," she said. "I've shown this to everyone and framed a couple of copies for my stall—you remember those little art deco frames I collected? I've been telling everyone that I knew you when tutors were saying you couldn't draw, and I taught you all you know about vintage and collectibles. Ha! I apologize but I have to get my kicks where I can. So, tell me, what it's like working with the King of Italian Fashion?"

I launched into a lament on the controversy surrounding the interview but Jean, as always, only dealt in the beauty of the transaction; she didn't want to sully it with talk of haggling or disappointed clients.

"Oh, nonsense, I bet he wonders how he ever managed before you came along. He recognizes a fellow taste maker."

Towards the end, talk turned to Lynda who had been caught by some of the Portobello stallholders taking sneaky photos of their merchandise, and one had called a passing copper to have her arrested for theft. Jean received the news of my encounter with Lynda at the fabric fair with a righteous sniff and said she would be passing it around the market to "lift spirits in challenging times".

"Anyway, I must go. Keep me abreast of elegant life in the big house. And, don't forget, if Adriani ever needs a vintage connoisseur who knows her Courreges from her Cardin, her Fortuny from her Vionnet…"

"You'll be my first call. I carry your card in my wallet."

"I don't solicit business, as you know. But me and him might just see eye to eye on a few things."

If only the same could be said for me and him, I thought when I hung up.

My phone beeped just as I was falling asleep, a message from Massimiliano. He wouldn't be over tonight as they were hanging around after closing to "work on some new material".

More like drink Jack Daniels and play air guitar till they fell over, I thought. But I was glad. I couldn't afford to be late again.

THE APOLOGY

"Signor Adriani has no one with him at present," said Anna who organized his appointments. She looked at me with the disapproving expression I was getting used to seeing. "You may knock and go right in."

I knocked three times with no response, so I pushed open the door into Signor Adriani's private sanctum and peeped my head around. I entered on tiptoe because the effect was not unlike when you step from the street into a place of worship. When the door clicked shut, the space hummed with eerie quiet. It was a minimalist haven of simple geometric lines, a temple carved from the bone marrow of Adriani's vision and dedicated to his relentless creative quest. It gave me a glimpse of Signor Adriani at his most defenceless, showed me an idea of him without minders or assistants, alone in the company of his thoughts, his restless eyes stilled but his brain surging. Cave Art of Early Man, Architecture of Le Corbusier, Exotic Flora and Fauna, Elsa Schiaparelli... The titles of recipe books he used for his special sort of alchemy were lined up to the ceiling on shelves scaffolded by ladders. This nude-walled, sunlit chamber was the mortar in which Signor Adriani ground and refined, sprinkled and purified. Here, the magic formula was captured and sealed with a stopper: the spirit of an era. The bottle's label read 'Zeitgeist'. The whole process had its beginnings right where I stood. I felt humbled to be breathing the rarified air.

But it struck me as strange I could not see him. Yet he kept an eye on me all the same, observed me from every side, staring out from the iconic photographs that documented his long career. Those of when he was younger were positioned at eye-level, current likenesses were arranged higher or lower on the walls. Strong-jawed and flinty-eyed, he confronted me from among a crowd of other famous Studio 54 faces, and smirked from an eighties silkscreen Warhol triptych. At the sight of the stark Peter Lindbergh black-and-white portrait which captured him under a lone spotlight, every hair on his arms illuminated, his lower body invisible except for the resplendent sneakers, I felt my breath catch. Arms wide apart, eyes downcast, it was his signature bow at the end of shows, but that didn't stop it from looking momentarily like Jesus on the cross.

I had seen photos of this room in magazines but never thought I would be standing in it. I almost forgot the less than auspicious circumstances that brought me here. I gripped the letter tightly, checked myself for breakfast stains, and cleared my throat.

Finally his voice could be heard at the other end, behind a half wall. I clasped my hands together and waited, careful to avoid brushing against anything. When he still didn't appear, I wondered if I should go back out to Anna. Maybe he'd forgotten about me; it wouldn't be the first time. But maybe this was some kind of punishment, I thought, and stood my ground. I heard mumbling; it sounded like him but might also have been a background radio. When his head sprouted from behind the wall, I was almost surprised to see him, so much time had passed, but that was nothing compared to his reaction upon seeing me: panic-stricken.

"Buongiorno, Signor Adriani."

He looked back, but of course this time there was no one bringing up the rear, no one to brief him on his next meeting or destination. Appearing resigned, he rounded the wall and approached his desk. He signalled me forward, and I handed him the letter. Using his finger, he sliced the top off the envelope as deftly as if he had used a blade and scanned the few lines while I listened to the overhead activity in the *Sala Grande* of the menswear department. It sounded like they were herding cattle. In reality, they would be fondling fine-ply yarn or comparing the geometric patterns woven into two tie fabrics, their biceps straining against Tencel jerseys. Empty vessels make the most noise.

He gave a tight, angry nod. He was on firmer footing now, his role clear. "Yes. I understand, and that's all well and good, however..."

He dropped the letter on the desk and, grunting as a sort of place holder, went to open a window, giving me a view of something most disconcerting. The tail of his navy, custom-made silk shirt was untucked from his trousers and billowing behind him like a small near-to-landing parachute. I wondered if I should say something. He was as particular about his personal appearance as he expected us to be about ours—more so because he expected us to disappoint him, but prided himself on setting a standard. *Fastidioso* to a fault, *impeccabile al'infinito*, this state of dishevellment was unprecedented. It was almost a sign of some calamity about to befall us. But when he returned from the window and faced me, he was as neat as always.

"While I appreciate your apology, I must warn you to be mindful... uh, Kat. Be more careful who you speak to. In this age of paparazzi, no-holds-barred journalism, gossip and rumour can be very dangerous to someone like me. You have to understand that I need to be able to trust my staff. I am a private person. That's just the way I am."

"Of course, Signor Adriani. I understand. The interviewer was a friend, and it was entirely unrelated to work, so I didn't think for one second that there'd be any problem. Had I known it was forbidden to mention even where I am currently employed, then I obviously wouldn't have done so."

A mere soupcon of sarcasm, it was out before I could control it, but it hadn't gone unnoticed. He looked me squarely in the eye, that rare thing.

"As a young designer, Kat, you need to make a choice," he said, his voice growing louder. "If you want to be the subject of interviews and appear in newspapers, then maybe you should go work for someone else. Or do your own line, if that's what you're after. In that case, a discreet, respectable organization like the one I've built over the years, a place to learn and grow, with integrity and humility, is not the place for you."

"Oh no, Signor Adriani, it is."

He had begun to rattle angrily. I imagined I heard the click of something shifting, a screw tumbling out, and something else dislodging. Soon his frame was wobbling dangerously, reeling towards the ultimate point he wanted to make. I could feel it coming.

"I know St Martin's graduates are hungry for fame. Attention seeking is the only thing they *are* taught there, it seems. Well, let me tell you, when I started I had nothing; I sold my first car to get the money to make a collection. I didn't go to fashion school to be filled with ideas about celebrity before I'd even put scissors to cloth! Now everybody wants to be the next... Alexander McQueen!"

Fashion graduates of what he referred to, in a rare stab at English, as the "sensation generation" infuriated him more than almost anything else. If he thought he might actually have one in front of him, here within castle grounds, he was liable to call the guards and have her thrown in the moat to be made an example of.

"Oh, no, Signor Adriani. My only goal is to have a long and rewarding career designing for someone whom I respect and admire."

He grunted.

"I want to do the best job I can for you, and I'm just happy to have the chance to demonstrate this."

"I hope this episode has helped you learn a valuable lesson," he said, somewhat mollified.

"Yes, Signor Adriani. Thank you."

I was waiting for the curt little nod that would indicate I was excused when a movement caught the corner of my eye. There was someone else in the room. A young man shot out from where Signor Adriani had emerged and swaggered our way. He had a roguish air, healthy colour and robust physique, upon which he slung a jacket with the casual ease of one of Adriani's catwalk models.

Patting his hair, he shot us both a crooked grin, and asked, "Anybody happen to have a cigarette?"

Signor Adriani's eyes bulged from his head. "Not through here!" he shouted. "I meant the door *over there,* you imbecile!" He grabbed the young man's wrist and whirled him around, his shirt billowing romantically behind him, like the smock of a great painter demonstrating to his life model exactly where he should pose. As he shoved the stranger in one direction, I took the opportunity to leave by another. But I couldn't resist one look back: the younger man had a bewildered but compliant smile playing about his lips while a tight-lipped Signor

Adriani frogmarched him across the floor, knocking against the austere lines of the furniture.

"Goodbye, Kat," said Signor Adriani, without looking around. "Get back to work. And for the future, don't forget what we talked about. Discretion. You only get one warning."

I slipped out—enlightened, like many who manage to squeeze a quiet moment at the local place of worship into their busy day—and ran immediately to find James. We were the only ones unsurprised the following week when the swaggering one was paraded onto the third floor and introduced as a new and vital member of the menswear team. Any experience in the area of fashion design was never alluded to, but his shirtless form was mentioned often, a 'qualification' that had impressed Signor Adriani right from the moment he'd laid eyes on him picking fruit in Mykonos where he had moored his yacht briefly during Easter.

James and I joined the others in extending the newcomer a hearty welcome.

ATOMIC CABARET

The first rays of spring had everyone out, but to the clientele of Atomic the only concession to warmer weather was to wear a layer less eyeliner. Feeling light and romantic in a floral dress, I pushed through the tightly packed bodies, a Massi-seeking missile. Lately, my troubles at work had led to some disagreements between us. Tonight I had in mind the simplest of evenings: enjoy a few drinks, have a dance if the live act was any good, and then bring Massimiliano back to mine. I'd even make eggs in the morning.

Massimiliano was slacking off. The surface of the bar was filthy with spills and unemptied ashtrays, and he was nowhere to be found. At the best of times, the only things that ever gleamed in Atomic were Massi's silver rings and the devilment in his eyes, but these resembled strike conditions. There was something unnerving about an unmanned bar; I could the see initial signs of anarchy in the faces of the thirsty.

Scouring the crowd, I noticed her bouffant first: peroxide blond and big as a bird cage, then his grinning face peering optimistically around it. Whispering in her ear; nonplussed by the rabble rising from the bar. A languorous drag of her lipstick-stained cigarette was her response. Buxom, in animal print, she was certainly striking as she blinked slowly through feline glasses that framed the intricate pencilwork around her eyes; the same pencil had probably been employed for the beauty spot teetering on the ledge of her red lips.

For all the cosmetic aid, she still had a face like a ploughed field.

"*Com'e stai, amore?*" called Massimiliano, seeing me coming and putting some distance between them. "Let me introduce you. This is the super talented front woman of a performance art cabaret act making their Atomic debut tonight. Kat, this is Bombshell. Bombshell, my girlfriend, Kat."

While Massimiliano gushed about the possibility of her joining his band for future gigs, I might have attempted to shake her hand, but she was already sliding off her stool in search of a new audience.

"Ciao to you too," I said to her retreating back, my mouth hanging open. Massimiliano planted a kiss on it as if plugging a sprung leak "You look beautiful. You know what? I'm going to make sure we get out of here early tonight. I've been busy recently with the band but I don't want my baby to feel neglected. First things first. What can I get my girl to drink? It's cabaret night!"

When he went behind the bar, there was a roar of relief from his forgotten people. He assured them that he'd make their drinks extra strong if they'd quit breaking his balls. A cocktail was sent over for me, extra strong.

When the entertainment, introduced as Bombshell and the Devastations, took to the stage to the sound of cymbals crashing, the first impression they made was as classy as the one Bombshell had made in person. The Devastations, dressed in sexy secretary attire and boxing gloves, lined themselves up at typewriters behind Bombshell, centre stage, while Massi watched her like she was his very own undiscovered overnight sensation, like the man who told Diana Ross: "Dump the Supremes, I'll make you a star."

Placing her feet as far apart as her pencil skirt would allow, she leaned back and began belting out the words to *Parole, parole,* an old favourite about a woman fed up with her lover's smooth words—his '*parole*'—while the Devastations sang the male part.

"You're my yesterday, my today, my forever—"

"Parole, parole, parole—"

"My turmoil, my angst—"

"Parole, parole, parole—"

Massimiliano dried the same glass for ten minutes.

A teddy bear and three water pistols were introduced on stage followed by the removal of The Devastations' garters while the crowd looked on perplexed. At least they no longer looked thirsty.

"Fantastica, non?" said Massimiliano, clapping energetically at the end. "Brava!"

"This ashtray needs emptied," I said.

He slid off along the bar with the overflowing ashtray and plonked it back empty so that it emitted a little cloud of exhaustion on impact. Massimiliano had already caused the owners of Atomic to be fined twice for allowing smoking on the premises; if they caught him again, the authorities had threatened to close the place down.

"Here you go, *Cioccolatina*," he said, placing a new drink in front of me. "To serve you, it is my greatest pleasure. So what did you think of the show?"

I could lob that ashtray clean through her beehive from here. "I wasn't as impressed as you seem to be."

"Now, *Ciccia*, I'm impressed as a fellow performer. Did you see how she had the crowd eating out of her hand?"

Later, as Bombshell was leaving, she blew a slow kiss to Massimiliano who, catching my eye, busied himself wiping down the beer taps.

"You're my beautiful, funny, sweet *Ciccia*," he continued. "You know that. I couldn't be interested in anyone else, right?" He raised my chin. "Do you hear me? I didn't think you were a jealous person." Then he threw the cloth aside and leapt over the bar. "*Ma la mia Dolcezza! Amore! Picciolina!* What are we still doing here?"

I gasped as he scooped me up in a fireman's lift and carried me out, fumbling to turn off the lights and lock the door as I dangled upside down. He dropped me into the front seat of the Fiat where I bounced on its loose springs. But not halfway to my place, a playful comment I'd made about how lucky he was to have no boss to answer to triggered an argument that had us knee-deep in *parole*.

"You shouldn't have written that letter," he said. "You let them control you. Apologize, my eye. Shit, it was great that you were interviewed. They should think themselves lucky you're being photographed and quoted. You need to set some boundaries."

"You don't go into the House of Adriani to set boundaries, Massi!"

"Then don't work there. Leave."

"But I came to Milan to work in fashion. I'd aspire to be recognized for something other than my knowledge of where they serve decent Guinness or where to find the best vintage shops," I replied, thinking back to the article.

"Yes, but they treat you like some kind of disruptive influence when you're just trying to do your job. At least my job is fun and no one's on my back, you said it yourself. Free drinks when I want, parties, tickets to gigs, cool people. Did I tell you about the time The Edge came into the bar and shook my hand as a fellow musician?"

I rolled my eyes towards the Fiat's rusty roof. "Many times. You serve drinks in a dive bar. Adriani is world famous, considered a living legend, you know? Oh, forget it." I fumed for a few minutes then glared his way. "I mean, do you honestly believe The Edge remembers shaking your hand?"

He looked at me steadily. Don't push it, the look seemed to say.

"I think you'd only think it was cool if I sold customized rock t-shirts from a stall in San Donato market. Next to the Algerians selling the fake designer scarves."

"All I'm saying is, is it worth all the hassle?"

"At least I'm not still living with *la mamma* who waits up for me at night when I'm done partying to see if I'm hungry for tortellini."

While we had been arguing, his phone had been beeping regularly, now it was ringing.

"Are you going to answer that?"

"No," he said. A period of hostile silence was broken by another series of beeps. "I've had a bit to drink and I'm driving. Just ignore it."

"I'll answer it for you and tell them to call back."

He lifted the phone, shoved it in his jacket pocket, and I sulked for the rest of the way. As soon as we pulled up in front of mine, I lunged for the door.

"Whoa... okay. Rewind," he said, reaching over to stop me. "*Cioccolatina,* I didn't mean to upset you. What do I know anyway? I'm just a barman. It's only because I care." He put his arm around my neck and pulled me close, squashing my nose against the edge of the phone in his breast packet. "Next time, I stay quiet. Promise."

"It's not like I disagree with *everything* you say."

"Still, I should keep my opinions to myself. You know what's best."

"I wouldn't go that far either."

The evening improved when he began tracing tiny kisses along the back of my neck, and around my earlobe till my breath quickened. Then he grabbed my head and kissed me hard and long and, as I fumbled for my keys afterwards, we were on track for the evening I had set out for. I dimmed the lights when we got inside and slid off his jacket. His phone rang again.

"Are you going to answer it this time? You're not in charge of a moving vehicle now."

He smirked. 'I kind of am, baby."

I stood, arms folded, by the kitchen counter. Sighing, he pulled his phone out.

"Eh! It's my dad," he said as if it would be obvious. "He wants me to help him with something at home tomorrow. It's not urgent. I'll call him in the morning. Sorry, babe. Look, I'm turning it off." He slipped it in his jacket which he hung by the door before going to my iPod and selecting something soft. "Just one second, baby." His lips grazed my forehead before he stepped into the bathroom.

At the click of the door, I flew across the room. Sliding his phone out of his pocket, with clumsy fingers, I turned it on. My heart raced waiting for it to come to life. Four missed calls, two voice mail messages. I hit 'Listen' while he whistled inside, knowing I would recognize immediately the hard, gravelly sound of her voice; I was prepared for it. She said what a fabulous time she had had the night before, and that she had hoped for more of the same, but when he hadn't come by tonight after closing as promised, she got lonely. She sounded like she was pouting as she spoke and she called him 'A*more*'. The voice in my ear bore no resemblance to the voice on the stage. But talking and singing were two very different sounds, I reasoned. Still, this flirtatious Italian purring had intonations of other origins, a strange gap in words of three syllables or more that reminded me of someone else. Then I heard a hint of the mockney affectation, acquired in London and doggedly maintained years later under the impression that it made everything sound cooler. I moved on to the next message and listened to the start of it, but hearing water running in the sink, I put the phone back.

He came out, fiddling with his watch. His whistling stopped.

"What's up?"

I stared at him.

"What?"

"Where did you say you were last night?"

"Come on, Kat, don't be like that." His face broke into that inane grin and I backed off. "Come on, Kat. This isn't you. I had band practice." He rolled his eyes, did a small dance of frustration. "I told you. Don't you trust me or something?"

"You liar! Chintzy!"

I waited for a denial even though, after hearing the message, I knew there could be no misunderstanding. However his refusal to utter anything just added insult to injury. Scratching his ear, he took a deep breath that implied he was tapping into the resources of his patience.

"Listen—"

"You've seen us together and everything," I said. "You've even been out with us. I mean, *Chintzy!*"

"Well, you should choose better friends," he mumbled.

"Oh really? Is that all you can say?"

"What else? She's the one came onto me. She made it clear what she wanted, and I didn't stand a chance. It was just the once—"

"Lecturing me about boundaries—the nerve of you! Didn't you think that getting off with my best friend was over-stepping some boundaries?"

Although less convinced that it had a right to be there, traces of the grin still flickered.

"But how could you think I wouldn't find out? I mean, are you stupid?" Even in my anger, I became conscious again of returning to that old role of shrill female unleashing on errant male. It wasn't in the street this time, but it was in the dead of night, and disrupting the neighbours all the same. "Oh, just take yourself back to mummy, you gobshite!" With no translation for gobshite, it stayed in English while I shouted everything else in an agitated, mistake-riddled Italian. But Massimiliano looked confused for a different reason.

"Why do you keep bringing up my mother?" he asked. "She's got *nothing* to do with anything."

I spluttered in utter disbelief, my frustrations only grow-ing as each word I spoke sounded even more ineffectual than the last. I hated him for assigning me this pathetic character to play, for making me come across so weak and typical. So much so that I was compelled to draw back my foot and bounce a chunky sole off his shin. The resounding crack off the boney limb convinced me it was one of the neighbours knocking on the door, briefly disorienting me.

Meanwhile Massimiliano was bent over, his face regis-tering shock, any sign of the grin finally banished. Under-standing that I could make my feelings clearer by physical remonstrations, I shoved him in the chest and sent him fly-ing backwards. He cracked his scraggy hip on the corner of the cupboard, tripped, and landed shocked and seated on the fourth stair.

It had only been a matter of a few months, and my poor unassuming neighbours, seeking little more than serenity in their twilight years, would already be petitioning to have me removed from the street.

"One last thing," I said, standing over him, "if I know Chintzy—which is debatable—she'll have you replaced with someone new by the middle of the week. You're worth less than a pair of shoes to her."

"I don't want her, I want you." He made tentative steps to get up but held his hands up to defend his torso and head.

"Why are you even still here?" I grabbed his jacket and pushed him towards the door.

He seemed genuinely surprised. "You're throwing me out? Kat, wait! We can at least talk about it. Don't be ridiculous." He pressed his heels into the floor but, by now, Callanetics had given me muscles to resemble his, and I easily dropped him on the mat, flinging his jacket after him.

"Check your messages for somewhere to sleep tonight." I slammed the door, then cringed at the thought of neighbours rattling in their beds from the vibration. But afterwards, as I climbed the stairs, I happened to look across the street. From Signora Rosa's upstairs balcony, I noticed the little reddening firelight of a burning cigarette. I remembered a conversation we'd had in which she lamented not getting to the theatre much since her son had moved away, and thought how, for one night and one night only, in her own private box, the best seat in the house, Signora Rosa might be enjoying the drama of our amateur operetta. For the second act, Massimiliano had stationed himself as a Rent-A-Romeo under my window: "... *Amore mio*... she meant nothing... it was just one of those things... I want you now more than ever... come to Calabria with me for the summer..."

Maybe I was spurred on by the idea of having an audience, or the notion that if we were putting on a show for the street, it should have a finale. I filled my green watering can—the one

I used on the geraniums in my efforts to have window boxes as glorious as every other resident of Via Gerolamo—and opened the window to a foolishly expectant Massimiliano. He howled as the water splashed off his artfully spiked head. He resumed his petulant dance of earlier, but picked up his heels this time. At number seventeen, a head in a hairnet peeped out. Other balcony doors squeaked open, and lights popped on in some windows: a somnolent standing ovation. Before there could be another encore, I closed my shutters and went to bed. I was almost asleep, when I heard a stern voice interrupt the ongoing soliloquy at my window: "That's enough now, son, go home. *La Signorina* doesn't want to see you. Things might look different tomorrow." So Rent-A-Romeo bowed out.

The next morning, I invited *le Signore* Fozzi, Rosa, Arpaia, and Micheli for coffee and brioche. I wanted to apologize and assure them that the previous evening's behaviour would not be a habit. But they seemed to harbour no hard feelings; indeed they were thrilled to learn the details and their eyes flashed in disgust upon hearing of Chintzy's betrayal. Obviously female solidarity becomes more important in one's later years—something to look forward to, at least.

SILVIA

"Kat! Come in," said Eva. "That's a lovely hat. Is it vintage?"

"Kind of. It's my Da's Market Saturday hat."

"Market Saturday?"

"The one he used to wear to take the cattle to market. You know, to be sold or slaughtered."

"Oh. But I see you've added your own touch with the striped ribbon."

"Da's Market Saturday tie."

"Right," she said, returning to matters on her To Do list. "Have a seat, Kat. Now, I know you've got a lot on your plate at the moment. What with the tailoring and the knits—"

"And the sportswear."

"*And* the sportswear, yes. What can I say? It was touch and go for a while, wasn't it? But things are working out. You should be happy we're placing—*Signor Adriani*—is placing such trust in you."

She paused. Insert gratitude here.

"I am. Of course."

"Good. So the thing is, Signor Adriani doesn't want to hire anyone else. He doesn't like new people. And Arturo, well, he says he's too busy with special projects for Signor Adriani, and James, he's good but he doesn't have your feminine hand… well, in a nutshell, we need you to take on the dress division, maybe even expand it if everything works out—" She held up her finger to silence me. "I've already spoken to Signor Adriani, and he thinks it's a great idea. Obviously, there'll be *some* compensation in your salary—"

"How much is 'some'?"

"I'll be honest, it won't be great. Signor Adriani has frozen the staffing budget until the end of the year, but we've managed to find a little something. Obviously, when the restrictions are lifted, that will change. What do you say? You're the only one for the job, Kat."

She had that same look on her face as the day she found me in the café. Her eyes sparkled like well-shined windows, and I could see the detailed operations of her brain inside: it was like a small, neat office. On a desk in front sat a Rolodex of Persuasion Techniques (she was whizzing through it right now because the cards flipped at high speed then stopped abruptly between two options: Steely Authority and Strategic Compliments). Next to the Rolodex was a thick, well-thumbed file marked Standard Responses to Everyday Questions; a page had come loose—it read: "*That's just the way it is in here.*"

"So, Kat, don't keep me waiting."

I panned back out, onto her earnest face.

"I appreciate everything you say, Eva, I really do. It's just that I don't know where I'd find the time. I've worked late every night this week. And last week."

"Kat, when Signor Adriani needs something, it is not that he is asking. If you don't want to do it, I suggest you go and explain why directly to him. My job is to tell you what is needed and your job, as I understand it, is to collaborate where possible."

Steely authority.

"Bear in mind," she said. "It's not often that Signor Adriani gets involved in these decisions. He usually leaves such things to be settled amongst us, the team. But he named you. What can I say? He likes what you do, Kat, and wants more of it."

Strategic compliments.

"I have no life outside this place as it is."

"So that's a yes?"

Dresses, though; now there was a novel idea. I would pelt the Adroids with frivolous fancies; frills and flounces would detonate with every step of their well-shined brogues; I would shock them with a display of knees that would recall Edwardian England's outrage at the first glimpses of female ankles.

"Okay then," I heard myself say. "I'll give it a go."

She gave a perfunctory smile. "I knew you wouldn't let me down. Now there's just one other thing. You'll be working with La Silvia."

Silvia Pavone, or Silvia La Polemica, as she was unofficially known. I hadn't seen that one coming. So Eva's eyes didn't reveal everything then. Silvia was the head of the technical department and a cantankerous, disagreeable old harridan. While our dealings up to that point had amounted to her blatant disregard of me, her long Adriani career was littered with underlings mowed down by her obstreperous character, reduced to road kill stains along the beige tracks. And her reputation extended way beyond the House of Adriani, into the farthest corners of the Italian fashion industry.

Previously the dress division had been represented by the other '*Responsabile Tecnica*', La Signora Martina: a gentle, upbeat woman, popular with everyone. But Silvia began to complain that too much of her workload had been delegated to Martina, unaware that people had been requesting to work with her. She threatened to cancel all "*le piccole intese e simpatie*", the *friendly understandings,* that she had forged throughout the industry during thirty years of tyranny, and which benefited the House of Adriani enormously: the bribing of fabric mills to deliver the impossible at cut price rates; the mistreatment of factory workers so that they worked day and night to meet her unreasonable deadlines; the late night calls for favours to the chairman of the *Camera Nazionale Della Moda*, the governing body of Italy's fashion industry.

Then there were the personal demands to CEO's of mills and factories: bouquets of her favourite flowers, expensive chocolates, cashmere throws, vacation invites… This job was Silvia's life's work; whatever whimsical satisfactions she could wrest from it, she felt deserving; whatever policies she could influence by throwing her considerable heft around, she felt justified.

So Signora Martina was fired.

In her defence, everything Silvia did, she did in the name of love, love for Signor Adriani. Her voice would dip into a whisper and her eyes would mist when she referred to him: *Il Maestro.* Her adoration was evangelical. She was like a Jehovah's Witness only frequenting the anointed classes, those who were already close to Il Maestro, shunning those unfit or unwilling to wholeheartedly follow his doctrines. She believed the day would come when a sort of Armageddon would strip away all the hangers on, the irrelevant, unworthy presences, and only the righteous would be left standing. A limited number of places were available, but in her heart she knew hers was secured. At least this was how Martina summed up the situation on the day we all gathered to wish her a regretful goodbye. No one saw any reason to doubt her. It explained much of Silvia's behaviour over the years.

Meanwhile, Silvia's earthly compensation for this devotion? Signor Adriani didn't give her the time of day. Despite their guaranteed future together in paradise, she was only human and experienced frustration at his daily lack of acknowledgement, which manifested itself in a long-term oppression of her department and more specifically her three much-pitied, ever-changing assistants.

Stepping over the threshold of her office was like crossing the gulf between a well-patrolled, curfewed, regulated autocracy into a mismanaged colony of lawlessness and corruption.

Just when I'd gotten used to the one extreme, now I was to acclimatize myself to the other?

If dresses had a general unifying characteristic, it was that they were honest and independent: what you saw was what you got. Dresses didn't come in two or more pieces or need assembling, they often didn't require company; fine on their own, they just wanted complimenting. And dresses separated girls from boys—no small feat in the House of Adriani.

It was in this spirit of candidness and straightforwardness that I introduced myself to Silvia as the new dress designer humbly in need of her services. I knocked on her glass door, and she looked up stiffly; her three assistants in the adjoining office looked up too, but surreptitiously, flicking their eyes at me, at Silvia, and back to their work without once moving their heads.

"*Si?*" she said, stretching the word so that it had a nursery rhyme quality. "*Entra.*"

She laid down her pen. "How can I be of assistance?" She might have hazarded a guess, as I knew Eva had already spoken to her but, obviously, she wanted to see how I would go about initiating things.

"How are you?' was my opening gambit.

"Fine. Thank you."

"Me too," I said and perched on the edge of the chair. Her eyes roamed over me. "Well, I won't take up too much of your time. I really just wanted to come say hello and to say I'm very excited we have the opportunity to work together. It's a privilege for me to be teamed with someone who is held in such high esteem, with such vast experience as yourself."

She sat perfectly still, evaluating me, her fingers crossed in her ample lap.

"I love designing dresses but, of course, I don't have the technical mastery you can provide. And one's no good without the other—I know you run a tight ship, so I'll be following whatever methods you find most effective. I'm very adaptable." I became concerned that my attempts to be unassuming and respectful, she found condescending, or worse, too deferential to be bothered with. I started to feel like a ball of yarn under a cat's stare. "I can't wait to start. I'm sure it'll be a successful and enjoyable partnership." I threw my hands up. "I mean, it's only frocks, right? Frocks should be fun!"

She sat forward in her chair. Her mounds and jowls jiggled as if processing everything. When they had settled, she beamed at me.

"I couldn't agree more!"

Relieved, I made myself comfortable in the chair; I'd been warned by James that she calculated her command of a situation by how much talking she got to do and, indeed, she immediately launched into a monologue on her standing within the industry, her years of experience, her knowledge of important people, followed by a description of the mutual respect that existed between her and Signor Adriani, clarifying with a tremor, "Il Maestro."

"...you see, I was used to being around important men from a very young age. When I was growing up in Bologna, the mayor often invited me over for tea. I get on very well with the opposite sex. Always have..."

As she talked, I used the time to study her; there was just so much to see. Her hair, various shades of grey irregularly globbed with blond, was clipped back in a dramatic crest. Strands stood out at erratic angles, poker straight and quaking from an earlier hairspray attack. Two pieces of fine gold jewellery were wedged insignificantly between two gigantic bosoms rippling inside a silk scooped-neck top. Three inches of cleavage escaped the confines of the silk, with a central canyon that trickled off into a series of hairline cracks made by the sun. There was no neck.

Despite her reputation for chaos, she was now sermonizing on the importance of discipline: "For example, I'll always wear a dark blazer every day. It looks smart and appropriate, and I know Signor Adriani appreciates it, which is good enough for me. You'll never see me without, no matter what fashions they happen to be sporting at the time..."

I looked at the evidence: a once-sharp, black blazer, stretched at every stress point, with buttons that hadn't met their holes in years, burnished silver at the elbows, lapels, and pockets. More than anything else, its purpose seemed to be to keep her gathered together. Parts of her looked like they were sneakily trying to escape, but the jacket rounded up these mindless, straggling elements, thwarting their plans of mutiny.

She crossed one slab of thigh over the other, holding onto the desk for balance. My eyes landed on the vertiginous slit in her calf-length skirt. It must have ripped, straining under the motion of one thigh maneuvering past the other. Or was it a sign there was still a dollop of sauce left in the old Bolognese pot?

She was interrupted by a knock on the door. It was one of the menswear designers enquiring after some suiting fabric. She tilted her head and looked out from under her eyelashes. Her tone of voice changed.

"Has Silvia ever let down one of her boys before? Hmm?"

"No, of course not," he said, smiling. "I just thought I'd check."

"An excuse to come up and see me, eh? My boys don't need any excuse. The fabric will be arriving tomorrow morning from the factory. It'll be here by 9 am. They sent it by courier. Now, what do you say?"

"Grazie, Signora Silvia."

She hoisted her bulk off the seat and sashayed over.

"Show Silvia some proper gratitude," she cooed. "Doesn't she always come through for her boys?" She inserted her hand under his half-open shirt, her painted nails slipping between the silk fabric and the smooth, tan skin, her crest tickling his nose. He appeared slightly bored. "Okay, you can go," she said and unhanded him.

I rose to do the same.

She opened her desk drawer and reached inside before walking me to the door.

"I'm very happy we had this little chat," she said. "It's not often I meet a designer who knows the importance of respect in this ego-driven industry. You appreciate how another person's skills can compliment your own. I know you're a talented designer, Kat. Of course, I know Signor Adriani likes your work. But it's your *methods* I like. What we must remember, and we'll not go far wrong, is that we both work for the same man, a most important man. Not because he pays our salary, but because he allows us to be near him, learning, sharing in his creativity."

She paused. "Il Maestro." It was like Amen at the end of a prayer.

"Il Maestro," I repeated.

Before closing the door, she pressed something into my hand. It was a small net bag of chocolate coins.

AT HOME WITH SILVIA

I t must have been Da's hat that had Arturo and Paola sniggering behind me. I felt one of them take a swipe at the tie and picked up my pace, our disagreeable cortege turning onto a corridor lined on one side with wide-open windows. The sun hitting the left side of my face at several second intervals hid the angry flush of my cheeks. A nest of birds sang up a storm from somewhere in the guttering. Their bucolic chirping drowned out Arturo and Paola, but I suspected Signor Adriani would have already issued the command to have them removed; they would be breaking some law, fluttering about, drawing attention to themselves like that. Another corner, and I nearly went slap-bang into the man himself unexpectedly coming from the opposite direction in his silent shoes.

He came to an effortless stop, the grips on his sneakers locking tight with the short hairs of the carpet. I skidded, managing to avoid physical contact by no more than an inch; I could sense his relief as he could probably sense mine.

"*La piccola gatta*," he said, looking me over.

The little cat again.

"Signor Adriani!" called Paola. "*Com'e sta?*"

"*Che bella sorpresa!*" said Arturo, all smiles. "*E una giornata splendida, vero?*"

I suddenly felt indebted to the pair of them.

Paola hurried between us and half-bowed. "You're not scheduled to work with us this morning, Signor Adriani. Shall I call Marco? Are you on your way somewhere? I think you're supposed to be with I*ntimo/Mare.*" She pulled out her phone. "Let me just check for you."

"I know where I'm supposed to be," he grumbled, pushing her aside. "Can't I take a walk by myself around my own premises without everyone making a scandal of it?"

"Certainly, Signor Adriani. I just wondered if—"

"Kat, where do you think you're going? Come back here!" he shouted.

I turned and sloped back.

"Arturo, a Polaroid!" ordered Signor Adriani. "Of Kat. Front, back and profile."

Arturo found a camera, and I stood in a slat of sunlight while he glared at me through the lens.

"*Che bei uccellini,*" said Signor Adriani, looking about him, bobbing slightly. *What lovely little birds.* Then he looked critically Arturo's way. "You're a man, aren't you?"

"*Certo!*" he replied, inclining his chin. "*Di sicuro!*"

"Then why am I getting better menswear inspiration from girls? Why aren't I getting such genial flashes from your wardrobe? Every day, the same thing—Arturo, you know what? You may be tall, muscular even, but you've no balls." Signor Adriani snatched the hat off my head and the Polaroids from Arturo. "And as for you Paola, you have the balls, but you haven't given me anything to think about in years."

He disappeared back around the corner, leaving the three of us to listen to the birds.

"Hello?"

"Hello, Kat. I thought I'd ring as you obviously weren't going to."

"No, Chintzy, I wasn't."

"I haven't seen you in a while."

"I've been really busy at work. That, and the fact that you slept with my boyfriend has kept me at a distance."

"Yes, I know. Massimiliano told me."

"Bully for him."

"So, I apologize?" It sounded like she was taking a guess at it.

"Are you asking me what's the correct procedure to follow after you've slept with your best friend's boyfriend?"

"Yes. I suppose I am," she said. "I want you as a friend. I don't want him."

"Well, that's just dandy. But this time there's no refund within fourteen days."

She responded with a prolonged intake of breath. She must have thought the passing of a few weeks would ease her way back in.

"So I was right, he was just a fling then?"

"Of course. He couldn't be anything else, Kat. For either of us." She paused for effect. "He was seeing other people too."

"Thanks for letting me know. So you were just looking out for me."

"Forget him, I say. He's a dickhead."

"And what does that make you?"

"I'm sorry, Kat. I deserved that. I…I suppose I just wanted to see what the attraction was. I know that sounds awful, but can we just put it behind us? We can't let a man come between us, can we?"

"It wasn't a man, it was just Massimiliano. But that was how little it took. Goodbye, Chintzy."

Although Silvia had always been a source of endless speculation, now, when the Adroids casually dropped comments about her, I tucked them away in my mind, to piece together later with my own observations. An average haul had to wash up some red herrings, but I could never be sure which ones they were: she ate a pound of *prosciutto di Parma* every night for dinner; Signor Adriani was her landlord; she'd been ostracized by the rest of her family and cried for days after visits with her nephews; she'd been forced into exile for a period in the eighties after an affair with a dangerous man; a tumor on the inside made her balloon on the outside; she had many lovers before ending up alone.

I learnt about her methods from watching the mistakes of others. Like the new designer from Jeans who didn't understand why he couldn't pin his own garments in fittings but instead had to articulate what he had in mind, before she would swoop in with her pins and scissors.

"*Ci sono modi e modi,*" she scolded. *There are ways and there are ways.*

Samples were ripped in two and imposter pins whipped out and flung to the floor leaving her assistants to crawl about retrieving them while Silvia padded about barefoot. The foolhardy Jeans designer's continued questioning led to her thrashing her tool belt onto the table and tossing her pin box high in the air.

"Not another pin will I put!" she shouted, squeezing her feet back into her shoes. "This boy is intolerable!" She stomped down the corridor, her mules clacking viciously against her fleshy soles. Everyone capered after her, a penitent procession picking pins out of their hair, the stunned designer desperate to understand what had happened. Through three corridors, she ranted "I will not work like that! Let him put his own pins and see how he fares without La Silvia! The factory won't even take his calls!" before locking herself in the bathroom.

The standoff resulted not only in the removal of the designer but also of half the collection, the factory claiming to be "booked solid" for weeks, leading to unprecedentedly low sales, and the Jeans team consulting Silvia on all future hires.

Ci sono modi e modi.

Late one evening, Silvia and I were sharing a taxi home from the train station after a day of fittings at the factory in Modena, a town in Emilia Romagna, where a large percentage of Italian fashion is produced. It had been a tiresome experience. I had been by her side for thirteen hours, and she had talked through seven hundred and eighty minutes of them. Standing next to a jackhammer would have been considered a meditative experience in comparison.

"We covered a lot today, Kat," she was saying. "Some of the protos were not up to my usual exacting standards, but I think that's because Rita has been slacking off. Her mind's just not on the job. Did you see the way she walked off while I was in the middle of talking to her?"

She paused for me to contribute then, shrugging, blazed on. "Well, I won't tolerate it. Because Signor Prodi—we're obviously on first name terms, but as a matter of respect I prefer to address him by his full title—if I asked, he would take a meeting with me at the slightest notice, you know. He may be the CEO of one of the largest luxury manufacturers in Italy, but if Silvia Pavone calls, he responds. A greater gentleman, you'd never hope to meet. If I had a word in his ear about La Rita, well, that would be that. She needs to watch her step, that girl. Mint?"

"No thanks."

"I'll get to the bottom of the matter. I won't have disrespect among my girls, not with my years of experience and standing..."

In an age of sourcing alternative energy, if she could have been strapped down and plugged into something, her gassing could have fuelled the train that took us to the factory and back, and powered a roomful of sewing machines while we were there. I stared out of the window away from her flapping mouth. As the day progressed, her breath became staler; I imagined it was because her taxed vocal chords were drying up. Throughout Porta Venezia, we passed bars and restaurants with clusters of people smoking in the doorways but when we passed Bar Atomic, there was no one. The door had a "Closed" sign nailed to it. After five smoking violations, authorities had ordered it shut. Massimiliano was out of a job and the rumour was that other bar owners were reluctant to hire him for fear of a similar fate. I never heard anything more about his band or the gigs he had lined up.

The taxi careered around the Piola roundabout throwing Silvia against me like a sack of potatoes. All I longed for in the world was to see her dropped off on her doorstep.

"Would you like to come up for some tea?" she asked.

"No!" I yelled, much too fiercely.

The beginnings of a pout tugged at her lips, lips that were still outlined with the morning's fuchsia although anything inside the line had been smacked away hours ago. The violence with which she jerked her bags from the taxi informed me that she expected my help. I stacked them at the lift but they were bulging with her equipment, and the only thing she seemed willing to carry was the bunch of lilies the girls had scraped together on our departure. As I transferred her stuff to the lift, the cab, like a white steed to take me away from all this, sped off without me.

We got out in a dark landing where she tinkered with the various keys of a triple-locked door. A resolute "Hah!"—almost as if she was surprised to have mastered it—and the door opened into a small, cool hallway. Even before she reached the light switch, I saw photographs hanging from every inch of the walls, the burst of light revealed most of them were of Il Maestro. Once again he was giving me the evil eye from all sides; I couldn't escape. Silvia obviously didn't want to, for this was like a small temple she'd erected in his honour for night worship when daily ministry at the central temple was over. Dropping the bags near a hat stand, I lingered between three doorways, relieved to see there were frames containing other subjects too: children, other people, invites, kids' drawings.

"Why don't you make yourself comfy, Silvia. I'll boil some water for tea." Finding my way around wasn't difficult. Her sparse provisions were huddled together in few cupboards.

"I keep the biscuits in the fridge so they don't go off," she called.

While the water boiled, I found a vase for her lilies and arranged them as the table centrepiece. A postcard from Sicily with a picture of a speedboat lay on top of two unopened letters. The message, in a child's print, read: "*Dear Auntie Silvia, We are on holiday. I brought the tractor you gave me to the beach and yesterday I made the biggest sandcastle and it is still there today. The sea didn't wash it away while we were sleeping. It has lots of walls and towers just like Bologna. Wish you were here. Love, Luca.*"

I carried a tray of tea and butter honey cookies into the living room where Silvia was seated in her nightgown and slippers.

"Oh, goodness!" I said, averting my eyes. "With all these photographs, it's like a gallery in here."

"Photographs give me pleasure. I like to be reminded of everyone. Even if we don't speak that often."

"Who are they? Why don't you speak often?" I left the tray down, drawn to a group of shots in the centre of the wall, both black and white, and colour, of a stunning woman, part Monica Vitti, part Catherine Deneuve, with a dash of Ivana Trump; a brilliant portrait of blonde ambition circa nineteen eighty-seven.

"Who's this?"

"Who do you think it is?" She smiled coyly.

The eyes were definitely familiar, an actress maybe, but I couldn't place her.

"*Quella e La Silvia*," she said in a hushed voice, like she was talking about someone who was no longer around. "May she rest in peace" would not have sounded out of place.

The difference in the Before and After was the stuff of fables. It was the result of eating the poisoned apple, a Brothers Grimm tale of spinning and pinning fabric into gorgeous gowns for a thankless old king until, one day, you wake to find you have spun your life away in the weave of those frocks. The woman in the photographs wore exuberantly printed dresses belted to accentuate a tiny waist, with padded shoulders to add power to her willowy frame. Her blond hair was pulled back in a crest but unlike today's skewiff quiff, which suggested a mind in disarray to go with a body in monumental decline, this woman oozed élan. She smiled widely, as one who was used to being smiled at, equally widely, by the other finely dressed individuals around her. She looked like a woman on the brink of life's great adventures.

"When I was your age, I was very attentive to my appearance," said Silvia. "I had a wardrobe full of French designer dresses, Thierry Mugler jackets, Ungaro and lots and lots of Chanel."

"And so many bright, fun colours." I couldn't tear my eyes away.

"Oh, I was a fun character—in *every* way. Ask anyone." She laughed. "Not like today, always in black. But I like to look professional, and I know how Signor Adriani appreciates it."

It was like being surrounded by a peep show into a bygone era, portholes through which to glimpse the nascence of the 'Made In Italy' label; when times were good and would only get better; when the world was clamoring for Italian luxury and the exoticism of European manufacture, and the lure of cheap Asian production was only for battery-operated toys; when the industry was stamped with a golden seal of elitism, driven by an unswerving dedication to glamour. With the passing of that golden age, the dishevelled old lady in front of me in her nylon blends, her legs drawn up uncomfortably beside her, looked like she'd been dazzled for eternity by that last flashbulb, unable to recall how it all came to an end so quickly, and confused as to why she no longer got sent invites to parties. Her eyes were emptied of their sparkle, wardrobe emptied of its colour, and without her daytime armour of lapels, scissors and cell phones, she looked tiny.

"And you never married Silvia?"

"Married, me? No." She added five slow teaspoons of sugar to her tea. "I've known many men, even been in love... once."

"And what happened?"

"Well, he wasn't mine to have," she said, all matter of fact. "He belonged to someone else. I had to let him go." Her gaze fell on various parts of the room until it settled on the fireplace and the ashes swept into a pile at the centre. It felt like the couch we were sitting on, with the flourishing cabbage roses, had divided itself in two, and her side was an upholstered carriage transporting her away from me and maybe up the chimney.

"Silvia?"

She tore her eyes back to me. "Hmm. You know, I've been thinking. That third dress today, the one with the dropped waist and shoulder tie, will have to be fitted again before they can proceed in actual fabric. It's better to be safe than sorry. Don't you agree?" She reached for my hand and raised herself up. The cabbage roses made a sucking sound. "Come, I want to show you something." She took me through the hall and into her bedroom; it was just like the other rooms: square, unfussy, monastic. A bed, a dressing table, and two wardrobes, those old fashioned dark wood ones with three panels and the little key and lock in the central door. She fiddled with the two keys and laid both wardrobes open.

"They're all in here. I've kept everything."

Plastic stacking containers each about twenty inches deep filled the wardrobes.

"Grab the top one down for me, can you, Kat?"

I hefted it onto the bed. She pried off the lid and grabbed a handful of vacuum-sealed bags, dropping them onto the coverlet like frozen pizzas.

All her lovely dresses! Exuberant florals, once-dazzling fuchsias and emeralds, the life sucked out of them; spots, stripes, leopard, jewels, stripped of their lustre; puffed sleeves, padded shoulders squashed into ungainly submission, buttons pressing into the plastic like fingernails, labels facing outwards like identification tags: Yves Saint-Laurent, Ungaro, Valentino. I picked up a couple, moved them about between my fingers, then let them slide out of my hands onto the bed. Designer clothes had never sounded so *supermarket*.

"What do you intend to do with them?" I asked.

"Oh, I don't intend to do anything with them. I'll never part with them, but I won't wear them. I know people would pay good money to get their hands on them, but they can't have them. They're for me any time I want to look at them."

"Like the photographs."

She started to gather them up. "It's getting late. Let's get them back where they belong."

When I replaced the boxes, I saw the three blazers on wooden hangers on the back of the door, inflated with the ghost of her, along with two white shirts, and a couple of grey silk tops. Along the wall: one pair of mules, one pair of court shoes, one pair of evening sandals, all black. She reached across me and closed the wardrobe door.

"That's how you're used to seeing La Silvia, eh? But I've shown you another side, now, haven't I?"

I washed up the dishes while she bustled about behind me. She seemed to be recharged. After making her promise to go straight to bed, I picked up my things. At the door, she once again squeezed a parting token into my hand.

"*Ti do i baci,*" she announced, smiling as I held the little box of *Baci* chocolates. Then she planted a wet kiss on my cheek. "*Vedi? Ti do i baci.*" *You see? I give you kisses.*

As I made the ten-minute walk home, I couldn't stop thinking about her.

SCISSOR SISTERS

Arturo had been bragging for weeks about the latest 'special project' he was working on: Signor Adriani had asked him to sketch dresses for Yansé Bowles, award-winning singer and actress, whom *Time* magazine hailed as "the most important and vital talent of our era." If previously he was smug, he had since become unbearable; we rarely spoke unless there was no other way around it. Eva had tried intervening, but he said he didn't treat me any differently than he would anyone else. If Signor Adriani knew of the situation, he never alluded to it. But little escaped his attention, so I often wondered. Either way, our differences went unresolved, by then replaced by indifference on my part. But the Yansé Bowles project changed all that.

A Bowles/Adriani union would be a coup for Signor Adriani because she only ever wore Dolce & Gabbana, Versace or Cavalli, labels with a reputation for showstopper gowns that enhanced her electric onstage persona. No one knew if the collaboration had been requested by her camp or ours, the only certainty was that it would be a mutually beneficial arrangement. *If* she fell in love with what she saw.

So Yansé Bowles became Arturo's *raison d'être*. He papered the walls of the communal workroom with sketches and insisted that none of us enter lest we disrupt his flow, locking the door when he had to leave. He took to wearing a white coat over his clothes like he was a scientist developing something important for mankind, and listened to Verdi and Puccini (not Bowles) on a loop. Rodolfo's anguished wail and Violetta's death aria sounded even more heart wrenching trapped behind glass. He passed my office more than usual, pounding his heels importantly into the carpet. He didn't seem to be coming from or going to anywhere; he was just taking his ego for a walk. I'd stare at the point between his shoulders, that little trench between two sculpted trapezoids straining the elastane of his cotton shirt, and all my irritation would be focused there like a sharpened arrow. Maybe he thought he was stalking about on stage. It wouldn't have surprised me if he requested a wind machine. He might have believed he *was* Yansé Bowles.

One morning, as I was losing myself in a delicious reverie of unbridled sabotage, imagining the thrill of trailing a fat red Sharpie across Arturo's wall of drawings, Eva arrived in my office carrying a sheet of paper.

"I'm really sorry to have to ask, Kat, but it's all hands on deck now we're one man short. This is a list of Arturo's appointments today. We need you to take the morning's, and James has agreed to take over the afternoon's. They're mostly just suppliers. He's snowed under with this Bowles business."

"I have a question, Eva. What exactly does Paola do here? Give his appointments to her."

"Paola can't do it. There's no one else."

"I'm snowed under too," I said, rising. "How long can it possibly take to draw up a few dresses? He's making a production of it. Yansé Bowles' world tours don't take this long to finish."

"There's no point arguing, Kat. The first appointment is already waiting in *Sala* A. Arturo's cell number is there at the bottom. He says you're not to use it unless absolutely necessary."

"Does he now?" I lifted the sheet, tore it into pieces, and dropped it in the bin. "I think I'll manage."

"Kat, I know you're annoyed but—"

I slammed my office door, leaving her standing inside looking out.

The day of the meeting between Bowles and Adriani began for me like so many others, in an interminable fitting with Silvia. The only notable difference was that we usually held our fittings in one of the row of cube-like offices on the third floor, sufficient for our needs. But Silvia had awoken that morning with an urge for draped windows opening onto gardens, and the soothing trickle of fountains, for grand high ceilings to lend authority to her voice, and plush carpeting to caress her tootsies. I knew better than to ask questions and, along with her assistants, hauled everything we would need three floors down to the *Sala Rosa*.

It was the final fitting of the dress collection before we broke for summer. The factory would close for the entire month of August, and we needed to have all three rails of samples back to them by the end of the day.

Nearly two hours in, I spoke as levelly as I could: "Silvia, do you think maybe, we could finish working on the dress that's been on the model for the past twenty-five minutes before you make another call?"

She froze, her quiff quivering.

"Kat, I'll have you know I am busy on more than just your dress collection. It is my job, and, indeed, why Signor Adriani respects my methods so highly, to keep many things moving simultaneously." She swung her head haughtily and, with stabbing fingers, dialled anew.

Nothing is moving, I refrained from saying. Except your gasbag chops. Except the air churning between your lips and the receiver. Except the ticking molecules of time that lock together to form minutes, the building blocks of hours, which stack up to form the very day that is now slowly packing up its old kit bag and heading west. That's what's moving; everything else is at a dead stop.

"Yes, hello. I'd like to make an appointment with Gigi," she began. "No, Gigi is the only one who understands my hair…"

Her previous call had been to her assistant to ask the exact measurements of the pear and chocolate tart that had arrived as a gift from one of the city's best *pasticcerie,* which compelled her to call the *pasticceria* to express her dissatisfaction at the paltriness of the gesture. Before that, she had telephoned regarding the availability of her usual window table for lunch the next day at the Grand Hotel et de Milan. In between, there was the flirtation with the new head of merchandising who, unfamiliar with the complicated telephone system, had dialled her number by mistake, and been detained fifteen minutes.

A mere three and a half hours later, we finished without any major confrontations, and she was ordering tea.

"*Una camomilla* is what you need, Kat. I'm sensing a bit of stress today."

"I'm fine, Silvia. Tea would be just the ticket though, thanks."

I managed to tune her out as the liquid warmed my throat and the steam caressed my closed eyelids. I'd always thought chamomile tea was what a country meadow would taste like if it could be put in a blender and liquefied: the concentrated essence of hedges, bees, pollen, butterflies, riverbanks, midges, wet ditches, rushes, dust motes, stacked hay, and daisy chains swirling in a china cup. I was grateful the holidays were approaching. I drained my cup and reached for the phone before she got to it again.

"What are you doing, Kat?"

"I'm calling one of the stockroom guys to come take the racks."

"You don't need to bother with that."

"But the sooner they go, the better. There's still a chance they'll get them this evening and can begin work." I squeezed the receiver until my fist hurt. "If we're quick, we'll make the last van." Can't you at least try for once to make things easier for the factory girls, I wanted to shout.

"Leave it to me. I want to double check some measurements before sending them. You run along."

The measurements were fine; they had been meticulously recorded, and checked. I knew because I had done it myself while she had been on the phone reprimanding Rita for forty-five minutes.

"Kat, can you come downstairs to the *Sala Rosa*," said Eva, "and bring your dossier with all the dresses you've put into work this season. Now." That was all she said before the line went dead. I abandoned my barely touched grilled veggie sandwich, suspecting it would be some time before we would meet again.

Eva did not like the dresses, I surmised, as the lift dropped. What I couldn't figure out was why she had waited until the last minute to mention it. It must have been brought on by something Signor Adriani had said; that was usually how it went. Maybe he'd had second thoughts; maybe he'd seen Arturo's drawings for Yansé and wanted him to design dresses.

The usually elegant *Sala Rosa* was in cataclysmic disarray. It was then that I remembered about the big Bowles meeting and guessed it must have been held there. Neither she nor Signor Adriani was present, but swarms of Adroids were moving about like startled survivors, reeling from some sort of aftershock. Eva appeared from the fray, clipboard protecting her chest.

"What's going on?" I asked.

"What's going on is Yansé Bowles has just chosen a selection of your dresses," she said, referring to her notes. "We need to get a second set of samples made for her to fit in September. Let me show you which ones." She grabbed the dossier from me. Every few pages she smacked a Post-it in the corner. "This one… and this one… yeah, this one… oops, forgot, this one too… Did she choose this one?—yes, yes, she did… that one, no… but this one, absolutely… loved it." Then she tore a page from her pad. "Just in case, I've missed any, I'll leave the list with you. Make a copy. Don't stand with your mouth hanging open, Kat."

"But what about Arturo's sketches?"

"Hated them. All of them. Not her style, apparently. She was on her way out when she passed your dresses. I'm not even going to ask what they were doing here. Of course, Arturo is convinced you were trying to sabotage him." Eva walked me over to the plundered racks. "Yansé was pulling them out at such speed, they've been dropped everywhere. We tried to be careful of the pins but some may have slipped out." She tapped the page I held in my hand with her pen. "Her measurements are all there at the bottom."

"These dresses should have been halfway to Modena," I said.

"Well, it's just as well they weren't or it would have been a PR nightmare." Eva shook her head in disbelief.

She turned away but, mid-step, looked back. "The factory will have to work day and night to get this lot ready for the second week of September. I don't care how you do it, even if you have to live down there and sleep under their machines, it better be done. What are you still standing there for?" She gave me a wink. "*Abbiamo fatto la bella figura.*" She was led away by her clipboard.

In Italy, *fare la bella figura,* the keeping up of appearances, was everything. Emerging unscathed from a disaster, surviving by the skin of one's teeth, gaining the advantage by being physically attractive, these were fundamentals of business and politics. More important than doing a job well was looking like you did it well or looking good while you did it not so well. The opposite: *la brutta figura,* was social death. I'd saved Signor Adriani from social death. All in a morning's work, and I'd been entirely oblivious.

I freed one of the racks and steered it to the heart of the maelstrom. Adroids hustled by not seeing me, shouting into phones, gesticulating; others sat on the sofas, at laptops, fingers skittering across keyboards, plugging in data. All the *Sala Rosa's* plush effects were draped in garments. Stunningly beaded archive dresses were being wheeled out of the way of an argument between members of the PR office on the importance of better preparation.

I scooped up each dress, laid it on the couch, and checked its vitals. Perhaps due to her unique methods, her *modi,* many of Silvia's pins had remained intact. Only when the dresses were all accounted for and ready to be wheeled out, did I notice Arturo. He was in a corner with Paola, whispering furiously. Now that's what *la brutta figura* looks like, I thought, as I watched his hand jump uneasily from his hips to his forehead, then drop to his sides, or clasp the back of his neck. Paola laid a comforting hand on his back, right there in that well-defined dip between his muscular shoulders, and massaged with her fingers. I could have left discreetly and allowed him to lick his wounds in private. But that would have displayed enormous ingratitude for the poetic justice at work. I steered my rail straight at them and, just before impact, swung right.

"Arturo! You were so excited to meet Yansé. Tell me, was she nice? Was it everything you hoped it would be?"

Paola turned first, her hand still on his back, and glared a warning. Then Arturo, his face puckered like it had been pulled too tight at the seams. He licked his lips and fixed his eyes just above my head.

"Still pretending I don't exist? It's a good job these dresses did though. Eva used the phrase 'PR nightmare'."

"Just fuck off, would you?" he said.

"You're not even supposed to be in here," said Paola.

"Oh, but I am. Eva called me to come get the dresses Yansé chose."

Arturo's face tensed further.

"So go do it," said Paola.

"Already done. I just wanted to come over and say better luck next time. No one can say you didn't put in the work. You were at it for what felt like weeks!"

He shot off across the room. Paola scowled and went after him, skirts rustling. "It's obvious she put those dresses here on purpose," I heard her say as she threw herself ahead to open the door for him.

I swung into reverse and headed for the other exit. Giddily, I pulled the rack through the courtyard, wheels bouncing off the pebbles, too impatient to call the stockroom for help or to follow the paths. A breeze whisked the hem of a fuchsia dress high in the air, spreading it brazenly against the calm blue sky before releasing it with a flutter against the red of the roof tiles and the stone of the *palazzo*. It resembled a dame of questionable repute kicking her heels up and flashing her knickers at her host after successfully passing herself off as a member of polite society.

The service lift was too slow, so I squeezed inside the smaller, faster one. Ping! I tumbled back out, steering carelessly, taking the corners with little concern for who might be coming in the opposite direction. Forgetting to knock, I announced my arrival by swinging open Silvia's door and crashing against the doorframes.

"*Cavolo*, Kat!" she said, standing up.

"*Cavolo*, Silvia!" I said. "*Ca-vo-lo!*"

Instead of the expletive '*cazzo*', she used '*cavolo*'. Cabbage. She could talk with the menswear team at excruciating length about their penises, but cursing was the one area in which she was prudish.

"What's come over you, Kat?"

"You'll never guess. You'd better sit down."

"Whatever it is, child, there's no need to take the door off its hinges. Arriving in here as wild as a gust of wind. Lucky I didn't have anyone important with me. And at this hour of the day, it's quite possible I would have. What were you thinking?"

"No time for thinking, Silvia! We have too much to do. Yansé Bowles wants to wear our dresses! Look!" I flung my arm out.

"Well, why didn't you say so?" she said, standing. "Who'd have expected that? And I thought that Arturo chap had it all under control, the way he was tap-dancing about. Let's take a look." She pulled out the sapphire jersey to examine the scale of the work. "This one will need to be resampled to her measurements. I mean, jersey yields but that girl... eh, she's all of a curve." She studied the notes on another. "Deepen V, two inches; shorten skirt, four; scoop out the back a further two... There'll be nothing left!" she hooted, and her whole upper body jiggled with mirth.

"You don't seem too surprised by all this," I said.

"When you get to my age, I tell you, there are few surprises. My motto is 'Expect nothing, be prepared for everything.' You should remember that."

I noticed she was puffing out her chest.

"You had a hand in this, didn't you?"

"You want to be careful who you're accusing."

"You left those dresses there. But how did you know she would be in that room?"

"If I had needed to, that wouldn't have been hard to find out." She looked at me from the corner of her eye. "If you were someone with my connections, that is."

"And I thought you were losing your marbles."

"My faculties are getting sharper with every passing year, my girl." She thrust her chest up over folded arms. "It's not what you know, Kat, it's who you know. I'm sick telling you that. When will you learn?" She squeezed until one bosom erupted jubilantly above the other. "I knew those dresses you designed were fit for a star. Turns out we had one, right there in the *Sala Rosa*." She was hugging herself.

"I don't know what to say. Thank you, Silvia. You've ruined Arturo's year! That was the nicest present anyone could have given me."

"There was nothing nice about it. You'd never have those dresses if it wasn't for me—and now I'll have the girls at the factory eating out of my hand. There's so much to do, you'll be cursing me for ever letting that Bowles creature lay eyes on them. So you better just come over here and give me a hug."

I had just time to gulp down one deep breath before I was plunged between those two great orbs and everything went dark.

NAPOLI

While the rest of the House of Adriani wound down for the summer, and Signor Adriani had already left to cruise the Mediterranean with half the menswear department in tow, and some devil-may-care Adroids, courageous in his absence, went ambling about without jackets, Silvia and I were working overtime. We made five trips to Modena to inspect sampling, including three nights sharing a hotel room because Silvia announced a sudden fear of the dark. She snored like a drunken pig farmer, hard to listen to even in repose.

Bowles' measurements were a configuration of magic numbers, a secret code. The samples assumed a sassy S pose even in their unfinished state, as if they were already inhabited by her stage presence, representing her while she took care of business elsewhere. Hanging next to them, the samples from the House of Adriani collection looked prepubescent.

"Yansé is a lot more *bouncy* than our usual girls," I joked with the dead-tired factory girls who didn't crack a smile. I told myself it was because their English wasn't good enough. On my last day, none of them knew if they'd even get a holiday. The factory would close, as was the custom, but 'Silvia's girls' were expected in until otherwise notified.

I got back from the train station late to find Edward at my door, perched on top of his suitcase, and smoking. There was a roundness to his face and shoulders that I'd never seen him sport before—it turned out it wasn't intentional, or welcome.

"I went back on the nicotine patches, but the only way I could get around the oral fixation was to shove Snickers bars in my gob. As you can see," he waved his cigarette, "I'm taking the necessary steps to be nice and trim for the wedding, don't worry. Oh, I'm hell-bent on having some fun, aren't you?"

The next morning, we would fly south for a few weeks' holiday culminating in Ginevra and Dario's wedding.

"To tell the truth, I'm knackered and haven't packed a thing."

He wheeled his suitcase into the bathroom as there was no room for it elsewhere. "Fear not. Leave it to me," he said. "I'm fresh as a daisy and just glad to be free. Give me a general idea where everything is, and I'll take it from there. I know your style better than you know it yourself. Who knows, I might even improve on it, if you pop open this bottle of wine."

"You're an angel."

I ordered a pizza while he rummaged about above.

"You'll be a porcelain Celtic goddess swept up on the Mediterranean beaches by day and a moonstruck femme fatale by night. How does that sound?"

"Fabulous!" I called and took a few sips of wine. The last thing I heard before I nodded off on the couch was: "...every eventuality covered in this one small case... like Grace Kelly... in *Rear Window...*"

For the next three weeks I would struggle to make outfits out of three mirrored sarongs, gold YSL sandals, a transparent white shirt, thirteen bikinis, a beaded boob tube, a studded belt, some *Dame Edna* sunglasses, an antique spider brooch, and a turban.

"I can't help it if he liked me, Edward. Get over it."

"He was looking at me first."

"You think everyone's looking at you."

He stopped to place his starlet-sized sunglasses onto his flaking nose. We had been bickering like this since we arrived in Naples.

"We have to come to some arrangement," he said. "We won't make it to Monteceleste if this keeps up."

"I never realized you were so competitive."

"Blame the French. Since Pascal and I split, I've realized they're just not my type. Then I come here, and they're all Huckleberry Finn in tight jeans."

It had started out peaceably enough. Sipping a lunchtime cocktail in Piazza Bellini, I was approached by a green-eyed native I'd been swapping flirtatious looks with for twenty minutes. Unfortunately, Edward had been equally excited to see him leave his gang of friends and expected me to make myself scarce, "instead of practically hopping onto his knee."

"Oh, never mind, there are plenty more where he came from," reasoned Edward. "This place is chock-full of gorgeous hooligans just reeking of trouble."

Napoli, a modern-day crime capital ran by generations of Mafiosi, and a stunning historic port town built on centuries of invasions, boasted a particular strain of southern Italian, not so much stallion as tomcat: buttery gold skin, light eyes, tawny hair, but turbocharged with testosterone, quick thinking, and a scrappy dialect. I imagined their chat up would be the same whether they meant to rob you or impregnate you. It was pointless grasping for a familiar word here and there because they wouldn't be men of their word anyway. But they were still more captivating than the bay, the castle, or the thin crust Regina.

I met Nando on our third day as I was photographing the view from outside our *pensione*. He offered to take a photo with me in it, we got talking, and then went for a stroll through the little *vicoli*, laundry flapping above our heads like bunting. The rooms of the overpopulated houses were so close to the street that some people chose to watch TV from an armchair outside, catching the evening's national programming as well as the neighbourhood's comings and goings. I squealed in horror as a sleepy senior citizen nearly got flattened during Wheel of Fortune by a speeding *motorino*. But the old guy didn't even uncross his legs, probably more disturbed by my outburst than anything else.

When Nando finished laughing, he said, "Have dinner with me."

I called Edward but his phone was still switched off. I hadn't heard from him since that morning, when I decided to sleep late, and he headed off to a museum.

Nando's eyes were so pale, it was like gazing into shallow water. I felt I could see into every corner of him, whereas the Calabrese eyes I'd recently spent too much time looking into had left me endlessly wondering, no end to their inky fathoms. Just as Nando had finished paying for dinner and offered to walk me back, he got a call from his grandma: she lived alone, had taken a tumble and needed his help.

"But can I see you tomorrow?" he asked. "I'll take you for a drive along the coast."

"Okay," I said, swooning.

I returned to the *pensione* to find Edward collapsed in the middle of the floor with his bags upturned around him.

"Oh, thank God you're back. I've been burglarized!"

"What happened?"

"It was a guy I had lunch with, I know it. He cleaned me out! Money, cards, phone, everything—he even took my passport!" He started flinging his loose belongings at the wall. "What am I going to do?"

I slid onto the floor beside him. "Well, calm down and stop throwing things for a start. It's not the end of the world. Now, have you cancelled your cards?"

He nodded.

"Well done. How much money did you lose?"

"About three hundred euro."

"Okay, well, I have about that in my purse. I can give you half to keep you going. We're not leaving the country, so you don't need your passport. See? We'll be alright." I grabbed my bag off the bed and unzipped the front pocket. "Who was this asshole? Haven't I told you to be careful?"

"I know. I should have *cretino* written across my forehead."

"It could happen to anyone." I opened the other pockets.

"It's only been three days," he said, "but I know this town'll be the ruination of me."

"It must be in my jacket." I went over to the bed.

"Right outside, practically on the doorstep, he was. And he seemed so nice."

After emptying out the contents of my bag, I flopped against the headboard. "Good God almighty and Holy Moses."

"What?"

Make up, guide books, keys, sun block, Frizz-ease, all spread out on the bedspread. But where was my wallet? "What did you say his name was?" I asked.

"Nando."

I closed my eyes. "We're both *cretini*."

"You met him too?"

"I don't believe it, there was a jealous tone to your voice."

"There was not!"

While I stared at my belongings on the bed, I could feel Edward staring at me.

"Where did you have dinner?" he asked.

"*La Trattoria del Pesce,* along the seafront."

"Where we had lunch. Did his dad need the car?"

"No. His grandmother had a fall."

"The crooked little sod."

"Right. Well, that's that. We have no money."

"True, but you know, Kat, you've made me feel heaps better. At least I wasn't the only mug taken in by him." A sudden realization flitted over his face. "Wait a minute!" He crossed the room to fish about in yesterday's clothes. He pulled some bills from his shorts. "Forgot about this," he said and started counting. "One hundred and eighty seven euro! Kat, we're saved! Now I won't have to sell you to the locals for half the price of a good milking goat."

The next morning we rose early. Edward was in much better spirits. We tried to place a complaint with the owner of the *pensione* about the ne'er-do-wells that roamed the grounds, but she led us to a sign by the stairs that read in five languages: "Tourists, be careful. Pickpockets operate in this area."

After breakfast, included thankfully in our upfront payment, we set off down hills so steep and constant that we felt six packs forming just from the effort of keeping ourselves upright. Sometimes, the streets turned into steps of fifty or sixty stone slabs leading down to the next descent. We were winded while elderly *Napolitani* tramped energetically by in the opposite direction, toting groceries and children, the women in heavy black clothes.

"Fresh tripe! Get your day's tripe here!" yelled a man in a stained apron whose tenement *tripperia* was at a junction where people milled around a cluster of stalls.

"This is more like it, isn't it?" I said. "Experiencing a typical morning in Napoli, like a pair of locals." I turned to find Edward wasn't beside me. I scanned the market and saw him back at a leather goods stall. Judging by the frown on the stallholder's face and the confusion on Edward's, their exchange wasn't a happy one. As I got near, I saw Edward shrug helplessly, repeating *"Io non capisco"*, a belt partway threaded through the waistband of his shorts. The stall holder, shaking his head, pushed Edward's hand away, and the fifty euro note it contained.

"E falsa—una banconota falsa! Non la voglio, io! Non la prendo, scemo! Dai. Via da qua!"

"What's his problem?" asked Edward. "I don't understand his accent. It's like he doesn't want to sell me the thing."

"He says it's a false fifty. Where'd you get it?"

"From the guy on the street selling cigarettes." He slid the crisp orange note out of the man's hand and looked at it with disappointment, then passed it to me.

"What do I know?" I said. "It looks fine, but he's not going to lie, is he?"

"Oh, Kat, I'll get some money wired this afternoon," he said, caressing the belt.

I handed over fifty euro. But the man's shouting escalated, and other stallholders began raising their heads. The owner of the next stall stepped over and examined the second note, holding it to the light and pursing his lips.

"Oh yes, It's a particularly good one," he said. "Practically artistry."

"Bloody foreign thieves," railed his neighbour. "Worse than anything we have at home."

A *carabinieri* officer stepped up and asked what the problem was.

"Give back the belt, Edward," I said.

"The young lady and gentleman tried to pay with counterfeit cash, Officer," said the second seller, triumphantly handing the notes over. "You'd swear it was the real thing."

"We had no idea," I said.

The officer looked us both over, asked for ID.

"You have to admit, their best bet was to try and pass it on," said the second seller to the first. "They go to the police, they look like the criminals. They go to the bank, they spend all afternoon filling in forms. And either way, they leave poorer."

"Come on, come on. Your ID, please." The *carabinieri* officer made impatient gestures with his hand.

"Our passports were stolen yesterday," I explained. "Someone called Nando. He also took money, my friend's cell phone—"

"Driver's licence. Identity card."

Before we knew it, the officer had lost patience and was piling us into a Panda that matched his uniform and ferrying us to the local *carabinieri* station.

"That's it. No more fraternizing with strange men," I said. "Ever. We will look at churches and eat gelato."

"At this point I prefer the French," said Edward.

"Don't be ridiculous."

"How long d'you think they'll keep us here?"

I didn't dare guess. The pace of activity in that particular law enforcement headquarters of that particular crime capital was anaesthetizing. I got up and approached an officer who was standing on one leg, his other laced through the back of a chair, dropping a fistful of nuts into his mouth one at a time.

"Excuse me, do you know how much longer we'll have to stay here?"

His colleagues all stopped talking and looked me over like they were seeing me in the *piazza* for the first time.

"Signorina, can you step back behind that line?"

I was guided backwards by two of them.

"Okay. Danger averted. I'm behind the line. I just wanted to know when we can leave."

"The *maresciallo* has gone out for lunch. He must sign some papers, and then you'll be allowed to go."

"Can't someone else sign them?"

"No. Take a seat."

Four and a half hours later, we walked out carrying a slip of paper with our names, addresses, nationality, nature of misdemeanor, *maresciallo's* signature, and an official stamp. As souvenirs of Napoli we thought them better than any postcard. We stood clutching our bags in Piazza Mercato, a marketplace famously little changed from Roman times, while the traffic roared, men talked like auctioneers, women sauntered provocatively, and the air seethed with *menefreghismo:* 'fuckyouism'.

"Let's go see if this'll get us a drink," I said, pulling out our last fake fifty.

A barman accepted the fifty, distracted during the *aperitivo* rush, so we had a little money until new funds arrived. We figured it would stretch farther away from the city, and the next morning we headed for Capri. I expected to see descendants of Brigitte Bardot and Audrey Hepburn, hopping off sailboats, flitting along bougainvillea-lined walks in striped tops and wide-brimmed hats. Instead, I saw grotesque subjects of an embalmment process that had stepped out of the formaldehyde early, painted their faces, and donned teenagers' clothing.

"*Dietro, liceo. Davanti, museo,*" commented Edward.

The women of Capri, suntanned, slim, with their golden hair rippling in the sun, exuded youth from afar. Up close, they were relics clutching with sheer desperation onto the last vestiges of the bella vita. *From the back: high school. From the front: museum.*

So we boarded a northbound ferryboat and alighted at Procida. Sleepy, wild, and full of adventure, we found we had much in common with the island. We ate catch of the day with spaghetti, local bread, and oil, washed down with cheap wine in squat little cups. We asked about room rates there but were told there were no vacancies and received a worried look. Undaunted, we strolled on, and then sunbathed where we fell on a patch of faded grass. In my mind's eye, I was the fiery village girl played by Maria Grazia Cucinotta in *Il Postino*, despite my sunburned shoulders and outfit of Edward's short shorts, beaded boob tube, and green turban set off with brooch.

It was only towards evening, when the last Bed & Breakfast door was closed on us, its sign that read *Ospitalità della Natura* swinging in our faces, that we confronted our plight.

"It looks like *l'ospitalità della natura* is exactly what we'll be at the mercy of tonight," I said.

"Who knew this poky little island would be such a popular destination," said Edward. "Are you sure we've been to all the hotels?"

"Procida's the size of my flat. We saw it all by our second lap." I shrugged off my rucksack and dropped onto the sand dunes, burrowing my legs into the warm sand to reach the cooler layers underneath. "Ah, that feels nice."

"Good. Tuck yourself in. I'll be back."

He raced off, leaving me trickling handfuls of sand onto my knees. I lay back and stared at the sky. It was the same blue as the robes of the Virgin Mary statue that welcomed (and turned away) guests at the corner leading to the last guesthouse. I would have had no trouble staying right where I was, just breathing in and out, tasting the robust air until I fell asleep. There was silence, except for muted communications between fishermen along the beach and some seagulls. It brought back memories of tramping about alongside Da, out in all weathers, bits of the earth lodged deep under my fingernails and the fresh air clinging to my hair and clothes.

Edward came panting through the dunes. "I know where we can sleep!"

I sat up, straightened my turban, and repositioned my shades.

"Come on!" He flew off again kicking up sand and I had no choice but to follow. I found him by an old upturned boat, one side propped up on four stones. "What do you think?"

"What?"

"It's almost a little hut."

I surveyed the flakey blue paint, the damp, exposed wooden slats, the tendrils of seaweed hanging over the 'doorway' like wind chimes on a front porch.

"I'm game if you are," I said. "But remember how you roared the place down when Ginevra trapped that mouse? Who knows what beasties the night will unleash? I say, it calls for some hard liquor. You make yourself at home. I'll go see."

"What do you mean, *beasties*? Where are you going?"

"Be right back!"

There was a little tavern in the central piazza, and I arrived at the same moment as the fishermen. When I explained our circumstances, the barman seemed quite decided and pulled from under the counter an unmarked bottle. "*Superalcolico,*" he cautioned. The fishermen greeted my query about the likelihood of snakes or scorpions on the beach with laughter.

"Well, if there weren't any before you drink that, there will be after."

As the sun was setting, Edward and I crawled inside our little bivouac.

"May the roof above us never fall in, and those gathered below it never fall out," I said.

We lay on our bellies, looking out at the swaying navy and silver waves, passing the bottle back and forth.

"Well, we wanted to see the other end of Italy. Milan can be kind of one-note. Monothematic: *la moda*," slurred Edward, extending his arms wide. "Whereas this is the *unseen* Italy. The corners that fashion forgot."

What I understood was: "Where is this unsheened tilly? The colours that flash are God."

"God?"

"We couldn't have organized it any better."

We cooled our eyes in butter.

"I think I'm going to be sick."

That came out clearer. He groaned and dragged himself over to the water's edge.

We woke the following morning flat on our backs, feet sticking out, to nothing more beastly than a hangover and a quizzical seagull. Before we left, we put a message in the empty bottle and sent it off to sea:

In this drunken bottle,
Best wishes from best friends
Who drunk its strange rum and got ill
For fear of the seasnakes night sends.

But the gulls of morning screech with laughter,
"What fools! Sure there be no fiercer beastie,

Nor wilier, more poisonous, nor craftier
Than the viprous landlubbing fashionisti!

"You're not going to start bawling all over the chapel and embarrass me, are you?"

"They're just getting married, Edward. I think I can handle it."

"It better not be one of those stuffy affairs with long-winded priests, disapproving old aunts, and monitored alcohol consumption. We need a good knees up. I know what these things can be like."

"And just how many rural Italian weddings have you been to?"

"I read the society pages. Weddings are the same wherever you go. If we were allowed to get married, we'd show you people how it should be done."

"But this is Ginevra and Dario. It's already special. I'm the reason they got together, don't forget."

"Oh, you are going to cry."

Monteceleste, the nearest town to the wedding chapel, some thirty miles north of Naples, proved to be territory even more uncharted by *la moda* than the island of Procida. Edward adopted David Attenborough's hushed tones narrating his expedition into the great unstyled wilds, describing his proximity to spiked mullets, platform-soled sneakers, and a dangerously large concentration of overdyed jeans featuring whisker-like creases emanating from the crotch. "One's eyes involuntarily travel there," he whispered. "They're like the arrows that indicate buried treasure."

I was just happy to be out of the clothes he had packed for me. I'd bought my dress an hour after we arrived in Naples, several days before we'd been divested of our money. It was yolk orange, and if all the freckles I'd gained in the intermittent three weeks joined forces, I risked becoming one with it, no telling where the dress ended and I began.

"Can you do my tie?" asked Edward.

I stepped back to look at him. "*Bellissimo.*"

"I'll melt as soon as we get outside."

"That's why it's at four. Hopefully the worst of the day's heat will have passed."

Edward turned to me. "And might I say you've pulled yourself together in a most ingenious way considering what little you had."

"With compliments like that, you really needn't bother."

"In your suitcase, I meant."

"The less said about my suitcase, the better."

Side by side in the mirror, we looked like one of those couples on old postcards, rendered in sepia but infused with blots of colour, like the violet flower in my hair that matched the one in Edward's buttonhole, or the matching pink of our cheeks, or the gold of my shoes and his cufflinks.

The Gianninis, a nice couple from outside Verona, whom we had met in the lobby bar, were giving us a lift to the chapel. We drove for twenty minutes through the countryside past ramshackle buildings, down winding lanes with overgrown hedges, finally crawling into a clearing in front of a spare, stone building. The only indication that it was a church was the cross made of two pieces of wood fastened above the sloping porch. Three bushes grew by the door behind a stone wall, a small sign on the gable read *Madonna de Barsento.* There was nothing or no one else around.

Soon cars arrived one by one. The women grouped easily together and a sudden breeze flipped the tails of their patterned dresses; the men shuffled their feet and adjusted their collars and cuffs. Only their glowing tans and lack of umbrellas separated them from a similar congregation gathering outside any Irish country church. The groom arrived and took his place amid slaps on the back and last minute bawdy outbursts, a squall of ribaldry that died down as quickly as it had flared up, just like the breeze. As we followed both parties inside, Dario's best man had to stoop to make it through the doorway.

The unassuming exterior concealed a breathtaking interior, like a dusty old stage curtain harboring an exquisitely designed set. We passed The Stations of the Cross, carved out of the walls, each one set off with a brass lamp containing a single flickering red flame. Women's heels on the floor made a noise similar to the sound the artists would have made chipping their vision into the stone. The centrepiece was a majestic gilt altar before a large mural of a wistful Madonna and child encircled by angels. But the most remarkable feature, and most surprising as it was inconspicuous from the outside, was a row of small stained glass windows close to the roof, which reflected an array of dazzling beams like moving spotlights as the guests filed into the pews.

The organ began to play, the doors creaked open, and everyone turned. Ginevra was at the centre of a ray of sunlight that had ushered her in and was now bidding its leave of her as the door closed again. Her dress we had found together in Verona, its caviar-beaded bodice strapless and boned to accentuate her splendid prow, its skirt a big taffeta *panettone*. She took her father's arm, giggled and began her walk. Dario lifted his eyes off her only once, and it was to throw a look of incredulity at his best man, as if to say, "*Can you believe she's with me?*" Tears dripped off Edward's chin.

The acoustics meant we couldn't hear much—the priest used no microphone—but some flubbed lines at the beginning caused nervous laughter between the couple and the first few rows. Several times Dario leaned in to Ginevra as if to share some private joke. Each photo I took featured some section of the bald pate of the man in front of me. I asked Edward to try from where he sat.

"Give me a minute," he said. "I seem to be a bit overcome."

Afterwards, the newly weds huddled, hand-in-hand, in the doorway under a shower of rice and blown bubbles. Mouths open, they seemed surprised to have stepped out into any of this, as if it had just been the two of them at the altar. They reluctantly let go of each other, and I got a great shot of Ginevra standing alone, regal and smiling, her head raised, eyes looking forward, bouquet of white roses held like a scepter.

When she reached me, she clasped my hands tight. "What do you think?"

"Terribly stylish," said Edward, before his tear ducts were swamped again

"Really beautiful, Ginevra," I said. "And you look perfect."

"I am happy, Kat." She turned to look at Dario who was being roughed up by his friends. "Isn't he's great?"

Edward blew his nose in agreement.

"Pull yourself together, Edward!" She took him by the shoulders. "The best man is single." She pointed out the tall fellow with Dario. "Handsome, no? Everyone's sure he's gay, but he hasn't come out. Antonio. I'm leaving it with you to crack the puzzle." *Pootzlay.*

Edward looked alert. "Oh. Much obliged."

"My father wanted me to marry him since I was five, so he comes recommended."

"And he resisted your considerable womanly charms since then, did he?" said Edward, musingly. "All those years. Interesting."

"What do you mean *all those years?*" said Ginevra.

The newly weds hopped into an open-topped sixties Fiat Ginevra's dad had restored, and our convoy trekked once again through the country roads, each driver blindly following the one before. Our destination was a fifteenth-century castle lit up with lanterns.

"That girl has class," said Edward, as we were escorted up its grand steps, through the central arches, to the back where candlelit tables had been placed all around a serene lake with swans.

The first toast: *"Per cent'anni!"* wished the happy couple one hundred years of happiness. No wonder, at thirty two, Ginevra was anxious to get started. The groom's tie was cut into pieces by his best men to pay the band, and the bride's veil was ripped apart to bring good luck. Dario, in his speech, joked, "I'm just thankful to Kat. She came to Italy to find a job, and I was there. She got fired from that job, and I was there. We never know where Kat's career will take her, but it led me to Ginevra." He leaned in and kissed her.

"Don't mention it," I yelled, and everyone laughed.

By the time all this was taken care of, plus five courses polished off, an endless variety of cake sampled, an unholy amount of wine guzzled, the DJ had set up on the roof. We would dance under the turrets until the sun rose the next morning. Edward spent most of the night with the bride's garter on his head, having been firmly knocked back by the best man, Antonio. I picked up where he left off with more success.

"Sloppy seconds?" he taunted, as he weaved around Antonio and I dancing.

"It's only seconds if someone else managed to get there first," I replied.

"Whatever—hey, anyone ever done a conga on a castle?"

MIDNIGHT

Back in Milan only a few days, and the September sky through my office skylight was the same colour as the robes of Our Lady on the side of the road in Procida. I remembered scrambling out from underneath our boat that morning and reaching up with my finger as if to trail a white line across the perfect blue like the ones aeroplanes make. The sky had seemed as close then as the ceiling was now.

Eva startled me as she passed, her staccato steps barely brushing the carpet. She gave me an easy smile and a few moments of small talk she wouldn't have time for by the end of the week. Her golden tan softened her, and I could see the girl who had first stepped into the House of Adriani nearly twenty years ago. Silvia, who had been in and out all morning, updating me on the Yansé Bowles project, seemed lighter on her feet too. In between visits to the factory, she'd spent time with her nephews in Sardinia. James, who'd spent the summer partying and catching up with friends in London, was as pale as the day he'd left, a smiling survivor of the Great British Summer. Paola had yet to return from wherever she was, and

337

Arturo looked like he had been there since July, hands clasped behind his back, waiting to be of service. All the other Adroids had been jacketed, stamped and herded back into their glass pens.

I had to keep checking the freckles on my arm to know that I had ever been away.

Yansé Bowles' dresses were shipped, and she put in a call to Signor Adriani to personally thank him. Her tour began, and photographs of her wearing House of Adriani, attending music award shows and walking red carpets, started appearing. By the time she made the Best Dressed lists, Adriani's celebrity clientele had swelled to include more prominent music and Hollywood figures. Several defected from long-standing relationships with other designers: Dolce & Gabbana and Roberto Cavalli were down three each; Versace lost four.

While I was present at the meetings, I learnt to stay in the background while Signor Adriani and his crack PR team bonded with the starlet over my sketches. I was a sort of protocol figure, like the ones making up the guard of honour during state visits of foreign dignitaries. Once, in the beginning, I stepped forward to explain the drape of a gown to an actress and received a crippling kung fu chop to the lower back from Natalia Andreoni, the head of PR, who continued to smile benignly as I grimaced in pain.

After the formalities, I was privy to the guffawed indiscretions that followed. Signor Adriani and his cohorts could give Joan Rivers a run for her money: "Thighs like a footballer. Better than anything Inter's got this season," he said, just as one singer's entourage swept from the room; of the actress whose languid doe-eyes had graced many movie posters, he said, "Her face is pulled so far back, she only has peripheral vision. I was standing right in front of her, just as I am to you now, and she had to look around to find me!" Then there was the young Hollywood bride, whose beauty had moved Signor Adriani to comment: "She's as radiant as the sun...Pity she has to wait for the echo to stop in her head every time she speaks." The lowest in the food chain, the actress whose body defied his waifish aesthetic, was known simply as the "catafalque."

Having built over the decades a loyal following amongst Hollywood's highest, most luminous stars, Adriani had become hungry to capture the comets, those short-lived but dazzling phenomenon, the whorey heiresses, rehab-reticent daughters of rock, and other paparazzi favourites; what Edith Wharton might have referred to as "the younger set." This led him to the idea of creating a new range of eveningwear with youth, sex, and hedonism as the ingredients. It would be called Midnight by Adriani. The order was torn from the pad and handed to me.

That'll be another side of frocks please. And make it snappy.

The launch of Midnight was to be an evening affair during which editors and major buyers would drink champagne and interview Signor Adriani, while models milled about wearing the collection. He wanted an intimate salon atmosphere, with a string quartet and spiffy waiters serving Japanese-inspired *amuse-bouches*. Every detail had been considered to imbue the event with the desired air of gentility and exclusivity. I wondered what all that had to do with the lifestyle of the eventual customer as she staggered from a club, flashed her knickerless nethers, violated her probation, and smashed her car into a lamppost. The dress wouldn't be seen in the mug shot.

The location was an eighteenth-century tearoom near the train station which still displayed the period's high ceilings, ornate mouldings, and chandeliers a blizzard of cut glass. Doors at the far end opened onto a flush courtyard dressed with furniture in the Adriani palette: eau-de-nil, oyster, sand, taupe—it was all beige to me. The vixenish junior editor of an influential French monthly and her darkly dressed entourage had claimed the spot to swig champagne and scatter cigarette ends while the late sun dappled the ground underneath her spiked, multi-zippered boot. An ivy-covered wall was all that separated them from the street beyond, where the criminal, lost, and desperate that loitered around Italian train stations went about their own shady business—in a fight, my money would go on the junior editor and her boys.

It was shaping up to be a great turn-out despite many of the most important guests having to fly in from various international capitals. Of course, if they had declined, Signor Adriani's wrath would have reverberated through their glossies in the form of a crippling advertising deficit the following sea-son. *You scratch my back, I'll back a four-page scratch-and-sniff perfume ad in your March issue.*

The quartet paused, and the trickling of the French foun-tain took over. The models in hues of berry and bloom began circulating between the tables; it was like a landscaped *jardin français,* and they were languid, exotic, swaying flowers.

"Black black is over," explained a passing American editor to her younger colleague. "But very black is on the way back."

The Midnight collection had every colour except black, very or otherwise.

Eva dashed by, dressed in a tuxedo. "Ciao, Kat. How's it going?"

"Great. Everything looks lovely, doesn't it?" But when I looked around, she was gone. I had started to think that if Eva wasn't in constant motion, if something happened that compelled her to stand still, it would be her undoing. She was a worker bee: sharp-shouldered, single-buttoned, tailored to the tasks of building the comb, keeping the hive friendly, the temperature right, but, above all, ensuring the pollen got from the drones to the king. Doubtless it was how she stayed so thin.

Another editor passed with her colleague. Her concern was looking chic throughout the relentless cycle of fashion weeks. "What I do is this. I choose the dress, be it Chanel, Lanvin or Prada. Then I have them make it in, say, ten different colours and overnight a few to each hotel I'll be staying in. I pack three suitcases of scarves, shoes, belts, and jewellery and just accessorize!"

Eva materialized again to give the nod. Various members of the PR office surfaced from strategic points, and we closed in and assumed position. We formed what the press derisively called "the Adriani wall of defence": in the eventuality the interview took an undesirable turn, with a few choreographed steps we would shield Signor Adriani from the unpleasantness.

To discreet applause, Signor Adriani walked apace to the front and welcomed everyone. To get things off and running, the microphone was passed to a popular presenter of Italian Fashion TV. Some overzealous photographers began snapping, so she had to repeat her question.

"Can you tell us about the idea behind Midnight, Signor Adriani?"

Twirling wire-rimmed glasses in his hands, he took a moment to reflect. It was his favourite pose for photographs: leaning forward, elbows on knees, squinting into the distance, and always, the glasses. They were a prop – his eyesight was sound.

"Well, it was quite a natural step," he said. "I wanted to offer the young woman of today an evening wardrobe for her lifestyle that evoked a modern spirit, a joie de vivre, but still maintained the distinct cachet of the House of Adriani. You see, what I have built during the thirty-five years of my womenswear business is a one-stop-shop for every generation, from grandmother to mother to daughter. I've shown this with my recent successful collaborations, in the worlds of popular music as well as film, ballet, and theatre, worlds in which I've hardly been a stranger." He gave a chuckle and his eyes darted around for affirmation. "Anyhow, Midnight is a continuation of that, the next natural branch of my empire."

The interviewer smiled in satisfaction. Adriani was on safe territory with the home press. They never challenged, misquoted, or took jabs at him; he was a source of unconditional national pride. The foreign press, on the other hand, were like the difficult, out-of-town relatives reluctantly invited over for Christmas dinner: *Aren't you over the hill for all this, Adriani? You don't want to be left on the shelf. When are you going to settle down and leave this fashion tomfoolery to the young folk? Pass the peas.*

As if in retaliation for the easy start, Peter Johnston, a respected British reporter specializing in arts and culture, spoke up: "So, Mr Adriani, tell me… " Already Signor Adriani would be bristling. He despised the use of 'mister', considering it prosaic and insolent; he was *Signor* Adriani in any language; was it too much to ask someone to step outside his rigid Englishness and respect that? "…this new venture, is it an indication that you are gearing up for many more years of this? Is the aim of this launch to effectively put paid to the rumours that you're ready to retire and are entertaining offers from international conglomerates, namely LVMH, to buy your company?"

The room held its breath. Signor Adriani looked about impatiently, and one of the PR guys stooped to translate, his palm pressed to his chest to hold his flapping tie, lending him a servile aspect that struck just the right tone. Comprehension registered on the designer's face, to be quickly replaced by irritation. I could see his thumbnail grow white from the pressure of bearing down on the glasses. I thought the sliver of metal might snap.

"Bravo! Bravo!" said Signor Adriani, with a sneer.

Mr Johnston looked bemused.

"As you've cleverly managed to answer your own question, I see no reason to go over it again. Next?" Signor Adriani turned stiffly away and pointed to another raised hand. But the snub was greeted with uncomfortable laughter. He could ill afford to alienate his audience, so he knew he had to back up. He stretched his thin lips into a lop-sided smirk, as if bracing himself against the elements. "If everyone answered their own questions, we'd be done in no time, and I could get on with the more important business of designing for next season." Spontaneous humour. He would try that. Anything to avoid answering the question.

A throaty, accented voice was up next. The French editor, her upper body rocking slightly as she bounced a foot off the seat in front of her, spoke an Italian that had no need of translation.

"I think it was George Bernard Shaw who said: 'It is all the youth can do for the old, to shock them and keep them up to date.' Has the oppressive media interest in young celebrities made you feel this way? And do you really feel that these *parvenues* you are targeting with this collection actually fit in with the House of Adriani philosophy, so often criticized for being elitist, even outdated? You have been quite outspoken in the past about other designers pandering to the masses. Perhaps you are now realizing it is a necessity in order to stay relevant?"

Even though his back was to me, I could almost feel the reverberation of whatever his eyes were doing. She stopped kicking her foot but maintained eye contact, in so much as I could tell; her head remained fixed in his direction, but her eyes were hidden behind thick bangs which quivered when brushed by her eyelashes. He turned to his PR team for a sign that this young dissident was someone he need bother with. "Is this person important?" was the unspoken query. Natalia nodded tersely. Another leaned in and whispered the name of her magazine.

"Well, Mademoiselle," he said, "Forgive me if I overlook something, you had several questions wrapped up in one. Firstly, I would concur with the eloquent George Bernard Shaw in that I have always been greatly inspired by youth. Whether you are aware of it or not." He smiled indulgently. "I surround myself with young people and they keep me on my toes. What you deem pandering to the masses, I consider an opportunity to dress the new icons, the faces of tomorrow, the young women that inspire other young women, especially if they challenge the prevailing standards of beauty. Striving to be relevant is my job, it's what I do, it's what I have always done, it's what drives me. That is why I am where I am today. Just as I learn from the young, it might benefit you to delve back into the archives and read up on *old* Signor Adriani and his many examples of *pandering to the masses* over the years." He raised his eyebrows in smug conclusion. "We have our homework to do at all ages, it seems, Mademoiselle."

She smirked and resumed kicking.

Twenty minutes later, an authoritative clearing of the throat curbed the growing restlessness. I strained to see as the room fell silent. Suzy Menkes, renowned editor of the *International Herald Tribune,* swaddled in her usual pillowy velvet, was still looking down at her notebook, her famous pompadour pointing straight at Signor Adriani almost accusingly, as if holding him there for questioning until her face arrived on the scene.

"First of all, my compliments on the collection, Signor Adriani. It's quite beautiful." She spoke with the earnest, fluttering voice of someone's batty, old auntie; one expected to hear her uttering exclamations of "Fiddlesticks! Poppycock! Toodleloo!" and "Jam on scones!" But her manner belied an intellect as sharp as the knitting needles she was rumoured to carry in her bag. Her diction, combined with the flattery, had already worked its magic on Signor Adriani who didn't even understand English. He was smiling and had relaxed his grip on the glasses.

"Signor Adriani, who amongst your team was the designer of this range? Are they here this evening? And if so, would you be so kind as to point them out?"

In the time it took to translate the question, my heart was drumming in my chest. I hadn't been briefed for this. I tried to catch Eva's eye, but she was staring straight ahead. I knew she would already have processed the question, lined up options, and selected a course of action. But I had no idea what to expect. It would be unprecedented for someone other than Signor Adriani to represent the House of Adriani. I would surely make a bollocks of it. I'd had no time to prepare. I noticed that Signor Adriani, who'd initially reacted as if he'd been skewered by one of her knitting needles, had resumed his composure and was now speaking.

"The process of designing this collection was no different than any other—uh, Suzy. It was created, with the help of my team, but like everything else that comes from the House of Adriani, it is entirely my vision."

"So there is no individual in particular you feel inclined to name that had more extensive involvement, let's say, in its creation?"

"Absolutely not. That's not how I work. I have a close, loyal team who follow my guidance and have enormous respect for my vision. That's all."

The press conference was over. Signor Adriani got up and was joined by Marco who updated him quietly on where he needed to be next. A few members of the Italian press came forward to congratulate him. Photographers spread out to get shots of the girls in the dresses. I moved off to the side, out of the way. My heart, which had leapt into my mouth during the last few minutes, slid back where it belonged.

Signor Adriani and Marco directed themselves to the exit but had to sidestep the braying photographers surrounding a blond model who'd had a glass too many and was hamming it up in a pink cocktail dress. His detour took him past me. He broke stride almost imperceptibly, gave the top of my arm a brief squeeze. "Brava, Kat. Brava," he said gruffly, through half-open lips and with lowered eyes. Then he continued to press forward, stepping into a waiting car outside as the doors swung closed.

"Excuse me," said a trendy young man. It was the British journalist. "I was just wondering..."

"Yes?"

"Where d'you get the champagne round here?"

I pointed him in the direction of the garden.

FASHION AND FARMING

Alacklustre sixties revival had been hanging around for the past three seasons, and the House of Adriani was about to present a show of such nonchalant modernity, it would scatter all trace of it. Based on the eroticism of Josephine Baker and the sultry ease of Cuba, where she performed at the American Theatre, it was a perfect pitch of floppy linen, embellished bustiers, men's waistcoats, Cuban heels, seashell jewellery, and airy wide-legged trousers.

"This could be one of those shows editors talk about for years," said Arturo. "Remember Spring 98?"

"A defining moment," agreed Paola. "This could be up there."

"It's really amazing what we can pull off when we all work together," I said.

I could see Arturo's head swivel a fraction on his neck before he decided to just nod in agreement. Paola, after looking questioningly at him, responded with a smile.

Our Spring/Summer collection had united us in a way that nothing ever had before, which had taken us all by surprise. It was as if we'd answered a silent call, mobilized, and come together in the name of something bigger: leading the House of Adriani to certain triumph. All we'd needed was the promise of a really great collection.

The only person who wasn't enjoying the camaraderie was Signor Adriani. He was happier when there was conflict; he thought it kept us on our toes, gave us an edge.

"What is this, a Sunday school?" he barked. "Will we be singing hymns next? I advise you all to grab hold of your *coglioni*. If I see anyone has lost their *coglioni*, I'll send you over to Miuccia Prada where you belong. Last thing I need is a bunch of imbeciles with no *coglioni*..."

As if to create friction, he began to complain there was something missing with the collection, an elusive *qualche cosa*. He paced the floor, looked to the ceiling, summoned us to him, cast us to the devil, all the while lamenting the need for "*un tocco di showmanship...un piccolo tocco*". He made fretful grabbing motions with his fingers as if what was missing could be freed from the air to fall accommodatingly at his feet.

"*C'e l'ho!*" he announced victoriously. "*Un sigaro! Un bel sigaro cubano!*"

He'd cracked it: Cuban cigars.

Women trailing ribbons of smoke on the catwalk hadn't been seen since the eighties and had an immediate frisson of something risqué, especially now, post-ban. But risqué was always in fashion. And considering the eighties were when the House of Adriani rose to power, and those yuppie businesswomen who first wore Adriani were often photographed with cigars held between painted talons, it could be a nod to his beginnings as well as a middle finger to current laws. It would certainly evoke images of Josephine gyrating onstage at the Havana club while her audience sat enthralled under a cumulus cloud of smoke. Signor Adriani was right; the cigar was the perfect prop. Fashion should be about the fearlessness of a complete vision, down to the last detail. It was courting controversy, but I had to admire the confidence of the gesture, the *coglioni*.

Arturo raced off to the catering table.

"*Perfetto!*" said Signor Adriani when Arturo returned brandishing a breadstick. He began demonstrating to Veronica, our house model, how to handle the breadstick like it was a Montecristo Joyita. "Don't bite it!" he shouted and the girl reared back.

Arturo patted crumbs from her front.

"But we'll use real ones for the show, right?" I interjected.

"And have them criticize me for promoting smoking? What's wrong with you, Kat? Bravo, Arturo. It looks just like the real thing." He bounded off for the evening, the picture of contentment. Eva shook her head in disbelief and left, too.

Arturo caught the appalled looks James and I wore, and defiantly said, "*Simpatico, non? Geniale.*"

"Other designers will be unveiling the new 'it' bag," I said, still trying to work out how this had happened, "and collaborations with precious jewellers; watches, sunglasses, luggage—Giorgio Armani, didn't he launch a limited edition car? And Hermes was linked to a yacht. What do we have up our sleeves? Breadsticks. Really?"

Arturo held his finger up warningly. "Any idea that's not yours, you feel the need to trample on."

"Nope. Only the bad ones."

"Well, mercifully for us, it's not what you think that matters, Kat. It's what Signor Adriani thinks."

"And what the editors think. Which affects what Signor Adriani thinks. Which affects us."

"Your job is to give him what he wants. So do your job, that's all."

James had just finished eating a banana and held up the skin trying to reclaim the morning's lighter mood. "Josephine wore a skirt of these too. Should I hold onto it?"

Arturo pounded across the *Pedana* and slammed the door behind him.

I turned to James. "Once again, in this very theatre, the curtain falls on good taste."

Kat, take a seat," said Signor Adriani. "I won't be a minute."

I smoothed my skirt under me and sat down. I had been summoned to his office with no explanation. He continued reading a many-paged document, picked up a pen, and jotted a few words in the margin. His fingers and thumb crowded the nib intimidatingly, like a finger scrum.

On the side of the desk sat the Suzy Menkes review I'd just been reading with James. I wondered if he'd gotten to it yet, if it had been translated. What had he made of her comment: "There was nothing remotely appetizing about the half-baked accessoire du jour: the breadstick! Dough, Signor Adriani! I write with Homer Simpson exasperation". He seemed calm. Maybe he had been mollified by her conclusion: "With any luck, the otherwise luxurious ingredients in this seductive collection might just be the bread and butter needed to keep this storied house fresh."

With a flourish, he signed the bottom of a page, flipped the document over, and looked up. His eyes seemed placid in that light. "You don't know why you're here, I'm sure."

Hadn't a clue.

"I feel we have come to a turning point, Kat. Things can no longer continue the way they've been going. You've come a long way since you arrived, there's no doubt. You've grown a lot, and I appreciate it. I want you to know that."

I managed a half-smile.

He got up to pace, lifting his wire-rimmed glasses. Coming to a halt directly under the Peter Lindbergh photograph, it was like he was looking down on himself looking down on me. It was disconcerting to be looked down on twice.

"I have just had a long overdue talk with Arturo. He is not happy. He has problems with your attitude."

"Uh-huh."

"You don't seem too surprised."

"I thought our differences might be in the past but…" I threw my hands up in resignation. "Oh, we just don't agree on a lot of things. Never have. But I don't see what I am expected to do about it." How could a man this powerful, this influential, be at the whim of Arturo's antics?

"Not a thing. But there will have to be some changes made." He drew near to his desk. "Arturo is jealous and resentful. He's competitive, which is something I like because it makes him want to do better, work harder." He shot me a look. Was it of warning? "He's been with me a long time and he has passion. I have to respect that. You understand that, don't you?"

I shrugged. "I suppose so."

"But I am also a businessman, and Arturo works for me. He must accept my decision as final and accommodate my vision. He will grow to understand. There is a need for renewal in houses like Adriani where people have worked for a long time. Loyalty is important, but renewal and relevance are what drives fashion. You offer the company all these things. Therefore, I think the time has come, Kat, to make you *Dirigente*."

Dirigente?

"Do you understand what I am saying, Kat?"

"No. I don't think I do." It was a word I'd heard bandied about but had never given more than a passing thought because it would never have been applied to me. It was a title reserved for the select few in the House of Adriani: the inner circle. Arturo was *Dirigente;* Eva was not. I always assumed that was down to Signor Adriani's misogynistic tendencies; the largest distribution of *Dirigenti* was to be found in the menswear department. Silvia, for all her devotion, was not *Dirigente*. I was as far from *Dirigente* as one could ever hope to be.

"This is a draft of the contract I am having drawn up for you," said Signor Adriani. "You will have it by this afternoon. It is, of course, a *contratto indeterminato*."

If the Adroids were to be believed, such a document hadn't been presented in years. A contract for life. I would be financially secure, could never be sacked, and would have as much power as Arturo. I looked into Signor Adriani's eyes—still calm—then at the words on the pages—jumping and dancing. What did it all mean? Would I be sworn in during some kind of ceremony? show allegiance by laying hands on the holy book? wear robes? kiss his ring?

"You'll take a couple of days to look it over," he said, rising to his feet. "Then give it back to me. Signed."

"It's an outrage!" Arturo paced the stone path while Paola leaned against a fountain with her arms folded. "After all the years I've given him!"

I ducked behind an evergreen and parted its branches.

"Always so grateful, so loyal. I had to earn that title. It's sickening!"

"It's a blatant insult, is what it is," said Paola. "I mean, that should have been me... if anyone." She looked up hopefully.

Arturo gave a derisive sniff and went pacing in the other direction.

I wondered how the news had reached them. I had told no one, not even James; I'd just come down here to think. Silvia's connections had been working overtime was my suspicion; she wouldn't have been able to contain herself with this intelligence.

Arturo's voice swirled up again. "It's quite a responsibility, you know, Paola, being the Creative Director of womenswear in the House of Adriani. After so many years, to keep the ideas coming, the creativity flowing. No one can say I don't work hard for it."

"Of course you do, Arturo," she replied. "What with all that bowing and snivelling you do alone—"

"But this—this is demeaning. There is no sense of proper order. It makes a mockery of the House of Adriani!"

"What about the pressure I am under," chimed in Paola, "Just in the day-to-day dealing with that man, trying to understand what he wants from me, his constantly changing mind, his catty criticisms, his temper, his..., his..."

"I don't know what he's thinking anymore," said Arturo.

"Just his shitty little character!" exploded Paola.

Arturo looked at her askance. "Settle down, Paola."

"Well..." she said, tucking her head into her chest.

"And here she comes in trampling over a system that's been in place for years," he said.

I shook the tree in frustration.

"You know, only the other day, he asked me if I was pregnant!" resumed Paola. "I mean, give me strength! I may have put on a pound or two on holiday but—"

"It's like anarchy has set in," said Arturo. "There's something to be said for the way things have always been done."

"We have been treated very shabbily," agreed Paola. "We cannot let this pass."

Arturo swivelled around to face her. Paola looked startled. If she—and I—hadn't known better, we might have assumed he had been struck by a desire to kiss her; every nerve in him seemed to pulsate with a longing as yet unspoken.

"From day one, I knew." He held his forefinger straight up: a one. "I had her pegged as troublesome. But I thought she'd be gone as quickly as she'd arrived. She was just so unsuitable. We could never have predicted this. You're absolutely right, Paola, it can't continue." He made a decisive ninety-degree turn and set off along another path, with Paola breaking into a trot after him. Their voices no longer carried as far as my tree. I turned and ran back through the gate, through the cobbled courtyard, took the back lift, and hurried to James's office. I told him of the latest developments while bringing him to the back of the building, to a window near the coffee machine. Arturo and Paola were still down there, heads locked together.

"What should I do? I'm not sure. Should I just go back down, tell him I heard every word, and have this thing out?"

"He looks fit to be tethered," said James. "Let him calm down first."

"I've tethered livestock more stubborn than him, if a fraction more intelligent. It should be no problem."

"I don't doubt it, Ellie-May, but settle a moment." His eyes were glued on the two animated figures below. "I've never seen him so worked up. You don't want to make things worse."

I thought a lot about what being *Dirigente* would mean. The court jester pulling up a chair on the King's private counsel? Now that required *coglioni,* and no mistake. But I was under no illusions. Even when I'd told James, I could see from the flicker in his eyes that he saw me differently. Things were going to change in ways I hadn't even foreseen.

The House of Adriani had come into prominence during the eighties when the battle of the sexes was raging, and Adriani was the first to provide the armour for both sides; it became the cornerstone of his success. But the residue of that war, the greed, ambition and cutthroat competition, had seeped in, and to this day clung to the walls of his empire unseen, coating the pipes and very engine of the place. The Adroids had been exposed to that air every day for years, so it wasn't surprising that some, who'd been there from the earliest, were compromised beyond repair.

It was time to bring things up to date; there was no reason why the behaviour within couldn't be as stylish as the product that came out. The yuppie business model was long irrelevant. Today we should take our cue from the organic farmer. It really wasn't so far-fetched. Seeds were planted, crops were tended, expectations were high. Come harvest time, verdicts were traded, orders were placed, and the whole earnest, optimistic cycle began again. Dependant on the environment and the elements, farmers studied the weather forecast, designers studied trend forecasts. Red sky at night was a shepherd's delight; red sky in the morning was Pantone colour card #12.

When I was old enough, Da brought me along to gather spuds with my cousins or help Uncle Eugene get his turf in; it was all manual work, done that way for generations, backbreaking. Nowadays, machinery has been introduced to ease some of the labour. Bowing and scraping to Adriani and his cronies was even more crippling than gathering spuds. If small

Irish farmers could embrace new ways of thinking, so could legendary Italian fashion designers. Nowadays, we lived in an environmentally-friendly, fair trade, energy efficient era. Fashion should reflect that. From the inside out. Respect for each other paired with respect for the storied House of Adriani would reap the most stylish harvest.

CHE COGLIONI!

"Who's responsible? Speak up or I'll fire you all!"
Signor Adriani recoiled in horror as the
model wearing the purple shift walked towards him. He seized
hold of Silvia who happened to be creeping across the Sala
Bianca to retrieve her tool belt and heaved her in front of
him like a sandbag. Peeping out over her left shoulder, he bellowed, "Who did this?" He flicked terrified eyes at the model.

Silvia stood slack-jawed, but I knew the blood was galloping through her veins.

"Is this your doing?" he screamed at her from behind.

"W-What, Signor Adriani?" she squeaked.

"That dress!"

"No, Signor Adriani." She hoisted her weight onto her
tiptoes, as if trying to occupy a more modest amount of space
while still shielding him. But pretty soon this close proximity
to Il Maestro would have her dissolving inside her blazer and
deliriously trickling away.

"Arturo knows why that dress is here," I said, stepping
forward and taking the model by the hand.

"Stay back!" Signor Adriani relinquished Silvia and ran behind the table. Cowering, he made a sign of the cross.

"I assure you I know nothing of the sort," said Arturo. "I haven't seen that thing in years."

Eva looked at both of us accusingly.

"Signor Adriani, Arturo ordered me to bring this dress for you—"

"You brought this here, Kat?" he asked. He sounded utterly disillusioned, like I had just admitted to pulling the wings off butterflies.

As I was responsible for dresses, it was natural an archive request would come to me or Silvia. But I should have known to double check. I'd been given enough glimpses into Arturo's mind to know how it stank in there.

"Don't come any closer!"

The model, who had been inching forward uncertainly, stopped and her lower lip quivered. She had no idea what she was doing to cause the great man such distress.

Signor Adriani was afraid of the dress.

"Burn it! Throw it out! Get rid of it!" he ordered. "I should throw you out with it, Kat!"

Out of range, Silvia had taken several deep breaths and collapsed sidelong onto a chair that moaned under her right buttock. She sat bolt upright again upon hearing my name in such pessimistic circumstances.

Dress style 'Naomi DSS89', so named because it had been worn by Naomi Campbell in the Spring/Summer 1989 show, at the dawn of minimalism, *was* pretty unremarkable by today's standards, especially without Naomi's Amazonian stature inhabiting it. It could be considered as much a leftover from another era as Silvia was, although held together better at the seams. But why the sight of it had reduced Adriani to such a quivering wreck, I couldn't guess. Clothes had the power to anger him—I'd seen that often enough—or make him laugh derisively; jackets calmed him—except the ones he referred to as 'hysterical'—but I'd never seen a garment strike fear in him before.

"I would understand if you brought me a selection of my most interesting pieces, favourites to revisit," he continued. "That would show initiative and an appreciation of the massive archive at your disposal. Are you all above celebrating what I have accomplished? Instead you attempt to infect me with this purulence, this purple verruca, this hemorrhoid in my back catalogue!"

"I'll have a selection of the best archive dresses for you tomorrow morning, Signor Adriani," said Arturo. "I'll take care of it personally."

"I don't want old styles reheated! I want n*ew* ideas!" He slammed his hand off the table, the incident prompting another of his favourite conspiracy theories: the one where everyone around him seeks to bring him down through bad design. "What do I pay you all for? Do you think I won't notice? You'll have to get up earlier in the morning to get one past me!"

As his ire expanded beyond me to the other eleven people in the room, he trembled with the force of it. To facilitate its release, he sent nearby odds and ends—pencils, magazines, an intern's sewing machine—flying off the work table. While everyone else froze, praying not to be struck by a stapler on the wing, Eva was ferreting through the papers on her clipboard which she carried like a portable in-tray.

"Oh, where is it?" she whispered, frowning.

"The night security could come up with better ideas than any of you!" revealed Signor Adriani. "I should hire him to design dresses. Do you hear me, Kat?"

"*Merda! Merdaccia!*" hissed Eva.

"I should replace half you other worthless wastrels with just one individual who'll carry his weight—"

"What's happening, Eva?" I whispered.

"That's the jinxed dress."

She said it like it should already mean something to me.

"The what?"

"The first exit in a show he got crucified for—the jinxed show. I'll never forget it—oh, where is this damned thing? It's bringing it all back. They said, entering the nineties, he had no place in fashion, that… he was a product of a decade now closed… remember it like it was yesterday… dark days— Ah, thank God!" She whipped something from between the layers, dumped the rest in my arms, and set off like a little schooner into the eye of the storm.

His wailing now contained a primal quality. The climax had to be near, for that noise could not be humanly sustained.

"—Do any of you realize what I do on a daily basis? My schedule would make all your heads spin— What is it, Eva?"

She thrust her hand forward. He snatched the magazine from her with a look that would have stripped the flesh from the bone of lesser mortals. Luckily, Eva didn't have the flesh to spare. It silenced him, whatever he saw there. Several Adroids inched forward, craning for a peek.

"Well, if it isn't the collection that keeps on giving," he said and flicked the magazine at them, sending them scattering. "Nosy—Nosy," he sing-songed. "Maybe I don't think you deserve to see. Maybe you should keep your eyes on your own affairs." He relented and held up a copy of American *Vogue*. It had Yansé Bowles on the cover, writhing on a giant gold balloon wearing a red, draped-silk dress from the Midnight range. Her feet, clad in gold Gucci heels, were extended forward while her head was tipped back, hair tumbling. "*Most Desirable Woman on the Planet*" ran along the bottom of the page.

Eva hurried the model wearing the jinxed dress out of sight. In a millisecond, the charmed Yansé had ousted the cursed Naomi, and all in the House of Adriani was still.

Then Signor Adriani flung the magazine over his shoulder like it was one of his fabric swatches. It skidded along three table tops and fell off the end. Although his head was still an angry red, his voice was steady.

"Good job, everyone. I think we're done here. Same time tomorrow."

The relief in the room was palpable. The tensed muscles, stiffened necks, interrupted breaths, and downcast eyes were released simultaneously in a chorus of giggles, creaks, and exhalations.

"Oh, and by the way, Kat, I forgot to mention," said Signor Adriani, on his way to the door. "The Cannes Film Festival is coming up, and one of your first *Dirigente* duties will be to accompany me. Eva, fill her in on the details, will you?" He pulled the door closed behind him.

The words hung in the air. Along with something else. I felt myself shudder and thought it was the draught from the door. I was conscious of an overspill of human energy that the Sala Bianca was unable to contain. I thought I felt someone breathing in my ear, then whispering into it, which brought on a weird sensation of déjà vu. I turned to locate the source of the grunting, and noticed the mannequin first, and the shears that protruded from its trunk like an arrow. It staggered on its wheels about to tip backwards while Arturo stood over it, his features pulled into a knot, his eyes burning with the same intensity as when he was in the courtyard with Paola. I found myself riveted by his every twitching movement: the bite of the lip, the lowering of the gaze, the attempt to extract the shears furtively like the incident might still pass unnoticed. This exposed the clean gash stretching almost from nipple-to-nipple—or axis-to-axis, to use the tailoring term. It cut the centre-front seam at a ninety-degree angle to form a cross. X marks the spot. Before Arturo's eyes, the thin cover that fitted as snugly as a nineteen-fifties turtleneck unravelled speedily to reveal the mannequin's smooth left breast. Suddenly the scene took on a perverse intimacy that made voyeurs of all of us.

The shadow of defeatism crossed Arturo's face at the same time as a ray of sunlight ricocheted off the blade. He examined the shears, held them up to the light, then raised his arm and plunged them deeper into the victim's breast. He dipped the mannequin like the lustful hero on the cover of a romance novel, the muscles of his back rippling under his thin shirt. Her wheels were jammed against the baseboard as he thrust the blade repeatedly into her beige flesh, exacting punishment on our dear old dress form. Cleverer than your average Adroid, she didn't deserve that end.

I realized I was squinting. X marks the spot where Arturo went bonkers. From the corner of my eye, I noticed others were peering through the same horrified expression. A skirt James had been draping earlier in the day hung in shreds from the unfortunate dummy's lower half, further impressing upon us an image of a lover whose ardour had ran amok during an erotic act, whose *passione* had turned dark. All we could do was wait for Arturo to exhaust himself.

And as suddenly as it began, it stopped. Arturo stood, his chest rising and falling, looking at the floor. He dropped the shears, and his arms hung by his sides. Then he reached up and took the tape measure from around his neck. He laid it on the table with a strange formality and doubled it over like a sash. Then he removed his white lab coat and laid it alongside. Finally, he slid the pin cushion from his wrist, placed it on the lapel like a brooch and, brushing down the front of his trousers three times, he straightened.

Without a word or sideways glance, he raised his head like a man confident of where he was going next: to the exit. At first, his heels made a hollow sound crossing the Sala Bianca floor, almost plodding, but in the last few steps he picked up pace. Freeing his hands from his trouser pockets, he wrenched open the double doors, and flung himself through them. As they swung wildly in his wake, he could be heard galloping up the hall like an animal turned loose. If, as Signor Adriani insisted, it was all a matter of *coglioni*, this was a creature hurtling off across the fields, reeling from castration, but finally tasting freedom.

When his footsteps died away, I became aware of everyone rooted to the spot, eyes now pinned on me.

THE RED SHOES

Silvia came ploughing through, using her humongous charmeuse bosom as a weapon to knock stunned Adroids out of the way and me back into a chair. Suspended above me, she petted my hair anxiously, which seemed to regulate her breathing. When I could handle it no longer, choking on her closeness and hairspray, I pushed her away.

"Are you alright? Are you bleeding?" She squeezed me around the shoulders and arms.

"It wasn't me on the wrong end of those shears, Silvia." The mannequin resembled an effigy of a hated public figure left smoking in a town square.

"The way I see it, the only difference in you and her," said Silvia gravely, "is that you weren't standing next to him." Then she began waving her arms like someone drowning because, having dropped to her knees, she couldn't get up. She huffed and puffed as her three assistants worked to right her. "Are you okay to be transferred?" she asked, upon standing, engaging in a brief tug-of-war with her clothing. Without waiting for a response, she propelled me out and through the corridors to her office where she backed me into another chair and wound me in three blankets from the best mill in Italy. A cashmere intensive care unit.

"Get Kat some water," she ordered an assistant. "You'll have some tea too?" Before I could answer, she added, "And some tea with lemon."

Eva stuck her head in, rolled her eyes while Silvia's head was turned and mouthed, "We'll talk later when you're, uh, free."

"Who was that?" demanded Silvia, head darting. "I'm going to organize a bodyguard. You can't be too careful. There are lunatics are on the loose."

The next day the corridors swelled with a constant pilgrimage to the foothills of my office. They brought flowers and chocolates and expressed such concern—and carried such good quality gifts—that I wondered if Silvia hadn't put them up to it. But what I found eerie was that no one said his name. Despite his being such a prominent and tenured Adroid figure, Arturo, after his systems malfunction, had been struck from the records forever. The process of wiping him from their collective psyches had happened overnight. The Adroids had amnesia.

Perhaps even more than me, or Silvia, it was Eva who had been knocked sideways by it all. Her day planner read: "11:30 Collection Review w/ Sig. Adriani, Sala Bianca; 1:00 Conference call w/ knit factory", but no note of Arturo turning into Norman Bates in the window in-between. Her eyebrows looked like they'd been removed and reattached a fraction too high. Of course, she took command the only way she knew how: with her chin inclined and her fingers gripping the sides of her clipboard, she ticked off a task at a time and put one brave little foot past the other.

"Right, Kat. Let's move on to more pleasant matters. You're off to Cannes. I have all the details worked out." She popped one bum cheek on the corner of my desk, something she had never done before. "You will be with Signor Adriani and his party the whole time. Here is the list—it's Marco, several models including Veronica, some members of menswear, Natalia from PR and her assistant. The celebrities will join him there; they'll be confirmed at a later point. Now, you'll be going on his yacht but you'll stay in the Carlton, where a suite has been booked for you. We will give you all you need in terms of wardrobe for the various parties, screenings, and events that make up the week. Obviously you must wear Adriani. All your expenses will be taken care of." She tapped her pen, scanned the page. "That covers it for now. Any questions?"

"What do you think of me being *Dirigente*, Eva?"

"Oh, well, of course, I'm delighted. I think it's very exciting. Congratulations!"

"Don't you think you deserve it too, after all this time?"

"Oh, nonsense! Me?" she said, blinking lavishly. "I'm not a creative!"

But we both knew of various menswear *Dirigenti* who were former pool boys, fruit pickers, and gogo dancers. In the House of Adriani, the 'creative' title could, at times, be tossed about rather creatively.

"What about Arturo?" I asked. "Has anyone heard from him?"

"No, and it's just as well. Our only interest now is to move on." She put the lid on her pen. "So far, the episode has been kept from Signor Adriani. We thought it best. We'll tell him Arturo is off sick for now. And if you want my honest opinion, the less said, the better. If it got out, I dread to think… But, you know, this could work out very well for you, Kat. All I'm saying is, let us know what you need, and we'll take care of it. Okay?"

"Okay."

"Anything at all," she said, and slid off my desk, straightening her skirt. "Just ask."

The dress was so weighty with beads it might sink the yacht. But it would fit perfectly with the gowns from Cannes I'd seen in magazines. Photographers would mistake me for someone important; only if they got too close would they see in my face my guilty secret: that I had no business being there.

I slipped it off and hung it with the rest: pink and black chiffon for opening night cocktails; green beaded jacket with white narrow trousers for dinner with Martin Scorsese; black tailleur for general functions; short black dress for dinner with Monica Bellucci, Vincent Cassel and Meryl Streep; sapphire draped jersey for the Gala Fashion Evening organized by the Italian and French fashion councils along with Donatella Versace, Roberto Cavalli, Valentino, and Karl Lagerfeld; floral mini dress with fur stole for the annual, much-feted Dolce & Gabbana boat party—Eva said I should be able to sneak away and, as long as I didn't brag about it the next day, Signor Adriani would be none the wiser. The last dress, the one with bands of glass beads was for my soiree with Sean Penn, George Clooney, Brad Pitt, and Julia Roberts. I'd looked at myself at least ten times in every outfit from every angle in a three-way mirror and still didn't recognize myself.

From current collections to archive treasures, I'd been told to choose whatever I wanted; there was only one condition which Eva repeated often: "No headwear, Kat. No hats, scarves, snoods, hoods, turbans, tiaras, Stetsons, bandannas or bows. Nothing inside out, upside down or back to front. In other words, no surprises."

Since Arturo's disappearance, Paola had been show-ing an unexpected side of her personality; an almost sororal desire to look out for me. I responded with my own unexpected side: I felt sorry for her. She'd fallen from Adriani's muse to Arturo's stooge, and now she'd been cast adrift by both men. The Adroids shunned her: she was he-who-shall-not-be-remembered's sidekick. But it turned out she had been to Cannes with Signor Adri-ani many years before and was happy to prep me for my turn.

"You'll have to get up really early. You'll have to get used to playing tennis every morning before breakfast. Signor Adriani loves a vigorous game of early morning doubles. He's most physically active that time of day. It's quite irritating, really. He also likes to swim in the ocean no matter how chilly the water and expects everyone to join him. Water skiing, have you ever done that?"

I shook my head.

"Well, you're a fast learner," she said. "You'll have to get your hair and nails done before you go. He expects glamour right from when you set foot on the yacht. I know the best people you can call." Her eyes sparkled. "Now, come with me. I have something to show you. You'll appreciate this." She led me to an area of the archives I'd never been to before.

"I can't believe, after all this time, there are still rooms I don't know about?"

"Not many people know about this place," she said, unlocking a door. Inside wasn't so much a room as a vault.

She hit some switches and it was awash with a half-light, a soft gold. At her coaxing, I stepped inside. On closely-stacked shelves either side of narrow aisles, little double decker caskets lined in velvet lay side by side. They were like miniature bunk beds and they held the most beautiful shoes I'd ever seen, rows of them, one shoe in the top berth, its comrade down below. They were shoe-shaped but they almost didn't look like things you would conceivably put on your feet.

"What are all these doing here?" I asked, reaching into the nearest shelf, caressing a soft pink leather sandal, its chiffon petals and beaded stamen trickling over my fingers.

"Every one of a kind shoe that was designed over the years, Signor Adriani had a second pair made," said Paola. "He keeps them all here. Those ones you have in your hand were worn by Julia Roberts at the Oscars, a few years back. Word is, he has been in talks with a major American museum to stage a retrospective, and these will feature alongside pieces from key collections throughout his career. You can choose a pair for Cannes."

"Are you sure?" I peeped at the sole; Julia and I did not wear the same size. "I mean, it's not forbidden or anything? Alarm bells won't go off as soon as I step outside? Barred gates drop from on high?" I couldn't help but eye her suspiciously even while my hand sneaked towards a turquoise satin platform with orange brooch.

"Don't worry, Kat. You're not going to get in trouble. Eva okayed it with Signor Adriani to take you here. She's excited to see what you'll choose."

I gasped at another pair that seemed transported from the costume department of old Hollywood: tall, open-toed, and ruby red, with a subtle sparkle and an interior of frosted pink velvet. I scooped them up and, despite others catching my eye, clutched them to my chest as I crept along the remaining aisles.

"It looks like you've made your choice," said Paola.

They sat on my desk like a pair of ornate boudoir vases. I ripped my shoes off and plunged my feet into the velvet. A perfect fit. I walked tall and straight out of my office along the carpet. There was no one around. They extended my legs by six inches but expected no effort on my part. Like a car that is described as a joy to drive, these shoes made of walking something else entirely. I paused, hand on hip, turned to the side, to the back, smiled coyly over my shoulder, and imagined the paparazzi. I turned the other way, angled my shoulder, and jutted my hip. I followed, the shoes led.

Gaining confidence, I broke into a strut, hands on hips and then swinging both arms. I happened to glance down and stumbled. The sight of the ruby against the beige shattered the illusion. They didn't belong on a beige carpet; it sucked the life out of them. It was remarkable how quickly they lost their sparkle. I reached for the door frame and took cautious steps back to my seat. I slid them off and put them back on the table.

Now two unusual things occupied my desk: the ruby shoes which were a temporary passe-partout to a glamorous, star-filled world and the *contratto indeterminato* which was the master key for permanent, unlimited access to Adriani's kingdom. The contract was as crisp as the second it had rolled out of the printer. I hadn't read it fully, it was still unsigned, and the HR office had left umpteen messages.

I knew now what I was afraid of. If I signed on the dotted line, I would be silenced for good, only taken out for special occasions, like the shoes. The rest of the time, I'd be shut away. It was already happening. I'd been interviewed by the *International Herald Tribune* and had to issue Signor Adriani an apology. I'd created the Midnight collection, and Adriani had denied my involvement. I'd been bribed to keep the Arturo affair quiet. I'd shrunk to fit into his world and now, when I looked around at it, even the beige carpet seemed like quicksand waiting to swallow the rest of me up.

"I sent you a check, mum. The Ballyloughin money. Will you pop it back in the bank when you're next in town?"

"Gladly, I will."

"So how's your week?" I asked.

"How's my feet?"

"Your week. How's things going?"

"Oh, my week! I was wondering how you knew about my feet because I've been in middling form with my corns these few days. Maybe it was brought on by the dancing last weekend. The band was great. I never sat once."

"Who danced you that you were in such demand?"

"A wee man from away down the country by the name of McEldowney: a great mover. Quickstep, waltz, old-time, he can do them all."

"Oh? And will this great mover be marking your dance card again?"

"He'll take me to Killeenan on Sunday night if I want. Heather Breeze are playing. Anyway, what do you intend for this money now? Are you thinking to start on your own wee house? This man's sons— or is it nephews? —own Mc Eldowney Contractors. Should I make some enquiries?"

"You can just put it back in the bank for now."

"I'm just noticing the clock, and you're one hour ahead out there. Everything alright? You're up late."

"So are you."

"Aye, but a wee hand of patience before I lie down sends me out like a light."

"I was just going to bed."

"Alright, Kathleen, off you go. And work?"

"Same old, same old," I began, then thought, Why am I withholding the news that will surely make her happy, just the sort of thing she'd been waiting to hear? So I said, "Actually, mum, they're making me all kinds of offers. A high position, a contract for life, great money, security. Adriani's even taking me to the South of France for a big event—"

"Oh, Kathleen!" she cried, followed by a laugh of pure delight. "Would you listen to that. Good God, that's just great! You're landed now. I knew it. Well done, Kathleen. That's the way!"

"It's big news, that's for sure," I said in agreement. It was what she said next that I found so disagreeable it kept me awake all night.

"Because people reward hard work in the end, Kathleen. They do. You minded the rules, showed respect to your boss and the workers, you appeared presentable, kept good time— you could be there till retirement. It's just like Daintyfit!"

Eva read the three sentences without expression. "Well, I didn't expect you to stick around forever, but I didn't think you'd choose now, of all times, to present me with this." She flicked the letter irritably like she hoped the words would tumble off the page. "Things were really falling into place for you. You *do* realize that, don't you?"

"I know, Eva. And I appreciate all the opportunities I've been given. But it just feels like the time to go."

"Is there anything I can do to change your mind?'

I shook my head.

"Where will you go? What will you do?"

"That's the part I haven't quite worked out yet."

"You must have something lined up," she insisted. Ever the efficient, well-oiled fact finder updating her files.

I shrugged.

"Have you got another job?"

"I might take some time off."

She looked down at her lap. "Are you going to speak to Signor Adriani?"

"I thought I'd get a letter to him first, make it formal. Then speak to him afterwards, when he's had time to digest the news."

"Right." Her tongue crept out and explored her bottom lip. "And where am I supposed to find another designer who can please both Yansé Bowles *and* Silvia Pavone?" A small laugh, without much humour, erupted from her. "Oh, fuck off, Kat! Really." She dropped her small fist onto the table causing several pens, a calculator, and BlackBerry to jump.

"You could try going back to the bar you found me in," I said. "That's as good a place to start as any."

"Don't you think I've been back many times? If there'd been others, I'd have found them."

❧

I had left a copy of the letter with Anna that morning asking her to slide it in with the rest of Signor Adriani's mail, somewhere in the middle.

Alongside the distinguished-looking envelopes with natty graphics from senior editors, CEOs, and glitterati, the plainness of my white 7" by 5" with the handwritten *Signor Adriani* in the fine-nibbed Micron 01, every House of Adriani designer's favourite drawing pen, was glaring.

"If he doesn't get to it today, that's fine."

"Do you need a response?"

"I guess not," I said, slinking out. I knew, no matter how politely worded my letter, he would read only ingratitude and disloyalty; I was cocking a snook at the exclusivity of his good graces. Hopefully, whatever piece of correspondence he opened before mine would contain happy news. Then I chided myself for this thinking. If he had taught me anything, it was that no one was indispensable. Except him. I was getting ideas outside my station if I thought my decision would spark anything other than minimal inconvenience.

I went next to Silvia, knowing that if I waited, Signor Adriani's secretary would get to her first. I thought I was already too late when she waved me in and asked: "So are you all ready to go? Is there anything Auntie Silvia can help you with?"

Then I realized she was talking about Cannes.

"Just have fun. Think no more about that business with Arturo. I was working on getting rid of him for you anyway, you know. He saved me the trouble. Good riddance." She put the four fingers of her right hand in a neat row under her chin and sent them flicking forward with an imperious toss of her head; it was a popular gesture meaning 'you're dead to me.'

"Signor Adriani obviously thinks very highly of you, Kat, and that's what matters. You're going to have a ball. I would have died to go to Cannes Film Festival when I was a girl. Look! These arrived twenty minutes ago." She got up and walked me through the vases of champagne roses that bedecked her office. "From a major Como silk manufacturer. I won't say which one." She was purring in a way that put me in mind of Elizabeth Taylor in an old White Diamonds advertisement. "Don't they smell magnificent?" A remarkably spry pirouette took her from one side of the table to the other. "What would you like? Tea? Coffee? I'll call down to the kitchen and have them bring something. Biscotti?" Her fingers hovered over the phone's numbers.

"Silvia, I have something to tell you."

She put the phone down, squeezed back into her seat, and dropped her hands into her lap. "*Dimmi tutto, Gioia.*" *Tell me everything, Joy.*

I opened my mouth but nothing came out. She pursed her lips, the heavy contouring giving way to the naked pink. I thought I saw her eyes waver as if they'd gotten wind of my news before I'd found the words to voice it. "*Allora?*" she encouraged and indicated a chair.

I took a small step forward and stopped.

"Now, Kat—before you go on—don't be telling me anything I don't want to hear. Okay?" She pressed two fingers to her lips and shook her head. "No," she said, and rose to go to the window.

And with her back turned, I blurted it out: "I've handed in my resignation."

Her head remained fixed on a point outside the window. I wasn't sure if she'd caught what I said until I noticed something in her posture had changed. She turned her head, and I saw her eyes brimming with unreleased tears.

"But... *why?*" She looked at me like I was throwing everything she'd done for me back in her face. Coming up beside her, I saw the tears spilling over like the water from the rim of the fountains below and I searched for the right words.

"Oh, please don't cry, Silvia. Or I'll cry too." I put my arms around her and stared into her crumpled face. *"Cavolo, Silvia."* She wouldn't even meet my eyes. "I know it's hard to take in but we're still friends, inside or out. There's a lump in my throat the size of a cabbage, I tell you. Will we look about that tea?"

She slunk out of my reach and pulled a tissue from the box on her desk. "I'm sorry. I can't," she replied, dabbing her face. "I have a menswear fitting and I'm late. I can't have Signor Adriani waiting for La Silvia. That won't do at all."

She had placed me at a distance farther away than just the other side of the desk. When she blew her nose noisily, I took it as my cue to leave, but when I closed the door and looked back through the glass, she was sitting in her chair, turned away, with her shoulders sloped. Her three assistants looked in but didn't move.

∾

Most people still hadn't returned from lunch so the third floor was empty. The twittering of birds and the tinkling of sprinklers created a touch of melancholy in me. I wondered if Signor Adriani had seen the letter. I had been rehearsing in my mind our parting conversation and hoped we could leave each other on a lighter note than I had left Silvia; I prepared myself to be summoned at any moment.

James tumbled through my door. He had just bumped into Silvia who had pulled him to her and informed him of my decision while smearing make-up and worse on the shoulder of his new Dior jacket.

"But—but I thought when they gave you that new contract, and it a thingummy one, well, that was it, you were in, sticking around. The outsider, on the inside, you know? Taking on the system. What changed?"

"Taking on the system sounds too exhausting."

"So you're deserting me? No, seriously, how come? Was it the Arturo thing?"

"It wasn't really any one thing. If I was a farmer, I'd say the big conglomerate that owns all the land around is squeezing me out. My soil is contaminated. Some of the shit they use to make their crops grow blew over and poisoned my ground, and all I really wanted was to grow a nice carrot."

"A carrot," said James.

I was laughing at his poor confused face and watched it change to one of indignation as he was pushed out of the way by a bank of people darkening the corridor and flowing into my office.

"Buongiorno, Kat," said Alessandra, head of HR. As one whose job title had the word 'human' in it, she took great pains to disguise she was of the species. Long-limbed, gaunt-faced, it was she who slid the contract towards me with the tips of her bony fingers on my very first day. I recalled my innocent enquiry about a clothing allowance, and how she reacted like I was something to beat away with a broom before scrubbing down the patch of ground on which I stood. Today she looked particularly hostile to have been wrenched from her natural habitat of number nineteen.

Beside her stood Marco; alongside him, Signor Adriani's personal bodyguard, whose name was Filelio, known as Fil, but I thought of him as Finn because he was a giant with hands like tyres. I'd never been that close to him before and couldn't for the life of me work out why he was currently occupying the length and breadth of my doorway. Bringing up the rear was the fruit picker Signor Adriani had discovered in Mykonos, whose name I forgot.

"Buongiorno, Alessandra. We don't often see you around these parts. What can I do for you all?"

"Signor Adriani wishes you to leave the premises immediately," said Alessandra. "You no longer work for him, so he asks that you clear your desk, gather your belongings and go."

"You mean you are here to escort me out?"

"That is correct," said Alessandra positioning herself in advance of the three men; she would be doing all the talking. "Naturally, you will be paid for the entirety of your notice period. But you will not be required to come to work."

I gawped, first at Finn, who looked down at his size twenty feet, then at Alessandra, sealed in tightly-belted beige, then at Marco, who had been rumbling into his cell phone but, during my silent stupor, had raised his voice: "One hundred-percent organic Indian cotton. One thousand thread count. From the Nagpur region. I don't care who else'll be there. Signor Adriani will not sleep on anything else. So if you want him there, make it happen." He shoved the phone in his pocket, looked around to see what he had missed, took it out, and dialled another number. "Yes, I'm calling about the shipment of twelve pairs of white Adidas Y-3 sneakers to Milan..."

It put things in perspective to think of myself slotted in between Furnishings and Footwear on Marco's To Do list.

"Well, you're—I'm going to need some time."

"We have been instructed to remain while you vacate," said Alessandra.

"In that case, you may pull up some chairs and grab a coffee," I said, heat prickling at the roots of my hair. "If you have so little to do with your time."

"I'll help you," said James, removing his jacket, widening his eyes as if to say *what the hell?* I pulled open a random drawer, much too violently as it turned out, because it bucked to the floor spilling stationary, tampons, a change of shoes, make-up and chocolate. I forked everything into two Prada shoeboxes I had.

"Just dump it all in," I urged James as he carefully collected old backstage passes into a rubber band. "Don't worry about it," I hissed as he tried to find the right lids for dehydrated markers. Alessandra scrutinized every movement.

Twenty-five minutes later, I was at the centre of an entourage making its way into the lift, down three floors, past the clock-in machine for the last time, and through to reception where I was stripped of my badge and keys and required to sign some papers. Marco held the door open for me, still talking on his phone. *Antipatica* Alessandra stood just inside the border with the outside world and watched as Finn and Mykonos, who had been carrying a box each, laid them on the street and averted their eyes. They muttered *"Arrivederci"*, and the whole party turned inside. The operation had been completed in less time than I thought.

As the gates slid towards each other, I looked up and saw all the Adroids gathered at the windows looking out. I stared at the tall black letters worked into the iron and heard the reassuring click as it closed.

The House of Adriani was united once more.

EPILOGUE

I turned the corner into rue du Gamin and saw that it curved off to the right. Number eighty-five would be just beyond the curve. The wheels of my two cases bobbed and spun over the cobbles but were otherwise bearing up well, considering I'd been wandering along streets like this for nearly an hour.

When I turned the corner, the sun splashed off the wet ground where someone had been washing the street. My sunglasses were buried in my case so I carried on blindly in a straight line and scattered a flock of pigeons. Sooner than I thought I came to number eighty-five. On a street lined with riotously coloured window boxes, the manifestation of the second floor tenant's horticultural prowess took a different form: egg boxes graced the two window ledges from which sprung a posy of cocktail umbrellas, candy canes, party poppers and swizzle sticks. Inside the window on the right, I could see a display of snow globes.

I rang the bell, waited; nothing. I rang again before stepping back to look up. The white gauzy curtains revealed his silhouette before he pushed them apart, opened the window, and stuck his head out. His hair was wet, with suds about the ears.

"Yes, hallo? Who is it?" Edward's voice rang out, proudly English for the benefit of anyone in the eleventh arrondissement who was in any doubt.

I waited for him to see me. "What the fuck are you doing here?" was his response when he did.

"I missed you?"

"Are on your way to Cannes?" he asked. A legitimate question, I supposed, as I hadn't spoken to him in a week or more.

"Not exactly. There was a last minute change of plan."

"What did you do? No, Kat." He grasped the railings and began to rock. "I was living for Cannes. That was all that was keeping me going. I was going to swing it to come down for a few of the parties." He stopped and looked distraught. "Tell me Cannes is still happening."

"Why don't you let me in, and I'll bring you right up to date."

"Are those suitcases yours?" he asked, not moving.

"Come on, Edward, I need a cup of tea. I've been lost for hours."

"Are you going to ask if you can stay?"

"And if I was?"

"We'd have to lay down some very serious ground rules, after last time. Like no nookie at my place."

"I can respect that."

"Wait right there." He returned inside, and I listened for the buzzer. I tried the door. He came back on the balcony with a cigarette and lit up. "So what were you saying?" he called down.

"Stop being evil! Admit it, you've missed me."

Of course he had missed me. I had missed him. He was Thelma, I was Sundance.

"I've had peace and quiet, Kat. What about Cannes?"

"I see you haven't managed to give up smoking though. Maybe the peace and quiet's grating on you."

"Nowadays, it takes a serene mind to have the courage to smoke," he replied, blowing nicotine high into the air.

"Oh, let me in. I agree to all your demands."

A well-fed pigeon on the wing from the eave of his building to the branch of a lush sycamore dropped the huge load she had been carrying on the crown of Edward's head. He stood perfectly still as the goop trickled down his hair and mingled with the soap suds. His eyes did enough moving for all of him.

"Look what you bring! You see?" He slowly unwrapped some of the towel and, with his mind on his modesty, dabbed gingerly at his head with a corner.

"You can't blame me for the pigeon. Anyway, that's good luck."

Edward with his eyes tightly closed in disgust patted his head. "Did you and the historic House of Adriani finally call it quits? Irreconcilable differences?"

"They threw me out."

The towel came to a stop. "Why?"

"Never mind that. I've had a revelation. Organic produce! Do you have a garden back there? I want to grow rhubarb, it's relatively simple. Gooseberries, the same. I got my mum's recipe for jam and for Ginevra's tart but I'll substitute the apricots. Duck eggs! Maybe I could get a small allotment—have you noticed any in Paris? Okay, listen, how's this for a name... *Dig Her Style*... eh? I could make some gingham totes, accessorize my small harvest, make the cartons for the eggs, you know? Green beans are supposedly easy to grow, tomatoes, and carrots for sure. I could sell from the back of a small van to begin with. If you're interested, I'll even let you in on it."

I smiled up at him, shielding my eyes with my hand. "You didn't say what you thought of the name…"

He gave a deep sigh. "The buzzer's broken. Let me get the keys." He pushed back the curtain, muttering, "She botched Cannes, and she comes to me with rhubarb…" The curtain wafted out through the window like a half-hearted flag of surrender, then he followed with a handful of metal.

"The one with the blue rubber tip is for the outside door. My flat is the only silver key on it. The others are the keys to the many exciting and glamorous facets of my new life—none of which, I might add, currently or in the future, involves an allotment. Now, catch!"

ABOUT THE AUTHOR

Jackie Mallon is an Irish writer and fashion designer currently living in New York. After studying at London's St Martins School, she worked in the world of high fashion in Milan for eight years, stockpiling stories for the novel she didn't know she was gearing up to write.

Jackie is a trained Irish dancer, a secret calligraphist, and needlework enthusiast. She enjoys sketching trees and rainy weather – not necessarily at the same time – and running marathons. She learnt Italian from reading Harry Potter with a dictionary on her daily tram commutes in Milan. She was once a dreadlocked petrol pump attendant and lived above a South London pub frequented by Cockney gangsters. She revels in the serenity of airports.

To learn more about Jackie and her characters, visit *www.jackiemallon.com; http://pinterest.com/maljax1/* and *www.betimesbooks.com*